The Collar

V. G. BRATT

THE COLLAR

Copyright © 2024 V. G. Bratt

All rights reserved.

THE COLLAR

DEDICATION

To my beloved, Chris.
You give me blue skies even on the cloudiest of days.

THE COLLAR

CONTENTS

	Acknowledgments	i
1	Dare	Pg 1
2	Lilyanna	Pg 17
3	Venture	Pg 26
4	Robin	Pg 34
5	King Dallin	Pg 46
6	Greystone	Pg 53
7	East Wing	Pg 66
8	White Cliff	Pg 79
9	Urba	Pg 89
10	Sprinter	Pg 98
11	Elrod	Pg 109
12	Maw	Pg 119
13	Sire	Pg 127
14	Swim Tail	Pg 142
15	Dread Wood	Pg 156
16	Sebastian	Pg 170
17	Tunnel	Pg 181
18	Rescue	Pg 193
19	Dream Wood	Pg 208
20	Patrol	Pg 219
21	Erosmay	Pg 230
22	Seeing-sight	Pg 245
23	Fire Breather	Pg 254
24	Wedding	Pg 264

THE COLLAR

ACKNOWLEDGMENTS

I would like to express my deepest appreciation to the following individuals:

May Rose Gregory for her collaboration and the use of her name in anagram form as the name of the little dragon, Erosmay.

Mike Gregory for designing the book cover.

Renee Johnson for her assistance and encouragement.

And lastly, I would like to thank my beloved, Chris, without whom I would not have had the opportunity to write this book. You are wonderful.

1 DARE

Dare gasped for breath. A split second earlier he had been standing on the battlements quietly watching the citadel's customs agents inspect a wagonload of goods being transported up from the docks, and now he stood winded with one arm pinned painfully behind his back and his face pressed against the fortification's rough cold stone.

'What's rule number one?' his assailant demanded in a hushed voice just behind his right ear.

'Never let your guard down,' Dare answered, as he squirmed and struggled for breath.

'Or what?' his attacker insisted, pressing the young smith a little harder into the wall of the battlement.

'You get a face full of cold stone,' Dare replied between clenched teeth.

Zarak laughed and released his hold, 'Better cold stone in your face than cold steel in your back.'

'That's true,' Dare said as he rubbed the circulation back into his arm. 'But next time, I'd appreciate it if you'd just pat me on the shoulder and remind me.'

'Why, where would the fun be in that?' the soldier countered good-naturedly.

With no family of his own, or at least no children he was aware of, Zarak had reluctantly befriended the young locksmith years earlier. It hadn't been a conscious decision on his part. But he soon found whenever he was stationed at the capital, Dare would just happen to appear and start tagging along behind him like a lost pup. And, by the time the soldier had twigged onto the fact their paths crossed too often to be mere coincidence, Zarak realized he genuinely liked the boy and hadn't discouraged him.

As to why Dare had picked him to be his mentor, Zarak still didn't know the answer to that one, but in his heart he was honored to have been chosen and wouldn't have had it any other way.

It also hadn't taken Zarak long to discover the lad was frustrated by, of all things, the fact he'd been born on the right side of the blanket into a good family with a respectable business. Whereas most people would've been elated by the prospect, it was obvious to the soldier the boy longed for adventure and was quietly seeking a way out of his would be dilemma.

So, before the young smith could do something silly like run off to sea or join a trading caravan, Zarak had sought permission from Dare's father to train the lad in the art of combat, believing this would provide an outlet for the youth's pent-up frustration.

Several years had passed since then and Zarak was pleased to have been proven right. The young smith had taken to the training like a duck to water. In-between running errands and working at the forge with his father, Dare had diligently practiced the moves Zarak had shown him and had slowly grown from a frustrated boy into a resigned young man. And Zarak had to admit, Dare handled weapons like a natural.

'By the pong, I should've smelled you coming,' Dare said, wrinkling his nose in mock disgust.

Zarak wasn't offended. He was well aware, despite the cold weather, he reeked of sweat, his own and of the horse he'd ridden nearly into the ground during his platoon's search for the princess and her abductors. But, because he'd been sworn to secrecy, he merely shrugged and replied, 'Downwind advantage.'

'So, when did you get back?'

'A few hours ago. I was on my way to the barracks bathhouse when I spotted you up here and just had to say hello.'

In spite of the rough greeting, Dare was glad to see his old friend and spent the next few minutes chatting with him as they made their way down the stone steps of the rampart. Then after reaching the crowded cobblestone street below, they bade each other farewell and went their separate ways, Zarak to the bathhouse for a badly needed wash and the young smith towards his father's locksmith shop.

By now Dare was running late and knew his father would be wondering where he was. So to make up for lost time, he darted down little used passageways and in and out of side streets whenever he could. And, he kept up his guard too just as Zarak had taught him, given that here in the capital you kept an eye out for both the effluent and affluent if you wanted to avoid a stink.

As he neared the center of the citadel, however, the young smith was forced to slow his pace and weave his way around the crowded market stalls just like everyone else. Because, ever since the king had announced his only heir, Princess Lilyanna, was to be married, merchants and craftsmen from all over the kingdom had been flocking to the capital in the hope of making their fortunes.

As son of the local locksmith, Dare was also well aware that along with this influx in trade there had been an increase in crime. And as a consequence, when he started to edge his way around a rather plump woman busy haggling with a merchant over the price of cloth and a man suddenly bumped into him, Dare thought the worst and assumed the man was trying to rob him.

Quick as a flash, the smith grabbed hold of the man's arm and held him fast until he was certain he still had possession of his coin pouch. Then, Dare released the man and said by way of apology, 'Sorry friend. I thought you were a pickpocket.'

Affronted, the little man snapped back haughtily, 'Do you know who I am?'

As part of his training, Zarak had taught Dare to anticipate his opponent's next moves, and the smith could tell "His Pompousness" was about to create a spectacle. So, he reacted the way any good swordsman would, he held his ground and cut the man down to size by saying, 'Why? Don't you?'

Unaccustomed to being challenged, the arrogant little man's eyes narrowed and it was obvious he fully intended to say more. But then, as he took in the smith's muscular frame, he thought better of it, shut his mouth and strode off in a huff instead.

As he watched his would be assailant disappear into the crowd, Dare shook his head and wondered if the uppity little man ever tripped over his own ego. Then, he turned and continued on his way, because now he was even more pressed for time than he was before.

Although several streets later, when he came across the newly erected booth of a beautiful young fortune-teller, the lack of time still didn't stop the smith from mischievously winking at her and saying he hadn't the time to have his palm read.

The dark-haired mystic played along and pouted in feigned regret as she lowered her tasseled shawl and dipped her shoulder in such a way the low cut neckline of her dress slid provocatively downwards.

Dare's eyes widened in surprise as he realized fortunes weren't all the young woman was willing to reveal.

She smiled when she saw his shocked reaction, and then raised an eyebrow and invited him into the empty booth with a tilt of her head.

With cheeks suddenly feeling flush, Dare knew he'd allowed the mystic's youthful appearance to belie her veteran status and decided a tactical withdrawal was in order. So after hurriedly mumbling an excuse, he strode away, leaving behind a little of his dignity along with the sounds of the seductress's mocking laughter and the jingling of her bracelets.

Normally Dare liked a joke just as much as the next fellow. However, since he was the butt of this particular one, it took him a few minutes before he could truly appreciate it. But once he did, he started to laugh. And when he noticed passers-by were starting to give him odd looks and a wide berth, he laughed all the more.

When he finally managed to compose himself, the smith replayed the encounter over in his mind as he walked and realized, in retrospect, he was glad his friend, Rhea, hadn't been with him to see what had happened, because that rogue would've ribbed him about it for weeks.

Rhea didn't hide the fact that he liked a bit of skirt and fancied himself quite the ladies' man, always boasting about his prowess with women even though Dare knew full well it was all talk and no action, and the smith was starting to get a little tired of hearing about it. And pondering this, it occurred to him he had the makings of a well-deserved practical joke, all he had to do was to get his friend to call upon the fortune-teller and she'd take care of the rest.

Dare was still busy devising the best way to go about this when he caught sight of the huge weathered padlock marking the entrance to his father's locksmith shop which had been skillfully carved from the trunk of an oak tree many years before and cleverly suspended above the door by a large chain, giving the impression it was the lock which secured the chain in place instead of the other way around.

When he reached the smithy and swung open the door, the little doorbell tinkled merrily in greeting as he stepped inside.

Seeing his father was busy with a customer, Dare nodded in greeting when they glanced his way. Then, he scooped up the small pile of broken keys that had accumulated in his absence and carried them to the workroom at the back of the shop.

After carefully selecting the blanks he needed from off the wall, the smith slipped off his jacket and donned his leather apron. Then, he sat down at the workbench and began the slow process of filing the blanks into replacement keys.

As Dare worked, he thought back to his encounter with Zarak earlier that morning. And although he knew the big man liked to keep his cards close to his chest, never volunteering much information about his work at the best of times, he thought Zarak had seemed even more guarded than usual.

When he'd asked the soldier where he'd been, Zarak had simply shrugged his shoulders and mumbled something about routine escort duty. And knowing Zarak as well as he did, Dare knew better than to push, even though he thought his friend looked a bit too travel worn for that. But since the smith seldom set foot outside the citadel gates, he decided to take his friend's explanation at face value and leave it at that.

Once he'd fashioned the first key to his satisfaction, Dare set it aside and began to work on the second, all the while thinking of Zarak and wondering what life would be like riding along beside him on the open road; the fact he'd never ridden a horse before didn't even cross his mind.

In his heart, the eighteen year old knew this was pure foolishness because his life had already been mapped out for him; he was expected to run the family business just as his father and grandfather had done before him. Yet, even though he tried his best to live up to this obligation, he still allowed himself the luxury of daydreaming like a young boy from time to time.

After all of the replacement keys had been cut, Dare stood and shook the metal filings from his leather work apron onto the stone floor. Then, aware his father liked to keep a tidy smithy, he went to fetch the broom from the corner of the room so he could sweep up the mess. And on the way there, he noticed the master locksmith had left his latest 'pick proof' lock lying at the far end of the workbench beside his toolbox.

Mischievous by nature and always up for a challenge, Dare was immediately seized by the desire to try and best his old man yet again. But knowing how hard his father had worked on the tamperproof design, he tried to ignore the temptation and got on with his sweeping instead, which was easier said than done because each time he caught a glimpse of the new lock the urge to try and pick it grew stronger.

Having inherited both his father's genius with the lock and the nimbleness his mother had possessed, Dare was a natural born picklock with a talent that had gotten him into trouble on more than one occasion, and today was no exception because by the time his sweeping had come to an end so had his resistance.

As he went to put the broom away, Dare glanced through the workroom doorway into the front of the shop to ensure his father was still busy. Then, he gave into the temptation, lifted the prototype, and began to probe it with one of his picklocks.

Dare quickly discovered the master locksmith had added several complex protrusions to the intricately bent wards seated within the device, and the added difficulty only served to fuel his enthusiasm. Guided by his natural instincts, the young smith skillfully worked his way past each ward, inwardly admiring his father's handiwork as he progressed.

Although the lock was a formidable affair, it didn't take the young smith long before he felt the last of the wards ease beneath his pick.

Pleased with his accomplishment, Dare checked to ensure there weren't any customers about. Then, he lifted the opened padlock by its shackle and strode cockily into the front of the shop. 'Father, this is your best lock yet.'

Looking up from his ledger, the master locksmith shook his head in resignation and said, 'Son, I don't know whether to be proud of you or worry you might be bad for business. If our customers only knew how easily you can do that, they might not bother to lock up their valuables at all.'

'I'm just following your advice,' Dare replied innocently. 'You said a good locksmith not only knows how to make em, but also how to break em.'

His father raised an eyebrow in disapproval and corrected, 'I said it's important to understand the internal workings of the lock in order to meet the customer's individual needs.'

'That's just what I said, isn't it?' Dare teased, knowing full well it wasn't what his father had said at all. Then before the master locksmith could chastise him further, Dare tossed the lock to his father just to keep him on his toes.

The master locksmith's reflexes were fast too. They had to be. As a single parent he'd grown accustomed to the sportive behavior of his son and he caught the lock effortlessly, but he refused to take the bait. Instead, he merely shook his head and said, 'Let's see if your key cutting is a good as,' he paused for emphasis, 'your other skills.' Then, he turned and headed towards the workroom at the back of the shop to check his rambunctious son's progress.

Pleased to find Dare had fashioned all of the replacement keys and that he'd tidied up as well, the master locksmith turned to him and said, 'You've done a fine job son.' Then, he nodded his head towards a wooden box filled with manacles sitting on the floor near the forge and added, 'If you deliver those to the dungeon, you can call it quits for the day.'

'Sounds good to me,' Dare replied, knowing full well he really didn't have a choice. And before his hardworking father had time to think of another task for him to do along the way, the young smith stripped off his apron, donned his jacket and hurried out the smithy with the heavy box.

It wasn't until after the door of the locksmith shop had closed safely behind him that Dare stopped to readjust the box he carried into a more comfortable position. Then, as he wondered for the umpteenth time why his father had never bought a barrow, he made his way to one of the lesser used side streets and disappeared down it.

Dare had been making deliveries and helping his father at the smithy for as long as he could remember. And once he'd grown tall enough to actually work the forge, the master locksmith had taught him how to hammer hot iron. As a result, of this and his combat training with Zarak, he'd developed a muscular frame and could've easily been mistaken for a soldier had his attire not marked him otherwise.

Despite the crisp winter air, Dare soon felt the first droplets of perspiration begin to form on his brow from the exertion of carrying the heavy box. But, it wasn't until the muscles in his arms began to burn that the droplets turned into angry beads of hot sweat and started to trickle, ever so slowly, down his forehead and into his eyes, stinging them and blurring his vision.

Forced to stop, Dare put down the box and wiped the sweat from his brow. Then, just as he started to rub the circulation back into his arms, he heard a familiar voice shout, 'Dare, what's in the box? It sure looks heavy!'

Glancing across the street, the young locksmith spied his friend Rhea. The two of them were very close in age and had been raised like brothers after the death of Dare's mother when his father, unable to rear a small child and run the family business single-handedly, would drop Dare off at Rhea's house each morning before opening the locksmith shop.

It had been Rhea's mother who'd rapped his knuckles with her wooden spoon and scolded him so he wouldn't burn himself when he'd tried to reach into the cooking pot hanging above the fire. And, it had been Rhea's mother who'd cuddled him and kissed away his childhood tears whenever he'd fallen and scraped a knee or bumped his head.

Dare genuinely liked Rhea, despite of the fact Rhea was a rogue and had a knack for getting the two of them into trouble. And because they'd grown up together, a strong bond existed between them regardless of their differences. Ignoring his discomfort, Dare shouted back, 'It's the latest in wrist attire! You know, what the well-dressed prisoner is wearing this year.'

By the time the young locksmith finished speaking, Rhea had made his way across the street. Wearing his usual conspiratorial smile, Rhea took one look at his exhausted friend and declared, 'You look like you could sure use a drink. How about stopping for a swift mug before you go to the dungeon?'

Seeing Dare was about to object, Rhea hurriedly continued. 'It would only be the one, just a short break before you finish your delivery. And, I'm sure the prisoners won't mind the wait.'

Although he was tired, Dare couldn't help but smile. It was true he needed a rest. And, he was thirsty, so he agreed. 'You're right. I don't think I can carry this box much further anyway.'

Rhea thumped his friend triumphantly on the back and said, 'Come on, let's get you that drink.' And, it was only then he offered to help Dare carry the box.

Normally, Rhea went out of his way to avoid physical work of any kind, relying instead on his charm and quick wit to get what he wanted. However, because of his close friendship with Dare, from time to time he'd make an exception and this was one of those rare occasions. Having learned the Oak Barrel had just changed hands, Rhea was already on his way there to see what it was like and was in need of a drinking companion. So, when he saw Dare from across the street with a need of his own, it made sense for him to lend a helping hand, once Dare had agreed to join him.

As they made their way to the tavern, Rhea chatted enthusiastically. 'You're sure lucky I bumped into you when I did. Why, by the look of you, your strength could've given out and you might've dropped that box on your foot and broken it. And then, where would you be? I'll tell you where, unable to make any more deliveries, that's where.'

Too tired to get a word in edgewise, Dare just grunted in reply, because at that particular moment he was still trying to decide which option was the worst.

Not waiting for his friend to comment further, Rhea continued with his narrative and was just about finished describing all of the pain he was saving Dare from when they entered the dimly lit tavern.

Because the afternoon was still young, there were several empty tables for them to choose from. And in unspoken agreement, the two young men carried the heavy box to the nearest one and set it down with a thud upon the stone floor.

By the unceremonious way Dare sank onto the wooden stool, Rhea could tell his companion was nearly done in. So without saying another word, an action totally out of character for him, Rhea walked over to the bar to order their drinks while Dare wiped the sweat from his brow and caught his breath.

When the tavern owner turned to serve him, Rhea noticed the man had a mouth full of chipped teeth, as well as several scars which he presumed were from settling brawls over the years. And by the look of the scar which started in the middle of the man's left cheek and ran backwards to where he was missing an earlobe, Rhea thought that particular fight must've been a good one and was a bit sorry to have missed it.

When Rhea returned to the table with the two mugs of ale, he immediately handed one of the drinks to his parched friend. Then after seating himself, he leaned closely towards Dare and said in a hushed conspiratorial voice, 'From the look of the new proprietor, this place could be even more lively than before and I think we might get to see some excitement before we leave.'

More interested in quenching his thirst, Dare downed several large gulps of ale before coming up for air. Then, after he'd set his mug down and he wiped his mouth with the back of his hand, he replied, 'We won't be staying long. And besides, you know how my father feels about us getting into fights.'

'I know, but a fellow has to let off a little steam once in a while,' Rhea said defensively.

'Rhea, somehow you let off more steam than anyone else I know.'

Rhea laughed at this and agreed, 'I just can't seem to help myself. Getting into mischief is one of the things I do best.'

'It sure is, but I keep hoping you'll grow out of it one day,' Dare said drily.

Their brotherly banter continued until they reached the bottom of their mugs. Then against Dare's better judgement, they bought another round.

As they talked and the circulation slowly returned to Dare's arms, the smith began to relax and paid little attention to the tables around him as they gradually filled with the evening crowd. And by the time they neared the bottom of their second mug, Rhea had successfully coaxed him into drinking yet another, on the condition he'd help deliver the manacles once they'd drank it.

After catching the tavern owner's attention, the burly man slowly made his way towards them, chatting with his customers and filling empty mugs as he went from a large clay pitcher which was just as chipped as his teeth. Then, when he reached their table and noticed the box of manacles setting on the floor beside them, he asked in a raspy voice, 'What's with the irons boys?'

Rhea wasn't one to miss an opportunity, especially when he thought a few easy coppers might be had. And, knowing Dare always carried a couple of spare picklocks tucked inside the broad protective leather cuffs he wore, Rhea slapped his unsuspecting friend on the back and answered as the smith choked on his ale, 'My companion here is an escape artist and these are his props.'

Too busy trying to catch his breath to object, Dare shot Rhea a dirty look in the hope his friend would shut his pie hole.

However, Rhea had other ideas and continued, 'He's much too modest to tell you, but his mother worked as a magician's assistant before she got married and became respectable. Then after he was born, she,' Rhea paused for a moment when Dare kicked him in the shin from beneath the table. But not letting a little thing like a new bruise stop him, he persevered, 'began instructing him in the magical arts just as soon as he could talk.'

Although it was true Dare's mother had assisted a local conjurer at the spring fete several times when she was a girl, the rest of Rhea's tale was a total fabrication. But by now, things had progressed way too far for Dare to do anything other than just sit there and hope the innkeeper would soon lose interest and go on about his business.

Unfortunately, the large man wouldn't let the matter drop. Intrigued, he turned to Dare and said, 'Let me get this straight. You chain yourself up and people pay you to free yourself.'

By now everyone else in the room was looking their way, which was exactly what Rhea wanted. And without missing a beat, he replied loudly, 'That's right.' Then, he stood up and announced, 'Would any of you be interested in witnessing this great escape artist at work?'

Dare's worst nightmare suddenly began to take shape before his very eyes as one of the unscrupulous looking men sitting at the next table enthusiastically replied, 'This I've got to see.' Then, as the man's drinking companions rowdily agreed, the man held up his scarred wrists and unashamedly displayed his lack of success in trying to remove the irons he'd once worn.

The situation quickly snowballed out of control after that, as more of the publican's drunken patrons said they'd like to see Dare's act too. Then, from somewhere at the back of the tavern, someone started to beat a slow tattoo with the flat of their hand on top of a table and, within a few heartbeats, the drumming spread across the room like wildfire.

Scared sober and outnumbered, the smith knew if he tried to leave the crowd would turn into an angry mob and he'd be forced into a fight he couldn't possibly win. Therefore, the only other available option was to try and give the performance of his life. And then, if he actually pulled it off, he'd live long enough to give Rhea a well-deserved thump on the nose.

Resigned to his fate, Dare took what he hoped everyone would think was a casual sip from his mug as he surreptitiously searched the room for a place where he could stand with his back to the wall during his impromptu performance. Then once he found the perfect spot, he set the mug back down, forced a smile onto his face, and stood up.

As the room quieted, the smith bent down and made a big show of fishing out the large ring of keys from the wooden box near his feet. Then, he held it high in the air for all to see, before handing it to the tavern owner with a flourish and saying, 'Look after this for me. But mind you,' he warned mischievously, 'I want it back when I'm finished.'

The burly man accepted the ring with a broken toothed grin and replied, 'I've always fancied myself owning one of these. And, knowing this lot,' he nodded his head towards his customers, 'it would be a handy thing to have around.'

While Dare's would-be audience hooted with laughter, the smith took advantage of the moment and looked the men over carefully. Then once they'd quieted back down, he asked one of the more respectable looking fellows, a dockworker wearing a woolly cap, to choose a pair of manacles from the wooden box. And to everyone's delight, the man with the knitted cap reached in and retrieved a pair from the very bottom of the box.

With all eyes upon him, Dare nonchalantly walked over to the location he'd spotted earlier. Then, he turned to face the raucous crowd and instructed the dockman to fasten his arms securely behind his back.

While the man obliged, Dare started to relax. Everyone there seemed to be in high spirits and the smith was surprised to find he was actually beginning to enjoy himself, now that he was in control of the situation. And no longer worried, he decided to ham it up. 'These are sure a lot heavier than the pair I practiced with at home.'

The man with the scarred wrist shouted back, 'You get used to them after a year or two!' Then while he and his companions laughed rowdily, Dare replied, 'I sure hope I'm faster than that.'

'Me too! I only have money for one more drink!' someone else shouted from across the room, which made the others laugh all the more.

Dare waited for the man with the woolly hat to retake his seat. Then, after everyone had quieted back down, he glanced over to the man with the scarred wrist and said, 'You're familiar with these things. Why don't you come over here and make sure they're fastened properly.'

The man's drinking companions thought this funny, and then they laughed uproariously when he stood up and announced, 'When I got up this morning, I sure never thought I'd be doing this.'

'That makes two of us,' Dare replied good-naturedly.

The scarred-wrist man did as he was bidden. Then, he confirmed loudly, 'They're as tight as a miser's purse.' And as he momentarily distracted the crowd by returning to his table, Dare seamlessly slipped one of the spare picklocks he always carried from the inside of his broad leather cuff and began to deftly probe the manacle's locking mechanism.

As everyone turned back to look at Dare, the smith pretended to struggle with the manacles a little and advised, 'Unless you have a hammer and chisel handy, I wouldn't recommend any of you try this for yourselves.'

While his audience laughed appreciatively, Dare then glanced over to the tavern owner and enquired, 'By the way, do you serve breakfast?'

Joining in the fun, the burly man shouted back, 'No, but for you I'll make an exception! Just don't expect me to spoon feed it to you!'

Although the locking mechanism was very basic and held little challenge for the young smith, Dare continued to ham it up by making exaggerated facial expressions and doing a lot of shoulder wriggling. And as his audience laughed at his antics, he swiftly finished picking both of the locks, and then slipped the picklock back into his leather cuff.

To make his performance last a little longer, Dare spoke loudly for everyone to hear. 'There are only two kinds of escape artists, skilled ones and very thin incompetent ones. The skilled ones make it their profession. As for the incompetent ones, they eventually find a new line of work, once they've lost enough weight for their shackles to slide off.'

He paused a moment for the crowd's laughter to die down, and then continued, 'And, now you'll see which kind of escape artist I am.'

The room fell quiet in anticipation.

Dare stopped moving and stood perfectly still. Then using his best showman's voice, he announced, 'Many a man has been fettered and chained, but lacked the skill to be free again. Fortunately for me, I'm not one of those men.' Then in one fluid movement, Dare thrust his arms dramatically forward and the manacles fell from his wrists with a thud onto the stone floor behind him.

As his high-spirited audience cheered and slapped the table tops in delight, Dare bobbed his head at them the way he'd seen trained performers do. And when the man with the scarred wrists shouted over and asked if Dare could teach him how to do it, the triumphant smith shouted back it was a trade secret and the magician's guild would make him disappear if he did, which caused even more laughter.

Dare bent down and collected the manacles from off the floor, along with several coins which had been tossed his way. Then between pats on the back, the smith allowed the tavern owner to clear a path back to his table. And as he followed in the big man's wake, he wasn't surprised to see Rhea pocket a few of the coins he was making a big show of helping to collect.

After Dare sat down, the publican returned the keyring to him. And, as he topped up the smith's mug with complements of the house, he said, 'That was sure a fine piece of handiwork.'

'It certainly was,' agreed a friendly voice from over Dare's left shoulder. 'How long have you been an escape artist?'

Not wanting to encourage the conversation, the smith turned towards the speaker, a tall dark-haired man with a beard, and replied. 'Not long. But, my heart isn't really in it, so this was my last performance.'

'What will you do next, if you don't mind my asking?'

Although Dare didn't want to advertise the fact his father was the local locksmith, he didn't want to appear to be rude either. So, he answered, 'I haven't quite decided yet.'

It was then Rhea materialized from out of the crowd grinning from ear to ear like a cat that'd just lapped up all of the cream and exclaimed, 'You were great! I always thought you were wasted working in your father's locksmith shop.'

So much for discretion, Dare thought as he shook his head. 'If my father ever finds out what I've done, he'll disown me,' he replied flatly. And for the merest instant, the smith thought he saw a glint in the dark-haired stranger's eyes. But then, Dare blinked and when he looked again the gleam was gone, making him wonder if he'd seen anything at all.

The dark-haired man laughed with friendly ease and said, 'Well, I guess we just won't tell him then. However, I can see you took your training seriously.'

Always on the lookout for new talent, the man neglected to mention he was responsible for instigating the table top tattoo that had forced the smith into his performance. Instead, he simply added, 'My name is Jerhal by the way. Mind if I join you?'

Since the harm had already been done, the smith decided to throw caution to the wind and replied, 'Sure, pull up a stool.' Then, he nodded his head towards his childhood friend and announced, 'This is Rhea. He's just come into some money and is going to buy another round.'

Knowing he'd been caught red-handed, Rhea shot Dare a sheepish grin and replied, 'That's just what I was going to say.' Then before Dare could reprove him further, Rhea excused himself and went to fetch the drinks.

Although Jerhal had seen Rhea pocket the coins too, he feigned innocence and looked enquiringly at Dare instead.

'That was payback,' the smith said by way of explanation. 'And now that Rhea knows sideshows aren't profitable, he'll have to find some other way to get his drinking money.' Then, after taking another sip from his mug, he concluded, 'My name's Dairen, but people call me Dare.'

'The name suits you,' Jerhal replied amiably.

The two of them were deep in conversation by the time Rhea returned with the drinks. Then, after making a toast to his roguish friend's good fortune, Dare let the matter drop, certain Rhea had learned his lesson and wouldn't be pulling another stunt like that one for quite some time.

It was late in the evening when the three finally decided to go their separate ways. Standing outside the tavern in the middle of the deserted street, the childhood friends bid farewell to Jerhal, who quickly melted into the winter darkness. Then left alone with their heavy burden, feeling greatly refreshed and a little too merry, Dare turned to Rhea and said, 'We'd better get these manacles delivered before my father decides we should wear em.'

Knowing the master locksmith as well as he did, Rhea picked up his end of the box and agreed. 'Yes, and I think the prisoners would suit these bracelets better than we would,' which was just the opening Dare had been waiting for.

Trying to keep a straight face, the smith added, 'Speaking of bracelets, I saw the most beautiful fortune-teller at the market,' knowing full well Rhea would make it his business to meet her the following day, just as soon as he'd recovered from the evening's exertions.

2 LILYANNA

Princess Lilyanna's eyelids felt heavy, her mouth dry. And, as she struggled to waken from her drug induced sleep, she couldn't understand why her bed felt as though it was swaying.

Through the haze in her mind, Lilyanna vaguely remembered ordering her bodyguards back so she could ride her horse freely to momentarily forget about wedding preparations and the politics at court. But then seemingly from nowhere, two horsemen had appeared and spooked her mount. There had been a struggle and, as she was being yanked from her saddle, a foul-smelling cloth had been pressed over her nose and mouth.

The princess slowly opened her eyes. As her blurred vision gradually came into focus, Lilyanna found she was in a small room. Then as she took a deep breath to help clear her head and stop the room from swaying, she noticed she could smell the sea.

Realizing she was on board a ship, her first reaction was to shout for help. But then, she heard the tread of someone's boots upon the cabin floor and knew she wasn't alone.

Paralyzed with fear, the princess closed her eyes and pretended to sleep. But after what seemed like an eternity and the person still hadn't left, she could bear it no longer and slowly turned her head to see who was there.

Alerted by her movement, a man with cold-dead eyes strode towards her and said bluntly, 'Good. You're awake. I'm glad you had the sense not to scream.

That would've made me angry, and you don't want to do that.'

Despite her drug induced grogginess, Lilyanna recognized the man as one of her abductors. But refusing to play the helpless victim, she determinedly pushed herself up into a sitting position and confronted him head-on. 'Why have you taken me?'

The man stood there a moment, appraising her like a serpent would before devouring its prey. 'You'll know soon enough. Just don't go making any trouble, or you'll sleep for the rest of the voyage.'

Knowing he spoke the truth, Lilyanna tried to swallow the lump that had suddenly formed at the back of her dry throat, and this was when she discovered the collar fastened around her neck.

'What is this?' she gasped, reaching up and trying to pull it off.

'Consider it a gift from your host,' her abductor replied without a hint of softness in his voice. Then, he strode out of the cabin and locked the door securely behind him.

Although Lilyanna sat there feeling nauseated and stunned, her clouded mind unable to comprehend what was happening, she knew one thing for certain; she was in BIG trouble.

◆◆◆

The only people Princess Lilyanna had seen in the two days since then had been her kidnappers. And although neither of the men had spoken much, she got the impression the leader was the man with the cold eyes whom, for lack of a better name, she'd mentally dubbed 'Dead Eyes' and the other man, because of his mop of wild-red hair, she'd unimaginatively named 'Scary Hairy'.

At first the princess had found the solitude nearly unbearable. Having grown up in a busy palace, there had always been someone nearby, if only a guard or retainer. And upon reflection, Lilyanna had come to the conclusion this was the first time in her life she had ever been truly alone. However, it was not in her nature to sit around and play the helpless female. So instead of waiting for a hero on a white horse to come to her rescue, she decided to pass the time more constructively and figure out where she was being taken to and by whom.

Thankfully Lilyanna had been a good student and had listened to her tutors well. She knew she could roughly determine the direction they were sailing by watching the sun and stars. So, she periodically climbed onto the berth and peered out of the small porthole to make observations.

This turned out to be a rather slow process, because the sky was overcast most of the time and she couldn't see very clearly. Although, after much dogged determination and patience, the princess discovered the ship was sailing in a northwesterly direction, which meant they were headed for Greystone and it was Elrod who had ordered her abduction.

When she was young, Lilyanna had been taught King Elrod was called the Black Hawk because it was the emblem on his coat of arms. But over the years, she had come to identify the name with the horrific deeds he'd done, first of which being the suspected poisoning of his predecessor. And now, she believed Elrod's heart was as black as the bird on his heraldry.

In an effort to fight off the rising panic within her, the princess reminded herself she was King Dallin's daughter, which gave her a sense of control over the situation. And then, she asked herself a question, 'What would father do?'

Knowing she must escape, Lilyanna began to review her options. But this didn't take very long because, with nowhere to run, there was little she could do while aboard ship. And even if she did manage to elude her captors, when they eventually caught her, she believed Dead Eyes would drug her for the rest of the voyage just as he'd threatened.

So for the time being, her best option was to pretend to cooperate with her captors, while lulling them into a false sense of security. Then when an opportunity to escape did arise, they would be caught off guard.

As the last of the evening shadows blended into the darkness, pleased she'd been able to figure out where she was being taken and had a semblance of a plan in place, Lilyanna laid down fully clothed upon the berth and quickly fell into a restless sleep.

When she awoke the following morning, the princess felt much better within herself, the lingering effects of the sedative she had been given having finally worn off.

Seeing someone had placed yet another bowl of porridge on the floor just inside the cabin doorway, Lilyanna got up and retrieved it. Because even though she truly detested the stuff, she knew it would be the only food she'd be given that day and she must keep up her strength.

As she lifted the spoon to stir some life back into the congealed oats, which looked more like rendering than something you'd actually eat, it occurred to her she had been so preoccupied with her predicament, she'd failed to examine the cabin closely for anything that might be of use to her.

Looking around the room with fresh eyes, it soon became apparent the previous occupant had vacated in a hurry, taking only a few items of clothing from the drawers beneath the berth. And, the small desk located in the corner of the room was so cluttered, there wasn't even enough space to set down a bowl of porridge, which up until now she had thought nothing about but it did explain why the bowls were being left on the floor beside the doorway.

Then, it suddenly struck her that she had overlooked the obvious; most sailors didn't have private quarters. So, whose cabin was this?

Excited, Lilyanna set down her unfinished bowl of porridge on the berth and went to investigate.

She started by rummaging through the clutter on the desktop, searching for anything which might come in handy during an escape or help her to determine if the cabin's previous occupant was friend or foe.

The princess quickly discovered several ledgers and opened one at random. From the listings, she could tell the ship was a merchant vessel employed to carry cargo, not passengers. So with a shortage of quarters, it made sense someone would have had to vacate theirs in order to accommodate her.

After closing the ledger and placing it back with the others, Lilyanna then came upon several large rolled documents, which she presumed were navigational charts.

The princess carefully unrolled one and quickly realized she was looking at the coastline around the western edge of her father's kingdom, so she discarded it and unrolled a second chart that was of no more use than the first. However, third time lucky, when Lilyanna examined the large document, she discovered it was far more than a mere navigational chart. It not only depicted the coastline around the Port of Hesketh, the southern edge of King Elrod's domain and what she presumed was the ship's destination, it mapped the entire kingdom of Greystone.

Lilyanna carefully tore off the portion of the map that showed the route from the port to Greystone Fortress, folded it as small as she possibly could, and tucked it into the hidden pocket within the folds of her riding dress. Then, she rerolled the chart in such a way that, at first glance, no one would have guessed it had been tampered with, and placed it beneath the others.

A quick search through the rest of the desktop clutter revealed nothing more of use, so the princess turned her attention to the contents of its two drawers.

Amongst the bits and pieces stashed inside the top drawer, Lilyanna found a small silver box so out of character with the other items she decided it warranted further investigation and withdrew it.

Even though the box bore no embellishments, Lilyanna admired the craftsmanship and thought it pretty because of its simplicity. It felt good in her hand. And, because the silver was burnished to such a high shine, she quickly realized she could see the collar she had been forced to wear reflected on the metal.

She already knew there were seven gemstones mounted on the collar. She had felt the settings, one large gem in the center and three smaller ones on either side of it. But, this was the first opportunity she'd had to actually see them and what she saw terrified her, because the blood-red stones pulsated with her heartbeat.

Once she had recovered from the shock and revulsion, Lilyanna tried to work the collar around her neck so she could see the clasp's reflection and unfasten the accursed thing. Yet no matter how hard she tugged, the golden collar would not budge. And in the end, when her skin began to redden and sting, she was forced to give up the effort.

Still determined to find something that might be of use to her, the princess turned her attention back to the silver box. But when she lifted its hinged lid and disappointingly found it contained a lock of hair bound by a silk ribbon, a cherished memento of the cabin's previous occupant but absolutely of no use to her, she closed the lid and carefully returned the box to its hiding place.

Lilyanna then reached down to pull open the bottom drawer, which she swiftly discovered had warped in the sea air. But, she was no quitter and just kept tugging and tugging on its handle until the stubborn drawer finally jerked open.

Her efforts did not go unrewarded, because placed on the very top of the rest of the drawer's contents sat the ship's log, bound in dark blue leather. Thus, her suspicion she was being held in the captain's quarters was confirmed.

She removed the log and carried it over to the berth. Then after making herself comfortable, she began to read the captain's clear script, only pausing now and again to force down more of the cold porridge.

The princess soon discovered the surname of the captain was Nagrom and the ship, christened Venture, had been commissioned five years earlier. But, the really interesting thing was that Venture's home port was White Cliff.

Lilyanna considered this carefully for a few minutes and realized, after her abduction, Elrod's men must have simply boarded the first available ship heading to Hesketh they encountered. The captain probably didn't even know she was on board. And, if her assumption was correct, he might be an unsuspecting ally.

Excited, Lilyanna began to peruse through the log and noted the captain had written daily entries up until four days previously, the day she had been brought on board. So it stood to reason, the captain would resume making his entries when he had access to his logbook once more.

Inspired, the princess decided to write him a secret message within the log itself. And if the captain was indeed the unsuspecting pawn she believed him to be, he would lend his assistance once he learned of her predicament.

Lilyanna walked over to the cluttered desk, retrieved the inkwell and quill she had spotted earlier, and carried them back to the berth. Then, she dipped the quill into the ink and began to write just beneath the captain's last log entry:

Dear Captain Nagrom,

I have been abducted. I write to you in the belief you had no prior knowledge of this. Please take the following message to my father, King Dallin, at White Cliff Castle. He will reward you for your efforts.

Please hurry, time is of the essence.

Sincerely,

Princess Lilyanna

Dearest Father,

I am well and miss you.

By now you will know I have been abducted. I believe by hirelings of King Elrod, as even now we sail in a northwesterly direction towards the Port of Hesketh.

Captain Nagrom had no knowledge of his part in this. Please look kindly upon him and reward him for delivering this message to you.

Please tell Urba I have been forced to wear a golden collar which I am unable to remove. The collar has seven blood-red gemstones that pulsate with my heartbeat. The largest gem is mounted in the center and there are three smaller stones mounted on either side.

Your loving daughter,

Lilyanna

To make the messages look official and to offer proof they had been penned by her, Lilyanna removed the candle from its wall mount beside the berth and lit the wick. Then once the wax had started to melt, she dripped some of the wax next to her signature at the bottom of the last message and pressed her signet ring into it.

Satisfied with the result, the princess blew out the candle and carefully returned everything back to its rightful place so no one would suspect her exploits. And for the first time since her abduction, later that evening when she lay down upon the berth, Lilyanna was able to sleep restfully, content in the knowledge she had finally gained some control over her situation.

The next morning when Scary Hairy unlocked her cabin door bearing the usual bowl as well as a small jug of water, Lilyanna had already risen, having been awakened by gulls as they neared port.

Seeing she was up, rather than placing the items beside the door, her abductor strode across the cabin and handed them to her. 'Here. You'd better eat. I don't know when we'll be feeding you again.'

Having been fed scarcely enough to keep a bird alive throughout the voyage, the princess nodded her appreciation for the warning and thanked him with a small smile.

Scary Hairy hesitated for the briefest of moments, as if he wanted to say something more. But then, he must have had second thoughts, because he turned around and left without saying another word and locked the cabin door behind him.

Lilyanna had made it a point to give Scary Hairy a small smile at least once whenever they were alone together, in the hope he would eventually warm to her. So far, he hadn't reacted to her ploy, but the princess took it as a good sign he had encouraged her to eat because he had not done this before. And, when he had hesitated, Lilyanna knew deep within her heart she was starting to get to him.

A moment later, when she glanced into the bowl, she discovered something even more amazing. Instead of the congealed oats she had expected, the bowl contained bread and cheese. And if she hadn't been so busy stuffing her face, she might have cried with happiness.

◆◆◆

Several hours later as the ship's crew prepared to drop anchor, Lilyanna wasn't surprised to hear the door to her cabin being unlocked. And when her abductors entered the small room and the man she called Dead Eyes thrust a hooded cloak towards her, she put it on without complaint, knowing the sooner she vacated the captain's quarters the sooner Nagrom would be able to enter the cabin and find the message she had left him.

What Lilyanna had not expected, was that just as soon as she had finished connecting the cloak's fastener, Dead Eyes would hold the foul smelling cloth over her nose and mouth for a second time. And that, as her world grew dark and her knees gave way, Scary Hairy would catch her in his arms and throw her over his shoulder like a bag of grain so he could carry her off the ship.

Dirk, the more experienced of the two, stopped him before he reached the door. 'Red, not like that. It'll arouse suspicion. Here, give her to me.'

The wild-haired man looked down at Lilyanna and hesitated, 'I sort of hate to part with her. She's the first woman I've held in years that's still got all of her teeth.'

'Yeah, the last woman I held didn't even have a pulse,' Dirk replied flatly.

Taking this for a joke, the wild-haired man was about to laugh, but then he saw the look in the other man's eyes and realized Dirk was deadly serious. So, Red decided to keep his yap shut and handed Lilyanna over to his partner, because the last man who'd antagonized Dirk now had to beg for a living and he liked walking just a bit too much to end up like that.

Distracted, Dirk didn't notice the redhead's reaction and told him, 'Pull her hood forward and let's get out of here.'

Red quickly did as he was bidden. Then, he opened the door and followed Dirk and the princess from the cabin.

Captain Nagrom was busy overseeing the unloading of his ship's cargo when he noticed his passengers upon deck. After giving Rowan, his first mate, a few last minute instructions, he walked over to the two men and enquired, 'How's the lady today?'

'She's still the same. She wakes rarely with little appetite and finds the light painful to her eyes.' Dirk lied with practiced ease.

'Hopefully the healers of Hesketh will be able to help her,' the captain replied earnestly as he gazed down upon the sleeping woman hidden beneath the voluminous cloak.

'That's our strongest desire,' Dirk agreed with mock sincerity as he cradled the woman even more protectively against his chest. 'Thank you for making an exception and allowing us passage on your vessel. But, please excuse us. The sooner we can get our mistress to the healer, the sooner she'll be recovered.' And with that, the two abductors dismissed themselves and headed towards the gangway with their helpless captive.

3 VENTURE

It was well past noon before all of the Venture's cargo had been offloaded, and by then Captain Nagrom and his hard working crew were ravenous; the fact Stewpot, the ship's cook, had a large cauldron of butterbeans and salted pork simmering away hadn't helped matters either, because for the last half hour the mouthwatering aroma had been wafting teasingly past their noses like the inviting perfume of an expectant lover which they could do nothing about.

Then finally, as their empty stomachs started to grumble in protest, the last of the wooden crates were lowered dockside. And once the cargo nets had been safely stowed away, the hungry men were able to make their way to the ship's galley.

Not standing on ceremony, Captain Nagrom joined the queue along with his men. And when it was his turn to be served, he grabbed a bowl from the top of the stack and handed it to Stewpot. 'Fill it to the brim. I'm so hungry I could eat the hind quarters off a sea monster and still have room to eat its brains for pudding.'

Having never seen a sea monster, Stewpot didn't know if the creatures even existed. But as he began to ladle the bowl full, he jokingly enquired, 'Oh yeah, what would you do with the claws? You know how I hate waste.'

'Why, I'd pick my teeth with them afterwards, of course,' the captain replied good-naturedly.

'Well, I'm fresh out of sea monster, so this will have to do,' Stewpot said as he began to hand the steaming bowl back to the captain. But as he did so, Nagrom's stomach rumbled loudly and the cook couldn't help but add, 'From the sound of things, I think the last sea monster you ate is still in there.'

'Aye, it's been trying to eat me from the inside out for most of the morning, so I thought I'd try to poison it with some of this,' the captain replied with a grin as he raised the bowl towards his friend and then turned and walked away.

Stewpot didn't take offence. From the small queue of hungry sailors waiting to be served, he knew they were just as eager as the captain had been to poison a few sea monsters of their own. So, he started ladling out the bean soup just as fast as he could, aware that once the men had eaten, they'd have other appetites ashore to satisfy.

As was his custom, Captain Nagrom carried the steaming bowl back to his cabin. And once inside, just as he always did, he pushed some of the clutter on his desk to one side so he would have space to place his bowl before he sat down to eat.

Although Nagrom had worked his way through the ranks, over the years he had gradually become accustomed to having his own private quarters and was glad to have the solitude of his cabin back, because for the past four days he'd had to share a small cabin with his first mate and, although Rowan was a good man, the sailor snored so loudly it was difficult to get any sleep.

Once he had finished eating, the captain set aside the empty bowl and jerkily pulled open the warped bottom drawer of his desk so he could withdraw the ship's logbook to update it. But after flipping through the book's pages, he was surprised to find someone, with an unfamiliar hand, had written two messages beneath his last entry; the first message was addressed to him and the second was oddly addressed to the writer's father. The penmanship was delicate and, without looking at the signature, the captain immediately knew they had been written by a woman's hand.

He leaned closer and carefully read the message addressed to him.

Dear Captain Nagrom,

I have been abducted. I write to you in the belief you had no prior knowledge of this. Please take the following message to my father, King Dallin, at White Cliff Castle. He will reward you for your efforts. Please hurry, time is of the essence.

Sincerely,

Princess Lilyanna

Dearest Father,

I am well and miss you.

By now you will know I have been abducted. I believe by hirelings of King Elrod, as even now we sail in a northwesterly direction towards the Port of Hesketh.

Captain Nagrom had no knowledge of his part in this. Please look kindly upon him and reward him for delivering this message to you.

Please tell Urba I have been forced to wear a golden collar which I am unable to remove. The collar has seven blood-red gemstones that pulsate with my heartbeat. The largest gem is mounted in the center and there are three smaller stones mounted on either side.

Your loving daughter,

Lilyanna

After a quick examination of the wax seal, Captain Nagrom knew with gut aching certainty he had been played like a fine fiddle and duped into assisting the princess's kidnappers. But what angered him the most was, it had never once occurred to him the two men might be anything other than what they appeared to be, the dedicated servants of an extremely ill woman who had pleaded with him for passage aboard his cargo ship, something he never allowed. And now, to make amends for this error in judgement, he would have to return to White Cliff just as quickly as possible and deliver the princess's message to the king.

His decision made, the captain slammed the logbook shut and strode out of the cabin.

A quick glance around the deserted weather deck confirmed his suspicion that most of the men had already gone ashore. However, Nagrom also knew there was always a straggler or two on the tween and lower decks, so he headed towards the hold. And sure enough, just as he reached the hatchway, the captain spotted one of the younger crewmen heading his way with a bag of dirty laundry slung over one shoulder.

'There's been a change in plans,' the captain informed him. 'Shore leave's been cancelled. Find the others and tell them to return to the ship immediately. We must sail with the morning tide.'

The startled sailor quickly regained his composure and replied, 'Aye aye captain.' Then, he disappeared back down the steps to rid himself of his laundry bag.

Confident his orders would be carried out, Nagrom next headed for the galley in search of Stewpot.

The captain smelled the smoke from the cook's pipe before he actually saw him. Having served a very late midday meal, the older man now sat resting upon a crate outside the galley door, escaping the heat of the stove and drawing on his pipe.

'I thought I'd find you here,' Captain Nagrom said as the cook looked up.

Stewpot removed the pipe from his lips and replied, 'Aye, my shoring and whoring days are long over. Now, I get more pleasure from my pipe and,' he added with a shrug, 'it takes a lot less work to spark up.'

The captain shook his head and smiled. 'We both know you're not that old. You just don't want to part with any of your pay.'

'That's true. I'm saving up. One day I'll find me a nice woman who wants nothing more than to cook for me. And then, I'm going to wed her and hang up my ladle for good.' Stewpot said with a grin. Then, he became more serious and asked, 'Anyway, you didn't look me up just to discuss my love life, so what can I do for you?'

The captain's expression sobered and he replied, 'We need to set sail back to White Cliff with the morning tide, so I'm having the men recalled.' Seeing that Stewpot was about to ask why, the captain held up his hand to forestall him. 'Long story. I'll explain later, but I need you to replenish the food and water supplies straightway. And because we won't be transporting any cargo this voyage, feel free to commandeer as many men as you need to help.'

Stewpot couldn't believe his ears. Sailing with an empty hold meant the captain, sole owner of the Venture, would incur a huge financial loss. But, a fast departure with less weight in the hold meant that, for this particular journey, speed was more important to Nagrom than wealth. Realizing the seriousness of the matter, the cook stood up and said solemnly, 'Aye aye captain.'

Nagrom nodded his thanks and then dismissed himself by saying, 'I'll leave you to it.'

As Stewpot tapped out his pipe, the captain started to make his way back to his cabin to sort out the paperwork caused by the unexpected turn of events. But, he hadn't even reached the door before Rowan, his first mate, came rushing up to him and asked, 'Is it true you've cancelled shore leave?'

'It's true. I'll explain everything in my quarters.'

Rowan, ever the professional, was aware rumors spread across deck faster than a ship could drop anchor, held his tongue and fell into step beside Nagrom.

After they had entered the privacy of captain's cabin, Nagrom walked over to the desk and retrieved his logbook. Then, he flipped it open, thumbed through the pages until he found the place where the princess had written her messages, and handed the book to Rowan.

Puzzled, the first mate took the logbook. Seeing the unfamiliar script, he read the messages carefully, and then looked back up and exclaimed, 'I didn't see this one coming!'

'Nor I. Who would've thought doing a good turn could drop us into such a mess?' Nagrom replied, shaking his head.

'I sure hope the king's in an understanding mood when we give him the princess's message.'

'Rowan, you're a true friend and loyal first mate. But as captain, I'm personally responsible for all of the decisions aboard the Venture. So, I'll see the king. And if he requires someone to fall on his sword, it will be me who bares his chest.'

'I sure hope it doesn't come to that.'

'Me too,' Nagrom replied wholeheartedly. 'However, let's keep this to ourselves until after we've set sail, because we don't know who the king's enemies are.'

As Rowan nodded in agreement, the captain continued, 'But first things first, we'll need to inform the harbormaster of our change in plans.' And sitting down at his desk, he dipped quill to ink and quickly scrawled a message to that effect which he then handed to his first mate for delivery.

While Rowan departed on his errand, Nagrom then hurriedly wrote several short letters of apology which he addressed to the merchants who had booked the Venture to transport their goods on what should have been the vessel's next voyage. In the letters, he explained there would be an unavoidable delay of about ten days and he would understand if they made alternative arrangements in the meantime. Then once the ink dried, the captain scooped up the letters and went out onto the weather deck in search of someone to deliver them.

Seeing several of his crewmen had already reported back for duty, Nagrom walked over to the one who could read, a sailor nicknamed 'Sail Cloth' because the man was usually three sheets to the wind while ashore but due to the fast recall appeared to be remarkably sober, and handed him the letters for delivery.

The first of the foodstuffs started to arrive shortly thereafter and, since the majority of his men had families living in White Cliff, the captain was pleased to find they did not mind being called back to the ship early, although it might have been a different story had their home port been Hesketh.

By late evening the last of the provisions were hauled on board. Impressed by the swift and efficient way in which Stewpot had organized the victuals to be delivered, Nagrom decided to seek the cook out and thank him personally for his efforts.

Having sailed with the cook for the last five years, the captain had never heard the older man whistle so much as a single note. But as Nagrom drew nearer to galley's open doorway, he was surprised to hear Stewpot whistling a jaunty tune and could not understand why the cook would be in such high spirits after working such a long day.

Brushing the feeling aside, the captain stepped into the galley and interrupted the cook's melody. 'I don't know how you managed it so quickly, but the ship is fully provisioned and I want you to know I appreciate your hard work.'

'Think nothing of it,' the older man replied happily, waving the captain's thank you away with his hand. 'You did me the favor. Remember that woman I told you about, the one I'm going to marry?' Not waiting for a reply, Stewpot continued, 'Well, I met her today. She's the miller's sister. Normally, she has already left for the day by the time I get there to buy supplies. But today, she was there. And get this, she's been working there for years but our paths just never crossed.'

The captain understood. He'd felt this strange kind of happiness the day he had met the woman he eventually married. And despite his tiredness, Nagrom smiled and asked, 'Is she pretty?'

'Aye, she's a handsome woman, with a good sense of humor too. When I first saw her, she had a smudge of flour on her cheek. So, just as bold as brass, I walked right up to her and said, "I'm going to call you Petal because there's a little flour on that pretty cheek of yours." Then, she looked up at me and we both laughed.' The cook shook his head and continued, 'I know. It sounds silly now, but it was a grand joke at the time.'

'So, she's pretty and she has a good sense of humor. But, can she cook? Remember, you told me you wanted to hang up your ladle.'

'That's the best part,' Stewpot replied with a grin from ear to ear. 'With all of that flour on hand, she bakes every morning. And, her pies have pastry so light, they just float right off the plate and into your mouth.'

'Well, I'm happy for you Stewpot. It isn't everyday a man meets the woman of his dreams.'

'It sure isn't,' Stewpot agreed as he bent down to move a stack of potatoes out of the way.

Seeing how busy the cook still was, Nagrom excused himself saying, 'I'd best let you get on with it.' And, as he strode away, he heard Stewpot resume his merry tune.

Although the captain was happy for Stewpot and his newfound ladylove, he was sorry to be losing such a fine ship's cook. And now, on top of delivering the princess's message and facing the wrath of the king upon their return to West Cliff, he would have to either start looking for a replacement cook or find someone suitable to apprentice to the current one, which was not going to be easy.

With an early start on the morrow and tired from the complications of the day, Captain Nagrom returned to his cabin and undressed. Too weary to bother with hanging up his clothes, he tossed the garments across the back of the desk chair and lay down on his berth, thankful to be spending the night back in his own quarters and glad he would not be disturbed by his first mate's snoring.

4 ROBIN

Three months earlier, Robin had started to hear a gentle whispering on the fringes of her mind and thought she was beginning to go mad. Having spent the past two years living in constant fear, she had suspected she would eventually lose her sanity as a result of the anxiety. And in an odd sort of way, she felt strangely relieved, because now she would not feel afraid anymore.

Over the following days, the whispering inside her mind gradually began to grow louder and more insistent, transforming from an incoherent whisper into a small voice which called out to her intermittently as she went about the fortress performing her duties. And although Robin knew it wasn't normal to hear a voice inside one's head, she was so very lonely; she welcomed it all the same.

Robin's life hadn't always been filled with fear and loneliness. Once she had lived a normal life and had friends just like everyone else. Then at the age of nineteen, she witnessed an evil so foul the shock of it had turned the color of her hair from the soft brown of her namesake to that of newly fallen snow. And ever since then, in their superstitious ignorance, the people of Greystone Fortress believed her to be evil and had ostracized her.

At the time, she had been so traumatized and withdrawn, she neither noticed nor cared how anyone was reacting to her. And by the time her dazed mind had finally realized what was happening, the white-haired woman hadn't a friend left in the entire world.

Now, like a mother attuned to her baby's cry, she found herself listening out for the small voice.

Through the process of elimination, Robin discovered the voice became louder the nearer to the king's private library she strode, which logically made no sense because, if she really was losing her mind, she would hear the voice clearly no matter where she went.

Realizing something wasn't quite right, Robin's aching loneliness and curiosity slowly overpowered her fear and she decided to investigate. And, because it was commonplace for her to be seen walking about the fortress carrying her sewing basket, Robin decided to enter the library on the pretext of mending the seat covers of the reading chairs inside.

With her decision made, the white-haired woman returned to her chamber and retrieved her sewing basket, although she left most of its contents on her small bed with the exception of a pair of scissors, a needle and several spools of thread which she would need if her story was to be believed. Then, she set off towards the library.

Not deceptive by nature, by the time Robin finally reached the library, she had to take a moment to calm her nerves and strengthen her resolve before she lifted her hand to rap upon the ornately carved door.

She waited several seconds. Then, when there was no response from within, the white-haired woman quickly opened the door and stepped inside.

The hairs on the back of her neck began to tingle in warning as Robin glanced around the room and found the interior of the library looked more like an apothecary's workroom than the peaceful place of learning she remembered from two years earlier when she had been there with Lady Allyce.

Her instincts told her to turn and run, but she knew she owed it to Allyce to find out what new evil Elrod was up to. So despite her misgivings, the white-haired woman slowly set down her sewing basket and bravely forced her trembling legs forward, her quest for the soft voice momentarily forgotten.

A long worktable occupied the center of the room where several freestanding bookcases once stood, and Robin spotted a large bookmarked tome resting amongst the stoppered vials and potion-filled jars which cluttered the table's surface.

Knowing the book held the key to whatever Elrod was working on, Robin walked over and reached for it. But just as soon as her fingers touched the cover, its gold lettering began to shimmer and change shape.

Startled, the white-haired woman pulled her hand back as if it was burnt. And when she did, the golden lettering reverted to its original form and the shimmering ceased.

Realizing the book was of the old magic, Robin grew even more frightened and was just about to bolt from the room when she heard the familiar voice say reassuringly, 'Don't be afraid. I'm here.' But this time Robin not only heard the voice in her mind, she also heard it with her ears, and it appeared to be coming from one of the upper shelves on the walled bookcase to her right.

Reminded of the original purpose for her visit to the library and not wanting to be in the room a second longer than necessary, Robin grabbed one of the library ladders and pulled it over to bookcase. Then, she hitched up her grey dress in an unladylike way and clambered up the ladder just as fast as her shaking legs could carry her.

When she reached the top shelf, Robin saw what looked like a clutch of six very large goose eggs and, from the thick layer of dust covering them, assumed they must have been placed there some time ago.

On impulse, she reached out her hand and ran it lightly over the surface of the first two eggs, which felt cold to the touch. But when her fingertips brushed across the third egg, she was surprised to feel a slight vibration. And then, she heard the familiar voice say, 'I thought you'd never get here.'

For the first time in over two years, Robin began to laugh. But, it was not happy laughter, it was the nervous kind brought on by suppressed fear and the realization she had gone completely mad because who in their right mind would be teetering on a ladder, scared half to death, in the middle of a converted library listening to a talking egg.

But before her laughter could turn into full-blown hysteria, the small voice from inside the shell scolded, 'Don't laugh. This is harder than it looks.'

Somehow this sobered Robin and she was able to stifle her laughter. 'I'm sorry. I couldn't help it.'

'I know. I can feel your fear,' the creature within the egg replied. 'I'll try to hurry.' And then, it started to make muffled tapping sounds.

Robin watched wide-eyed as the egg began to wobble and a small crack appeared on the surface of the shell, then another and another. Then all of a sudden, the shell burst apart and there, sitting on the shelf in the middle of the broken shell fragments, was a tiny winged creature which Robin realized must be some kind of strange reptile because it had iridescent scales that shifted in color between copper and sage green depending upon which way it moved.

The little creature looked straight into the white-haired woman's eyes and greeted her with a kind of rumbling purr before saying, 'That was hard work.'

'I bet it was,' Robin replied, still trying to figure out what kind of creature she was talking to as it stood up. And then, as it stretched out its limp wings, she recognized it for what it was, a very small dragon.

Filled with wonder, she reached out and tenderly stroked the top of the little dragon's scaled head with her forefinger. 'Do you have a name?'

'Erosmay, and I'm hungry.'

Wondering why she seemed to be the only person who had heard the dragon's voice in her mind, Robin was about to ask, but before she could Erosmay piped in, 'We are linked companions. We can communicate telepathically and with speech. You need more practice, but I can hear you clearly right now.'

Albeit this concept was new to her, Robin did feel a connection with the little dragon and held out her hand so Erosmay could step onto it. Then, she protectively cradled her new linked companion against her chest and began to descend the ladder.

Once they had safely reached the floor, Robin gently placed her passenger down and said, 'I have to climb back up and retrieve the broken shell because, if Elrod sees it, he'll know you've hatched and come looking for you.'

'That's true. I had to delay my emerging because of him,' Erosmay replied.

'Are you linked with Elrod too?' Robin asked in surprise.

'No, but I can sense him and I don't like what I feel,' the little dragon answered matter-of-factly.

'That makes two of us, so we're going to get on just fine,' Robin agreed.

'Yes we are. But first, we need to get out of here, and I'm hungry.'

Robin couldn't help but smile. She liked the forthrightness of the little dragon. And with her heart filled with happiness, she hastily grabbed her sewing basket and climbed back up the ladder to retrieve the shell fragments, while Erosmay stayed where she was and fanned her wings to dry them.

Once the white-haired woman reached the top shelf, she scooped the broken shell into her sewing basket and blew the dust across the surface of the remaining five eggs so it would not appear as if they had been disturbed. Then, she clambered down the ladder again and returned it to its original position.

When Robin rejoined Erosmay, the little dragon's wings were no longer wrinkled and limp like a butterfly fresh from its chrysalis. However, because she did not want to run the risk of someone spotting her new linked companion in flight and reporting it back to Elrod, the white-haired woman lifted the lid of her sewing basket and said, 'Climb in and I'll carry you to my room. But be careful, there's a needle and pair of scissors inside.'

Being linked, Erosmay understood Robin's concern. And with a beat of her leathery wings, the tiny dragon rose into the air and said, 'I still need something to eat.' Then, she darted into the basket.

'What would you like?' Robin asked, curious as to what she should fetch the newly hatched dragon.

When a picture of a full-grown horse suddenly appeared in her mind, Robin laughingly replied, 'I don't think you could manage a whole one, but I'll see what I can find.'

So instead of going straight to her room like she had planned, the white-haired woman picked up the sewing basket and headed towards the kitchen. And for the first time in two years, Robin was actually glad she had been shunned because there was no need for her to seek permission to enter the pantry once she got there, although she did notice a few raised eyebrows.

After ensuring no one else was inside the large larder, Robin lifted the lid of her sewing basket so Erosmay could peer out and see what foodstuffs were on offer.

The little dragon showed little interest in the bread, fruit, or fresh vegetables. But, when she spotted the cooked meats, she started to flap her wings and bounce about like an excited puppy, which made Robin's heart race for fear someone might hear the commotion and come to investigate.

To quiet Erosmay, the white-haired woman quickly grabbed a couple of roast quail and dropped them into the basket. And when the dragon pounced ravenously on them, Robin realized one of her fingers could have easily been bitten off by accident. So when she added a small meat pie for herself, she was a lot more careful.

After closing the lid of the basket, the white-haired woman stepped back into the kitchen. And just as she had expected, the kitchen staff fell quiet and busied themselves with their duties to avoid speaking with her, which suited Robin just fine. So, with her chin up and shoulders back, she strode boldly out of the kitchen. Although once she reached the safety of the hallway, her feigned confidence melted away like snow on a warm day and she hurried back to her room just as fast as her feet could carry her.

Robin's hands were shaking so badly by the time she had closed the door behind her, she had to set the sewing basket down before lifting its lid to peer inside. And when she did, she was surprised to find Erosmay lying fast asleep amongst the scattered remains of the quail she had just devoured, her belly so distended it looked as if it might burst, which was hardly surprising given the birds were nearly as big as she was.

Smiling down at her new friend, Robin felt a deep love for Erosmay and knew she would do everything within her power to protect the tiny creature from harm.

The next few days passed quickly. Robin threw the broken shell down one of the kitchen's refuse chutes to lie hidden amongst the other broken eggshells already there. And while she went about her duties like normal, Erosmay stayed hidden in their small room and, in-between eating and sleeping, practiced her flying to strengthen her wings.

They also worked together improving their telepathic communication, or mind-speech as Erosmay called it. In this instance, the dragon was the tutor and the white-haired woman the pupil.

Robin was a clever student and quickly learned to picture an image in her mind while expressing the emotion, if there was one, and mentally saying the word or words that best described what she was trying to convey. So, if she felt tired and wanted to go to sleep, she released the fatigue within her while picturing herself yawning and closing her eyes as she mentally said 'I'm sleepy.'

At other times, their roles were reversed and Robin was teacher and Erosmay the student.

As their mind-speech developed, it became stronger. Robin soon found she could communicate with her linked companion wherever she was within the fortress. And by doing so, her days of isolation came to an end even though everyone else at Greystone Fortress still ostracized her.

Robin also discovered that, although Erosmay was like a young child in many respects, the dragon possessed an innate wisdom passed down by the generations of dragons before her. And even though the white-haired woman found this combination of youthful innocence and old sage knowledge surprisingly odd, she began to understand and appreciate it all the same.

Then late one evening, after Erosmay's wings had become strong enough and she had mastered her flying technique, the dragon informed Robin she was going to start hunting her own food.

At first Robin was pleased, because she thought the kitchen staff was starting to wonder why she was making so many trips to the pantry. But then, her maternal instincts took over and she became concerned she would be unable to protect Erosmay if the little dragon needed her.

Because they were linked, Erosmay felt Robin's apprehension. And being a dragon, the most courageous and noble of creatures, not to mention arrogant, she found this amusing and made a rumbling sound deep in the back of her long throat before she told Robin so in no uncertain terms.

Chastised, Robin realized her linked companion had actually laughed at her. But before she had time for hurt feelings, the dragon darted out of the window and into the evening shadows so quickly, the white-haired woman was left standing by herself gobsmacked.

When the little dragon returned a few minutes later, she had a dead mouse clenched between her razor-sharp teeth, which she then proceeded to gulp down right in front of Robin. And by the expression on Erosmay's little scaled face, Robin realized the dragon was proving a point; they were equals, despite her small size, and she expected to be treated as such.

As time passed, Robin slowly grew accustomed to Erosmay's nipping in and out of their bedroom window faster than a fiddler's elbow, usually returning with a kill or full belly. But sometimes, late in the evening or in the middle of the night, the dragon would go exploring and return so excited that she would wrap her scaled tail around Robin's wrist and, like a pet on a lead, take her on an impromptu excursion.

Never being much of a sleeper, Robin did not mind the odd hours. And valuing the companionship they shared over sleep anyway, she enjoyed experiencing things from the little dragon's perspective.

To better accommodate Erosmay, Robin started to wear her long white hair in a single plait at the back of her neck, so the little dragon could ride on her shoulder. And together, they would explore parts of the fortress, like secret passageways and hidden tunnels, which Robin hadn't even known existed. Then, when they returned to their room in the early morning hours, they would cuddle up together on Robin's small bed and fall fast asleep.

For the first time since her hair had turned white, Robin started to wake up looking forward to the coming day, feeling happy within herself, and the dark circles under her eyes gradually began to fade.

Time flew by and, even though the two friends could not openly spend their days together, they were in constant contact via the mind-speech they secretly shared.

As Robin went about her daily duties, she would tell Erosmay where she was and what she was doing. And, the little dragon would reciprocate, by telling Robin about what she had caught to eat or what she had seen during her explorations.

Once, when Robin was in the dining hall busy mending a wall tapestry and one of the serving maids walked past her wearing a new dress, the little dragon commented in mind-speech, 'Her bum looks big in that.'

This, being the closest thing to girl talk the white-haired woman had experienced since her shunning, came as a bit of a surprise and she had to suppress a giggle. Robin casually glanced over to the poor girl. Then, she slowly looked around for Erosmay and eventually spotted the dragon sitting in the shadows on top of one of the far curtain rails.

'Erosmay, have you been listening to this girl's private conversations?' Robin asked in mind-speech.

The little dragon replied proudly, 'I have been watching and learning.'

'I see,' Robin said disapprovingly, knowing this was how Erosmay justified her eavesdropping. 'Did she ask someone if her bum looked big in that dress and they told her no?'

'Yes, but they were wrong. Her bum does look big,' the little dragon answered with conviction.

'Sometimes people say things that aren't true in order to spare the other person's feelings,' Robin explained.

'Humans lie,' Erosmay stated flatly.

'It's more complicated than that,' Robin replied in mind-speech. 'Remember when I tried to explain that everything isn't always black or white, but that sometimes things are a shade of grey. This is one of those times.'

Grey was not a concept the young dragon would accept, and Erosmay wasn't having any of it. Instead she boasted, 'Dragons don't lie. We are truthful creatures.'

'You are also very crafty,' Robin fondly teased back in mind-speech.

'Yes, truthful, crafty, and hungry,' Erosmay added. Then, she lifted her leathery wings and flew out of the room, abruptly ending the conversation.

Robin smiled to herself. She found it endearing most of their conversations ended with Erosmay telling her she was hungry, which made sense because the dragon was growing so rapidly.

When the dragon had first hatched, she could easily fit in the palm of Robin's hand. And in the past three months, Erosmay had doubled in size, which started to worry the white-haired woman because she did not know how large the dragon would grow before she reached maturity. But one thing was certain, the larger Erosmay became, the harder it would be to hide her.

Even though Robin lived in fear for her life at Greystone, with no money of her own and nowhere else to go, it seemed her only option had been to stay at the fortress and work for her room and board in hope the Black Hawk would eventually consider her too insignificant to warrant his attention.

But now that the welfare of her linked companion depended upon her, Robin's thinking became bolder and she realized, in order to protect the growing dragon, they would eventually have to leave the fortress. So that evening, after they had eaten their meagre supper, she broached the subject with Erosmay. And when she did, her linked companion rumbled with dragon laughter and replied she had been thinking the same thing.

Robin lovingly hugged the little scaled creature to her chest. Then, she shared her ongoing dilemma, the fact she hadn't a copper to her name to purchase the food and supplies needed for their journey.

Eager to help, Erosmay offered to catch their food. But, Robin quickly dismissed the notion by saying she didn't think she could eat a rodent.

The little dragon understood, because she would have preferred not to eat vermin either and told Robin so. But until they left Greystone, rodents and small birds were the only animals she could catch that people would not notice disappearing.

Up until now, Robin hadn't even considered this and she complimented the dragon for her wisdom, which pleased Erosmay to no end because there was one thing she liked even more than knowing what a clever creature she was, and that was hearing Robin tell her so.

In high spirits, Erosmay also offered to help gather the things they would need for their departure, providing they were small enough for her to carry in flight. All Robin had to do was describe the item and tell her where it could be found, and she would take care of the rest.

So over the next few days, as Robin went about her work, the white-haired woman did exactly that. When she saw something she thought might be useful, like a long forgotten half empty bottle of black dye she could color her distinctive white hair with, she told Erosmay via mind-speech what it looked like and where it was.

The little dragon would wait so her linked companion could distance herself from the theft, before stealthily making her way to the location and lurking in the shadows until she was certain no one was about. And then, she would spirit the item away to their hiding place.

Just when everything seemed to be going according to plan, a servant knocked unexpectedly on their chamber door one evening and told Robin that Elrod wanted to see her in the Great Hall.

Hearing this, the white-haired woman's heart filled with dread. But, she bravely stepped out into the hallway and closed the door behind her, so Erosmay would not be able to sneak out and follow.

As she made her way down the long corridor, Robin tried to figure out the reason behind her summons: did Elrod want to resume the cruel game of cat and mouse he liked to play with her, or had he found out about Erosmay despite the precautions she and her linked companion had taken?

When she finally reached the Great Hall, there was no need for her to give her name to the guards at the entrance. Everyone at Greystone already knew who she was by her distinctive long white hair and, when her presence was noticed, heads began to turn her way.

Court had already ended for the day and the Black Hawk stood casually talking with a small group of courtiers. He glanced over at her with his predatory gaze and she quickly bent her knee in homage. However, he did not acknowledge her and turned his attention back to the men he was conversing with.

Having played this game numerous times before, Robin knew Elrod would only speak to her when he was good and ready, and not a moment before. So, she stood and quietly waited, trying to hide her fear and thankful her shoes were comfortable.

Now and again Erosmay would send her encouragement via mind-speech by telling her to 'Stay brave'. And when the little dragon did this, the white-haired woman was reminded of the day they had first met, which made the waiting bearable.

By the time Elrod finally beckoned Robin to him, her feet were just beginning to ache. She walked rather stiffly towards him, curtseyed, and nervously greeted him in a voice which sounded oddly strange to her ears. 'Your Majesty.'

The Black Hawk motioned for her to rise and step a little closer. Then once she had, he reached out and lifted her head up by the chin so he could examine her face more closely. And despite the warmth of the room, when Elrod's bony fingers touched Robin's skin, a shiver ran through her.

Seeing the fear reflected in the white-haired woman's eyes, Elrod decided it had been much too long since he had last summoned her.

He held her gaze a bit longer. Then, he lowered his hand and said accusingly, 'You look different.'

Scared stiff, Robin didn't know how to answer and just stood there.

Elrod let the awkward silence hang in the air as he savored her discomfort, and then he said, 'I'm expecting a guest in a few days. Make ready the private rooms in the east wing.'

Robin was stunned. Ever since she received the Black Hawk's summons, she had feared for the little dragon's safety. But now, it appeared some other poor soul was the subject of Elrod's attentions, and she felt a guiltily relief as she hurriedly muttered 'Yes sire' and bobbed a curtsy.

When she glanced back up, Elrod still watched her. And for an instant, the white-haired woman thought he had noticed her reaction. But, he surprised her again by dismissing her with a flick of his wrist.

Robin did not need to be told twice. She curtsied and then made a hasty retreat out of the Great Hall, down the long corridors, and back to her small room where Erosmay greeted her excitedly with a hero's welcome.

5 KING DALLIN

The early light of dawn was just beginning to appear on the horizon when King Dallin decided to get out of bed. Having spent yet another sleepless night restlessly tossing and turning over fears for the safety of his missing daughter, he wearily threw back his bedcoverings and sat up, electing instead to face his fears on his own terms rather than struggle with them as shifting phantoms conjured by his imagination.

Because it was too early for his servants to have stoked up the fire, the king's chambers had chilled and he could feel the winter coldness on the soles of his feet through the carpets as he walked over to the basin to wash himself with yet even colder water. But Dallin was not a soft king, he had endured far worse, having been tempered defending the kingdom with his father as a youth. And ignoring the discomfort, he splashed the cold water onto his face to help clear his mind from morning grogginess.

He dressed quickly, in a simple tunic and trousers, before walking over to the mirror and running a comb through his thick dark hair. Although there were only a few strands of grey near his temples, the dark circles under his eyes and the gauntness of his cheeks made him appear much older than his forty three years.

Ever since his daughter, Princess Lilyanna, had disappeared five days earlier, Dallin could think of little else and finding her had become his obsession. Yet despite extensive searches carried out by both his army and spy network, the king knew no more than he had on the day of the abduction and the lack of information left him feeling frustrated and helpless.

He had only felt this way once before, two years ago when his son had suddenly fallen ill and passed away unexpectedly. And now, his only remaining child's life was in danger and, until his men discovered her whereabouts, there was nothing he could do to help her.

As the king swung open the door and stepped into the hallway, the guard stationed outside his chambers snapped to attention. Dallin greeted the soldier in a soft voice and continued on his way towards the tower in the west wing of the palace, unaware the observant guard, who now discreetly followed him down the deserted corridor, had noted his careworn appearance with concern.

Although Dallin was a fit man, five days without proper food and sleep were beginning to take their toll and, by the time he had climbed the tower's circular stairway, he began to feel lightheaded. So, he stopped and took a few moments to steady himself before he ascended the last few steps to the wizard's chambers.

As the king lifted his hand to rap upon the door, the wizard's apprentice, Garan, opened it before Dallin's knuckles had even touched the wood and indicated, by holding an index finger to his lips, that his master required silence.

Dallin didn't find it odd that he should be taking orders from the young aspirant, for here he held no title and his close friend and confident ruled. He merely nodded his head and entered the room quietly just as he had been bidden.

The old man sat meditatively, cross-legged in a swirl of black robes upon the rug covered floor. His eyes were closed and his head was tipped slightly back, already deep in his searching.

Like a wolf sniffing the air for the scent of prey, the king knew that Urba's seeing-self was reaching out, scouring the land in search of Lilyanna's aura, and his heart quickened just as it did each morning when he watched this procedure. But knowing how dangerous a search of this nature was, Dallin stood statue still so he would not distract his friend.

Minutes seemed to turn into hours as the wizard sat unmoving in the middle of the cluttered room. And when at last Urba broke his trance and began to collapse, Garan was there to catch the old man in his arms and gently cradle him while the king held a goblet of wine to the wizard's pale lips.

As Urba took a small sip to steady himself, the king noted, not for the first time, how small and frail the wizard looked. These past five days had aged them all, but Urba seemed to be shrinking with each search he performed.

'I couldn't see her,' the wizard told Dallin weakly. 'It's as if the earth has swallowed her whole.' He shakily took another small sip of wine. Then, after allowing Garan and the king to help him to his favorite chair, the wizard added, 'This is no ordinary abduction. Someone has gone to great lengths to conceal Lilyanna's whereabouts.'

Dallin was not surprised; he had been hearing similar statements from Urba each morning. And knowing there was nothing more he could do to assist them, the king excused himself from the room so Garan could tend his exhausted mentor.

As Dallin descended the stairway, he mentally reviewed the implications of the kidnapping, just as he had done the five mornings previously. It was clear the abduction had been an act of political sabotage. Whoever had taken his daughter did not want her marriage of state to take place. But, which of his enemies had the most to gain? Was it a new enemy, someone he had mistakenly over looked? Or, was it an old one, like Elrod the Black Hawk, self-appointed king of Greystone?

In any case, with only eight weeks to go before the royal wedding was to take place, he thought it best not to throw the kingdom into turmoil by announcing his daughter had been abducted. This would have only unsettled the populous and dashed his plans for uniting the kingdom with that of his long-time ally and friend, King Gestmar. So instead, he had circulated the rumor that the princess had gone into seclusion to prepare for her upcoming nuptials. This had not only satisfied the gossips at court, it had also eliminated the need for Lilyanna to make any public appearances until after the happy day.

Additionally, since preparations for the wedding had already thrown the palace into a state of confusion, the king, ever the strategist, had informed his servants he was commandeering several rooms in the west wing to plan a surprise for his daughter and her new husband which were off limits until he told them otherwise. And, it was to these rooms he and his loyal bodyguard now strode.

When the two men finally reached the impromptu command center, the soldier standing outside the door snapped smartly to attention and allowed them both to enter unchallenged.

With one sweeping glance, Dallin took in the fatigued faces of his handpicked team and could tell no significant progress had been made during the night. And as the men started to rise in deference, he forestalled them with a wave of his hand. 'Good morning gentlemen. I know you're tired, so please don't stop what you're doing on my account.' Then, he strode purposefully towards the map on which they plotted their progress, or lack thereof, so he could examine it closely.

Over the past five days, the king had anxiously watched as small black-flagged pins began to appear on the map, marking the locations which had been eliminated by his search parties. And as the number of black flags steadily grew, spreading across his kingdom like blight, Dallin knew that soon, if not already, his beloved Lilyanna could be lost to him forever.

Yet stubbornly, he refused to give up hope and turned to Lord Talmen, his head of intelligence, for an update, which he already knew wouldn't amount to much but wanted to hear anyway. Then after the short briefing, the king left the command center and headed to his council chambers because, despite the kidnapping, he still held court and presided over the day-to-day running of the kingdom to maintain the impression nothing untoward had happened.

As the weary king strode down the corridor, he found himself wondering for the umpteenth time, just who in their right mind would actually choose to be a king? Sometimes, like today, he wished he were a simple craftsman, working with tangible objects instead of dealing with matters of state. But, wishing for something that would never happen was a luxury even a king couldn't afford, so he pushed the thought from his mind.

This morning, he was scheduled to settle a matter between the houses of Tevon and Steed. Both families claimed to be the rightful successors to the hereditary fishing rights of the coastal area known as the Breakers and had been squabbling for years. But last month tensions had escalated and, when blood had been drawn, he decided to put an end to the dispute once and for all before someone got killed.

It was noon by the time Dallin had fully heard the grievances of both parties and had made his final ruling. Feeling mentally drained and badly in need of a sanity break, he left the council chambers and went to seek out the company of his good lady wife, Queen Leah.

He found her sitting at the small table in their private rooms trying to eat her midday meal. Since the abduction of their daughter, neither of them had much of an appetite. And by the look of her plate, Dallin could tell she had consumed very little and was merely pushing the food around the dish with her fork.

As he walked over to her, she gave him a sad smile, one that spoke of love and loss. He understood her well and she him. They had originally married out of duty. Yet over the years, they had grown to love each other deeply and Dallin did not know what he would do if anything ever happened to her.

After kissing his wife tenderly on the cheek, Dallin sat down wearily at the table opposite her and waited as one of the servants brought him a plate of food and a goblet of wine. Then, once the servant had left the room, he sadly confirmed what she had already suspected; there had been no progress in the search for Lilyanna.

Although the king too ate very little, his heart always felt a little lighter after spending time with his wife, and today was no exception.

Because Dallin wanted to stop by the command center before he returned to his council chambers to listen to more petitions that afternoon, he did not stay long. And regrettably, as had become their new custom, before leaving he promised Leah he would send her word if there were any new developments regarding their missing daughter.

The corridors seemed much longer than usual to Dallin as he headed back to the makeshift headquarters for the second time that day, and he was thankful he'd had the foresight to locate it in the same wing as the wizard, their close proximity saving him much valuable time and energy.

As the king neared his destination, he could see Lord Talmen, his head of intelligence, standing in the corridor speaking privately with a tall bearded man, just out of earshot of the guard by the door.

When they became aware of his presence and started to bow, Dallin signaled for them to rise with a nod of his head. And once they had, Talmen introduced his companion to him by saying, 'This is Jerhal. He's one of mine.'

The king understood; the man was one of Talmen's spies.

Although the bearded man appeared to be outwardly relaxed as he bobbed his head to Dallin and said 'Your Majesty', the king noted an astute alertness reflected in Jerhal's dark eyes. But, even he didn't suspect that the man standing before him was the spymaster's top agent.

Before Dallin could ponder this further, Talmen leaned a little closer to him and confided, 'For the time being, I'd prefer not to introduce Jerhal to the others.'

Realizing Talmen wanted to keep Jerhal's identity secret, Dallin nodded and replied, 'Join me inside once you're finished here.' Then, leaving the two men to complete their business, the king strode the final few steps to his temporary command center.

Just as he had done earlier that morning, upon entering the room, Dallin held up his hand to indicate everyone should continue their tasks and walked over to inspect the map.

There were several more black-flagged pins than there had been the last time he had looked, eliminating locations even farther afield.

'It's a slow process, but we'll find her Your Majesty,' Talmen said confidently over the king's shoulder as he joined him.

'Let's just hope we're not too late,' Dallin replied.

'The princess is much too valuable a prize to discard lightly,' his head of intelligence stated reassuringly. 'Her abductors will keep her alive as insurance, whatever their plans may be.'

'That stands to reason,' the king agreed. 'But, other than for Elrod increasing his military strength, what new information have we gleaned?'

'Frustratingly, nothing of any significance in regards to the princess.' Talmen answered. 'However, we've discovered the bakers are becoming increasingly disgruntled over the rising price of grain which, I've just been informed, is being caused by unusually high foreign exports to Greystone.'

'Interesting, I'll issue an edict effective immediately banning all exports of grain and metal to Greystone. I don't want Elrod's people to suffer, but I don't plan to feed and weaponized his army either,' the king said decisively.

'A wise precaution Your Majesty,' Talmen agreed.

Having already spent too much time at the command center, Dallin started for the door. But then, he turned back to Talmen and enquired, 'Was,' he hesitated slightly before continuing, 'my new acquaintance helpful?'

'Very,' answered the head of intelligence. 'He's the one who informed me about Elrod's growing army. And today, he connected Greystone to the rising grain prices.'

'Cleaver man,' the king replied.

'Yes, and resourceful,' Talmen added. 'I've asked him to remain in White Cliff for the time being, just in case we need his services later.'

'Very well,' the king replied. And then, he exited the room to begin the long walk back to his council chambers where he planned to spend the rest of the afternoon listening to petitioners.

6 GREYSTONE

For the second time in five days Princess Lilyanna slowly woke from a drug induced slumber. Her vision was blurred, her surroundings cloudy. Fighting back nausea, she sluggishly realized she could smell leather and felt the rough jarring of wheels upon a potholed road rather than the rhythmic swaying of the ship.

Wondering how long she had been unconscious, the princess struggled to push herself upright, groggily comprehending the leather smell was from the carriage seat she was sprawled upon.

Even in her befuddled condition, the princess thought it odd she was neither bound nor gagged, but when she pulled back the curtain she understood why her abductors had not bothered. They had already left the coastline far behind and were travelling through dense woodland so sparsely populated screaming for help would have been pointless.

The sinking feeling in the pit of her stomach told her the carriage doors were locked. Yet, she still reached out and tried to turn the handles just to make certain. And when they held fast, she was at least satisfied she had tested them.

Lilyanna then turned her attention back to the windows. It didn't take her long to discover they had been tampered with too. And try as she might, she could only open them slightly, but it was enough to ventilate the carriage and help alleviate the side effects of the sedative.

Still wearing the heavy cloak her abductors had made her don, the princess clumsily unfastened the clasp at her neck. Then, leaving the discarded garment in a crumpled heap, she scooted closer to the window and took in a deep breath of the fresh woodland air to clear her thinking.

While aboard the Venture, she had deduced she was being taken to Elrod's fortress deep within the Greystone Mountains. And, although her father was undoubtedly searching for her, he still might not have discovered it was the Black Hawk who had taken her. So at present, her only real hope of rescue rested with Captain Nagrom finding the messages she had written in his logbook and acting upon them.

Incapacitated as she was, Lilyanna also knew she was in no fit state to attempt an escape. And, until the drug she had inhaled wore off, the only thing she could do to help herself was to continue her charm offensive, assuming Scary Hairy still travelled with her.

Drowsy, nauseous, and thankful the carriage was not swaying like the ship, the princess sat back more comfortably on the leather seat, closed her eyes, and nodded off.

Her sleep wasn't restful, more of a light doze. What with the nausea and the potholes, Lilyanna assumed the carriage was being driven along some little used back road.

Having studied the map of Greystone while on board the Venture and subsequently noticing the moss on the northern side of the trees through the carriage window, it took her dazed mind awhile to realize she was traveling on the major trade route from the Port of Hesketh to Greystone Fortress. Then, when she did, her feelings of repulsion for Elrod turned into anger.

As heir to the throne of White Cliff, Lilyanna had been taught for a kingdom to flourish, its people had to prosper. Commerce was the key to this, and it was the crown's responsibility to encourage trade by maintaining the realm's infrastructure.

It was obvious the usurper had spent very little money, if any, from his royal coffers on the road system he had unscrupulously acquired, making the lives of his subjects unnecessarily difficult.

Filled with indignation, the princess scooted closer to the window and took in a deep breath to calm herself. Then, she tried to recall if she had heard anything to explain what Elrod was spending his money on. But try as she might, she drew a blank, because her recent conversations had centered on wedding plans and her father had dealt with the political side of things.

Knowing her anger served no real purpose, Lilyanna tried to let it go by turning her thoughts to her intended, Prince Arlo.

The two of them had always known they would wed, their fathers had arranged the union many years before. And surprisingly, this wasn't an issue for either of them.

They had met as children and played together in the palace gardens beside the fountain. And one evening, as she was being tucked into bed, Lilyanna remembered telling her mother she liked the new boy because he thought the same way she did.

Her mother had given her a smile, the kind of smile Lilyanna now knew her mother gave when she was secretly pleased about something, and merely replied, 'That's good darling. Have sweet dreams.' Then, the queen had kissed her goodnight on the forehead and slipped out of the room.

Because Arlo was the only person near her age who fully appreciated what it meant to carry royal responsibility, their friendship had swiftly developed. Then later, as adolescences, they had started to exchange personal correspondence, each taking pleasure in sharing thoughts and ideas with a likeminded individual. And, it was through these letters the bond between them had grown.

Lilyanna found she valued and trusted Arlo's council, which was a rare thing because the majority of the people at court said whatever they thought she wanted to hear, and this wasn't helpful when she was trying to make an important decision.

She was uncertain when it had happened. But as time passed, Lilyanna started to daydream more and more about Arlo, wondering what it would feel like when his lips touched hers. And even though she had tried to hide it, whenever she received a letter from the handsome young prince, her heart would beat just a little faster.

It wasn't until the evening of her eighteenth birthday she found out he cared for her romantically. And, she remembered every detail as if it were yesterday. They had left the crowded ballroom and gone out for a bit of fresh air. Strolling quietly in the palace gardens, they talked about everything and nothing, simply enjoying each other's presence.

At the time, she didn't know Arlo had planned it, but they ended up standing beside the fountain and he told her, 'I've always liked this garden.'

'Yes. It is lovely,' she had agreed.

'The first time I saw you was in this garden,' he said as he smiled at her with a look in his eye Lilyanna had never seen before.

She had stood transfixed, suddenly finding it hard to breath and not understanding why.

He leaned down and kissed her gently, yet passionately on the lips. Then, he looked deeply into her eyes and continued, 'So, it seems only fitting our first kiss should be here.'

As tired as she was, Lilyanna still felt a flush come to her cheek when she thought of that kiss.

Then, her eyes misted over, and the princess found herself fighting back tears as the reality of her situation came crashing down on her. Instead of this being a special time in her life, full of wedding plans and bridal gown fittings, she found herself in the middle of nowhere, wearing the same dress for the past five days, and robbed of all future happiness.

As strong as she was, it took all of Lilyanna's willpower to stop the tears. She wiped them roughly from her cheeks with the backs of her hands and reminded herself she was King Dallin's daughter, heir to the throne of White Cliff, and that it would take more than Elrod's twisted scheming to ruin her royal destiny and life with Arlo.

◆◆◆

It was evening by the time the carriage finally rolled to a stop and, despite the soft leather seat, every muscle in Lilyanna's body ached from the constant jarring.

The princess heard muffled voices as the driver and his companion dismounted. Then, she watched numbly as the man she had nicknamed Dead Eyes unlocked the carriage door, stuck his head inside the vehicle, and warned her in a harsh voice, 'You won't get any help here. You're in Black Hawk country now and folk know better than to anger him. So, don't get any ideas or, tomorrow instead of riding your horse, you'll be asleep strapped across its back. Understand?'

Lilyanna knew exactly what he meant and, because her mouth was too dry to speak, nodded her head.

Satisfied, Dead Eyes continued, 'Good. You can get out now.' Then, he turned and strode off to help Scary Hairy unharness the horses.

Tired of being confined inside the carriage all day, the princess refastened her cloak. Then, she rose stiffly from her seat and stepped out of the vehicle onto the stony ground below.

They had stopped in a small hamlet, consisting of several houses and an inn, all of which were crudely constructed of timber from the local woodland. It looked a peaceful place. And under normal circumstances, Lilyanna might have liked it, but she was too hungry, thirsty, and bone-weary to care.

She stood and watched as a lanky stable boy appeared from around the back of the inn. After a brief discussion, her captors gave him a couple of copper pieces and he led their tired horses away to be fed and watered. Then Dirk, the man the princess called Dead Eyes, turned and motioned for her to join them.

Since the abduction, Lilyanna's kidnappers had given her very little food, deliberately starving her into submission. And, their tactic was working, because the princess numbly followed the two men into the Wayfarer's Rest, detesting herself with each obedient step she took, yet knowing she must comply in order to keep up her strength.

Despite her low spirits, Lilyanna felt her mood brighten the moment she entered the inn. It was warm and welcoming. But most of all, she could smell the aroma of hot stew wafting from the kitchen.

Looking around, the princess noticed Dirk watching her with cruel amusement in his cold eyes, the first sign of life she had seen reflected in them since they had met.

Holding her gaze, he stipulated, 'If you behave yourself, you can eat with us.'

Lilyanna wasn't sure she had heard correctly, but she was famished and would have agreed to dine with the Black Hawk himself if it meant a full belly. So, she nodded her head for a second time that evening.

The innkeeper, a plump middle-aged man, greeted them ingratiatingly with an overfriendly smile full of large white teeth and an oily voice, 'Welcome to the Wayfarer's Rest. What can I do for you?'

In those two simple sentences, Lilyanna's faint hope of finding an ally at the inn was dashed, for it was apparent discretion was also one of the services the innkeeper profited by.

Dead Eyes answered, 'We require hot meals and a room for the night.'

'Do you want to eat first or see the room?' The man asked, flashing yet another of his toothy smiles.

'We'll eat first. It's been a long day,' Dead Eyes replied.

'Very well. This way,' the innkeeper said, ushering them into the adjoining room with a sweep of his hand.

The three hungry travelers didn't need to be told twice. They stepped past the innkeeper and entered the room as directed.

'Go ahead and find a table,' the innkeeper said from behind them. 'I'll tell my good lady wife you're here.' Then, he disappeared towards the kitchen.

Although a couple of the tables were already occupied, there were still several vacant ones to choose from.

Leading the way, Dead Eyes strode purposely to an empty table at the far end of the room and seated himself with his back to the wall, so he had a clear view of the doorway and the inn's other patrons.

Lilyanna was not surprised by his choice of seating. It was a defensive one, and any fighter worth his pay would have chosen it.

She followed Scary Hairy to the table and wearily sat down on the wooden chair opposite him, preferring to face the wild-haired redhead rather than

Dead Eyes during the meal.

The cook, a short woman every bit as plump as her innkeeping husband, arrived a little later bearing a wooden tray heavily laden with steaming bowls of venison stew and a large plate piled high with sliced dark bread.

Lilyanna was so ravenous, it took all of her willpower to sit there and not snatch a bowl from the tray. But she had too much self-respect to do it and suspected if she did, Dead Eyes act of kindness would evaporate like the steam from off the bowls and he would cruelly take the food away, leaving her to go without.

Scary Hairy had other ideas. He was hungry and did not care who knew it. He reached out and grabbed the first bowl to touch the table. Then, faster than a weaver's shuttle, he began shoveling the stew into his mouth before the woman had even set the next bowl down.

Because she was so thirsty, Lilyanna was surprised to find her mouth-watering by the time the woman left to fetch them ale and Dead Eyes had finally picked up his spoon. Nevertheless, it was only then she allowed herself to lift hers.

The stew was thick, with plenty of meat and vegetables, and the fresh dark bread was delicious. However, even though Lilyanna wanted to wolf them down just like Scary Hairy was doing, she knew, having eaten so little over the past five days, she had to pace herself in order to avoid making herself sick.

As they ate and sipped ale, the princess began to relax and observe her abductors. This was the first time she had seen the two of them interact for more than a few minutes. And she swiftly discovered, they weren't friends because neither man spoke much to the other, which shed a whole new light on her predicament.

When she finished the stew and it felt like her belly would burst, Lilyanna used the last of her bread to wipe the bowl clean like her captors had done. Then, as she lifted her mug to wash it down, the princess noticed Dead Eyes watching her and suddenly realized she was being played like a fine fiddle.

So as not to arouse suspicion, he had allowed her to eat with them like an ordinary travelling companion. And, because the alcohol would affect her quickly in her dehydrated state, he had bought her ale because an inebriated captive is far less likely to attempt an escape than a sober one.

Thankful she had managed to keep her wits about her, the princess decided to play along, but with a ruse of her own. She lifted the mug to her lips and pretended to take a big gulp. Then, to give the impression she was much more intoxicated than she really was, she swayed a little as she placed the mug back down and glanced across the table at Scary Hairy to see if he had noticed, but the wild-haired man was more concerned with the dwindling contents of his own mug.

Lilyanna waited a bit. Then, she picked up her mug again and pretended to take another large sip. But this time, as she returned the mug unsteadily onto the table, she feigned a hiccup and looked up at Dead Eyes in embarrassment.

Although the princess couldn't read her abductor's face, the deception must have worked because shortly afterwards Dead Eyes ordered their mugs be refilled. Then, as he stood and fished out a couple of coins to settle the bill, he told Scary Hairy he was going to make arrangements for the morrow and strode out of the room, leaving Lilyanna and the wild-haired man alone with their mugs.

The two sat quietly, Scary Hairy trying to forget the rigors of the day by pulling heavily on his ale, and the princess, sipping lightly on hers, deliberating the best approach to ask him for help.

By the way he slouched in his chair, Lilyanna could tell the ale was beginning to take effect. So with nothing to lose and little time before Dirk returned, the princess decided to try her luck. She leaned towards him and said in a slurred conspiratorial voice, 'If you help me escape, my father will reward you.'

Scary Hairy kept his eyes on his mug and replied, 'Money's no good to a dead man.'

To hide her surprise, Lilyanna faked another hiccup and asked, 'What do you mean?'

'If I fail to take you to Greystone, that's what I'll be. Because, if the Black Hawk doesn't kill me, Dirk will.'

Lilyanna's heart sank. She had known the man might refuse to help, but it had never occurred to her he would be killed if he did not deliver her.

Scary Hairy then looked her straight in the eye and ended their conversation. 'We'll talk no more of this.'

Knowing better than to press him, Lilyanna changed tactics and pushed her mug towards him. 'Would you like this? I'm full up.'

Not as devious as his accomplice, Scary Hairy picked up her mug and emptied its contents into his.

Shortly afterwards, when Dead Eyes returned from his task, he found them both sitting quietly just as he had left them, only now their mugs were empty.

Dirk walked around the table and sat back down in his chair. Then, as he reached for his mug, he told his partner, 'I've swapped the team and carriage for fresh horses and supplies.'

'Good. The carriage was a right bone rattler,' Scary Hairy grumbled. 'I've still got a cramp in my backside the ale couldn't reach.'

'It served its purpose though, since the lady couldn't sit a horse.'

'Yeah. Even in Hesketh, a few eyebrows might've been raised if we'd have ridden out with her slung across its back.'

'But, we're not in Hesketh anymore,' Dead Eyes added as he shot a warning look at Lilyanna.

'No, we aren't,' the wild-haired man agreed.

'And this time, there's no ship's captain around to ask awkward questions,' Dead Eyes continued, still looking at the princess.

'No. There isn't,' Scary Hairy confirmed.

Dead Eyes then quickly downed the rest of his drink and announced, 'We'd best turn in. We've got a long ride ahead of us tomorrow.'

Lilyanna had sat slumped in her chair like Scary Hairy during the exchange. But unlike him, she was only feigning her intoxication. And when her abductors got up from their chairs, she slowly staggered to her feet and walked unsteadily with them back through the adjoining room and up the stairs to the room Dead Eyes had organized for the night.

Like the rest of the inn, other than for the mound of travelling supplies dumped in one of the corners, the room was furnished with the barest of necessities, containing only two beds, a washstand, and a small stone fireplace which had been lit to remove the winter chill.

Noticing the lack of sleeping facilities, the princess staggered over to the single bed and claimed it for herself, making it perfectly clear she had no intention of sharing the larger bed with either of her captors no matter how drunk she was.

Her actions amused Dirk and he smiled, which wasn't pretty because he'd had so little practice. Then, he turned to his partner and said, 'Red, it looks like we're sharing the big bed tonight. But first, let's move Her Highness's across the doorway.' And as if Lilyanna was as light as a feather, the two of them lifted the small bed with her still sitting on it, carried it across the room, and set it down right in front of the door, blocking the only escape route.

Her plan dashed, Lilyanna tried not to let the disappointment show, and kicked off her shoes. Then, after spreading her cloak like a blanket for extra warmth, she climbed into the small bed fully clothed and pulled its coverings up snugly under her chin.

Having slept in a private room her entire life, the princess was unaccustomed to sharing one with anyone else, let alone two full-grown men. So, in an effort to ignore them, she turned her face towards the blocked doorway and closed her eyes. Although, she did not relax until her abductors stopped moving about. And just when she thought she might get some sleep, the snoring started and Lilyanna realized she was in for a very long night.

Lying there, she turned her thoughts to Arlo and wondered if he had been notified of her abduction. Then it occurred to her, even if he had not, he would know something was wrong when he stopped receiving her letters.

She also thought of her parents. The unexpected death of her brother had hurt them deeply and she would have done anything to have spared them further distress. But she had no control over her situation and, try as she might, she could not think of an alternative escape plan.

When the princess finally drifted off, it was not a sound sleep. And all too early the following morning, she was awakened by the crowing of a cockerel.

Bleary-eyed and feeling as if her head had barely touched the pillow, Lilyanna heard her abductors starting to stir and knew they had been awakened by the rooster too. Yet, because the room was cold, the bed warm, and she wasn't there of her own accord, the princess pretended to sleep even though she knew it would not be much of a lie-in.

Dirk, just as deadly as the weapon he had been named after, didn't care if Lilyanna was tired or not. To him, she was just another job Elrod had given him to complete. Only this time, there weren't any perks, because he had been ordered not to violate her. However, this still didn't stop him from walking over and shaking her roughly by the shoulder when he told her to get up.

From the tone of Dirk's voice, the princess could tell he was deadly serious and sat up. Then, while her abductor walked away, she slipped her cold shoes onto her stockinged feet and pulled the cloak she had used as a bedcovering around her shoulders to ward off the morning chill.

She wasn't surprised to see the men had also slept in their clothes. She even found herself feeling a bit sorry for Scary Hairy when she noticed the large holes in his dirty socks. But, the most interesting thing was the number of weapons each man carried about his person. She had always known Dead Eyes was dangerous, but she had no idea he was a walking armory. And, as for Scary Hairy, he wasn't as harmless as his quiet manner had led her to believe.

Dead Eyes looked over and saw her watching them. 'If you behave yourself and help carry the supplies downstairs, you can eat with us.'

Having eaten a hearty meal the evening before, Lilyanna didn't feel as listless as she had the previous day and replied defiantly, 'I'll not lift a finger to help you.'

'If you don't, not only will you go without food, but you'll also go without your blanket tonight,' he replied gesturing towards the bedrolls lying on the floor.

Knowing Greystone Fortress was located in the mountains and that sleeping on the ground at higher elevation would be even colder than the chilled room she was currently in, Lilyanna's survival instinct prevailed over her desire to make her captors' job more difficult. And so, she walked over and picked up one of the bedrolls.

'All three,' Dead Eyes ordered sternly as he and Scary Hairy began to collect the remainder of the supplies.

Detesting herself for helping them, Lilyanna begrudgingly bent down and picked up the other two bedrolls from off the floor. Then, the heavily laden trio headed downstairs.

Despite the early hour, the ingratiating innkeeper was there to greet them wearing his usual toothy smile when they reached the small reception room. 'Good morning. I trust you slept well.'

Dead Eyes answered for them all. 'Yes, we did. And, while we break our fast, we'd like the boy to saddle our horses so we can get an early start.'

'Very well, you know where the tables are. You can leave your things over there and go on through,' the innkeeper replied as he pointed to an empty spot near the door.

The smell of fried eggs and bacon filled the air and Lilyanna's stomach growled in anticipation as she followed her kidnappers through the doorway and across the adjoining room to the same table they had eaten at the evening before. And because the food smelled so good, she was glad she had helped carry the bedrolls, even if it meant aiding the enemy.

They were the first to arrive. But as they waited to be served, several other sleepy-eyed travelers entered the room.

The little cook arrived at their table a short time later bearing her familiar wooden tray. But this morning, along with the customary plate of sliced bread, the tray held three plates. And, upon each plate were two sausages, two rashers of thick bacon, and a couple of fried eggs.

The cook served them quickly and efficiently, too busy to flash any insincere smiles like her husband had.

As she hurried back to the kitchen to fetch their rosehip tea, Dead Eyes callously reached over and relieved Lilyanna of one of her sausages.

The hungry princess could not believe her eyes. And quick as a flash, before she could protest, Scary Hairy helped himself to the other sausage on her plate.

As her captors exchanged conspiratorial smirks and the cook returned with the tea, Lilyanna swiftly pre-empted a raid on her bacon by snatching up both pieces and stuffing them into her mouth.

Noticing only eggs remained on the princess's plate, the little cook raised an eyebrow. But to her credit, when she saw Lilyanna's cheeks bulging like a squirrel carrying nuts, she didn't say a word. Instead, she simply set the steaming mugs of tea on the table, gave Lilyanna an odd look, and headed back to the kitchen while the two men snickered in amusement.

Luckily for the red-cheeked princess, Dead Eyes wasn't the jovial type. And by the time she had swallowed the mouthful of bacon, he and Scary Hairy had turned their attention back to the food on their own plates.

Knowing it might be a longtime until her next meal, Lilyanna did not let the embarrassing incident stand in her way. While her kidnappers munched away on her sausages, she ate her eggs and wiped the plate clean with a slice of bread. And as an added precaution to stave off future hunger, when her abductors weren't looking, she stealthily slipped a second piece of bread into the concealed pocket of her riding dress.

Afterwards, when the plates were bare and their hunger satiated, Dirk settled the bill. Then, they loaded the supplies onto their horses and began the grueling trek through the mountains towards Greystone Fortress, the Black Hawk's seat of power.

7 EAST WING

Ever since the death of Lady Allyce, Robin had avoided her former mistress's private rooms in the east wing of Greystone Fortress. However, now that Elrod had commanded her to make ready the apartment for his impending guest, the white-haired woman had no other choice than to obey him. So, early the following morning after his summons, with a heavy heart and a large basket in hand, Robin obediently went to the fortress storerooms to obtain the necessary cleaning supplies.

When the keeper of stores glanced over and saw her standing in the doorway, he begrudgingly set aside the list he was filling and asked her what she wanted. And just as she had known it would, when Robin told him she was there on orders from the king, the storeman's attitude instantly shifted from disdain to wary attentiveness and he hurriedly began to gather the cloths and polishes she needed. Then a short time later, she emerged from the storerooms with her basket nearly overflowing.

In her heart, Robin still grieved over the loss of her friend, Lady Allyce. She had been one of those rare individuals with a gift for making people feel welcome and at ease no matter how lowly their station. And along with countless others, Robin had grown to love her.

With the passing of time and the help of her linked companion, Robin was normally able to cope with the terror of her friend's death. But this day, as the white-haired woman made her way down the long corridors, the vivid memory of her mistress's last moments sprung afresh to Robin's mind and she began to feel panicked.

In an effort to block out the unbidden memory, Robin turned her thoughts to Erosmay and she asked the little dragon what she was doing via mind-speech.

Erosmay replied, 'I'm watching a bird and trying to decide if I should eat it now or save it for later.'

Knowing the little dragon was growing quickly and hungry most of the time, Robin cautioned, 'It might not be there later.'

'I know where it lives,' Erosmay replied confidently.

Robin couldn't help but smile. 'I won't worry about you going hungry then.'

'You worry too much,' the little dragon informed her matter-of-factly. 'I can take care of myself.' Then in afterthought, the dragon added, 'And, a room can't hurt you.'

Realizing her linked companion could sense her trepidation, Robin agreed. 'You're right. I should be brave. It's only a room.'

They continued to chat in mind-speech as Robin walked and, before the white-haired woman knew it, she had arrived outside the apartment and Erosmay was reminding her for a second time, 'It's only a room.'

Comforted by the dragon's encouragement, the white-haired woman set her feelings aside and opened the door.

The apartment was dark, cold, and musty.

In no-nonsense fashion, Robin boldly stepped inside and, after setting her heavy basket on a nearby table, strode purposefully across the main room, pulled back the dust-covered curtains and opened the large double window so fresh mountain air could flow inside. And then, in the cold light of day, she turned to face the room.

The dark wooden furniture was still there, just as she remembered. But to her immense relief, all of Allyce's personal effects had been removed.

Next, Robin walked over to the sleeping chamber and inspected it with a critical eye. As with the main room, everything was covered with dust, there were no soft furnishings other than the curtains, and the floor was in need of a good mopping.

Realizing she had a lot to do, Robin decided to work methodically from the top-down and rolled-up the sleeves of her faded grey dress.

With the aid of a wooden chair, the white-haired woman stood on tiptoe and unfastened the curtains which she let drop onto the floor in small dusty heaps. Then, she gathered up the fallen drapery and carried it over to the balcony where, despite the light drizzle, she commenced to shake the dust and cobwebs from the fabric over the balustrade.

Robin tried not to think of Allyce as she worked. But the two of them had spent so much time together inside the apartment and sitting out on the balcony, it wasn't long before the white-haired woman's eyes began to fill with tears for the loss of her friend and over frustration the murderer had gone unpunished because, as king, Elrod was above the law.

Through blurred vision, Robin clumsily folded the last of the curtains she had been shaking and placed it on top of the others. Then sniffing back the tears, she picked up the stack of drapery and carried it back inside the apartment where she deposited it onto the small table beside her sewing basket.

'Are you alright?' Erosmay asked, full of concern in mind-speech.

'I'm fine,' the white-haired woman answered as she removed the handkerchief from her pocket and wiped the tears from her eyes. 'I was just thinking about Allyce and Elrod.'

'It would be impossible not to,' her linked companion replied sympathetically. 'Just remember, we are nearly ready to leave this terrible place.'

Robin sniffed again and smiled. No matter how bad she felt, the little dragon was always able to lift her spirits and help her regain perspective.

It was true; they were nearly ready to make their escape. They had already acquired dye for her hair, food, and a pair of old shoes. But because it went against her principals to cause anyone hardship, they still had not been able to obtain the shirt and trousers she needed to finish her street urchin disguise.

Robin blew her nose and absently glanced down at the stack of curtains as she stuffed the soiled handkerchief back into her pocket. And suddenly, she realized the answer to their clothing dilemma was sitting on the table right in front of her. 'I think I know where I can get the clothing!'

'Where?' Erosmay asked excitedly.

'The fortress laundry,' Robin explained. 'This dusty drapery needs to be washed and ironed before Elrod's guest arrives. So when I drop it off, I'll see what I can find.'

The irony was not lost on Erosmay and she let out a rumble of dragon laugher.

'What's so funny?' Robin asked her linked companion.

Still rumbling, the little dragon answered, 'The Black Hawk will provide the disguise you need to escape him.'

'I hadn't thought about it like that,' the white-haired woman replied, pleased she could finally strike a blow, albeit a small one, against Elrod. And shortly thereafter in the hope of obtaining the clothing she needed, Robin set off for the fortress laundry with an armload of curtains.

The plan was a sound one and might have worked, had it not been for the dusty tickle which began to play at the end of her nose on the way there. And by sheer bad luck, just as Robin stepped over the laundry room threshold, the tickle transformed into a full-blown sneeze so loud all the women there turned to look at her. But then, once they saw who it was, they all looked away again except for Morag, the indomitable head laundress, who strode over to her.

By the brisk way Morag took charge of the curtains, Robin understood why the woman's subordinates called her 'The Iron Maiden' when her back was turned. And because the head laundress had not asked her any questions, Robin realized she had been expecting her, which meant the keeper of stores had already whispered the latest fortress gossip into Morag's ear.

As Morag began issuing instructions to her staff, Robin used the opportunity to slip discreetly into the adjoining room to acquire the clothing to complete her disguise. But, this too was the head laundress's domain and she ruled it with an iron fist. Before the white-haired woman had a chance to locate the items she needed, Morag arrived and commenced to hand Robin the freshly laundered towels and bedding she deemed suitable for Elrod's impending guest, and then she sent the white-haired woman swiftly on her way.

Once back at the apartment, Robin set aside the fresh laundry, rolled up her sleeves, and got on with her work. Time passed quickly for her and it was well past noon before she realized she had not stopped for a midday meal, and this was only when Erosmay interrupted her cleaning to comment upon it.

Having nearly finished mopping the sitting room floor, Robin asked the dragon if she would like her to bring back something from the fortress kitchen. And as usual, Erosmay replied she wouldn't mind a snack, which Robin knew really meant she had already eaten but, being a greedy gut, would like to scarf down a little more.

The white-haired woman smiled to herself and replied fondly in mind-speech, 'I'll see what I can find.' And true to her word, after she finished mopping the rest of the floor and had set the mop and bucket out of the way beside the door, she wiped her hands on her faded grey dress and set off for the kitchen.

Too busy to think about food, Robin had not realized how hungry she was until she was striding down the corridor. And then when she did, her stomach realized it too and started to grumble at her, so she quickened her pace.

As she neared the kitchen, Robin began to hear snippets of female laughter mixed with the familiar clinking of crockery as the scullery maids washed up after the midday meal.

Knowing their conversation would cease once she entered the room, the white-haired woman mentally prepared herself and stood a little straighter. Then, she walked into the kitchen like she owned the place just as one of the scullery maids was saying, 'I told him I wasn't that kind of.' And when the speaker fell silent, Robin knew without looking the girls had seen her.

Alerted by the sudden silence, the more senior kitchen staff seated at a table further into the room, sipping tea and resting their feet while deciding what to prepare for the evening meal, sat stone still as she walked past and avoided making eye contact with her lest she hex them.

With Erosmay depending upon her, Robin had started to use such superstitious ignorance to her advantage. Aware she was being watched, the white-haired woman liberally helped herself to a large bowl of leftover stew along with a piece of sliced venison which she placed onto a plate for her linked companion. Then pretending to be much bolder than she really was, Robin turned around and strode out of the kitchen, knowing full well none of the people there had the guts, or any other piece of anatomy for that matter, brave enough to challenge her.

Being linked, Erosmay had sensed Robin's trepidation as she had entered the kitchen as well as her relief when she had left, and it pleased the dragon to know the white-haired woman was regaining her self-confidence. Then to top it off, when Robin told her in mind-speech about the snack she was fetching back, Erosmay was absolutely ecstatic.

While still fresh from the egg, the dragon had cleverly taught herself how to open their chamber door by flying up, wrapping her tail around the door handle, and pulling on it. But in her youthful exuberance, one day she opened the door before Robin had drawn close enough for it to appear as if the white-haired woman had opened it herself and several of the servants, having witnessed the door seemingly open of its own accord, had assumed Robin wielded magic to make it do so. Thus, via the fortress rumor mill, the white-haired woman was transformed from a traumatized outcast into a spellcasting sorceress.

Knowing there was no truth to the rumor, Elrod was secretly pleased, as he derived cruel pleasure in seeing Robin's increased isolation. And ironically, Robin was pleased as well, because the fear generated by the rumor gave her greater freedom to move about the fortress with fewer questions being asked of her.

Now older and wiser, Erosmay had learned to be a little more patient and, even though her mouth was beginning to water by the time Robin arrived outside their chamber, she ensured no one was about before swinging open the door to allow the white-haired woman admittance.

The room they shared was no larger than a broom cupboard, but it was private and for the time being served them perfectly well.

Robin walked across the chamber within a few strides and placed the food on the small wooden chest which held her few possessions and also served as a bedside table.

After giving Erosmay a few loving strokes all the way down from the top of her little scaled head to the tip of her tail, and receiving several nuzzles in return, Robin set the plate of venison on the floor so her linked companion could enjoy her snack.

'My favorite,' Erosmay said in mind-speech as she walked over to the plate.

Robin laughing replied, 'You always say that, no matter what meat I bring you.'

'Yes, meat is my favorite.' The dragon earnestly agreed.

'I thought you liked some meats better than others.'

'I do. I like big pieces better than little ones,' Erosmay replied forthrightly, showing a mouthful of razor-sharp teeth.

The mischievous little dragon never failed to put a smile on the white-haired woman's face, and today was no exception. Happy to be in her linked companion's company, Robin sat down on her small bed, the only other piece of furniture in the room, and picked up her spoon.

While they ate, Robin told Erosmay about her thwarted attempt at the fortress laundry to obtain the clothing for her disguise.

The little dragon did not reply, but she did stop eating long enough to politely look up at Robin to confirm she was listening before turning her attention back to her plate.

It wasn't until after all of the venison had disappeared down the dragon's long throat that she finally spoke, 'Sergeant Sorkin has lots of clothes.'

Assuming Erosmay meant she could obtain the garments by filching them off the sergeant's drying line, Robin replied, 'I don't want to cause anyone hardship.' Then as she set her empty bowl aside, she added, 'Life here is difficult enough for people without us stealing from them.'

'Yes,' agreed Erosmay as she lifted her wings and flew up onto the bed. 'Life here is difficult.'

Accustomed to nestling in Robin's lap after meals while the white-haired woman gently stroked her, Erosmay made herself comfortable and continued, 'He won't notice the clothes missing.'

Perplexed, Robin stopped midstroke and asked, 'He won't? I don't understand?'

With a gentle nudge of her head, the dragon prompted Robin to resume her stroking and replied, 'They're not really his.'

Robin had learned early in their relationship, if Erosmay was anything to go by, dragons were curious creatures by nature. And even though Erosmay chose to only communicate with her, the little dragon understood human language. So, she asked tactfully, 'Erosmay, have you been watching and learning again?'

The dragon replied proudly, 'Yes. I like learning.'

Knowing she was in for an interesting tale, Robin cuddled her linked companion closer and said, 'So, tell me about this clothing Sergeant Sorkin won't notice missing.'

It transpired Erosmay had been venturing much farther from their chambers than Robin had suspected. And at some point during these excursions, the little dragon had noticed dozens of young men, dressed in all manner of clothing, enter the army garrison. Then later, when the dragon saw these same young men again, they were wearing the blood-red uniform of Elrod's army.

This news alarmed Robin because it was the first she had heard about the Black Hawk's increasing military might, which was not surprising since she was no longer privy to fortress gossip. But not wishing to distract her linked companion, she only asked, 'How does Sergeant Sorkin fit into all of this?'

'I wanted to see the men turn red, so I flew to the building and watched.' Erosmay paused and shook her head disappointedly, 'But, they didn't shed their skin. They just changed into red clothes and put on red hats. Then after they marched around like ants, Sergeant Sorkin sold all the clothes that weren't red and bought ale. It made him happy and he sang.'

'I see, and you want to sneak a shirt and pair of trousers out of the garrison without this Sergeant Sorkin noticing?'

'Yes, but I need to think about it.' And with that, Erosmay lowered her head onto Robin's lap and closed her eyes to contemplate.

Robin smiled lovingly down at the little dragon as she continued to stroke her. The rhythmic motion relaxed them both and, except for the dragon's soft rumblings, they sat in comfortable silence.

Erosmay had proven herself to Robin time and time again. So when the dragon told her that she would do something, the white-haired woman no longer doubted her linked companion or worried for her safety. Instead, Robin was simply thankful she had such a loyal friend.

As usual, their time together passed all too swiftly and it was not long before Robin found herself giving Erosmay a final hug and gathering up their dirty dishes so she could drop them off at the scullery on her way back to the east wing.

Erosmay, on the other hand, was facing a much more enjoyable task. She loved sneaking about the fortress and had finely honed her evasive techniques: keeping to the shadows, moving just out of a person's field of vision, and freezing suddenly to become one with her surroundings. But now, with a secret mission to accomplish, the sneaking was going to be even more fun.

Too excited to wait for the evening shadows, Erosmay darted out the small window and into the nearby foliage the second Robin stepped out of their chamber.

By cautiously flying short distances between one concealed area to the next, Erosmay slowly zigzagged her way to the army garrison.

When she finally arrived, the dragon noticed there were a lot more young men in blood-red uniforms then there had been during her previous excursion.

Despite the winter drizzle, Erosmay settled herself comfortably within the concealing branches of a nearby tree, perfectly camouflaged by her iridescent copper and sage green scales, to wait for an opportunity to fly across the grounds of the garrison.

Although the little dragon already knew red men liked to follow orders and march around in columns like ants, she still found it entertaining. And when one of the soldiers turned the wrong direction and started to march off on his own, she nearly fell from her perch trying to suppress her laughter. But then, when he was made to do press-ups in the dirt until his arms gave way, she regretted her mirth.

It was dusk before the compound had cleared enough for Erosmay to even consider flying across it. Then when she finally did venture forth, she flew very low to the ground as an added precaution.

It did not take the dragon long to reach the building where she had observed the recruits change into their new red uniforms.

She landed quietly beneath one of the building's open windows, tucked in her wings, and listened for sounds of movement coming from within.

Hearing an unfamiliar voice, Erosmay stood perfectly still. 'I wonder what the recruiter promised this gullible lot.'

Sergeant Sorkin replied, 'The usual, a full belly and a place to sleep with a roof over their heads.'

'They better enjoy it while it lasts. Once they're posted, food and roofs will be the least of their worries.'

Sorkin snorted in agreement, 'That's true enough. But, let's not ruin the surprise.'

'I won't. I've enough on my plate cleaning up after them.'

'You know what they say about one man's rubbish being another man's treasure,' Sorkin reminded his subordinate.

'I sure do,' the soldier replied a bit more enthusiastically. 'And, it almost makes this job worthwhile.'

'That it does,' Sorkin agreed. 'Start filling the baskets and I'll get the wagon.'

The little dragon heard the door open and close as Sorkin left, followed by sounds of the other man filling the baskets as he had been ordered. Using the opportunity to better position herself, Erosmay moved stealthily towards the front of the building to wait for the sergeant's return, which she knew would not be long because Sorkin liked to park the wagon close by.

Erosmay heard the shod clip-clop of the horse's hooves before she actually saw the beast, and she crouched perfectly still in the evening shadows as the wagon rolled to a stop in front of the building.

The two soldiers quickly loaded the large clothes filled baskets onto the back of the wagon. Then as they went to seat themselves at the front of the vehicle,

Erosmay flew onto the back while Sorkin told his colleague, 'Let's turn these rags into riches.' And with that, the sergeant snapped the horse's reins and the wagon lurched into motion, totally unaware he had acquired an extra passenger.

The little stowaway waited until they had left the garrison before she crept silently between the baskets to start looking for the items she needed.

Quickly spotting a shirt-sleeve dangling over the edge of one of the baskets, the dragon reached up and slowly pulled the garment free with her teeth. The shirt obviously had not been washed in a very long time. It smelled terrible and tasted worse, but Erosmay couldn't afford to be picky. However, had she been capable of spitting, she gladly would have in order to rid her mouth of the shirt's horrible stale sweaty flavor. Yet out of love for Robin, she persevered and dragged the disgusting garment to the back of the wagon.

It took her a bit longer to find the trousers the white-haired woman needed. And to the dragon's dismay, they were just as repugnant as the shirt, but her commitment to Robin did not waver and she stoically pulled the trousers to the back of the wagon next to the shirt.

Admittedly, Erosmay would have preferred to have flown the clothing to the fortress despite its foul odor, however, this wasn't an option because the garments were much larger than she was and, even if she made two trips, their sheer weight made flight impossible.

Yet familiar with the route, the little dragon knew the wagon would eventually trundle past the Far View Inn on its way to the fortress's poor quarter. And when it did, this would be the most convenient location for Robin to meet her. So, she quietly hunkered down with her ill-gotten gains at the back of the wagon and contacted the white-haired woman via mind-speech. 'I have the clothes, but they are heavy and I need you to collect them.'

'Alright, where are you?' Robin asked.

'I'm on a wagon now, but I'll be waiting for you in the bushes beside Far View Inn soon. But be warned, the clothes stink.'

Knowing the little dragon had an acute sense of smell, Robin smiled and replied, 'I hope you didn't find the odor too offensive.'

'I'll live,' Erosmay retorted.

'Good. I'd miss you terribly if you didn't,' Robin teased. 'See you at the gate.'

The little dragon carefully peered around the baskets every now and again to check on the wagon's progress. And when Erosmay saw she was nearing the inn, she pushed the stolen garments off the back of the vehicle, glided down onto the deserted road beside them, and dragged the foul-smelling clothing into the bushes at the side of the building as the two soldiers, oblivious of the theft, drove on.

To pass the time while she cleansed the disgusting taste of unwashed human from her mouth and waited for Robin to arrive, Erosmay positioned herself beneath one of the inn's bedroom windows so she could earwig on the room's occupants. But, it quickly transpired they were more interested in getting ready for bed than talking, so the disappointed dragon crept back to her place beside the garments before Robin could discover what she had been up to. And by the time she got rid of the terrible taste, she sensed the white-haired woman's approach and greeted her in mind-speech, 'Well met. You walked quickly.'

'Yes. I didn't want you to take any unnecessary risks,' Robin answered as she appeared in the darkness draped in a hooded cloak and carrying her familiar sewing basket.

Erosmay didn't need to be linked to be in total agreement. And, rather than run the risk of tasting the disgusting clothing again, she stepped out of the way.

The white-haired woman retrieved the stolen garments from the bushes and stuffed them inside her sewing basket. Then before she closed its lid, Robin looked down at Erosmay and offered, 'There's room inside if you'd like a lift back.'

'Now that really would kill me,' the little dragon replied.

'Oh, I'm sorry. I forgot about the stench.'

'You won't come laundry time,' the dragon warned. 'I'll fly back. I need fresh air and I'm hungry.'

'I'm glad to see the smell hasn't put you off your food,' Robin teased fondly.

'Me too,' the dragon earnestly agreed as she spread her leathery wings. Then with one powerful downward stroke, she took flight and disappeared into the night sky.

8 WHITE CLIFF

The wind had blown in their favor throughout the entire voyage and, sailing with an empty hold, the Venture managed to make the return journey to White Cliff in four days instead of the usual five the crossing normally took.

Standing on the upper deck with his first mate, Captain Nagrom watched as the white-cliffed harbor slowly came into view.

'We made good time', Rowan stated the simple fact.

'Aye, we did, but even so the king may not agree,' Nagrom replied as he adjusted the lens of his telescope. Then, as the dock came into focus and he saw a vessel already moored alongside the pier, he added, 'Someone's beaten us in. We'll have to drop anchor in the harbor and row ashore.'

'Consider it done,' the first mate said, trying to sound cheerful. 'The men and I can sort this lot out. You'd best ready yourself. It isn't every day one meets a king.'

'You're a good man,' Nagrom replied by way of thanks. 'If you need me, you know where I'll be. But under the circumstances,' he said with a shrug, 'I must admit I'm not looking forward to the introduction.' Then, leaving his first mate in charge, the captain headed back to his cabin to dress for the most important meeting of his life.

During the return voyage, Nagrom had made what preparations he could in anticipation of the occasion. He had aired and brushed the small specks of lint from his best set of clothes, painstakingly polished and buffed his boots to a high shine, and had Stewpot, the ship's cook, trim his curly dark hair.

He also had plenty of time to mull the situation over and had decided to tell the simple truth, as there was no denying his inadvertent involvement in the princess's abduction. Then, if the king chose to punish him for his actions, he would face the consequences like a man. He just hoped the king would be lenient and not tar his crew with the same brush, because they were all honest seamen who did not deserve to be punished for sailing under his command.

Having tracked their course carefully, the captain had known they would reach White Cliff that day and had laid out his clothing accordingly. So when he reached his cabin, it did not take him long to change clothes and slip-on his highly polished boots. Then, he took out his penknife and cut the page containing the princess's messages from the ship's logbook, folded the page neatly, and tucked it safely inside the breast pocket of his jacket.

Nagrom had just finished combing his hair when he heard the familiar sound of the chain, as the Venture dropped anchor in the harbor, signaling their arrival. And being a man of action, the captain didn't waste any time. He just tossed the comb onto his berth, donned his hat and strode out of the cabin.

When he stepped back on the weather deck, he was surprised to see Stewpot standing beside Rowan, waiting for him.

'So captain, you can look professional when you set your mind to it,' the cook remarked dryly.

The unexpected comment stopped Nagrom in his tracks. Stewpot had an uncanny knack of saying the right thing at the right time, and today was no exception.

Wound tighter than an anchor chain, Nagrom began to laugh. And, as he laughed, the stress flowed out of him like a great wave.

Feeling much more relaxed, the captain admitted, 'To tell the truth, I feel like a bridegroom on his wedding day.'

'Well, you know what they say about bridegrooms,' Rowan interjected. 'They shouldn't keep the bride waiting.'

'You said it,' Nagrom agreed, feeling much lighter of heart, but glad he wouldn't be delayed any longer than necessary. 'Is the gig ready?'

'Aye, launched and manned,' his first mate answered.

As the three walked over to the ship's railing, the captain told Rowan, 'I don't know how long I'll be, but give the men two day's shore leave in any case. They've earned it.'

'I will,' Rowan replied. 'And, good luck.'

'Aye, good luck captain,' Stewpot echoed.

Nagrom thanked them with a nod of his head. Then, he turned and climbed down the rope ladder to the awaiting gig below.

After the captain had taken his seat, the sailor they had good-humoredly nicknamed Fish Bait, because he had the misfortune of falling overboard the first time he sailed with them, lifted his oar and pushed off from the Venture. And with practiced ease, the strong-armed oarsmen put their backs into it and began to row.

As the gig glided towards the pier, a couple of squawking gulls swooped down to investigate. But finding nothing edible aboard the little craft, the troublesome birds flew back to the shore in search of richer pickings.

It did not take the crewmen long to row the captain dockside. And, aware of the gravity of the situation, when he climbed out of the gig they all solemnly wished him good luck.

With the princess's messages tucked safely inside his breast pocket and the familiar aroma of curing kippers from the nearby smokery in the air, Nagrom thanked his men for their good wishes and then started to make his way towards the harbor road.

Under normal circumstances, he would have enjoyed the walk. But on this particular day, he could ill afford the delay. So when he spotted a youth driving a weather-beaten wagon loaded with fishing nets, the captain waved him over and shouted. 'Hey lad, if you give me a lift to the castle, I'll pay you a silver piece.'

'We'll have to take the long way. Citadel center's blocked with market stalls,' the boy reliably informed him as he pulled his horse to a halt.

Having been there less than a fortnight earlier, Nagrom was aware of this. 'I understand, but let's hurry. I've important business to attend to.'

Eager to earn the silver piece, the boy lifted the reins in his calloused hands and, just as soon as the captain had sat down beside him, commanded the horse to 'walk on'.

Concerned for the welfare of his crew, Nagrom didn't begin to relax until they had cleared the congested waterfront and the boy had flicked the reins to quicken the horse's pace. Then, in an effort to put the meeting with the king from his mind, the captain sat back and commented, 'Nice horse.'

'It belongs to my uncle,' the boy answered amiably. 'We have an arrangement. I feed and muck out after it and he loans me the horse and wagon.'

'I see,' the captain said, instantly liking the lad's friendly forthright nature. Then nodding his head towards the nets in the back of the wagon, Nagrom asked, 'So, is your father a fisherman?'

'He was, but he drowned,' the boy replied. 'Now ma and I earn a living by mending nets and doing laundry.'

Noticing the boy's ragged clothing and that his worn-out shoes were too large for his feet, Nagrom realized the lad and his mother were living hand-to-mouth, so he stopped asking questions in case he inadvertently embarrassed the youth.

The two fell into a companionable silence, with only the clip-clop of the horse's hoofs and the cry of gulls breaking the quiet, as they slowly left the harbor behind and began to travel up the steep winding road towards the citadel.

Because it had rained the night before, the aggregate road was a bit rough in places where the stones and chalk had washed away. And every once in a while, when one of the wheels struck a rough patch, the wagon's passengers would bump shoulders.

When they eventually neared the summit, outside the walls of the citadel where the ground had started to level but tribute to the crown was minimal, they came upon several rather rickety dwellings the captain had seen a hundred times before but had never paid any attention to.

As they began to ride past the hovels, the lad smiled and waved to an equally rickety pipe smoking old man sitting outside one of them and, after removing the clay pipe from his lips, the wrinkled old man grinned and waved back.

Having observed the youth, Nagrom found himself wondering why his affable companion was wasting his time working for coppers when he had the potential to earn so much more aboard ship. But not wanting to pry, he managed to hold his tongue until after they had entered the citadel and completed the diversion. Then, the captain's curiosity finally got the better of him, and he just had to ask, 'Have you ever thought about going to sea?'

'Only every day,' the boy replied flashing him a smile. 'But, my ma doesn't want me to be a fisherman, or a deckhand either for that matter. She says she couldn't bear it if I went the same way as pa.'

Nagrom wished he could offer the honest hardworking lad a placement on his ship, as he had no doubt the youth would be an asset to his crew. However, until he met with the king, he didn't want to make any promises he might not be able to keep. So, he simply nodded his head and didn't say anything more until after the boy had reined the horse to a halt outside the castle gates. Then, he asked the boy his name.

'Archie,' the lad answered frankly.

'Well Archie, I'm Captain Nagrom. And if you wait and give me a lift back to the dock, I'll give you another silver piece for your trouble. But mind you,' he warned, as he handed the lad the first silver coin he had promised, 'it may take most of the day.'

The boy shot Nagrom a grin and promised, 'I'll be here. I can mend nets while I wait.'

Nagrom stepped down from the wagon, walked over to one of the soldiers standing guard outside the castle gate and, because he didn't know who was aware of the princess's abduction, simply told him, 'My name is Captain Nagrom and I've a message for the king from Princess Lilyanna.'

Suspecting Nagrom to be a cracked pot, the guard curtly replied. 'Whatever message you have for the king, I'll make sure he gets it.'

Aware the soldier was there to defend the castle and restrict admittance, the captain looked him straight in the eye and answered politely, but firmly.

'Thank you, but no. The princess instructed me to give the king her message and that's exactly what I'm going to do.'

After giving him the once-over, the guard decided to take Nagrom seriously and let the captain pass through the gate. Then, a second soldier who had witnessed the encounter escorted him across the courtyard to a small office where Nagrom met his second obstacle, a quill-dipper sitting behind a desk.

The soldier told the quill-dipper, 'This is Captain Nagrom. He wishes an audience with the king.' Then, the soldier turned and left the room.

Annoyed by the interruption, the man begrudgingly set his writing quill back into its holder beside a matching inkpot and looked up at the captain. 'So, you want to see the king.'

'Yes, I do,' Nagrom replied seriously.

'And the reason behind your request?'

'I've a message from Princess Lilyanna.'

The quill-dipper lifted his right eyebrow, having been ordered to stay alert for anything unusual pertaining to the princess during her seclusion. 'The princess has her own messengers. Why didn't she send one of them?'

'That's a question you'd best ask the princess,' Nagrom answered politely.

The quill-dipper decided to try a different tactic. 'The king has no time to waste, so leave the message with me and I'll pass it onto him.'

'No. I can't do that. The princess instructed me to give the king her message. And, if it takes me all day or all week, that's exactly what I intend to do. As for wasting the king's time, the longer this takes, the more of the king's time **you** waste.'

The man looked up challengingly at the captain and the captain returned 'the look' right back. They locked gazes in a test of wills for several seconds. But Nagrom was deadly serious and, in the end, it was the quill-dipper behind the desk who looked away.

Satisfied with the exchange, the man wordlessly lifted his quill and scratched a few quick words onto a piece of paper. Then, after dusting the ink with pounce to dry it and folding the note, he summoned a servant by ringing the small handbell on his desk.

When the out of breath retainer stepped into the room a short time later, the quill-dipper handed him the paper with his ink stained fingers and instructed, 'Escort Captain Nagrom to Lord Talmen's office and give Talmen this.'

'As you wish,' the servant replied obediently, thankful he hadn't been admonished for his tardiness. Then turning towards the captain, he said, 'This way.'

Pleased to have passed his second obstacle, the captain nodded and followed the retainer out of the quill-pusher's office, down a long corridor, up a spiral staircase, along another long corridor, and into a small office area where two men sat hunched over paper strewn desks.

Although both men stopped working and looked up when they entered, it was the older man whom the retainer addressed and handed the folded paper. 'Master Tindal asked me to escort Captain Nagrom here and to deliver this message for Lord Talmen.'

The older man unfolded the paper and perused it quickly. Then, after he had dismissed the retainer, he looked up at the captain and asked, 'Do you know who Lord Talmen is?'

'I assume he's the third obstacle I have to contend with before I can speak with the king,' Nagrom replied dryly.

'Lord Talmen is the king's head of intelligence. So if this is a hoax, be warned, this is your last opportunity to change your mind. Otherwise, you might spend the night behind bars.'

'I stand corrected, Lord Talmen isn't my third obstacle. You are.'

'Very well,' the man said. Then, he lifted his quill and wrote a few lines of his own at the bottom of the note he had received from Tindal and handed it to his colleague. 'Markus, please take this directly to Lord Talmen.'

As Markus left on his errand, the older man stood up from his chair and told the captain, 'I'll need to frisk you for weapons. It's standard procedure.'

Having wisely left his weapons on board the Venture when he dressed that morning, Nagrom lifted his arms, pleased to be finally making some progress.

The man adeptly ran his hands over the captain's body in search of any hidden weapons. Then once he was satisfied Nagrom was unarmed, he returned to his desk and said, 'Lord Talmen will be joining us shortly.'

Relieved, the captain replied, 'Finally. I was beginning to wonder how many more songs I was going to have to dance to before someone took me seriously.'

'Well, if your feet ache from all the fancy footwork, you can sit down on one of the chairs over there,' the man replied, pointing to a spot behind Nagrom.

The captain turned around and walked over to the small row of wooden chairs lined up against the wall. But instead of sitting down, he casually picked one up, carried it over to the man's desk, and set it down, bridging the gap between them.

If the man thought this forward, he didn't let it show and proceeded to calmly stack the papers he had been working on into a neat pile and set it to one side. Then, he withdrew a blank sheet of paper from one of his desk drawers, placed it on top of the desk, and sat back in his chair to wait.

Shortly afterwards, the sound of approaching footsteps could be heard from the hallway. And when Markus and a lean man, about ten years Nagrom's senior, strode briskly into the room, Nagrom and his companion both stood.

The spymaster didn't waste any time. He walked straight up to the captain and said, 'I'm Lord Talmen. Please sit back down and tell me why you're here.'

Although direct, this was the first greeting Nagrom had received since stepping foot inside the castle that wasn't hostile. Realizing he must have passed some sort of vetting process, the captain retook his seat and began his account.

'As you know, my name is Nagrom and I'm captain of the merchant ship Venture. Nine days ago, as we were preparing to set sail for Hesketh, two men approached me pleading their mistress required urgent medical treatment in Hesketh. I explained my ship wasn't equipped for passengers. But they continued to press me and, in the end, I relented because I didn't wish to cause the lady any unnecessary suffering.

I moved my belongings out of my cabin and allowed the lady to reside there undisturbed throughout the voyage, her servants taking care of all her needs.

On the fifth day, after they'd disembarked and we'd offloaded the cargo, I returned to my cabin intending to update the ship's log. And when I opened the log, I discovered this,' Captain Nagrom said reaching inside his breast pocket and extracting the folded page he had cut from the logbook.

He handed the page to Talmen and he continued, 'Realizing I'd inadvertently aided in the kidnapping of the princess, I set sail on the next tide for White Cliff. The return journey only took four days because we sailed with an empty hold. But even so, her abductors now have a nine day lead.'

As the spymaster unfolded the paper, his eyes were immediately drawn to the princess's signature and seal at the bottom of the page. Recognizing the document as authentic, he read both messages over carefully. Then, he looked over to Nagrom and asked, 'Did the princess look mistreated in anyway?'

'I never saw her face. They carried her covered with a cloak.'

'She must have been drugged,' Talmen stated matter-of-factly. 'Did she get enough to eat?'

'I don't think so,' Nagrom answered truthfully. 'They said their mistress's illness had put her off her food and she only ate a single bowl of porridge on a good day, which is what they brought her.' The captain shook his head in regret and continued, 'I am truly sorry, but I had no reason to question what they told me.'

'Understood. Is there anything else you think we should know?'

'They drove the princess away in a curtain drawn carriage, if that helps. At the time I presumed they were travelling to the healers, but now I know differently.'

Talmen nodded. Then, he glanced over to the man who'd been recording Nagrom's statement and said, 'Karl, we're finished here. Dry the ink.'

While Karl put down his quill, Talmen then told Markus, 'I've an urgent message for the king's ears only. Tell him "Wedding plans are going smoothly".'

As Markus left the room to deliver the message, Talmen turned back to Karl and continued, 'Once we've finished here, I'd like you to find Jerhal and tell him to meet me at the command center.'

Shaking the pounce for the transcript and then handing it to his superior, Karl replied, 'Okay. Then afterwards, do you want me to join you there or man the office?'

'You'd better come back here. I want to keep up the appearance it's business as usual,' spymaster replied as he stuffed the princess's messages and the transcript into his leather document case.

The captain had sat quietly throughout the exchange, preparing himself for the moment of truth ahead. And when the spymaster told him it was time to see the king, Nagrom stood up, surprised he felt slightly weak at the knees.

9 URBA

For a fleeting moment, King Dallin had considered cancelling the meeting with his treasury chancellor, Lord Hargreaves. But then, he dismissed the notion, knowing he needed to keep busy lest he spend the time fretting over the safety of his missing daughter.

The meeting had been lengthy and was nearing conclusion when someone knocked upon the council chamber door and interrupted Hargreaves before he could finish expounding the issues surrounding the new bridge construction at Fast Rapids and the actions taken to rectify them.

Glancing towards the doorway, Dallin and the chancellor watched as the door swung inwards. Then Issar, one of the king's personal guards stepped smartly into the room and announced, 'Your Majesty, pardon the intrusion, but there's a messenger here to see you.'

'It's alright Issar,' the king replied, glad for the interruption. 'You can let him in.'

When Markus entered, Dallin's pulse quickened. He had received messages from this particular messenger before and knew he was employed by Talmen, his head of intelligence.

Markus gave the king a quick bow. Then, after Dallin had motioned for him to approach, he walked over to the king and whispered, 'Wedding plans are going smoothly.'

On the day of Lilyanna's abduction, Talmen had promised he would send

Dallin this simple five word phrase to let him know when his daughter's whereabouts had been discovered. Nine days had passed since then, and Dallin was beginning to wonder if the spymaster had made a promise he could not keep. But now, after all this time, Talmen had proven true to his word.

Filled with excitement, the king forced himself to appear outwardly calm and thanked Markus. Then as the messenger left the room, he turned to Lord Hargreaves and abruptly ended their meeting. 'It sounds like you have the project at Fast Rapids well in hand, so let's wrap this up until our meeting next week.'

Aware he held his position at the king's pleasure, the bewildered chancellor stood and replied, 'As you wish, Your Majesty.' Then as he began to collect his ledgers, the king strode out of the room and, with Issar beside him, headed towards the makeshift command center in the castle's west wing.

When they got there, the room was abuzz with excitement and everyone stood clustered around Lord Talmen and an impressive looking stranger dressed in sailor's garb.

Just as the king always did upon entering the command center, he pre-empted formalities with a wave of his hand. Then as Dallin strode forward, the men parted, clearing a path between him and the spymaster, and Talmen introduced the man with him as Captain Nagrom of the merchant ship Venture.

The captain immediately dropped to one knee, 'Sire, please forgive me. I unknowingly transported the princess to the Port of Hesketh.'

Dallin stopped in his tracks. Although he heard what the man said, it took a moment for the news to sink in. Then keeping his face expressionless, he looked the captain directly in the eyes and commanded, 'Stand. Tell me everything, from the beginning.'

Captain Nagrom did as he was bidden. And when he had finished, Talmen handed the king Lilyanna's messages.

Upon seeing the familiar script, Dallin's eyes filled with tears of relief and he pretended to read the messages several times, so he could clear his vision. Then, no longer bound with invisible chains of frustration, the king turned to

Lord Talmen and ordered a messenger be sent to the queen informing her of the news.

With a nod of Talmen's head, one of his men vacated the room to carry out the king's request.

Turning his attention back to the captain, the king said, 'My daughter requested I reward you.'

Nagrom replied, 'Sire, there's no need. It was my mistake the princess was transported to Hesketh and I shall bear the cost.'

Whereas most rulers would have been pleased to keep their royal coffers full, King Dallin would not hear of it. And in the end, an agreement was reached. The king paid the crew's wages but, at Nagrom's insistence, the captain did not receive a copper.

With his mission completed, Captain Nagrom was dismissed, much to his great relief. And although the captain did not know it, he would later receive a royal warrant of appointment, gaining him a considerable amount of new business. However, at the time, he was simply thankful his crew hadn't been punished because of his actions and he could now offer the industrious net mending boy, Archie, an apprenticeship aboard his vessel.

As the captain departed, the king walked over to the map and, with a sweep of his hand, brushed away all of the tiny black-flagged pins which had marked their search radius. Then, he pulled his dagger from its sheath and, since Elrod wasn't available, plunged the blade deep into the map where Greystone Fortress was located instead.

Although the gesture was symbolic, everyone in the room knew the first blow had been struck against their enemy.

'Gentlemen, the situation is more serious than the simple ransom demand we first suspected,' the king said gravely.

As the men murmured their agreement, Talmen, always one step ahead of his counterparts, added, 'Precisely. And by now, the princess will be deep within the Black Hawk's domain, if not already at Greystone Fortress itself.'

Although the king's worst fears had just been realized, knowing his adversary's identity strengthened him. Pushing his fatherly concern aside, the king stated flatly, 'We cannot allow Elrod's scheming to interfere with the royal wedding.'

Everyone there knew failure meant the crippling of plans for unification the king had spent the past two decades striving to achieve. They also knew they needed to devise a plan to ensure this did not happen. But after deciding a sea route would be faster than travelling by land, it soon became apparent this was all they agreed upon.

Talmen sat quietly listening to the others. And, although he thought several of their suggestions showed some merit, the head of intelligence also knew the ideas lacked the finesse of first-hand knowledge. So when Jerhal arrived, the spymaster indicated, with a tilt of his head, for the operative to join him a short distance from the others.

Jerhal acknowledged with a barely perceivable nod of his own and casually strode over to be appraised of the situation.

As he stood listening to his superior, Jerhal's dark eyes took in every detail of the room. He didn't ask any questions, because there was no need. He knew Talmen was a professional and would provide all the information he needed.

After briefing his operative, the spymaster returned to the others and introduced him. 'This is Jerhal. He's lived in Hesketh for several years and is familiar with the area. He will be included in the rescue party and is aware of the situation as it currently stands.'

Recognizing Jerhal from before, the king told him, 'I'd be interested in hearing things from your perspective. What course of action would you propose?'

Jerhal did not hesitate. He returned the king's gaze and replied, 'Since time is of the essence, I agree sailing will be faster than a land route. There's a small harbor a half-day's ride up the coast from Hesketh where a shallow bottomed craft could drop anchor under the cover of darkness. We'd require strong horses, Greystone Steeds to be precise, assuming you have some in your stables. They're strong swimmers. They'd be easy to offload without any unnecessary delays. And since they're native to the area, they'd be able to bear a rider through the rough terrain of the Greystone Mountains at a fast pace without looking out of place.'

It was obvious Jerhal was much more than the simple man Talmen had introduced him to be and Dallin liked the idea of such swift action. Caught up in the excitement, the king added, 'Yes, that sounds good. The rescue party will need to be small. Too large a group will arouse suspicion.'

Jerhal was in full agreement. By now Elrod would have already doubled his guard and posted spies everywhere. So, the fewer people involved in the rescue the better.

Getting to and from the fortress would be relatively straightforward. The difficulty lay in the rescue itself. First, they would have to locate the princess, but the spy was confident he would be able to do this. He was familiar with the layout of the fortress and he had a few contacts who might be of help.

Secondly, because of the increased security, the rescuers would have to deal with unexpected patrols. Although confident in his own fighting skills, Jerhal knew he would still need someone he could count on to guard his back in a close fight. And, if that person just happened to be as strong as an ox and able to carve up an opponent like a roast on Feast Day, so much the better.

The spy immediately thought of Zarak, the stocky professional soldier he had worked with several times before. The man was an exceptional fighter, trained in the use of all manner of weapons and able to fight just as well on horseback as he could on foot. Physically, he was very strong, and his mind was as sharp as his sword. But best of all, Jerhal knew Zarak was in White Cliff, because he had seen him a few hours earlier.

The final obstacle lay in the fact the princess would be held under lock and key. Although Jerhal was capable of picking a lock, some of the more complicated ones were pretty tricky and the rescue party would not have time to waste. They would need to get in, grab the princess, and get out of the fortress before anyone knew they had been there.

It was then the spy remembered Dare, the young locksmith he encountered at the Oak Barrel. He had no doubt the smith was very skilled and he had been impressed by the way Dare had kept his wits about him when his friend had egged him to perform under pressure.

Inspired, Jerhal quickly formulated a rescue plan which he then shared with the others members of the room. The strategy was simple, involving only three people: a soldier, a picklock, and himself.

With the king's consent, the men then began to work out the logistics while Talmen and Dallin took Jerhal aside 'to discuss some minor details'.

Once out of earshot of the others, the spymaster turned to Jerhal and said, 'We'll need to monitor the rescue party's progress. Because, if for some reason the mission should fail, we'll need to initiate a contingency plan.'

Jerhal was well-aware of the danger. The distance to be travelled was far and any manner of mishap could befall them along the way. He nodded in understanding and quietly inquired, 'What do you have in mind?'

◆◆◆

A short time later, Jerhal found himself sitting in a cluttered room with the magician, Urba. The king had commanded he deliver the princess's letter to the wizard, brief him on their current course of action, and ask him to make the necessary preparations for monitoring the rescue party.

After carefully reading the letter and listening to the spy's update, the wizard sat back more comfortably in his chair and began to explain the basic principles behind the monitoring process. 'Each person is surrounded by colorful swirls of energy, as distinctive to the individual as the unique prints upon one's fingertips, called an aura.'

Intrigued, Jerhal leaned forward so he could better hear what the haggard old man with the wispy chest length beard was saying.

'Once a seer has familiarized himself with an individual's aura, the seer can then enter into a meditative state, focus upon that particular aura and, using his seeing-sight, locate the individual. Thus, by doing this several times a day, the seer can effectively track a person's movements.'

Without missing a heartbeat, Jerhal ask, 'What if there's no movement?'

'That's a good question,' the wizard replied. 'The seer can tell a lot from the speed of the energy swirls within the aura. For instance, if they slowdown, this indicates the individual is resting. Conversely, if they speedup, this reflects physical exertion of some sort.'

'How can you tell if the person is in trouble?'

'In addition to the speed of the energy swirls, certain colors within the aura intensify and glow more brightly allowing the seer to distinguish between mental and physical stress,' the wizard answered.

The spy had learned a longtime ago to trust his instincts, and he had the uneasy feeling the old man was not telling him everything. So, he pressed further. 'That's all well and good, but how would you actually know what kind of trouble the person is in?'

Forced to elaborate, the wizard continued, 'Desperate times require desperate measures. On very rare occasions, the seer might be forced to merge his seeing-self with his subject, therefore enabling the seer to know what the individual is actually experiencing.'

Jerhal was accustomed to operating in secret. Until today, he'd never heard of this type of monitoring and, the more he learned about it, the more invasive he found it to be. 'Is this type of monitoring common practice among you wizards?'

Detecting growing anxiety in the spy's voice, the older man did his best to reassure him. 'No. The ability to search out an aura is a very rare talent. There are only a handful of people born each century with the gift. It's a dangerous practice and, without proper training, a seer can lose his way and not return to his body. When this happens, the seer dies. As for merging with another person, this is even more hazardous and not done lightly. If the seer doesn't withdraw his seeing-self completely, his body will die and the person he merged with is left with a split personality.'

Although the spy agreed with the king monitoring was necessary, even if it was safe, his finely honed instincts rebelled against the prospect of someone sensing his thoughts and emotions no matter how far away they were, and his usually unreadable face reflected as much.

Having seen the same look many times before on the faces of his subjects, Urba chuckled quietly and told the uneasy operative, 'You think this is bad, one day we'll be able to hear conversations long-distance.'

Not waiting for a reply, the wizard absently scratched his head, ruffling his unruly white hair all the more, and admitted, 'I've been working on that for years, but haven't had much success yet.'

Realizing Urba had taken the time to explain how the monitoring process worked in order to build his trust, Jerhal replied, 'Hopefully when you do, you'll also develop a way for spies like me to guard against it.'

The wizard stated, 'For every action there is an equal and opposite reaction. Take the case of Princess Lilyanna for an example, I am familiar with her aura and under normal circumstances would have no difficulty honing in on it. But, she has been forced to wear the collar of concealment and the very pumping of her heart has begun to awaken the dormant creatures within the collar's gemstones. As a result, their auras are distorting her own, making it unrecognizable, and thus hiding her location.'

'I was wondering why you hadn't been able to locate her. You've been searching for an ever-changing needle in a moving haystack.'

'For someone unfamiliar with the science of seeing magic, your grasp of the situation is very sound,' the old man replied with a nod of approval. 'Now thanks to the princess's quick-thinking, we know where she is being taken. So, there's no need to search for her by magical means and I can rest for a few days to regain my strength.'

Jerhal could see the wizard was obviously exhausted. And if the need arose for Urba to merge his seeing-self with Jerhal, the spy wanted the sage to be fully rested before he made the attempt.

'Now back to the matter of monitoring,' Urba instructed as he gestured for Jerhal to stand up from his chair. And in spite of his apprehension, Jerhal did as he was told.

After positioning himself directly in front of the spy, the old man explained, 'I'm going to familiarize myself with your aura. It's similar to a blind person feeling an object in order to understand its shape. The procedure is painless and won't take long. Just close your eyes and try to relax.' Then, the wizard extended his hands so his palms rested just above the spy's head.

Jerhal could feel a tingling sensation dance gently across his scalp. It wasn't unpleasant, merely the whisper of a touch. But even so, he didn't like it and hoped the procedure wouldn't last long.

The two stood in silence, with eyes closed facing each other, the wizard deep in concentration and the spy in resigned tolerance.

As Urba slowly moved his hands across the surface of Jerhal's aura, he expected to find the yellow color patterns denoting high intelligence, cunning, and abstract reasoning. But, the intensity of other colors surprised him, especially the vivid blues which signified integrity and unwavering loyalty.

When the exhausted wizard finally lowered his hands, he was pleased, and greatly relieved, he and the spy were working on the same side.

10 SPRINTER

After eating a hearty supper, the master locksmith dozed contentedly in his chair, with legs outstretched and arms crossed over a full stomach, on the opposite side of the fire while Dare ran the small whetstone down the blade of his practice sword, just as he did most evenings since Zarak had given him the weapon. Only now, instead of the blade being pitted and dulled by rust, it was razor-sharp and glistened in the firelight.

Their home above the locksmith's shop was comfortably warm despite the cold drizzly winter weather outside and, having lived there for so long, the two had grown accustomed to its sparse furnishings and lack of a woman's touch.

Dare spat on the whetstone to begin another downwards stroke on the sharp blade. But just as stone touched steel, someone suddenly started pounding on the shop door below and he nicked his finger.

His father woke with a start. Seeing his son was busy, cursing and sucking on his cut, the master locksmith got up from his chair with a grunt and went downstairs in the dark to see who was causing the disturbance.

When he answered the door, he was surprised to see Zarak, his son's soldier friend, and a tall bearded man standing before him. By the serious expressions on their faces, the smith could tell they weren't there on a social call and quickly invited them inside.

Once the door was closed behind them, Zarak turned to the smith and apologized. 'We're sorry for disturbing you at such a late hour. This is.'

'Jerhal,' Dare interrupted in confused recognition from halfway down the stairway, 'I didn't know you knew each other.'

Zarak glanced up and replied, 'I didn't know Jerhal knew you either, until an hour or so ago.' Then turning back to the master locksmith, he stated flatly. 'This wasn't my idea.'

Before the older man could ask Zarak what he meant, Jerhal interjected. 'We're here on the king's business.'

The bearded man paused just long enough for father and son to realize he was deadly serious. Then, he continued. 'Princess Lilyanna was abducted nine days ago, and we've just discovered it was the Black Hawk who's taken her.'

Both Dare and his father stood in stunned silence. They had heard whispered rumors about Elrod's sadistic acts of cruelty, but never believed he would have the audacity to abduct the king's sole heir.

Mindful of what Zarak had said, the master locksmith grew suspicious and demanded, 'Why are you telling us this?'

Jerhal returned the older man's gaze and answered, 'We require your son's skills.'

With a sinking feeling in the pit of his stomach, the master locksmith already knew which particular skills Jerhal was referring to. But fearing for his son's safety, he asked anyway. 'And, what skills are those?'

'Lock picking,' Jerhal replied.

The desire to protect his son outweighed any fear over his own safety. The master locksmith countered, 'I taught him everything he knows. Take me instead.'

Jerhal replied kindly, but firmly, 'You're too old and have no combat skills.' Then, before the master locksmith could protest further, Jerhal continued. 'Your son will be part of a three man extraction team comprised of Zarak and myself.'

Sensing his father's growing panic and realizing he loved his father far more than he longed for adventure, Dare boldly demanded, 'Do I have any say in this?'

Zarak answered apologetically, 'I'm afraid not. I've already spoken on your behalf, but it appears you're the linchpin of the operation.'

Jerhal cut the conversation short. 'We sail with the morning tide on a ship called the Sprinter. Pack your tools, a warm set of clothes, and try to get some sleep.'

'Best bring your sword too,' Zarak added, as they turned to leave.

Although the master locksmith didn't like the sound of any of this, he knew two things with certainty; you don't disobey your king and Greystone was a dangerous place. So if he was ever going to see his son again, Dare would need his sword for protection.

As the little bell tinkled and the door closed behind their unexpected visitors, the stunned father and son looked at each other, both knowing their contented life at the smithy had just been shattered.

The master locksmith recovered first. 'Jerhal's right. Greystone Fortress is located high in the mountains, so you'll need warm clothing.'

Understanding his father was putting on a brave face, Dare swiftly added, 'Yes, and thick woolen socks for my work boots.'

After gathering an assortment of picklocks, the two climbed the stairs back to their private rooms so Dare could pack for the journey, which didn't take long because his wardrobe was limited and the only weapon he owned was the sword Zarak had given him. Then to add a sense of normality, they bade each other goodnight, just like they usually did, and went to bed.

Neither of them got much sleep, however. Dare tossed and turned with feelings of regret, because he had foolishly longed for adventure and discovered too late how much his father meant to him, never once realizing his father had struggled with the same yearnings as a young man. And, his father lost sleep because, he was worried for his son's safety and powerless to protect him.

The following morning when Dare's father gently shook him awake, it was still dark outside. And by the dry gritty feeling of his eyes, the younger smith was surprised he had slept at all.

After mumbling that he was awake, Dare sat up and rubbed the sleep out of his tired eyes. Then, he rolled out of bed, washed, dressed, and went to join his father in the main room.

It was obvious the master locksmith had been up for some time because, instead of its usual morning chill, the room was warm and welcoming.

When his father saw him, he smiled and handed Dare a plate with eggs, bacon, and a stack of hot oatcakes.

From the dark rings beneath the older man's eyes, Dare wondered if his father had slept at all. However, before he could voice his concern, his father told him, 'Best eat up, before it gets cold.'

'Thanks. It smells great,' Dare replied enthusiastically, aware this was the last meal they would share together for some time.

While the master locksmith dished up a plate for himself, Dare sat down at their small table, drizzled honey on his oatcakes, and took a big bite. He wasn't disappointed, the food tasted even better than it smelled.

The master locksmith watched with loving amusement, as Dare wolfed down forkful after forkful. His son always had a healthy appetite, and this morning was no exception.

Although he had never cosseted the boy, Dare was the only reminder the locksmith still had of his wife. And despite his son's masculine appearance, from time to time, he would glimpse a trace of her with a tilt of Dare's head or when her smile was reflected in his son's eyes.

In truth, he had never got over the loss of his wife and had suppressed the grief deep within himself. But now, knowing his son might not return, he was heartsick with fear of losing him as well.

After serving his son a meal that should stick to his ribs for the better part of the day, the master locksmith gathered the dirty dishes and placed them in the washing-up tub while Dare went to collect his sword and the small sack of clothing he had packed the evening before.

When Dare returned to the main room, his father was waiting for him. 'I always intended to give you this,' the master locksmith said as he handed his prized pocketknife to his son. 'And, it seems like now is the right time.'

Knowing the knife was a family heirloom and highly treasured by his father, Dare accepted it and replied solemnly, 'Thank you father, but wouldn't it be safer here?'

'No son. You might need it. Now, we'd best get going.'

Knowing his father's mind was made up and there was no changing it, Dare followed him down the stairs and out of the smithy.

Although it was no longer dark outside, it was still early and the streets were deserted.

In unspoken agreement, father and son headed towards the harbor in silence, the only sounds they could hear were those of their own boots upon the cobblestones and the occasional chirping of an unlucky male cricket still calling out for companionship from amongst the daybreak shadows.

With few obstacles to impede their progress, the two smiths were able to set a fast pace down the narrow streets and reached the citadel's lower baily in a fraction of the time the journey normally took.

Following the internal road, they skirted the rampart until they reached the barbican, where they turned, passed beneath the portcullis and exited the citadel.

The cobblestones abruptly came to an end at this point and, in its place, the road was surfaced with hard packed aggregate, comprising of stones, gravel and chalk which had been bedded in over the years by those travelling upon it.

Without the protective walls to shelter them, the two smiths were immediately buffeted by the brisk coastal wind and simultaneously pulled their jackets tighter about themselves.

Had it been warmer, they might have stopped for a moment to admire the vessels in the harbor and take in the view, because from the clifftop a person could see for miles and it was easy to understand why the first king of White Cliff had chosen this defensive location upon which to build his castle.

Shrugging off the morning chill, the two walked swiftly and eventually reached the crudely constructed hovels Dare had spotted from the battlements. And seeing the rickety dwellings close-up for the first time, he was surprised the wind hadn't blown them down long ago.

Shortly afterwards, they reached the fork in the road and took the left-hand turning which lead downwards to the deep natural harbor below.

There was the odd bush growing amongst the tufty grass along the steep roadside, but no trees. Whether this was due to the chalky soil or the wind, Dare wasn't farmer enough to know. Although, he was impressed by the way workmen had skillfully cut the road deep into the cliff-face, which would have taken years to complete.

His father had been mulling over his own thoughts and suddenly said, 'You know, I'm going to buy that barrow you've been banging on about.'

Dumbfounded, Dare could not believe his ears. He had been trying to convince his father to purchase a barrow for ages. And now, when he wouldn't be there to use it, the master locksmith had relented. But before Dare could ask why, there was a sudden flash of white wings as two greedy seagulls fighting over the same scrap of food swooped down in front of them. Then, just as quickly as they had appeared, they were gone and his father commented, 'A fisherman I know said gulls are the rats of the sea.'

'I hadn't thought about it, but I think he's right,' Dare agreed.

No sooner had the words left the young smith's mouth than, a juicy splat of bird poo landed on the ground between them. And then, he added with a lopsided grin, 'You know, if I was the paranoid type, I'd think those gulls overheard us and took offence.'

His father chuckled and replied, 'We'd better quit while we're ahead then.'

'Yes,' Dare answered. 'I only packed one change of clothes.'

Preoccupied with plummeting poo, the two hadn't noticed the slight shift in wind direction until the smell of curing fish wafted upwards from the port's smokehouse. Still in good spirits, Dare inhaled a deep pungent whiff and said, 'Ah, nothing like fresh sea air.'

'Ripe sea air is more like it,' his father corrected lightheartedly. 'And now you know the first of two reasons why we're smiths instead of seafolk.'

'Because being covered in soot and sweat is so much nicer than scales and fish guts,' Dare jokingly replied.

His father laughed with him and then asked, 'And, the second reason?'

'I don't know. You tell me,' prompted Dare.

Not having the heart to tell his son the truth, the master locksmith replied, 'It's simple, ladies prefer brawn over brine.'

'Since when do you know so much about women?' Dare challenged skeptically.

'You forget I was young once too. But then, I met your mother and she forged me into a one woman man. So now, I couldn't change even if I wanted to, which I don't by the way.

Dare had often wondered why his father never remarried. And now without even asking, he had the answer.

By the time they reached the coastline, the master locksmith's legs were beginning to feel the strain from walking on the downwards slope and he was thankful to have that part of their trek behind them.

Of the three vessels they'd seen anchored in the harbor during their descent, they quickly located the Sprinter, which wasn't difficult because she was moored directly to the pier. And, even to laymen like Dare and his father, it was obvious she had been built for speed, with sleekness in design the larger more squat cargo bearing vessels lacked.

Seeing the Sprinter's crew were busy hoisting thick cargo nets filled with equipment and supplies over the railing and into her hold when they arrived, the two smiths tried to stand out of the way, amongst the organized chaos, so the sailors could get on with their work.

A few minutes later, the clip-clop sound of hooves drew their attention back up the pier where they saw five restless horses with shaggy grey and white coats being led towards them.

'They're called Greystone Steeds,' the familiar voice of Jerhal informed them from seemingly out of thin air. 'They're stocky sure-footed animals, prized for strength and high altitude endurance. And since their native to Greystone, they won't draw attention.'

Dare nodded, then asked, 'Why do we need five horses?'

'On the first half of our journey, three horses will be ridden while two carry supplies. On the way back,' he hesitated a moment before continuing, 'our new companion will ride one of the pack animals, leaving the remaining horse free to carry the provisions. To lessen the likelihood of injury and to give each animal opportunity to rest, we'll rotate mounts. But if the unfortunate should happen, we'll distribute the supplies evenly amongst ourselves and ride the pack animal.'

Dare's father had stood quietly listening to the exchange. And, impressed with Jerhal's efficiency, he realized the spy was a master craftsman in his own right.

'Glad to see you could make it,' Jerhal said by way of greeting to Zarak as he strode up to them.

'Wouldn't have missed it for the world,' the soldier replied. 'Besides, it'll be interesting to see how long it takes,' he nodded his head towards Dare, 'for this young pup to get his sea legs.'

Dare noticed the knowing look pass between the two men but, since he wasn't a proven sailor, he wisely held his tongue.

Once the horses and last of the provisions had been hoisted on board, the master locksmith wished his son's travelling companions a safe journey. Then, he turned to Dare. But before he could utter a word, his son hugged him awkwardly, but hard, and told him reassuringly, 'Don't worry. I'll be back before you miss me.'

'I'm counting on it,' he replied, too choked up to say anything more. Then after his son released his hold, the master locksmith sadly watched Dare follow the other two men up the gangway and onto the ship, where he turned and waved one last goodbye before disappearing from view.

Although the master locksmith would've liked to have stayed and waited for the Sprinter to take in her lines, he could not afford the luxury because he had been instructed to go about his business as usual. So with a heavy heart and a lump in his throat, he turned around and began the steep upward trek back to the citadel, all the while hoping Dare wouldn't discover the real reason their family had chosen smithing over a life on the sea. But then, his son would either get violently seasick or he wouldn't. In either case, there wasn't anything he could do to help him.

◆◆◆

After stowing his things, Dare found a quiet spot on the weather deck near the stern where he could stand and watch the citadel gradually shrink from view while he worked up the courage to broach an awkward truth with Zarak.

'Did you leave your girl behind?' a gruff voice asked from over his shoulder.

Glancing around, Dare discovered the speaker was one of the older members of the ship's crew. And, from the sailor's tanned skin and the deep crow's tracks marking the corners of his eyes, it was obvious he'd spent most of his life at sea, a proper 'old salt'.

Not wishing to share his private thoughts with a complete stranger, the smith played along and jestingly replied, 'I guess I'll just have to meet another at the next port like you sailors do.'

'That's the spirit lad,' the man said with a wink. 'Remember, it's the woman's place to stay home and wait for you to return. And then, whatever you do, don't tell her you missed her or she'll have you wrapped around this,' he held up his little finger, 'the rest of your miserable henpecked life.'

'So I take it, you're married then.'

'Not me. I'm as slippery as an eel and have escaped the net more than once,' the sailor proudly boasted. Then, before he could continue, a shouted command rang out and he dutifully hurried away.

Although the distraction had helped, Dare still hadn't worked up the nerve to speak with Zarak. So delaying the inevitable, he decided to familiarize himself with the ship.

Unlike her heavier counterparts, the Sprinter swiftly sailed on the crests of the waves instead of ploughing laboriously through them. Yet even so, the young smith wasn't a natural seaman and it was not long before he started to feel the color beginning to drain from his cheeks.

Hoping some fresh air might help to relieve the queasiness, Dare stopped his explorations and headed back to the weather deck. But, he scarcely reached the railing when he was struck with a wave of nausea.

Unaware the sailor he had spoken with earlier was watching him hurl his morning meal, the seasick smith recognized the familiar gruff voice when the man drily commented from behind him, 'In my younger days, I fed the fish a few times myself.'

The very thought brought on another bout of nausea and, as Dare doubled helplessly over the railing spewing his stomach contents for a second time, the sailor added good spiritedly, 'That's it lad. Better out than in.'

Mercifully for Dare, by the time he'd finally lifted himself from the railing, his unwanted observer had gone. And feeling a little better, he managed to make it below deck with the intention of sleeping off the seasickness. But, his stomach had other ideas, and he spent rest of the day listlessly hugging a bucket wishing he would just die and get it over with.

Zarak and Jerhal knew there wasn't much they could do to help their young companion other than leave him alone until his body grew accustomed to the swaying motion of the ship, so that's exactly what they did.

It wasn't until the following day Dare's seasickness started to abate and he was able to force down a little bread from the ship's galley. Then, because he still needed to have a private word with Zarak, he went in search of the battle-hardened soldier.

Failing to find his friend on the upper deck, Dare methodically worked his way downward and eventually spotted Zarak grooming the horses in the bottom of the ship's hold.

Although the mixed smell of damp hay and horse dung made the smith's queasy stomach churn, Dare steeled himself and determinedly strode towards the makeshift stable.

Noticing the horse he was currying perk its ears, the soldier knew someone was approaching and glanced towards the hatch. Seeing it was Dare, Zarak greeted, 'Glad to see you've returned to the land of the living.'

'Only just,' the smith replied with a shake of his head. 'I still don't feel entirely myself.'

'You've nothing to be ashamed of,' Zarak reassured his companion as he ran the brush across the horse's shaggy coat. 'The sea doesn't discriminate, and I've seen many a man humbled by her.'

Pleased his friend wasn't disappointed in him, Dare decided to push on and tell Zarak the reason he'd sought him out. So after a slight hesitation, and for lack of better words, he took a big breath and just blurted, 'I've never ridden a horse.'

Zarak understood. Having grown up in the citadel, Dare had never needed to. But the soldier had trained enough raw recruits in his day to know what to do; he stopped grooming the horse midstroke and handed the smith the curry brush. 'You'd best get acquainted then.'

11 ELROD

The princess's rain-soaked cloak no longer protected her from the incessant drizzle and she was wet through. Yet chilled to the bone as she was, when Lilyanna caught sight of Greystone Fortress in the distance, the shiver that ran through her was not caused by the cold.

Up until now, she had clung onto the faint hope she would escape her abductors, even though the two attempts she'd already made had both failed and she only still drew breath because Dead Eyes feared Elrod more than he was angered by her.

Filled with foreboding, the princess reined her mount to a halt and stared up at the massive stone structure, slowly realizing she might never leave its dismal grey walls.

Misinterpreting the reason why Lilyanna had stopped, Scary Hairy rode his horse up alongside hers and commented, 'Impressive, isn't it?'

The princess was well versed with the history of Greystone Fortress. It was constructed of the local dark-grey hardstone. Defensively, it was impenetrable. And, the only time Greystone's ruler had ever been overthrown was from disloyalty within, Elrod's treachery to be precise.

Her teeth chattering, Lilyanna begrudgingly replied, 'It's well named.'

Before either of them could say another word, Dead Eyes shouted back over his shoulder, 'Get a move on. I want to sleep in a warm bed tonight.'

Grateful for the interruption, Lilyanna gave her mount a light nudge with her heels and rode on before Scary Hairy could notice the tears amongst the raindrops rolling down her cheeks.

The three travelled in relative silence the remainder of the afternoon, slowly zigzagging their way along the muddy road ever deeper into the heart of the Greystone Mountains.

As the riders neared the fortress, the crudely fashioned stone houses they had seen dotted sparsely about the landscape began to appear more frequently and they started to encounter the occasional traveler.

At dusk, when they finally passed the guard post and entered the peripheral bailey of the fortress, it lived up to the princess's expectations, in that it was just as depressing as she had imagined it would be. Everything was grey, except for the blood-red uniforms of the soldiers, from the towering stonework to the mud beneath their horses' hooves.

Her fingers so numb, Lilyanna could hardly grasp the reins as she rode her horse behind Dirk's and in front of Scary Hairy's, just as she had done throughout the entire journey. But, the animal must have been as frozen as she was, because it didn't notice her lack of control and plodded steadily along the fortress's narrow streets, past people, all dressed in grey, who looked as cold and miserable as she felt.

In a futile attempt to warm her fingers, Lilyanna periodically transferred the reins from one cold hand to the other so she could breathe heavily onto her frozen fingertips. It didn't help much. Although, it did give her something to do while she scolded herself for not wearing riding gloves on the day of her abduction.

Her captors had come better prepared. But having been exposed to the elements for so long, their clothing looked as soggy as her own. And, she was inwardly pleased to see Dead Eyes, once so tall and proud in his saddle, now rode hunched like an old man before her.

Her horse suddenly jerked its head back and she was jolted from her musing in time to glimpse a greenish blur swoop dartingly past them. It happened so fast, Lilyanna assumed it was some kind of strange bird but couldn't see it properly in the dim light and was too busy fighting for control of her spooked horse to chance a second glance.

Seeing the princess was in trouble, Scary Hairy rode up rapidly from behind her, grabbed hold of her horse's bridle, and brought the startled animal under control.

The incident was over within a few heartbeats. And miraculously, the princess remained seated.

'Are you alright?' the wild-haired man asked.

Lilyanna nodded, thankful for his quick intervention.

'Good,' Scary Hairy replied. 'Now we'd better catch up with Dirk, or a skittish horse will be the least of our worries.'

The two rode side by side a short distance until the red-haired man was satisfied the princess's mount had calmed down. Then, because the streets were so narrow, he fell back, bringing up the rear.

The scare helped shake some of the cold-induced lethargy from Lilyanna and she began to notice, the further they journeyed upwards into the heart of the fortress, the more improved the living conditions of the people became. The buildings were better maintained and their occupants looked healthier. But most noticeably, the streets were paved with cobblestones.

After reaching the innermost portcullis, the three bedraggled riders passed under it and into the fortress's private courtyard where they reined their horses to a halt and the men dismounted.

Lilyanna tried to do likewise. But her legs were so numb, they were incapable of the act, so Scary Hairy walked over and unceremoniously assisted her from the saddle. Then encumbered by heavy wet clothing, when she tried to stand, her legs buckled and she would have fallen had the wild-haired man not been there to support her.

The abductors swiftly relinquished their charge to a couple of awaiting guards who proceeded to manhandle Lilyanna towards the Great Hall where Elrod was dining.

Humiliated and outraged over what the usurper had put her through, Lilyanna soon found her feet and was able to walk unaided by the time they reached the large double doors of the hall.

Before entering, the princess commanded her guards authoritatively, 'A moment.' And to her surprise, they stopped while she adjusted her wet cloak and pushed a strand of damp hair from her face. Then once she was ready, she nodded for them to open the doors and boldly strode into the room as regally as she could, given the fact she hadn't bathed or brushed her hair properly in nine days.

Having grown weary with the diversions at court for some time now, Elrod had been eagerly awaiting Lilyanna's arrival.

When he glanced up from his plate and saw her approaching, a rush of excitement, the like of which he had not felt since the death of his wife, ran through him, although the smile that touched his thin lips was barely perceptible.

When the princess reached him, she stood tall in her sopping wet clothes and addressed him defiantly. 'I have no doubt you're an evil man, a cruel king, and that your heart is truly hawk black. And,' she paused for effect, 'I also know, you'll never get away with this.'

Elrod wasn't disappointed. He had been told, despite her soft feminine beauty, Lilyanna was a strong-willed woman with some fight in her, which was exactly what he craved because it meant the slow breaking of her spirit would provide him with months of entertainment.

He took a casual sip from his goblet. Then, after setting it back down, he replied condescendingly, 'My dear, I already have.'

'That's debatable. It's early days yet,' Lilyanna countered. 'But for the time being, what do you plan to do with me?'

Cocking his head to one side like some kind of predatory bird, the regicide answered, 'I haven't decided yet. I don't know whether to marry you or bury you.'

He'd hoped to provoke a reaction. But when princess didn't bite, the usurper continued, 'When I do, you'll be the first to know.' Then believing her too travel-weary to be of amusement, he ordered the guards to take Lilyanna away.

As frozen as Lilyanna was, Elrod still made her skin crawl. And not wishing to be near him a moment longer than necessary, she turned without uttering a word of protest and strode from the hall as regally as she had entered.

Fearing she would be taken to the dungeon, the princess did not begin to relax until after they had walked down several opulent corridors and, upon reaching the stairway, they started to climb upwards.

When her guards finally stopped, it was in front of one of the numerous ornately carved wooden doors somewhere high-up within the fortress.

Relieved and a little perplexed, Lilyanna bravely stepped into the chilled unlit room and discovered she now stood in a large private suite which smelled of furniture polish. Then totally spent, as the door was closed and locked behind her, she walked over to the nearest chair, wearily sat down, and fell fast asleep in her wet clothing.

A short time later, the princess was roused by the sound of someone knocking. Bleary-eyed, she glanced towards the door and watched as it slowly swung open and a pretty young woman, about her own age with long white hair, stepped into the chamber.

Filled with anxiety, Robin hadn't known what to expect when she entered, she had merely been sent word she was to serve as lady-in-waiting to the chamber's new occupant.

Now, looking upon the disheveled state of the woman sitting before her, Robin's kindly heart went out to her and she said, 'You look all done in. Don't move a muscle. I'll have a hot bath drawn and will get you something to eat.' Then with that, she turned and left the room, her earlier trepidation totally forgotten.

Lilyanna didn't know what to think. After so many days of mistreatment, her instincts warned her not to trust this white-haired woman of Elrod's. But, she also knew she was sorely in need of food and a hot bath, so she simply sat and waited to see what would happen next.

Within minutes, two servants arrived with pails of steaming hot water. They did not speak, merely knocked upon the door to announce their presence, entered, and carried the pails into the adjoining room where they promptly emptied them. Then, one of the servants lit the candles and collected the empty pails while the other started fires in the hearths.

Once they had left, Lilyanna forced her weary body upright and walked into the next room, which turned out to be a large bedchamber with the steaming hot bath she had been promised.

Robin arrived shortly thereafter carrying a big tray of food. When she saw Lilyanna struggling to unlace the back of her dress, the white-haired woman quickly set the tray on the bed and hurried over to assist her. 'Here, let me help you with that.' Then, to make her travel-worn charge feel at ease, she tried to sound cheerful as she began to loosen the lacing and introduced herself. 'My name's Robin, by the way.'

Having been a seamstress, Robin couldn't help but notice, although the dress was in as terrible a state as its owner, it was made of high quality fabric and adorned with expensive lace. Hence, she concluded, the bedraggled woman standing before her was of the aristocracy, which made sense; Elrod wouldn't have gone to so much trouble over a commoner.

Once the lacing was undone, Robin walked around to face the tired woman and gently started to slip the dress from her new mistress's shoulders. But when the dress slid downwards and exposed the collar locked around her companion's neck, the white-haired woman froze.

Noticing Robin's shocked reaction, Lilyanna watched the color drain from the white-haired woman's face and decided she might be able to trust her. So, the princess looked straight into Robin's eyes and confided, 'I can't take it off.'

Realizing she was about to relive the same terrible nightmare she had spent the last two years trying to forget, Robin nodded her head and tried to concentrate on the unfortunate woman before her instead of the collar she wore. 'I know. I think Elrod is the only one who can,' she replied gravely. Then not wishing to cause further alarm, Robin brushed the moment aside and briskly continued, 'But, it's a problem for another day. For now, let's get you into that bath.' And despite her trepidation, she pulled the dress down to the floor, and ushered her new mistress towards the hot bath.

After the princess was settled comfortably, Robin prompted, 'My lady, you haven't told me your name.'

'Lilyanna,' the tired lady answered. 'Princess Lilyanna, heir to the throne of White Cliff.'

Robin curtsied respectfully and then asked, 'Your Highness, what would you have me call you?'

'In private, Lilyanna, I don't feel very regal just now,' the princess said as she lathered her face with a soapy sponge.

Robin smiled. 'Well Lilyanna, after you rinse those bubbles off, you can have a nice soak and I'll wash your hair.' And, that is exactly what she did.

A short time later, as Lilyanna sat on the bed wrapped in a warm blanket hungrily munching through the food Robin had brought, the white-haired woman towel dried and brushed the princess's freshly washed hair. Then, once all of the snarls had been removed and Robin saw Lilyanna was finding it difficult to keep her eyes open, the white-haired woman removed the tray and tenderly tucked the princess into bed.

As her charge fell fast asleep, Lilyanna told her about the map inside the pocket of her dress. So after the newly reinstated lady-in-waiting added more fuel to the fires in both rooms and blew out the candles, she picked up Lilyanna's discarded clothing from off the floor, found the map, and quietly left the princess to her dreams.

Under normal circumstances, Robin would have dropped off the clothing at the fortress laundry and collected a change of clothing either from there or from one of the seamstresses. But, the hour was late and maintaining the pretense of cheerfulness while actually being scared stiff had left her feeling mentally exhausted, so she headed back to the sanctuary of her room instead.

Attuned to Robin's feelings, Erosmay had sensed the white-haired woman's growing anxiety throughout the evening. And at one point, the little dragon had even contacted Robin via mind-speech to find out what was wrong. But, her linked companion had gently rebuffed her, saying she was busy and would explain everything later.

Time passed by much slower for the little dragon after that. Robin had never distanced herself in such a way before and, not knowing what to make of it, Erosmay became more agitated as the evening progressed.

It wasn't until Robin had nearly reached their shared chambers she finally felt calm enough to contact her linked companion via mind-speech. 'Erosmay, I'm sorry about earlier.'

Relieved to hear Robin's voice, Erosmay asked, 'Are you all right?'

'No,' Robin stated numbly. 'Elrod's guest is wearing the collar.'

No further explanation was necessary. The little dragon immediately understood and replied solemnly, 'I understand. Hurry home.'

Erosmay knew all about Robin's past, because the white-haired woman had told her. She knew Robin had grown up in an orphanage where she had been taught to sew and then later apprenticed to the fortress dressmaker, through which she'd met Lady Allyce and had become her friend and lady-in-waiting.

Robin had explained how, after her mistress had lost the child she carried, Elrod had pretended to reassure his wife by giving her a jeweled collar as a token of his love. And when her mistress's health started to decline shortly afterwards, Robin hadn't realized the collar had been slowly draining Allyce's life force until the day of her friend's death.

Grief-stricken, Robin had watched as Elrod took out a tiny golden key and unceremoniously unlocked the collar fastened around the neck of her dead friend. Then when he tried to remove the collar, he couldn't because it was adhered to Allyce's skin, so he had tugged and tugged until it finally came away, revealing tiny serpentlike creatures dangling from each of the collar's open-backed settings. By the deep holes burrowed into Allyce's flesh, it was obvious they were the cause of her death. And, as the vile creatures slithered back into the gemstones from whence they came, Elrod had laughed cruelly and threatened Robin. 'If you breathe a word of this, you'll join your friend. Now, prepare the body for burial.'

When the horrific day had finally ended, Robin had told Erosmay, she had gone back to her room and cried herself to sleep. And by the following morning, her hair had been turned totally white by fear. However, the little dragon knew something about Robin the white-haired woman didn't even know herself. Robin was pure of heart, which was why Erosmay had chosen her as a linked companion and the reason Robin's body had reacted so strongly to the evil she had witnessed.

Sensing her linked companion's presence, the little dragon flew up to the door, wrapped her tail around the handle, and pulled the door open so Robin could enter. Then, after white-haired woman had dropped the armload of dirty laundry she was carrying onto the floor, Erosmay comforted her in the only way she knew how. She landed lightly upon Robin's shoulder and nuzzled her little scaled head affectionately against her linked companion's cheek.

Robin reciprocated in kind. Then, she walked over to the bed, sat down and wearily kicked off her shoes.

The two sat for a long time, Robin upon the bed and Erosmay nestled comfortably in her lap, quietly enjoying each other's presence while Robin absently stroked the little dragon, the act calming them both.

'In all good conscience, I can't just leave the princess here. She'll die if I do,' Robin finally blurted out loud.

'I know,' Erosmay replied matter-of-factly in mind-speech.

'You do?' Robin asked in amazement as she stopped petting the little dragon and looked down at her.

Returning her gaze, Erosmay answered, 'Yes, it would be against your nature.'

'But, I have no idea how to help her,' Robin confessed.

Speaking with the wisdom of the dragons of old, Erosmay then surprised her by saying, 'The creatures in the collar are cold-blooded like me. They seek heat and sustenance.'

'I see. So if we block their heat source, they might stay dormant,' the white-haired woman surmised excitedly.

'Yes, I believe so,' Erosmay agreed.

'Wool is an insulator! When I collect the clothing for Lilyanna tomorrow, I'll get her a woolen shawl as well, and no one will suspect a thing.'

'Yes. She can tuck it beneath the collar when she is alone, and that should buy her more time.'

'Now, all we need is a new escape plan, and I haven't a clue as to what it should be,' Robin added.

'Me either. But, we will watch and learn,' the little dragon answered.

'Yes we will,' agreed Robin.

'And in the meantime, I'll try not to grow too much,' Erosmay replied drolly.

12 MAW

Having spent the better part of the last four days, between bouts of seasickness, in the hold feeding and mucking out after the horses while trying to rectify his gap in equestrian training, Dare had decided stable work was another occupation he didn't fancy.

At first, the smell had made his queasy stomach churn horribly but, because he did not want to run the risk of letting himself down in Zarak's eyes for a second time, he had persevered. And when the soldier had approvingly jested the last time he had seen anything Dare's particular shade of green it'd had leaves, the smith knew he hadn't lost Zarak's respect even though he still had not ridden a horse yet, since there wasn't enough space in the hold to make the attempt. However, to ensure a successful outcome when he finally did, he had been secretly feeding the Greystone Steeds apples from the galley to gain their trust.

As the afternoon wore on, the horses began to grow increasingly restless and nothing Dare did seemed to calm them. So, unsure as what to do, the young smith sought out his companions on the upper deck to voice his concerns.

After hearing him out, Zarak calmly replied, 'They're probably sensing the coming storm.'

Preoccupied with the horses, Dare had not noticed the wind had picked up until the soldier pointed it out. Then, he asked, 'Do you think it'll be a bad one?'

'It's too early to tell,' Jerhal answered before Zarak could.

As the spy expertly guided their conversation away from the weather, it never occurred to Dare his companion had knowingly withheld information and, because Jerhal was in command of their mission, Zarak had allowed it.

If it had been up to the soldier, he would've handled things differently, preferring to have prepared Dare for a rather rough night. But, the decision wasn't his to make, and he understood why Jerhal didn't want to alarm the smith unduly.

The wind continued to grow stronger and the sea more choppy with each league they sailed.

By evening, the weather was so bad the cook didn't attempt to prepare a hot meal but doled out portions of cured pork and dry bread instead, which Dare and his companions carried down to the tween deck and ate while sitting on the canvas hammocks they had been assigned above neatly stacked supplies.

Dare had never experienced anything like it, he'd found sleeping in a hammock comfortable enough on a calm night as well as a good use of available space. But, trying to eat and sleep on one during a storm was entirely a different matter.

As each wave struck against the hull of the ship with greater force than the wave before it and his hammock swung even more wildly, all he could do was thank his lucky stars his stomach had settled. Because under the circumstances, it would've been impossible for him to retch into the seasickness bucket he'd held onto longer and hugged closer than the pretty lass he had met at the winter festival.

Having grown accustomed to the rhythmic creaking of the ship's timbers during the voyage, the smith couldn't help but notice the stressful change in sound and glanced over to his travelling companions, but they remained calm. So, he tried to follow their example and not let his apprehension get the better of him, which was easier said than done whilst being tossed about like a leaf in the wind.

To blank the storm from his mind, Dare attempted to visualize himself riding on the back of one of the Greystone Steeds he had been taking care of. Then, it occurred to him they must be even more anxious than he was. So, he sat up and shouted to Zarak above the howling storm, 'Should I see to the horses?'

'Never mind the horses,' the soldier shouted back. 'With these waves, they could lose footing and accidentally crush you to death.'

'Yes,' Jerhal agreed loudly. 'Believe it or not, right now it's safer to be in a hammock than out of one.'

As if in confirmation, the ship abruptly listed starboard and they heard a popping sound as the strap securing the supplies beneath them snapped under the strain. Casks and crates came crashing down. Then as the ship struggled to right itself, the loose stores began to dangerously move around the deck faster than nutshells in a game of chance.

Outside, the captain stood tied to the helm so he wouldn't be swept overboard by the storm as walls of water hammered against him in the darkness while he fought to control the ship.

The Sprinter's smaller size and weight normally enabled her to ride the top of the waves instead of resting deep in the water and ploughing through them. But, it was impossible for her to outrun a storm of this magnitude, and the captain feared these sleek features would be her undoing.

White-knuckled, he steered the wheel with a vice-like grip. Yet with each course correction he made, another ferocious white capped wave would counter it and force the Sprinter a little closer towards the treacherous 'Maw', a notorious rock-strewn body of shallow water which had gutted many a ship.

Unaware of the captain's valiant efforts, Dare and his companions remained safely cocooned in their hammocks on the tween deck listening to the sounds of devastation beneath them as careening casks shattered into sliding wooden crates and the panicked horses on the level below whinnied in fear.

Suddenly, as a terrible scraping sound reverberated from the bottom of the ship and it felt like Dare's hammock was being yanked from under him, the Sprinter's bow pitched upwards and she lurched to a shuddering halt.

Realizing they had run aground, Jerhal was the first to react and swung himself out of his hammock. But just as his feet touched the deck, another huge wave struck the ship and he landed facedown, hard upon the jagged debris.

Fearing he had been impaled, Zarak and Dare scrambled to the spy's aid and carefully lifted him from the splintered crates. And miraculously, when they examined their wheezing companion's chest in the swinging lantern light, they saw no obvious sign of injury.

'Are you alright?' Zarak asked above the roar of the storm.

Ashen-faced and struggling for breath, Jerhal gasped, 'Cracked a couple of ribs.'

'We've got to get out of here,' the soldier advised. 'Do you need help?'

'No,' Jerhal answered, pushing through the pain. 'I can make it. You lead.'

Wasting no time, the soldier turned and started to pick his way across the debris strewn deck with the wounded spy, holding onto his injured side, and Dare following close behind.

It was hard going. The once level flooring now slanted steeply downwards and was made slippery from spilled foodstuffs and cold seawater gushing through gaps in the fractured hull.

When they reached the ladder leading to the upper deck, they had to wait while the panicked crewmen who had got there before them pushed and shoved their way up its tilted rungs. Then when they finally stepped out onto the gale swept deck, they discovered the gigs had already been launched and, realizing it was everyman for himself, the remaining crewmen were frantically salvaging and fighting over anything they could use as a makeshift raft.

Seeing this, Dare asked his companions above the howling wind, 'What do we do now?'

Jerhal thought for a moment and then shouted back, 'We could use the casks! Emptied, they'd be buoyant enough to support our weight!'

While the mountainous waves continued to hammer the broken ship deeper onto the jagged rock and she groaned in agony, the three men turned as one and began to retrace their steps back into the hold.

Once they got there, Jerhal ordered Dare, 'Fetch three hammocks while we empty the casks.'

Dare hurried to comply, his leather work boots splashing noticeably deeper in the flooding seawater than they had minutes earlier.

While the smith rushed to do as he'd been bidden, the spy and Zarak pulled out their knives and immediately began to work the stoppers from the first casks they came upon.

Despite his injury, Jerhal was the first to succeed. But, the floodwater had risen as he worked and, because of his cracked ribs, he couldn't lift the heavy wooden barrel high enough above the waterline to empty it.

Seeing the spy was struggling, Zarak shouted over, 'We'll do that! Start on another!'

As Jerhal splashed his way in search of a third, the soldier shoved the bung he'd just removed into his pocket and began to empty the cask he was working on.

By the time Dare returned with the hammocks, Zarak was already hammering the stopper back into his cask with a piece of wood from one of the broken crates. Then as the seawater continued to rise around them, Dare bound the barrel in one of the hammocks while his friend went to empty the cask Jerhal had just abandoned. And working together, it did not take long before all three casks were emptied, restoppered, and bound securely.

With no time to spare, Zarak began to climb back up the ladder onto the upper deck so he could assist from above while Dare and Jerhal passed the casks up to him.

Buffeted by the storm as he emerged from the hold, Zarak couldn't see anyone in the darkness and assumed everyone else had abandoned ship.

He immediately kneeled down beside the top of the ladder and reached into the opening to retrieve the first of the casks his colleagues were pushing up to him, but he couldn't get a proper grasp. So, he dropped to his belly upon the wave drenched deck and tried again.

This time, the soldier's fingers found the rope binding and, gripping onto it tightly, he gritted his teeth and hoisted the cask upwards onto the deck beside him.

Fighting against the gale-force wind and already soaked to the skin, Zarak pulled the cask up the sloped deck where he hastily attached its rope to the starboard railing so it wouldn't roll and be swept away. Then, as he turned to retrieve the other two casks, he glimpsed someone approaching in the darkness.

Realizing he wasn't alone, Zarak blinked to clear the salt from his stinging eyes. And when he looked again, he saw the dark silhouette of a knife in the man's hand.

Knowing the man was about to attack, Zarak assumed a fighter's stance, legs apart and knees bent. Then, because he was a professional and didn't want to kill the guy unless he absolutely had to, he warned him off by shouting, 'The cask will support both of us! There's no need to force my hand!'

The man wasn't in a sharing mood and snarled, 'I'm not going to chance it!' Then, he raised the knife menacingly and ran towards the soldier.

Zarak held his ground until the last possible moment. Then, just as the sailor lunged towards him with his knife, the soldier stepped sideways, turned fluidly, and pushed his attacker hard from behind. The sailor's momentum finished the job, and carried him over the railing.

It all happened so fast, the man hardly had time to scream before he disappeared beneath the waves.

With no time for a second glance, Zarak hurried back to the hatch to retrieve the other two casks.

Although Jerhal hadn't uttered a word of complaint while they passed the heavy wooden barrels to Zarak, Dare had noticed the ashen pallor of the spy's face in the swinging lantern light and could tell his companion was in great pain, so the smith had taken the lead and lifted the majority of the weight. Then once they were finished, he had waited at the bottom of the ladder while Jerhal climbed up, just in case the spy needed assistance.

The floodwater had risen to Dare's waist by the time it was his turn to exit the tween deck, and he was relieved to be leaving it behind. However, as he emerged onto the wave drenched upper deck and into the full force of the storm, the smith knew he hadn't yet escaped a death by drowning, merely its location.

Pumped with adrenalin, Dare followed Jerhal in the darkness up the sloped deck to where Zarak was waiting with the canvas covered casks.

As giant waves came crashing down and the rain lashed their faces, the three hurriedly tied the casks tightly together, forming a crude triangular shaped float. Then, so they wouldn't be swept away, they commenced to secure themselves, each to a barrel, with the excess rope.

Just as the men were finishing, a sharp cracking sound suddenly rang out. And when they glanced in the direction the sound came from, they saw the foremast slowly lean to port and come crashing loudly down onto the deck.

Her timbers weakened, the Sprinter let out an anguished moan and began her final death throes.

Knowing they were out of time, the men from White Cliff quickly pulled the float down the sloped deck towards the submerged port side of the bow and Jerhal shouted, 'Don't forget to hold your breath!' Then as one, they launched themselves into the storm-tossed sea.

Although Dare was already chilled to the bone, when he hit the cold water it still nearly took his breath away and, as the powerful waves crashed over him, he was thankful he had been told to hold his breath.

Forced deep under the water, the smith had never been more terrified in his life. But amazingly several heart-pounding seconds later, he and his companions, coughing and spluttering for breath, popped back up like a cork onto the surface of the raging sea.

The storm was relentless. No sooner would the men catch their breath than the next huge wave would crash over them. Seawater went up their noses and salt stung their eyes, but worst of all was the teeth chattering cold.

They lived in the moment, numbly grasping onto the rope bindings and canvas tarpaulin while the pummeling waves ripped them from the float and the rope tethers cut into their saltwater softened skin.

From time to time Dare and Zarak would hear Jerhal let out a loud groan, and they knew the spy's injured ribs had once again been battered against the cask he was holding onto. But, there was nothing they could do to help him.

Hypothermic and preoccupied in their struggle for survival, none of them noticed the swift current was steadily carrying them toward land in the darkness.

To buy himself more time before he drowned, Jerhal used the last of his strength to slip the end of his trouser belt beneath one of the upper rope bindings on the float, to raise himself a little higher out of the water, and re-buckle it. Then, he slipped into unconsciousness from the pain.

Unaware of their companion's helpless condition, Dare and Zarak continued to fight for their lives. Physically, they were both strong men, the smith made muscular from hammering hot metal at the forge and soldier from hours exercising on the practice field. Yet even so, they too were nearing the end of their endurance.

Lips blue and shivering uncontrollably, they now swallowed more seawater than they spat out.

It wasn't until one of the large breakers lifted the float higher into the air that Dare thought he glimpsed a rocky shore in the darkness. But then, the float dropped and the shore was gone. So to be certain, with the next huge wave, he looked again. And this time, it was even closer.

13 SIRE

After the current had carried their float onto the rocky shore, Zarak and Dare, both chilled to the bone, slipped off their tethers and numbly unfastened Jerhal from his cask. Then, they dragged his unconscious body behind the shelter of a large outcropping, where they too succumbed to exhaustion and collapsed beside him.

Dare had no idea how long they had lain there, wet clothed and unmoving. But the next time he opened his eyes, he saw a gaunt man leaning closely over him who seemed surprised he was still alive and had exclaimed, 'You're a lucky man! The sea has chosen to cast you away.'

The smith hadn't felt very lucky. He'd swallowed a bellyful of saltwater and the stench of decay emanating from the gaunt man's rotten teeth would've made a maggot gag, if it had been dumb enough to get that close.

Lightheaded and nauseated, Dare had retched violently and, as his stomach muscles cramped with pain, he'd heard the rotten-toothed man say something about the sea either swallowing you or you swallow it. But, he'd been way too busy throwing up to pay much attention.

Afterwards, the man had pulled Dare upright and tried to help him walk, but the smith's weak legs wouldn't support his weight. So, the man had half dragged half carried the smith into the warmth of a small hut and laid him down on the dirt floor beside the central fire, where Dare had fallen into an exhausted sleep while he was stripped of his wet clothing and covered with an old woolen blanket.

Hours later, when Dare finally began to stir, every muscle in his body seemed to ache. Then, as memories of the shipwreck came flooding back, he awoke with a start and tried to sit up, but a hand reached out and gently pressed his shoulder back down while a soft disembodied male voice said, 'You're safe now. Rest, and I'll get you something to eat.'

There was a rustling sound as the speaker stood and walked around him to the opposite side of the fire. But, it wasn't until the man stopped beside a roughly constructed driftwood cooking tripod and turned to pick up a large wooden spoon that Dare caught his first clear glimpse of the man's gaunt face and recognized the man as his rescuer from the beach.

Strangely comforted, the smith lay still beneath the tattered woolen blanket and watched as the rotten-toothed man began to stir the contents in the badly dented cooking pot suspended above the fire. Although admittedly, it did take Dare a moment to realize the cooking pot was actually an old battle helmet suspended by its leather chinstrap.

Seeing his patient's bemused expression, the gaunt man gave the smith an enigmatic rotten-toothed smile and said softly, 'The sea is a great provider.'

Uncertain if the man was talking about the pot or its fishy smelling contents, Dare changed the subject and asked, 'How are my friends?'

The man lifted his index finger to his lips and answered in a hushed voice, 'Big Fellow's alright. He left a little while ago to fetch more firewood.'

Dare wasn't surprised; Zarak wasn't one for sitting around when there was work to be done.

'But, that one,' the rotten-toothed man looked towards a spot somewhere behind Dare, 'was nearly graveyard dead when I found him.'

Following the man's glance, Dare turned his head and saw Jerhal's motionless body lying upon a crudely fashioned bed a short distance away.

'He was knocking on death's door when I found him. But,' the man paused as he started to ladle steaming soup into a bowl-sized clam shell, 'it wasn't his time and he seems to be resting comfortably now.'

'He had a bad fall and cracked some ribs,' Dare said quietly by way of explanation.

'Yes, I've seen the bruises. And, Big Fellow told me,' the man replied as he carried the soup over to Dare.

Realizing he didn't know his rescuer's name, Dare decided an introduction was in order and started to introduce himself. But, he got no further than 'My name is,' when the rotten-toothed man interrupted him.

'I know your names. Big Fellow, Ribs, and you're,' the gaunt faced man paused and looked at Dare appraisingly, 'Little Fishy.'

Unable to believe his ears, Dare couldn't hide his reaction, which was exactly the response the mischievous rotten-toothed man had expected. He chuckled softly and added, 'Because the sea threw you back.'

Although Dare was no fisherman, he understood the man was implying he was too little to keep. And under different circumstances, he might've found it funny, because he was tall and muscular. But just then, he wasn't certain if his rescuer was oddly eccentric or merely pulling his leg.

He was also mindful of the fact they owed this strange rotten-toothed man their lives. So even though he disliked the new name, the smith forced himself to regain his composure and asked politely, 'What shall we call you?'

'Why, Sire of course,' his rescuer replied, as if he was stating the obvious. 'Now, eat your soup before it gets cold.'

Having been cooked in a battle helmet and served in a clam shell, Dare didn't know what to expect of the fish soup other than it also contained some kind of green floaty bits. So prepared for the worst, the smith lifted the shell bowl to his lips and took a tentative sip.

To his relief, the soup didn't taste half bad. So, he took a second sip, and discovered the unfamiliar green bits had a parsley flavor.

For one brief moment, the soup's soothing warmth reminded him of home and of Rhea's mother who, even though he was long grown, still occasionally stopped by the smithy with a large bowl of potage or a loaf of freshly baked bread just to ensure his father and he were looking after themselves. But then, Zarak entered the hut, arms heavily laden with driftwood, and interrupted his thoughts.

'Sire, I bring thee tribute,' the soldier quietly greeted the gaunt faced man before striding over to the side of the room and depositing his burden on top of the dwindling supply of firewood already piled there.

Sire, who'd been gathering up Dare's dry clothing, looked over and softly replied, 'And greatly received it is.'

Seeing Dare sitting up with the shell bowl cupped in his hands, the soldier smiled at him approvingly and said, 'It's a great day to be alive.'

Pleased to see his friend, Dare flashed him a lopsided smile and replied in a hushed voice, 'Every day is a great day for that.'

'True enough,' Zarak agreed quietly. Then, he asked, 'But, how do you feel?'

Considering what he'd just been through, Dare felt fairly well within himself and answered lightheartedly, 'I've still got some water in one of my ears.'

'Me too,' Zarak replied cheerfully, 'and webs between my fingers.' Then, he became more serious and asked, 'Do you feel up for a short walk?'

'I think so,' the smith answered. And, raising the bowl to his lips, he started to gulp down the rest of his soup, green floaty bits and all.

When the bowl was empty, the rotten-toothed man handed Dare back his dried clothing. 'It wouldn't do for you to die of a chill, after I went to all the trouble to save your life.'

Well aware he was only wearing a smile and his leather cuffs, Dare accepted the clothing gratefully. Although, he did hold his breath during the exchange, so the stench of his rescuer's breath wouldn't cause him to spew up the soup he'd just swallowed. Then, ignoring the discomfort of his aching muscles, he hurriedly dressed and followed the soldier out of the hut.

The sky was overcast and the air felt crisp. And like Zarak, Dare too thought it really was a great day to be alive.

They walked in silence until they were far enough away from the dwelling the sound of their voices wouldn't wake Jerhal. Then, his curiosity got the better of him, and Dare asked, 'Aren't your muscles aching?'

'Sure they are,' Zarak replied candidly. 'But, this isn't my first shipwreck, and I've found it best just to get on with things. Your muscles will warm, and you'll feel better for it.'

The smith had always known, because of Zarak's profession, there were things his friend hadn't told him. The soldier wasn't exactly secretive, more the strong silent type. But even so, it'd never occurred to Dare to ask his friend if he'd ever been shipwrecked.

As they walked, the sound of the waves gradually grew louder and Dare realized Zarak was leading them towards the shore.

'So, what do you think of Sire?' the soldier casually asked.

'Nice man with a heart of gold. Too bad about the breath,' Dare replied unhesitatingly.

Zarak agreed, 'My thoughts exactly.'

'I'm still trying to decide if he's in his right mind though,' the smith added.

'Sire is as sane as you and me,' the soldier assured him. 'He's just got a strange sense of humor.'

'And an unusual way of living,' the smith added, remembering the battle helmet cooking pot and the seashell bowl.

'Not really. We talked quite a bit before you woke up. And, once you know his story, you'll understand why he lives the way he does.'

'Enlighten me,' Dare said. 'The anticipation's killing me.'

'He's a castaway too. His ship ran aground near here about ten years ago,' Zarak explained while trying to keep a straight face. 'And since nobody else seemed to want the place, he's claimed it and proclaimed himself king.'

'And that's why he told me to call him Sire,' Dare replied in astonished disbelief. Then in spite of his sore stomach muscles, he started to laugh.

'Yes. He thinks it's funny. And, because there's no harm in it, we're going to indulge him,' Zarak laughingly replied. 'His birth name was Syros, by the way.'

When Dare finally came up for air, he asked, 'So, why do you think Sire confided in you and not me?'

Zarak shrugged his shoulders and, for lack of a better reason, lightheartedly answered, 'I woke up first.'

They were still in high spirits when they reached a narrow pathway leading down to the rock-strewn shore which Sire had inadvertently created over the years by his comings and goings.

Seeing it was too narrow for the two of them to walk side by side, Zarak took the lead and they commenced their descent in single file. However, after only a few steps, the soldier stopped abruptly and held up his right hand, signaling for Dare to halt.

The smith froze in his tracks. Having been combat trained by Zarak, his response was immediate and unquestioning.

Zarak then formed a V shape with the index and middle fingers of his upraised hand, pointed the two fingers towards his eyes, and then swept them downwards to where the far side of the slope met the shore.

Dare looked in the direction Zarak was indicating and couldn't believe his eyes, because there on the rock-strewn shore below stood one of the Greystone Steeds he'd tended while aboard the Sprinter.

The horse looked a sorry sight. Its shaggy grey and white coat was all matted and there was a bit of seaweed tangled in its long mane. Yet against all the odds, the hardy animal had managed to survive.

The soldier whispered, 'Let's catch him.'

'Just tell me what to do, and I'll do it,' Dare whispered back, fully aware up until then the only thing he'd ever caught had been a cold.

'We're in luck. The float is still there,' Zarak said softly with a grin from ear to ear.

Then, confident what the smith lacked in experience he'd make up in determination, he added, 'We can use the hammock ropes. Just avoid eye contact and don't make any sudden moves.'

With their strategy in place, the two White Cliff men resumed their descent to the rocky shore, cautiously trying to avoid stepping on any loose stones which might shift beneath their feet and alert the horse of their presence.

In the end it wasn't noise that gave them away, but their scent carried upon the wind.

For one heart pounding moment, they froze in place and watched as the bedraggled horse raised its head to sniff the air. Then, it looked directly at them. But more interested in the grass it had found growing out of a small crevice, the hungry animal lowered its head and resumed grazing.

Realizing he'd been holding his breath, Dare slowly exhaled and shot Zarak a quick sideways glance. And seeing his friend had been holding his breath as well, the inexperienced smith felt a little more confident.

When they finally reached the abandoned float, both men knelt down and began trying to remove the water-sodden hammocks from the wooden casks. But they quickly discovered, seawater had swollen the hammock ropes, tightening the knots to such an extent they were nearly impossible to untie.

Finally, after much tugging and against Zarak's better judgement, the soldier pulled out his knife and, using its blade as a lever, commenced to work it under one of the loops of the knot he was working on.

Seeing this, Dare started to reach for the pocketknife his father had given him, but the soldier knew how much the knife meant to the smith and stopped him. 'No need, wouldn't want to snap the blade.'

So, Dare persevered, trying to untie the knots in his rope with his fingers while Zarak tried to pry apart the knots in his rope with his knife.

The soldier's technique was faster and he'd just managed to free his rope when they heard the sound of hooves approaching.

Both men slowly glanced in the direction of the noise and saw the haggard Greystone Steed walking directly towards them. 'Keep working and try not to spook it,' Zarak advised softly.

While Zarak adeptly tied a bowline knot at one end of his rope and then passed the other end of the rope through the loop he'd just fashioned to form a makeshift lasso, the horse reached them and nudged Dare in the back with its nose.

Realizing the Greystone Steed must have recognized his scent on the wind and thought he'd have an apple in his pocket, Dare slowly turned and tenderly began to stroke its neck. 'I'm sorry fella. I don't have any apples for you today.' Then ever so gently, he slipped the lasso Zarak passed to him over the animal's head.

Having been halter trained as a foal, the horse was accustomed to a lead and didn't pull back.

'Now keep hold of the rope and pass its free end beneath the lasso and then back all the way through the loop you've just made,' the soldier instructed calmly. 'This way the lead won't cut into his neck.'

As Dare did as he was told, the soldier softly added, 'I'm glad to see all those apples you snuck out of the galley paid off.'

'You knew about that?' Dare asked, surprised his thefts had been noticed. 'Why didn't you say anything?'

'It's always good to learn a new skill,' the soldier replied with a smile as he walked over and began to check the horse for injuries. 'But as a thief, you definitely need more practice.

Dare wasn't offended and laughing agreed, 'I guess I do.'

'I still can't believe this horse made it all of the way off the ship and onto dry land,' Zarak said in wonder as he lifted one of the horse's hooves to check for stones. 'Why, he must've even swum with his tail.'

As if to confirm that was exactly what he'd done, the horse suddenly whickered and tossed his head.

'I think he just said "Yes",' Dare chuckled, tightening his grip on the lead.

'Swims with his tail and talks, talented animal,' Zarak replied dryly, as he finished checking the last of the horse's hooves. 'He needs to be fed. Lead him up the slope and find him some grass near the stream. I'll sort out the other rope and meet you there.'

Dare nodded. Then, he turned to the horse and said, 'Come on Swim Tail, let's get you something to eat.'

As the smith started to lead the horse away, the soldier queried, 'Swim Tail?'

Dare paused and replied, 'It's either that or Apple Eater.'

'Swim Tail it is then,' Zarak agreed. Then, he knelt down beside the float and took out his knife.

The exhausted horse obediently followed the smith up the rocky slope to where the grass was more plentiful and began to graze, while Dare kept hold of the lead rope in one hand and used his other to brush Swim Tail's matted coat with a large clump of grass.

Zarak joined them not long after, carrying the second rope and three sheets of canvas he'd cut away from the casks. 'I doubt Swim Tail's in any condition to roam far,' he said, dropping the canvas onto the ground. 'But to be on the safe side, we'll hobble him. This way we can remove the lead and he can graze without one of us keeping an eye on him.'

What Zarak said made a lot of sense to Dare. And, since he had no experience of his own to draw from, the smith watched interestedly while the soldier tied the two ends of the second rope together, twisted the loop into a figure eight, and then lifted the bottom half to create one double banded loop.

With his preparations completed, the soldier walked over to Swim Tail, lifted the stallion's left front hoof and slipped the double banded loop around. Then after setting the hoof back down, he twisted the double loop twice in the middle, lifted the horse's other front hoof and slipped what remained of the double banded loop loosely around it.

The simplicity of the hobble's design didn't go unnoticed by Dare. He swiftly realized with two simple twists, Zarak had not only turned one large double banded loop into two much smaller ones, he'd also shortened the rope to restrict the length of the horse's stride. And, since Swim Tail didn't seem to mind and there wasn't a paddock nearby to keep the horse in, the smith decided this was an excellent temporary solution.

After they'd removed the lead rope and Dare had affectionately stroked the grazing Greystone Steed one last time, the two castaways picked up the salvaged canvas and headed back to the hut.

Although Dare had always considered himself capable and streetwise, since stepping onto the ship everything he'd experienced was new to him. But to the smith's credit, he was a willing and fast learner, absorbing everything shown to him like a sponge. And, curious to know what Zarak intended to use the canvas for, he asked him.

As they walked, the soldier explained, until they replaced their equipment, they could use the canvas as blankets at night and, by cutting a small slit in the middle of each piece large enough to slip their heads through, as ponchos for warmth and protection from the rain during the day.

Although Dare hadn't forgot about their rescue mission, after waking up and finding he'd survived the shipwreck, he'd just sort of set it aside as a priority in his mind. But now, he saw Zarak, ever the professional, was actively making preparations to resume their journey. And in the few hours the soldier had been awake, he'd already captured one horse, fashioned blankets-cum-ponchos from the canvas hammocks they'd bound the float together with, and showed his appreciation to Sire for rescuing them by replenishing the man's firewood.

Realizing he should be following his friend's example, Dare vowed to himself, from that moment onward, he would do everything he possibly could to help.

When they reentered the hut, Sire was busy stuffing four freshly caught fish with some kind of green plant while Jerhal, having awakened, was sitting up in his bed watching him.

The spy hadn't dressed yet and, even though the room was dimly lit, Dare couldn't help but notice the large angry bruise on Jerhal's side.

Seeing the concerned look on the smith's face, Jerhal tried to make light of his injury by using the same kind of friendly banter he'd used when they'd first met. 'It looks worse than it feels.'

Having seen healthier looking sides of ribs for sale at the butcher's shop, Dare didn't believe him. But before he could respond, his empty stomach rumbled so loudly Sire turned towards him and said, 'Little Fishy needs some food.'

Remembering what Zarak had said about the man's strange sense of humor and that he should try to indulge him, Dare played along and pointed to the largest fish the rotten-toothed man was preparing. 'You better believe it. Why, I'm so hungry I could've eaten that one from head to tail while it tried to wriggle off the hook.'

Sire looked up at him with an odd twinkle in his eye and, for one horrible moment, Dare thought his rescuer was going to hand him the raw fish so he could do just that. So, he hurriedly added, 'But, it's stopped moving now, so I'll wait until it's cooked.'

Pleased by the way the smith was handling himself, Zarak set down his armload of salvaged canvas with a satisfied smile, because all in all, the day had been a good one and he was glad it was ending well. Then, he strode over to Jerhal and said, 'Glad to see you're feeling better.'

'I'll be back to my old self in no time,' the spy replied in the same light-hearted manner he'd used with Dare. Then, he looked Zarak in the eyes and asked more seriously, 'How bad is our situation?'

'Not as bad as you might think. Surprisingly, we found one of the Greystone Steeds, exhausted but uninjured, down on the shore.'

Although the spy's side hurt when he moved, he sat a little more erect, eager for Zarak to continue.

'We hobbled it with a rope from the float and left it grazing in a grassed area near here.'

'Strong horse,' Jerhal replied appreciatively, aware of how powerful the waves had been.

'Yes,' Zarak agreed. 'Another day of rest and it'll be ready to carry a rider.'

'Good. Hopefully with another day of rest, I'll be able to ride.'

The fish had turned a warm golden brown by this time and Sire called the men over to eat. But as Jerhal started to get up, the rotten-toothed man waved him back and handed Dare a skewered fish to take to him.

When the smith returned to the fire to collect a cooked fish for himself, he asked the rotten-toothed man, 'How did you manage to catch so many fish in such a short period of time?'

Sire tapped the side of his nose with his index finger and replied, 'I call it cable-fishing, don't know the real name for it. But if you're interested, I'll show you how it works in the morning.'

'It would be my privilege Sire,' Dare replied, remembering his earlier decision to be more useful.

After stuffing the fish, Sire had run a wooden skewer through each one before seasoning them with a sprinkle of sea salt and roasting them over the fire until they had turned crispy, resulting in four very tasty fish.

Dare hadn't been lying when he'd said how hungry he was. And, even though he didn't particularly like fish, it seemed to melt in his mouth. Whereas, the green plant stuffed inside, which turned out to be the same plant the soup had been flavored with, added a slightly crunchy texture.

While they ate, the discussion turned to the three White Cliff men's need to resume their journey just as soon as possible, although they didn't explain why, and the best way for them to go about procuring supplies.

Sire said he could provide enough smoked fish to last them several days. But, he didn't have any spare waterskins or warm clothing.

Zarak thanked him for his offer of food, but explained they wouldn't require any additional warm clothing because they planned to use the canvas salvaged from the float for that. He also said he didn't think water would be an immediate issue if they travelled upstream along the nearby river until they came upon a road. Then, they should be able to purchase waterskins from someone living alongside it.

As Sire tossed the skewered remains of the fish he'd eaten into the fire and began to lick its juices from his fingers, the conversation turned to the men's need for replacement weapons.

The rotten-toothed man didn't say anything until his fingers were clean. Then, he told them whenever he found a weapon washed upon the shore, usually attached to a corpse who didn't need it anymore, he'd bury the body and throw the weapon onto his pile of accumulations, because you never knew what might come in handy. However, they were welcome to help themselves to anything they found there.

The following morning after breaking their fast with more fish soup, Zarak went to check on Swim Tail and have a rummage through Sire's pile of accumulations while Dare carried a large empty basket and followed their host, armed with a hooked walking stick similar to a shepherd's crook, towards the small cove where he cable-fished.

The smith was surprised by Sire's brisk pace, but his muscles no longer ached and he matched the gaunt faced man stride for stride, occasionally spotting small clusters of plants growing amongst the rocks that looked like the same parsley tasting ones Sire used in his cooking.

When Dare asked the rotten-toothed man the name of the plant, the smith was told it was called glasswort, because it was used in glassmaking, and that his host ate it most days along with the fish he caught.

Dare was already well aware of this, because they had eaten some combination of fish and the plant at every meal since the shipwreck. And in all honesty, he wouldn't have been the least bit surprised to find they were going to have fishcakes sprinkled with glasswort for pudding later that evening.

It transpired the cove wasn't far from the hut. And, it was much smaller than the smith had expected.

'See those floats,' Sire said pointing to two short chunky pieces of wood bobbing in place at opposite sides of the small bay, 'They mark the ends of the cable.'

'I see,' Dare said, looking to where the rotten-toothed man was pointing.

After descending the rocky slope, they walked along the water's edge until they came alongside the float nearest them. Then in one smooth motion, Sire deftly reached out with the hooked end of his walking stick, caught hold of the cable just beneath the float, and pulled it towards them.

Realizing the cable must be weighted down, Dare quickly asked, 'Do you want my help?'

'No Little Fishy. I could do this in my sleep.'

So, as Dare watched his rescuer haul the cable onto the shore, he discovered a loaf sized rock, serving as a weight, had been attached to the cable roughly two strides inwards from the float. Then at regular intervals from the weight, about a stride apart, the rotten-toothed man had attached baited hooks, fashioned from old nails, onto the cable via odd lengths of rigging he'd painstakingly spliced together.

'Do you always catch so many?' Dare asked, impressed because there were fish hanging from all but two of the crude hooks.

'Depends on the time of year,' Sire answered. 'In the summer when it's hot, fish like to swim near the surface and I do alright. But in winter when it's cold, they swim deeper. And since I don't have a boat, I catch fewer. That's why I smoke the extras I catch.'

'Oh, I see,' Dare said, wondering how many fish the rotten-toothed man would catch if he just breathed on the water. Then instantly regretting the wicked thought, the smith asked, 'Can you spare the smoked fish you're going to give us? We wouldn't want to cause you hardship.'

Sire nodded as he commenced to unhook the first of the fish and, as he tossed it into the basket Dare carried beside him, he assured the smith, 'Don't worry. It's early in the season. I still have plenty of time to replenish my stores.'

After all of the fish had been unhooked, the gaunt man had Dare carry the basket over to the water's edge where they began to gut and wash their catch, the smith using his treasured pocketknife and Sire wielding a much larger blade acquired from one of the wrecked ships.

Working together, it didn't take long before the fish were cleaned, the hooks baited, and the cable reset. Then, they picked up the fish filled basket and headed back to the hut.

The sound of metal being scraped reached their ears before the two of them actually saw Zarak and Jerhal sitting outside the small dwelling busily trying to remove rust from a couple of weapons the soldier had retrieved from the pile of accumulations with wave smoothed hardstones.

'Looks like you've got your work cut out for you,' Sire casually commented as they drew near.

'If we keep at it, we should have serviceable weapons by evening,' Zarak replied matter-of-factly. 'Not that we're looking for trouble, but at least we'll be able to protect ourselves if some should come our way.'

Having been in a few scuffles in his early days, Sire understood. 'So, are you still planning to leave tomorrow morning?'

'Yes,' Jerhal answered good-naturedly. 'We wouldn't want to overstay our welcome.'

Although Sire didn't mind helping out a man in need, he'd grown accustomed to his own company and the spy's comment wasn't far off the mark. But instead of saying so, he flashed a rotten-toothed smile and turned to Dare, 'You'd best get to sharpening. I'll deal with the fish.'

While Sire disappeared into the hut with their catch, Dare picked up a rusted long knife along with one of the hardstones Zarak had found on the shore, sat down beside his colleagues, and began to sharpen the blade's blunt edge.

As the soldier had predicted, the White Cliff men spent the remainder of the day honing blades, repairing handgrips, fashioning sword belts, and making knife sheaths out of anything they could find that would do the job. And by nightfall, they were no longer defenseless.

14 SWIM TAIL

When Dare awoke to the familiar aroma of fish soup, he knew without even opening his eyes Sire would be standing nearby tending the helmet pot. And even though the strange cauldron only held enough for them each to have but a single serving, their host had a way of ensuring the soup was robust enough to sate their hunger.

He sleepily recalled asking the rotten-toothed man the day before why they'd broken their fast with soup, and their rescuer had simply replied he liked something hot to drink in the morning, which made sense in an odd kind of way.

Although the dirt floor he was lying on was hard and uncomfortable, the hut itself was warm and dry. And because they were to resume their journey after breaking their fast that morning, the smith knew he'd miss the hut's small comforts when they were sleeping out in the open the following night.

In truth, Dare would've liked nothing more than to have rolled over, pulled his sailcloth blanketing more closely about himself, and gone back to sleep. But mindful of their decision to make an early start, he forced himself to sit up instead.

Having slept fully clothed, he had only to run his fingers through his unruly dark blonde hair to comb it and pull on his boots to ready himself. And, as he did exactly this, he heard the rustling sounds of his companions and knew they too were awake.

He turned and asked the rotten-toothed man if there was anything he could do to help, but their host merely shook his head and told him he had everything in hand. So, after exchanging a few words with his colleagues as they folded and stowed away the odd assortment of bedding, he went outside to relieve himself.

Having put the small hut back to rights, Zarak and Jerhal joined their host beside the fire. And whilst the spy didn't utter a word of complaint, from the grimace he made as he sat down, it was obvious his ribs still pained him greatly.

'One more day won't make much difference if you'd rather leave tomorrow,' the soldier told him quietly.

Jerhal lifted an eyebrow and replied, 'And to others, one day could seem a lifetime.'

Zarak knew the spy was referring to the princess, but made no comment.

'I think we've stayed here long enough,' the spy went on. 'And besides, my ribs are going to ache while they mend no matter where I am.'

'Alright then,' Zarak agreed. Then, he turned to the rotten-toothed man and asked, 'Are you sure you won't come with us?'

'I'm sure,' Sire answered as he handed the soldier a bowl of soup. 'I'd have to work for a living, and I just don't have the energy for it. Whereas here, the sea provides all of my needs.'

'Well, if you ever change your mind, you're always welcome at White Cliff,' Zarak told him seriously.

'Yes. A man with your skills is always welcome,' Jerhal added.

Sire didn't understand what the injured man meant by this. But before he could ask, Little Fishy reentered the hut and the moment was lost.

As usual, it had taken longer to prepare the soup than it did for them to consume it. And in no time, their fast was broken and the men found themselves gathering up their supplies and heading for the grassed area where they'd left Swim Tail to graze.

To protect themselves from the drizzly weather, the three White Cliff men each donned one of the ponchos they'd fashioned from the canvas hammocks which had once bound their raft together. And, for protection from almost everything else, they wore the weapons they'd refurbished from their host's pile of accumulations.

True to his word, the rotten-toothed man provided enough smoked fish to last them several days, which he'd thoughtfully wrapped in two canvas parcels and attached to a short length of old rope, one parcel at either end, so they could be transported across the back of their horse like saddlebags.

In spite of the damp weather, they were all in high spirits, the three White Cliff men because they were resuming their rescue mission and, although he wouldn't openly admit it, the rotten-toothed man because he preferred his solitude.

As they neared the Greystone Steed, the stallion whickered softly, as if he too was ready to continue their journey. Rested and fed, the sheen had returned to his coat and he stood proudly with his head held high, looking entirely different than the bedraggled horse they'd found upon the shore the day before.

Talking softly, Zarak walked up to Swim Tail and gently slipped the lasso around the horse's neck. Then just as before, the soldier passed the end of the rope beneath the lasso and pulled it back through the loop he'd just made, so the lead wouldn't tighten and cut into the animal's neck.

While Zarak removed the hobble and checked the Greystone Steed's hooves for stones, Jerhal thanked the rotten-toothed man one last time. 'We owe you our lives and that's a difficult debt to repay. But if you're ever in need, you can seek us out at White Cliff.'

Although Sire knew Ribs was deadly serious, he had no intention of ever leaving his home and replied politely, 'The sea supplies all of my needs, and then some. But, I'll remember your words.'

When it was time to say farewell, Sire called each of them by their proper birth name as he solemnly shook their hands and wished them a safe journey. And, this was when Dare finally decided he agreed with Zarak their host was of sound mind.

After making a stirrup with his hands and helping Jerhal onto Swim Tail's back, Zarak then took hold of the rope and commenced to lead the small rescue party towards the river.

At first, the going was easy. The estuary was wide and because it was tidal, saltwater mixing with fresh, the rocky riverbank was sparsely covered in grass. But as the morning progressed and the three men travelled further upstream, the grass was gradually replaced by larger vegetation which grew more densely and slowed their progress, making the journey increasingly difficult.

From time to time, Zarak would point out a bush or tree to Dare, tell him its name, and then explain something interesting about it. The smith quickly learning things like, even though the ash and alder often grew in the same area, their wood was entirely different. The ash was a tough hardwood which absorbed shock without splintering, whereas alder was rot resistant and only strong when kept wet. Hence, ash was used for hammer and axe handles and alder for boatbuilding.

Although Dare was attentive, he didn't walk over and inspect any of the vegetation closely until the soldier pointed out a couple of hazel trees. Then, because he was starting to get hungry and was growing a bit tired of fish, the smith hurried over to them in the hope of finding some nuts. But, it was the wrong time of year and there wasn't a single nut to be found.

Shortly after this, Zarak and Dare began taking turns to lead the horse. And it was during one of the smith's stints, he asked Jerhal a question he'd been pondering. 'Back on the ship, how did you know tying the casks together with hammocks would work?'

In need of something to take his mind off the growing pain in his side, Jerhal was pleased for the distraction and answered. 'To pass the time, I've developed a mental exercise to keep my mind sharp called "If-Then".'

From the perplexed expression on Dare's face, Jerhal continued. 'You know. If this happens, then what would I do?'

Zarak, having been listening to their conversation, smiled and interjected good-humoredly, 'If you step into quicksand, keep hold of your horse's reins.'

'It worked,' Jerhal replied in mock defense.

'Only because there was a fallen tree nearby,' the soldier countered lightheartedly.

'I still think the reasoning is sound. If only the horse would've been a bit smarter.'

'Are you saying my horse was stupid?'

'I'm just saying an intelligent horse would've tried to swim.'

Up until then, Dare had been trying not to laugh. But when he saw the offended look on Zarak's face, he couldn't contain himself and burst out laughing.

Both men stopped talking and looked towards him. Then, realizing how silly they must have sounded, they started to laugh too, which was terribly painful for Jerhal because his injured side was so tender.

Distracted by the merriment, Dare wasn't paying attention to his footing and tripped on a tree root. Suddenly finding himself falling, he let go of the horse's lead and tried to catch himself before he tumbled down the riverbank through the bracken covered undergrowth. But, his reaction was already too late. And a couple of seconds later, he landed abruptly at the river's edge, with a few minor scrapes and his boot filled with water.

After shouting he was alright to his companions so they wouldn't come after him, the smith emptied the water from his boot and scrambled back up the slope, his pride more bruised than the rest of his body.

The remainder of the afternoon passed without further incident, allowing Dare plenty of time to regain his dignity and think about Jerhal's 'If-Then' game. And, even though the spy hadn't answered his question, he got the impression, up until the night of the shipwreck, the cask float had been another of Jerhal's untested scenarios.

When it was finally time to stop for the night, the men from White Cliff made their camp in a small clearing. And because the weather had steadily improved throughout the day, they were able to find enough dry resin rich dead branches to fuel a fire.

As they ate their cold ration of smoked fish, Zarak and Jerhal discussed the plan for the following day and agreed it would be best to continue traveling upstream in the hope they'd come upon a road or smallholding, because if they found one they'd surely find the other. Then, they would obtain what supplies they could and travel in the most northwesterly route available to them.

With a clear strategy in place, they stoked up the fire, wrapped themselves in their canvas blankets, and bedded down for the night.

Recently shipwrecked and with the added exertion of a full day's travel, all three men were exhausted and quickly fell asleep, secure in the knowledge they were alone and no harm would befall them.

During the night, their small fire burnt itself out and the ashes were cold when they awoke the following morning. So, Zarak pulled his fire starting implements, a piece of flint and rusted nail he'd found on the shore, from his pocket, struck a spark, and restarted the fire so they could warm themselves while they ended their fast with more of Sire's smoked fish.

Having already slipped on their versatile canvas ponchos to ward off the morning chill, it didn't take them long to break camp. Other than for a quick face wash at the river's edge while the horse drank his fill, all they had to do was kick a little soil over the fire to smother it, and then they were ready to set off for another long stretch of the legs.

As they travelled steadily upstream and the elevation slowly began to rise, Dare noticed the ash and alder Zarak had pointed out the previous day were gradually being replaced by conifers which grew in much closer together than their lowland counterparts.

By midmorning the woodland had thickened to such an extent, the pale-faced spy was forced to dismount, because dodging the low-hanging branches while on horseback strained his injured side more than walking around them on foot did.

And so it was, Zarak began to guide the rescue party in single file ever upwards deeper into the forest.

From time to time, the soldier withdrew his rusty sword from its homemade scabbard to hack his way through bushes and brambles blocking their path, while Jerhal, Dare, and Swim Tail followed behind. All of them becoming hotter, hungrier, and more scratched up as the morning progressed.

When Zarak tired, Dare replaced him at the head of the small procession and they resumed their trek just as before. And other than stopping for a short meal break, they trudged on into the afternoon, soldier and smith alternating between leading the column and leading the horse.

It wasn't only rough terrain and thick vegetation the rescue party had to contend with, but swarms of hungry midges. Attracted by the smell of the men's exertions, the vile little insects flew around their faces, up their noses, and bit exposed flesh, making an already uncomfortable situation even more unbearable. But apart from swatting them, there was nothing they could do to rid themselves of their maddening tormenters.

At the front of the column, Dare got on with the business at hand and snapped off yet another dead branch blocking their path, the backs of his calloused hands covered with small cuts and abrasions as the vegetation he was attacking fought back.

As the smith tossed the limb aside, Jerhal thought he heard a sound in the distance and asked, 'Did you hear that?'

They all stopped and listened.

The sound came again. There was a very short pause. Then, it came again. And all three recognized it, the rhythmic sound of someone chopping wood.

'Finally,' Zarak declared, the relief showing plainly on his unshaven face.

'What did I tell you?' the spy replied with a grin. 'If you walk far enough long enough, sooner or later, you're bound to meet up with somebody.'

'I'm just glad it was sooner and not the later,' the soldier said. 'We're nearly out of smoked fish.'

Although it meant a change in direction, their need of provisions momentarily outweighed their need for progress. So, the White Cliff men began to work their way towards the sound just as quickly as they could before the man wielding the axe finished chopping.

Luckily the farther from the river the rescuers walked, the thinner the undergrowth became and they were able to travel much faster. At first, the men assumed this was because the densely packed trees blocked the light so the vegetation beneath struggled to grow. But then, they noticed small cloven hoofprints amongst the fallen pine needles and realized some kind of foraging animal had been feeding upon it.

Had the men spotted the tracks earlier, they would've hunted the animal down to replenish their dwindling food supply. But as it was, they hurried on in the hope of finding the man with the axe.

They eventually came upon a clearing and spotted the woodsman busily felling one of the dead trees growing along its far edge. His back was turned to them and, from his muscular frame, it was obvious the man wasn't afraid of hard work.

'We'd better let him know we're here,' Jerhal advised his companions.

'Yes,' Zarak agreed. 'We wouldn't want to startle him and get our hair parted with his axe.'

Although they'd chuckled at the soldier's jest, they also recognized the truth in his words. So Jerhal, not fancying a new hairstyle, cupped his hands around his mouth and shouted across the clearing, 'Hello friend. We come in peace.'

The woodsman lowered the axe and turned to face them. Then, he shouted back in kind and, still carrying his axe, began to walk cautiously towards them.

When the White Cliff men drew close enough to talk without shouting, Jerhal took the initiative and spoke with friendly ease, 'We're glad to see you. The ship we were on sank a few days back and we've no idea where we are.'

Their battered appearance hadn't gone unnoticed by the woodsman. And, from the poor state of the three men's rusted weapons and obvious lack of supplies, the woodsman would have believed them had it not been for Swim Tail. 'And the horse?' he asked skeptically.

'The horse too,' the spy answered earnestly. 'I know it's unbelievable, but that's the truth of it.'

Standing beside him, Zarak and Dare both nodded their heads in confirmation. Then, the soldier found his tongue and eagerly added, 'I'm Zarak, this is Dare, and the talkative one is Jerhal.'

Deciding the men weren't a threat to himself or his family, the woodsman began to relax. 'I'm Erwin and, by the look of it, you could use something to eat.'

Relieved they'd found someone willing to share more than information, the White Cliff men thanked the woodsman appreciatively and followed him across the clearing.

'You're in luck,' Erwin told them as they walked. 'Yesterday my feral pig rushed me, so there'll be pork in the pot this evening.'

'Does that happen often?' Dare asked, remembering the tracks they'd seen and glad they hadn't unknowingly killed one of the woodsman's animals.

'No. The pigs normally stay in their sty. But, a couple of sows escaped a few years back. I managed to recapture one, but the other got away, mated with a wild boar, and gave birth to boarlets. They're all vicious and, let's just say, I carry my axe for more than chopping wood.'

As they neared the edge of the clearing, the woodsman's log cabin became visible through the trees.

Dare thought it looked a peaceful place, with chickens contentedly scratching the ground in search of grubs and a freshly tilled vegetable patch.

Movement at the front of the cabin caught the smith's eye. He watched as a woman, a bit younger than Erwin, stepped through the doorway carrying a young child on her hip. When she glanced over and saw her husband approaching, she smiled and greeted him. 'I didn't expect you back so early.'

'Be honest Rose, married to me you never know what to expect,' Erwin replied good-naturedly.

Still wearing the same happy smile, Rose turned to the three travel-worn strangers and explained, 'Yesterday, he went to fell a tree and brought back a butchered pig instead.'

Before any of the White Cliff men could respond, her husband added, 'And today, I've brought you three men who taste so bad even the Maw spat them out.'

They all laughed. Then, the woodsman introduced the shipwrecked men to his good lady wife.

After giving them the formal greeting 'Welcome to our home' in return, Rose tilted her head towards the child she was holding and cheerfully announced, 'And, this little imp is Holly.'

Hearing her name, the little girl bashfully squirmed higher in Rose's arms and hid her face in the warm protective curve of her mother's neck.

Rose hugged her daughter reassuringly and told her, 'It's alright. They don't bite.' Then, she turned back to her unexpected guests and said, 'There's a stream behind the house where you can wash yourselves and water the horse. When you're ready, come inside and there'll be food on the table for you.'

Dirty, tired, and hungry, the men mumbled their thanks and, with Swim Tail in tow, disappeared behind the cabin.

They washed quickly and saw to the Greystone Steed's needs. Then feeling greatly refreshed and looking a little more respectable, the men from White Cliff headed back to the front of the cabin.

When they rounded the corner of the building, Erwin was standing just outside the front door to meet them, holding his little daughter instead of his axe.

Out of respect for the woodsman and his family, Zarak politely asked him, 'Would you like us to lay down our weapons before entering?'

'No,' Erwin replied as he lifted his daughter playfully into the air. 'You'd best wear them. The way this one gets about, they're safer on you than left unattended out here.' Then, after lowering the toddler back down and tickling her cheek with his beard, he concluded. 'Now, come inside and let's eat.' And with that, he turned and led them into his home.

The cabin was small with only one room: a kitchen at one end, a bed at the other, and a fireplace positioned against the back wall in-between to service them both.

In the center of the kitchen area stood a small rectangular table with a bench on either side. And to cater for their unexpected guests, the woodsman's wife had thoughtfully moved her husband's chair from its usual place beside the hearth to the head of the table.

As the three hungry men entered, each respectfully wiped his booted feet on the rag rug at the entrance and greeted Rose warmly. Then, they quietly took their seats at the table while she began to fill hand carved wooden bowls with hearty pork soup and Erwin entertained their fidgety daughter.

After everyone had been served, Rose filled a bowl with soup for herself and carried it over to the table. But, as she sat down on the empty seat beside her husband, Holly decided it was her mother's turn to hold her and held out her chubby little arms.

Rose laughed, and the sound was as light as spring rain and as warm as summer sun. Then, she lifted her daughter from Erwin's knee and set the child in her lap.

The evening passed quickly for them all. The food was good and the company interesting. From time to time, even little Holly added a few words in baby talk, which none of the White Cliff men could understand but her parents did.

Erwin traced an invisible map on the table top with his finger to show his guests where they were in relation to Greystone Fortress and Inbe, the nearest village which he and Rose jokingly called In-between amongst themselves because it was located in-between the back of beyond and the deep blue sea.

Understanding the truth of the matter, the three men laughed appreciatively.

The woodsman went on to explain Inbe was a good day's walk in the general direction they were travelling and there was a small shop there where they could purchase supplies.

Her belly full, listening to the familiar sound of her father's voice, the little toddler eventually fell asleep in her mother's arms.

Having lost his own mother at an early age, Dare watched Rose slowly stand and carry the sleeping child across the room where she gently tucked Holly into her cot.

Living with his father, the smith wasn't accustomed to the kind of cozy family lifestyle the couple enjoyed. And seeing how lovingly Rose cared for their little daughter, tenderly kissing her goodnight on the cheek, Dare was surprised to find himself thinking it might be nice to marry and start a family of his own.

Realizing his mind had wondered, Dare turned his attention back to the conversation at the table just as Jerhal was saying, 'don't have waterskins.'

Erwin replied, 'We've a spare one. If you sip sparingly, you'll have enough water to reach Inbe.'

'Thank you,' the spy replied sincerely. 'We'd really appreciate it.

When Rose returned to the table, she had a patchwork quilt slung over one arm and a small container with a bird carved on its lid in her other hand.

'Rose, do we have any dried venison left?' Erwin asked his wife as she sat down.

'Yes,' Rose answered, understanding why her husband had asked. 'I'll wrap some up for our guests in the morning.'

With their food and water needs momentarily taken care of, Jerhal allowed himself to relax and he began to enjoy the evening.

The five of them talked quietly about a great many things, including the latest kingdom news. And the spy soon discovered, because their hosts lived such an isolated lifestyle, some of the things they mentioned were inaccurate and several months out-of-date, but he politely feigned ignorance and didn't correct them.

Then as the evening neared its end, Rose pushed the little carved container into the middle of the table and said, 'There's balm inside, made of beeswax, pine resin, and lard. Treat your cuts and scrapes with it before you go to sleep tonight, and they'll feel much better in the morning.'

Taking her kind gesture as a signal, the travel-weary men stood and helped her clear the table. Then trying not to disturb the little one, they quietly moved it and the benches to the side of the room to make more space for them to sleep and spread the quilt on the floor for padding.

After his guests had been seen to, Erwin wished them a good night and went to join his wife, leaving the White Cliff men to slip off their boots and bed down beneath their canvas ponchos.

By now Dare was accustomed to sleeping fully clothed, although he still missed his bed and feather pillow, even if he was too proud to admit it. And despite his tiredness, he lay there a long while listening to the heavy breathing of his sleeping companions, silently envying their ability to sleep anywhere they laid their heads, before he too finally fell asleep.

At the crack of dawn, when he was awakened by a crowing cockerel and the sound of a child's voice, the smith lay there bleary-eyed groggily wondering if it had been Holly who'd woken the cockerel or if the cockerel had woken her.

Then, as Dare sat up and began to pull on the first of his boots, it occurred to him the toddler must wake up around this time every morning and this was why Erwin had smiled when they'd told him they wanted an early start and he'd assured them it wouldn't be a problem. And, by the time the smith had finished pulling on the second boot, he'd decided he liked his sleep way too much to even consider starting a family of his own within the next few years.

With only their canvas ponchos and the quilt to gather up, it wasn't long before the cabin had been put back to rights and Rose began to serve them a substantial fry-up consisting of rosehip tea, fried eggs, bacon from the unfortunate pig that had charged Erwin, and fried bread.

Afterwards, Rose and Erwin gave the White Cliff men a small cloth wrapped parcel containing enough dried venison to tide them over until they reached the village of Inbe as well as the waterskin they'd promised.

Grateful for everything the couple had done for them, Jerhal offered to pay for the food they'd eaten and the supplies. But, the woodsman shook his head and wouldn't hear of it. So later, when the spy went to collect their ponchos while his companions got the horse and filled the waterskin, Jerhal left a silver coin on the mantelpiece for their hosts to find later.

When Zarak and Dare returned with Swim Tail, little Holly got very excited when she saw the horse. And being the thoughtful father he was, Erwin carried her over so she could pat the Greystone Steed on the nose.

While their daughter chatted away in baby talk to the horse, her smiling mother turned to the soldier and commented, 'Your horse is sure good with children.'

'Swim Tail is a remarkable animal. He's also gentle and dependable,' Zarak replied sincerely, totally unaware these were the same qualities he'd told his colleagues several days earlier he liked in a woman.

Hearing this, Jerhal and Dare exchanged a meaningful look, but didn't say anything.

After donning their ponchos, Zarak helped the injured spy onto the Greystone Steed's back. Then, the White Cliff men said their heartfelt farewells to Erwin, Rose, and Holly, knowing the encounter had been a chance one and they'd probably never meet again, and began their trek to the village of Inbe.

By the time they were out of the woodland family's earshot, however, Jerhal decided he'd held his tongue long enough and it was time to pull Zarak's leg. 'So, you value the same qualities in a woman as you do in a horse?'

Ever a man's man, the soldier replied without missing a beat, 'And good qualities they are too. Although, I never said she should look like one.'

15 DREAD WOOD

Three days after skillfully haggling in Inbe to re-equip themselves, Dare and his companions reined their horses to a halt and dismounted. After a short discussion, they decided to leave the main road skirting the Dread Wood and cut across the forest to make up lost time.

Having only heard the Dread Wood spoken of in children's stories, Dare hadn't realized the forest was a real place until the shopkeeper mentioned it when giving them directions. But then, not wanting to appear ignorant in front of the man, he hadn't said anything.

It wasn't until the smith was alone with Zarak and Jerhal he'd asked them about it, and learned the Dread Wood had once been part of the Drea Wood, a large ancient forest which had been contaminated and cataclysmically rent in two during the War of Magic eons before. And now a deep unpassable canyon, known as the Great Rift, separated it from its other half, the Dream Wood.

Although neither of his companions had ever travelled through the Dread Wood, they'd read eyewitness statements of people who had. All of the accounts reported enormous trees with trunks as large around as Sire's hut. And having seen a few strange things in their travels, both men believed the contaminated forest had undergone some kind of bizarre transformation, because several eyewitnesses had also mentioned seeing termightiest, large wolf sized termites, which they claimed travelled in tunnels crisscrossing the forest floor just beneath its surface.

Both Zarak and Jerhal admitted they'd no idea if such a huge insect actually existed. But if push came to shove, they thought the three of them would be perfectly capable of defending themselves if they should happen upon any aggressive ones.

Having been raised in a citadel made of stone, Dare had never seen a termite. But from the sound of things, he was certain he wasn't going to like meeting its next of kin and had spent each evening since sharpening the blade of his sword, as had his colleagues.

Now in the cold drizzle, the smith found himself leading Swim Tail in single file off the road and into the dappled light of the Dread Wood behind the two older men and their recently acquired mounts onto an unused footpath so narrow it looked more like a game trail.

Whether it was bravery, stupidity, or sheer stubbornness, Dare wasn't certain. But knowing King Dallin and Princess Lilyanna were relying on him, he tried to shake off the feeling of trepidation.

Then later when the smith eventually began to relax, he silently chided himself for letting his imagination get the better of him, because this forest looked just like the others he'd seen. The trees were of normal size and the ground was firm beneath his feet, nothing at all like what he had expected.

Zarak must have felt the same way, because a short time later Dare heard the soldier mutter, 'Mountains out of molehills. Or in this case, termite mounds.'

'Are you disappointed?' Jerhal asked.

'Yes and no,' Zarak replied honestly.

Dare understood what his friend meant. Although he would've liked to have seen a termightiest, he was glad they hadn't been attacked by one.

Preoccupied with fighting their way past branches and through brambles just as they had days before, none of them noticed the forest was gradually changing until much later when Dare commented, 'Is it my imagination, or do the trees seem bigger?'

Zarak answered drily, 'It's either that or we're shrinking.'

'I was afraid you were going to say that,' the smith replied, trying to sound lighthearted even though the uneasy feeling he'd shook off earlier was starting to return.

'At least we knew what to expect,' Jerhal reminded them.

'And the termightiest?' Dare asked.

'Oh, there's still plenty of time for that,' Zarak remarked flippantly. 'The tree trunks aren't even hut sized yet.'

Aware he spoke truly, the men fell silent and resumed their trek down the narrow path.

The further they journeyed into the heart of the woods the larger the trees became. And several hours later when Zarak suddenly stopped, held up his hand, and then cupped it to his ear, Jerhal instantly repeated the soldier's hand gestures so Dare, acting as rearguard, would understand what was happening.

They stood quietly frozen in place, listening. For the first time, the spy and smith hearing the faint droning sound Zarak had noticed. It was barely audible, yet seemed to emanate from all around them.

To Dare, it seemed as if he could actually hear the huge trees growing upwards in search of light. However, he also knew the idea was ridiculous and looked to his companions for a more plausible explanation, but they didn't recognize the sound either and merely shook their heads.

Having elected to cut across the Dread Wood instead of going around it, the rescue party had no other option than to move cautiously deeper into the woodland, the thick canopy high above them blocking the drizzle and the light, making it increasingly difficult to distinguish shape from shadow.

At one point, Dare thought he saw the forelegs of a termightiest emerging from one of the tunnels his travelling companions had told him about. But then an instant later, when the smith realized it was actually the upended roots of a fallen tree, he was relieved he hadn't shouted out in warning and made a fool of himself.

Apparently, Swim Tail didn't want to spend any more time in the Dread Wood than he did. Because the next thing Dare knew, the Greystone Steed was nudging him in the back with his muzzle. And realizing the horse was showing a great deal of common sense, the smith plodded forward.

As the trees grew steadily taller, their branches grew proportionally higher. So much so, the men from White Cliff were eventually able to mount their horses and ride beneath their lowest boughs. The only drawback being, with little undergrowth to edge the path, it soon became difficult for the riders to distinguish the path from the forest floor in the dim light. And eventually, Zarak was forced to rein his horse to a halt and tell his companions, 'Just to be on the safe side, I think we should blaze our trail.'

'Good idea,' Jerhal replied. 'But whatever you do, don't mark it with and X.'

'Why not?' the soldier asked, curious as to why it mattered.

'Because, someone already has,' the spy answered, indicating the mark on a nearby tree.

'Point taken,' Zarak agreed with a nod of his head. 'And to be extra careful, we'll use a double slash on the off chance someone else has used a single. Then if the markings align, so much the better.'

'And if they don't?' Dare quietly probed.

Zarak lost his smile and replied seriously. 'Then, either we've made a mistake or our predecessors have.'

'When will we know?' Dare asked, already knowing the answer in his gut.

'Only time will tell,' Zarak candidly answered as he slipped the hatchet he'd purchased in Inbe from his pack and blazed the bark of the X marked tree with a double slash of his own.

The small column then warily proceeded deeper into the Dread Wood. But strangely, other than for the faint background droning and occasional chopping of Zarak's hatchet, the only sounds the three riders heard the rest of the afternoon were made either by themselves or by their horses.

Fully aware they would have to spend two nights, possibly three, in the Dread Wood, none of the White Cliff men relished the prospect. So despite their tiredness, the rescuers forced their mounts onwards until it became too dark for them to travel without losing their way.

When they finally stopped for the night, they decided to err on the side of caution and eat their evening meal cold. They also decided to take turns standing watch, something they hadn't done before.

Although Jerhal hadn't complained, it was obvious the spy's ribs still pained him by the way he sat slumped in the saddle and, because Zarak had lead the column all day, Dare volunteered to take the first shift in order to give his colleagues the opportunity to rest.

To keep himself alert, the smith took to walking the perimeter of their encampment and checking on the horses. But other than for the soft breathing of his sleeping companions and the incessant droning they'd grown accustomed to, the night was quiet. So unnaturally quiet, Dare stopped walking and listened, really listened, and for the first time noticed faint cracking sounds, similar to snapping wood, intermixed with the strange droning.

As the hairs on the back of the smith's neck started to rise, it suddenly all made sense. Having been told termites ate decaying plant material, it stood to reason their next of kin would eat a similar diet. And, the sound he was hearing wasn't droning at all, but chewing, as thousands of termightiest fed upon the dead wood of the Dread Wood in the tunnels beneath them. Then, remembering the total absence of animal life, he shuttered as he realized what else the termightiest must eat.

Knowing the horses would have been restless if they sensed any predators nearby, the smith bravely resisted the urge to awaken his sleeping companions and decided to keep his suspicions to himself until he was relieved of guard duty. Although from then onwards, he started to walk a much tighter circuit around the campsite and kept his right hand at the ready on the hilt of his sword.

When at last it was Zarak's turn to stand watch, Dare quietly shared his thoughts with the battle-hardened soldier.

'Makes sense,' Zarak replied seriously. 'Glad to see you've kept your wits about you. Now, try to get some sleep. If things are as you say, tomorrow might be an eventful day.'

'I sure hope I'm wrong,' the smith told Zarak earnestly as he walked over to his bedroll. But after he lay down, sleep was a long time in coming.

The soldier's stint at watch was just as uneventful as Dare's had been.

Although, it did provide him plenty of time to mull over the smith's suspicions. And the more he listened to the strange droning, the more plausible the smith's ideas became. So much so, when it was finally Jerhal's turn to stand watch, Zarak quietly shared Dare's suspicions with him.

After hearing his colleague out, Jerhal responded decisively. 'Go put your head down and, just as soon as it's light, we'll break camp.'

'Agreed,' Zarak concurred in a hushed voice. And without saying another word, the soldier returned to the blankets he'd vacated a few hours earlier.

During his previous travels, the spy had spotted termite colonies harmlessly working away at decaying logs and such like. They were small, hence the 'mite' part in their name. And, they looked a lot like a white ant, having a head with antenna, three legs attached on both sides of the thorax, and an abdomen.

As Jerhal guarded the camp, he thought long and hard about the termites he'd seen, little by little recalling even more facts. They were either blind or had very poor eyesight, which made sense because they preferred the dark. And oddly enough, they had soft bodies, not hard exoskeletons like other insects. So he reasoned, the termightiest might share these same vulnerabilities and, if so, dispatching them might be as easy as slicing a knife through butter.

On the other hand, the spy cautioned himself, the termites he was thinking of hadn't been altered by magic. And having seen how the trees of the Dread Wood had been affected, if Dare was right, the termightiest might have been transformed into a much different more aggressive creature altogether.

In the past he'd used fire, torches in particular, to ward off frenzied wild animal attacks. However, swiftly realizing light from the torch might actually attract the shortsighted insects' attention like moths to a flame, Jerhal discounted the idea.

Then, the spy was struck by another disturbing thought. Termightiest either didn't require sleep, because if they did the incessant droning would have stopped, or they worked in shifts, which meant the creatures could relentlessly harass their prey until it succumbed to exhaustion.

Thus far, the rescue party's cautious approach, traveling silently and not lighting any fires, had been the correct course of action. So Jerhal surmised, if they continued as they were, they just might make it out of the Dread Wood unscathed.

A fine mist had settled in the low contours of the Dread Wood by the time it was finally light enough to travel.

When Jerhal gently shook his companions awake, he reminded them, with a finger to his lips, to keep the noise down. Then as they broke their fast with cold rations, he quietly told them what he'd remembered about termites, as well as his conjectures regarding the termightiest.

Having only to pack their bedrolls and saddle the horses, it didn't take long for them to strike camp after they'd eaten. Then in unspoken agreement, the three retook their places in the small column and, with Zarak in the lead, resumed their journey through the Dread Wood.

Because the mist obscured the path, their progress was painfully slow. At times, the soldier was forced to dismount and walk ahead in search of the way, leaving Jerhal and Dare sitting on their horses in the cold looking out for termightiest. Then, Zarak would return and they'd travel a little further until the path disappeared again.

As the morning wore on, the mist slowly began to dissipate and the men were able to travel a little faster in the subdued light, riding up and down steep slopes, maneuvering their horses past large boulders, and zigzagging their way around huge trees even larger than the ones they'd seen the day before.

To satisfy their hunger, they ate dried venison. And to quench their thirst, they sipped from their waterskins. But, they did all of this on the move, because the constant droning was beginning to unsettle their nerves and they didn't want to spend anymore time in the Dread Wood than was absolutely necessary.

The only times they actually stopped were either to search for the path and, once found, blaze their double slash into the bark of a nearby tree, or to leave a more personal slash of their own behind one.

By the afternoon, the travel-worn men were so weary they mistook a small group of light-colored shapes deep within the forest shadows for a flock of grazing sheep. And it wasn't until their horses caught the unfamiliar scent and tried to bolt, the riders recognized the shapes for what they really were: foraging termightiest. Concerned the huge insects would attack, Dare and his companions struggled to regain control of their frightened mounts. But once the dust had settled and the men could spare a second glance, they were surprised to find the termightiest seemed not to have noticed them.

Still pulling back on the reins, Jerhal shouted over to his companions, 'We're in luck fellas! It looks like they're blind and deaf!'

'That still leaves smell, touch, and taste!' Zarak shouted back as his restless horse pranced beneath him. 'And, I'd prefer not to get intimate.'

'You didn't say that at Stone Bridge,' the spy retorted, finally reining in his mount.

'That was different,' the soldier laughed. 'I thought the young widow wanted to cook me dinner, not have me for dinner.'

'Black widow was more like it,' Jerhal replied, flashing a wicked grin. 'You should've asked me about her. I could've warned you she was a man-eater.'

'I don't recall you volunteering any information at the time.'

'That's because a man should keep his sword honed my friend, and I thought yours was beginning to rust.'

'So, we're friends now are we?' Zarak jokingly asked.

Ignoring the soldier's question, Jerhal continued, 'Besides, I remembered how much you enjoy grappling in the dark.'

Zarak laughed, recalling the night on a previous assignment the grappling hook he'd insisted on bringing had saved their lives. Then, he replied in mock understanding, 'So, you had my best interest at heart. Well, if I had to choose between her and the termightiest on this mission, I'd rather take my chances with the termightiest, fewer grasping limbs to contend with.'

Dare had travelled with the two men long enough by now to know this was how they released stress. Although, it was the first time he'd heard mention of Zarak's escapades at Stone Bridge. And had he not been busy trying to keep Swim Tail under control, he may've joined in the banter. But by the time the Greystone Steed had calmed, Zarak and Jerhal were already spurring their horses forward and he had to hurry to catch up.

Knowing the termightiest couldn't hear them was a great relief. The men no longer had to communicate in hushed voices or with hand signals. And despite the incessant droning, they were able to relax a little and their spirits began to rise.

As they travelled deeper into the Dread Wood, and unknowingly nearer the termightiest's nest, the men began to encounter the huge insects in greater numbers. But, because the termightiest didn't bother the riders, the riders didn't bother them, even the horses grew accustomed to the strange creatures' unfamiliar scent.

The trail still disappeared in places. Yet, with Zarak's expert guidance and the aid of whoever had blazed the X into the bark of the massive trees years before, the small rescue party was able to follow the route despite the dim light.

It wasn't until the path collapsed beneath Zarak's mount they understood the danger, and by then it was too late. Jerhal and Dare could only watch in horror as both horse and rider plunged into the trapping pit hidden below.

Fearing the soldier had fallen to his death, Dare and Jerhal jumped from their horses and ran to the deep hole.

With their hearts in their mouths, the two men looked over the edge of the pit and saw Zarak gasping for breath in a crumpled heap below them, trying to avoid the thrashing hooves of his injured mount.

'Hold my legs!' Dare ordered Jerhal. Then trusting the spy would grip him securely, the smith dropped onto his stomach and leaned unhesitatingly into the pit as he shouted down to his friend, 'Grab my hands! I'll pull you up!'

At the sound of Dare's voice, Zarak staggered to his feet and lifted his arms. But, his reach was short and he was unable to clasp the smith's hands. So to make up the distance, he jumped.

Zarak's feet had scarcely left the ground before several enormous termightiest scurried into the pit from connecting tunnels just beneath the soldier's dangling feet. They were darker in color than their smaller counterparts and obviously much more powerful. But, it was their enlarged jaws and fearsome hornlike snouts, both of which the smaller termightiest lacked, that caught Dare's attention.

Sensing danger, the smith clenched his teeth and pulled Zarak upwards with all of his might, for the first time thankful for the years he'd spent hammering hot iron on his father's forge.

The injured horse below suddenly started to let out loud agonizing snorting noises, and both men knew without looking the termightiest were savaging the wounded animal.

The sounds of the slaughter were horrific and Zarak, usually calm under pressure, began to frantically run his feet over the pit wall in search of a toehold which would help support his weight.

As Dare struggled to pull the weapon laden soldier upwards, he could see the injured horse flailing in pain at the bottom of the pit. Its blood was everywhere, mingling with the thick toxin sprayed from its attackers' horned snouts.

As Jerhal sat straddled across the back of the smith's legs, pushing down firmly to anchor him, he could feel Dare's body slowly sliding deeper into the pit. Fearing he would lose both companions, the spy dropped his full weight onto the back of the smith, ignoring the shooting pain in his injured ribs.

Coupled in a human chain, Dare stopped sliding, his arms and legs stretched to breaking point. Then just when he thought his shoulders were going to dislocate from their sockets, Zarak found the toehold he needed.

Pumped with adrenaline, the soldier was able to push himself upwards. And using Dare as a human ladder, he scrambled up the smith's arms and over the backs of his colleagues to safety.

Jerhal continued to hold Dare securely as Zarak caught his breath. Then, they dragged their dangling companion away from the trapping pit and collapsed beside him.

The three sat panting together sprawled upon the forest floor, happy to be alive. And when Dare told them between gasps he thought his sleeves would need to be lengthened, they all laughed.

Once the men had recovered, they picked themselves up and walked back to the trapping pit for a close inspection.

Remarkably, the termightiest had sealed the top of the pit with a thin layer of pulped plant material barely strong enough to support the sprinkling of topsoil they'd scattered across its surface as camouflage.

Lulled into a false sense of security while observing the smaller worker termightiest passive demeanor, they'd mistakenly underestimated how deadly the matured insect could be.

With the entire Dread Wood serving as their larder, the termightiest didn't have to hunt for food. The vegetation they fed upon was all around them. And through the clever use of trapping pits, the meat they ate consisted of any unsuspecting creature misfortunate enough to fall in.

'Simple, but effective,' Jerhal said, stuffing the small specimen of pulped material he'd retrieved from the broken pit cover into his shirt pocket for the spymaster and wizard, Urba, to examine upon their return to White Cliff.

Having just had his mount butchered beneath him, Zarak was in no mood to admire the termightiest work. 'Brutal,' he replied instead, shaking his head and gazing down at the blood-soaked pit floor. 'What a waste of a good horse.' Then as an afterthought, he added with disgust, 'The only thing they left behind is the buckle from my pack. I guess they couldn't chew it.'

Knowing what a keen horseman Zarak was, Dare couldn't help feeling sorry for his loss and placed a comforting hand on his friend's shoulder. 'Come on. Let's leave this place.'

'Yes,' Zarak agreed. 'There's nothing here but the stench of death.'

As the men went to retrieve the two remaining horses and the hatchet Zarak had dropped when he'd felt the ground giving way beneath him, several of the smaller light-colored termightiest scurried past them, oblivious of their presence, and began to repair the shattered pit covering.

'Efficient too,' Jerhal remarked to no one in particular.

'Way too efficient for my liking,' Zarak conceded, as he bent down and picked up the discarded hatchet.

Other than for a few minor scrapes and bruises, the soldier was in remarkably good condition after his fall and insisted on leading their small party. Albeit, as a precaution and because they were unable to purchase a rope in Inbe, he now wore a canvas tether constructed of hastily torn strips from their ponchos and prodded the ground for trapping pits with a walking stick fashioned from the branch of a nearby tree.

Surprisingly, their pace wasn't much slower than it had been that morning. However, the X marks emblazoned on the trees they'd previously found so reassuring were suddenly conspicuous by their absence.

Although none of the men said anything, they all suspected their trailblazing predecessors had never made it out of the Dread Wood. And aware of their own mortality, they spent the remainder of the afternoon travelling ever up the steep gradient in the futile hope they'd cross the forest before nightfall. But when it finally became too dark to distinguish the path, the rescue party was forced to stop in the Dread Wood for a second night.

At their insistence, Dare and Jerhal volunteered to take turns standing watch so Zarak could rest the full night.

Without their ponchos and only two woolen blankets between them, because the termightiest had made off with all but the buckle of Zarak's leather pack, the three men spent a very cold and miserable night.

By morning a fine damp mist had settled once more upon the ground. But frustratingly for the rescuers, they had to linger near their horses for warmth and wait for it to clear.

When the path was finally revealed, however, their patience didn't go unrewarded. Because no more than twenty strides from where they'd made camp, it suddenly ended, only to resume again a short distance away just as it had done countless times before. But this time, Zarak had a gut feeling something wasn't right, and over the years he'd learned to listen to his gut.

The soldier drew cautiously closer, his tether momentarily tightening before going slack again as Jerhal followed behind on his horse. Then, there it was, ever so faint, the same unmistakable stench he'd smelled the day before at the bottom of the pit.

Rather than prod the questionable area with his walking stick, Zarak picked up a stone and tossed it midway between the broken path segments. And like ripples on a pond, the camouflaged seal collapsed at the point of impact outwards, revealing the trapping pit hidden below.

Fascinated, all three men approached the deep hole and looked in just as several of the larger horn-snouted soldier termightiest entered from adjoining tunnels with their antennae twitching in anticipation of dispatching newly captured prey.

'You're right. They're easy to appreciate from up here,' Zarak commented drily.

Although the beginnings of a smile played at the corners of Jerhal's mouth, the spy didn't say anything and continued to watch the termightiest as they picked through the seal fragments with their enlarged jaws in search of whatever had fallen into the pit.

It wasn't until the enormous insects had given up their hunt and disappeared back into their tunnels Jerhal spoke, 'I didn't mean to be insensitive yesterday. I was caught up in the moment gathering information for my report.'

Being a professional soldier, Zarak understood, in his occupation paperwork was also a necessary evil. 'I'm glad I could help.'

Having already witnessed the worker termightiest repair a pit cover the previous day, there was no need for the rescuers to linger. So after remounting their horses, Jerhal and Dare followed Zarak cautiously around the large pit and up the path.

The remainder of the morning passed uneventfully and by midday, when the men from White Cliff stopped to water the horses at a nearby stream and to feed them the last of their dwindling oat supply, Dare asked Jerhal, 'Why don't the termightiest ever venture out of the Dread Wood? It's not like they're fenced in here.'

The spy thought about it for a moment and answered, 'I'd have to get the king's wizard to confirm this, but I think it has something to do with magic. Because the termightiest were created by magic, they probably need the magic of the Dread Wood to sustain them. And, if they were to ever leave, they'd most likely perish like a fish out of water.' Then Jerhal looked over at Zarak and asked, 'What do you think?'

'Sounds right to me. But then, I really don't know much about magic,' the soldier admitted with a shake of his head.

Dare thought Jerhal's explanation made a lot of sense too. And after his fishing experience with Sire, he understood what the spy meant about taking a fish out of the water.

Once the horses had been fed and rested, the men resumed their journey. Yet having grown accustomed to the constant background droning, the further they travelled, they failed to notice the noise was starting to fade and the trees were slowly reverting to their natural state.

As more sunlight penetrated the leafy canopy, the undergrowth began to flourish and Zarak was able to distinguish the path more clearly. But it wasn't until the riders had to dismount and lead their horses, because of low-hanging tree limbs, they realized they were nearing the edge of the ancient woodland.

With the last rays of sunlight, they stepped out of the Dread Wood and back onto the bordering road they'd vacated three days earlier. And in the distance silhouetted against the evening sky, they could clearly see Greystone Fortress jutting formidably before them high on the mountainside, confirming Zarak had guided them ever true.

16 SEBASTIAN

Feeling a little peckish, Erosmay had flown to the stables to catch a mouse or two to tide her over until her evening meal. And as was the dragon's custom, she'd perched herself high upon one of the rafters, hiding amongst the shadows, to wait patiently for her snack to arrive.

She hadn't been there long before she heard voices coming from outside, one of which she recognized straightway as belonging to the owner of the stables. So when he stepped through the doorway, she wasn't surprised to see him or to overhear him explaining his charges for feeding and grooming the two horses belonging to the travel-worn men with him.

Vexed the men were going to scare her snack away, the little dragon hadn't paid much attention to them until after a price had been agreed and the stable owner had gone to fetch fresh water for the horses. Then, she overheard the tall dark-haired man with a beard say to the others, 'While you buy horses and supplies, I'll have a snoop around and find out where they're keeping her. Then, I'll meet you at the inn.'

When Erosmay heard the word snoop, her ears perked and she was immediately interested. Because, after eating, her second favorite thing to do in the entire world was snoop.

Unable to resist the urge of snooping on a snooper, something she'd never done before, the young dragon quickly decided the tall bearded man required closer observation and she could wait a little longer for her snack. So when the other two men went to purchase horses and supplies, Erosmay followed

Jerhal instead.

Stealthily darting from one concealed area to the next in the light drizzling rain, she tailed the spy all the way from the stables to Far View Inn. And since the man hadn't done any snooping on the way there, Erosmay assumed this was where he planned to do it, because an inn was an awfully good place to keep someone.

Just as Jerhal stepped over the threshold, Erosmay landed on the ground behind him and, in the shadowed wake of his booted feet, followed him inside. Then while the innkeeper walked over to greet him, she darted away and hid herself on the far side of a thick wooden chair near the doorway, her iridescent coppery sage green scales providing the perfect camouflage.

Filled with expectation, she was disappointed when she discovered Jerhal wasn't going to do any snooping at the inn, but had only gone there to arrange lodgings for himself and the other two men as well as collect a small travel chest he'd paid the innkeeper to store for him.

When the spy picked up the chest and began to carry it upstairs, Erosmay nearly flew back to the stables. But then, she remembered he hadn't done any snooping yet. So when the innkeeper wasn't looking, she snuck back outside, found a comfortable vantage point, and waited to see where Jerhal would go next.

Shortly thereafter, when the spy stepped back onto the street, Erosmay was amazed to discover he'd totally changed his appearance. Instead of the tattered clothing and muddy boots he'd worn on his arrival, Jerhal was now freshly groomed and foppishly dressed as a low-ranking noble with a silly little hat tilted jauntily to the side of his head.

He even walked differently. Instead of the brisk no-nonsense stride he'd arrived with, Jerhal now strode with a pretentious strut. And in this new guise, had the dragon not been keeping an eye out, she wouldn't have recognized him.

Erosmay was intrigued. With this change in clothing and mannerisms, the tall man now gave the impression he was vain and foolish, exactly what he wanted people to think. But having observed him earlier, the dragon knew better.

Curiosity piqued, Erosmay stealthily followed Jerhal along the streets of

Greystone. And when he finally turned and headed towards the fortress itself, she wasn't surprised because, other than for an inn or the garrison's prison, if a person was going to be kept anywhere it was most likely in the fortress dungeon.

The little dragon overheard Jerhal exchange a few words with the guard, and then watched as he was admitted into the fortress. But rather than proceed towards the dungeon like she'd expected, he headed in the opposite direction. So, inquisitive as always, Erosmay followed him all the way to the fortress laundry where he was greeted warmly by, of all people, the indomitable head laundress, Morag.

Taken aback, Erosmay let out a gasp in amazement, to which her linked companion, Robin, responded by asking if everything was alright. The dragon quickly reassured her it was but, not wanting to miss anything, said she'd explain later and abruptly broke contact.

Hidden amongst the shadows, Erosmay watched in wide-eyed disbelief as Morag, acting totally out of character, hastily stripped off her apron and grabbed her shawl. Then, after issuing a few quick instructions to her subordinates, she left the laundry early on the arm of Jerhal and wearing a smile from ear to ear.

Surprised to see the Iron Maiden with a male companion, the other women in the laundry were just as gobsmacked by this unexpected turn of events as the dragon was. And just as soon as the formidable middle-aged spinster was out of earshot, they started twittering amongst themselves like startled birds in an aviary.

Jerhal, or rather Sebastian as he was known in Greystone, had learned early in his career courting a woman for information was a lot like swordplay; you had to be nimble, quick-witted, and able to anticipate the next couple of moves well in advance.

In his role as Sebastian, he'd been feigning interest in Morag off and on for about a year now, pretending to meet her by chance and filling her ears with flirtations, but always leaving her wanting more by keeping the encounters purposefully brief. Only now, out of duty to his king and against his better judgement, he'd publically sought the woman out.

Walking down the hallway arm in arm, they were both aware they'd be the subject of conversation for anyone who saw them. And although the spy knew Morag would be inwardly pleased by this, as it would only serve to enhance her reputation, he played the innocent and said, 'I hope my meeting you like this won't cause you any difficulty.'

Knowing how quickly rumors swept through the fortress, having started so many herself, Morag giggled demurely and reassured him, 'Don't worry Sebastian. I know how to take care of myself.'

Of this, Jerhal was also well aware. In her position as head laundress, Morag overheard the idle chatter of servants and staff alike. And as a result, she knew everyone's dirty laundry and wasn't afraid to air it, which made her a valuable source of information as well as a vindictive enemy.

Talking softly, they left the fortress and strolled leisurely, despite the light drizzle, until they came upon a small haberdashery situated along one of the less travelled side streets, never suspecting the small dragon followed. And when Sebastian suggested they go inside, Morag coyly agreed.

After a quick look around, Sebastian asked the shop owner if he had any green scarfs. The man replied he had and, eager to please, ducked behind the counter, only to reappear a few moments later holding several green scarfs of varying shades.

Sebastian carefully examined the scarfs, selected one, and paid the haberdasher for it. Then, he turned to Morag and said, 'This is for you, so you can tie your hair back at work. But, just for today, may I take the liberty?'

Surprised by the unexpected gift, Morag was speechless. And although she had no idea what he was asking of her, she nodded her head granting him consent, because she was so flattered she would've done anything to please him.

As Sebastian stepped closer to her, so close he nearly brushed up against her, Morag could feel her pulse quicken. Afraid to breath for fear of breaking his spell, she stood perfectly still as he lifted the scarf and gently draped it around the back of her neck. Then ever so slowly, he slid his hands down the scarf and tied the ends into a loose knot that rested provocatively at the top of her cleavage.

Satisfied, Sebastian stepped back and looked at her appraisingly. Then, he smiled and told her, 'It matches your eyes perfectly.'

Morag had never known a moment like it. This man made her feel beautiful. Speechlessly, she raised her trembling hand and tenderly touched the scarf, as if it was made of the finest silk.

From the look on the laundress's face, it was obvious she was pleased. Still smiling, Sebastian replied, 'I'm glad you like it.'

Finally finding her voice, Morag spluttered, 'I do. It's lovely. Thank you.'

The couple walked out of the shop arm in arm. And by the time they entered one of the more respectable taverns, no one would have ever suspected the head laundress had been dumbfounded a short while earlier.

After they'd seated themselves at a secluded corner table, the proprietor arrived and Sebastian pretentiously ordered two glasses of the establishment's finest red wine, knowing full well the man would make a great show of serving them the same cheap plonk he always served and charge him double. But, Morag would be impressed and that was all that mattered.

When the wine arrived, Sebastian fished a couple of coins out of his pocket and paid the man as if the exorbitant price was inconsequential. Then, he raised his glass and toasted Morag, who smiled bashfully at him like a young girl.

With eyes only for each other, the two sat quietly chatting and sipping wine. In his guise as Sebastian, Jerhal spun an apologetic yarn to explain his absence and said, because he had to leave on business early the following day, he'd wanted to spend the evening with her.

Although saddened her companion was leaving so soon, Morag was flattered, that of all the women in the fortress, he'd sought her out and pleased to be spending even this one evening in his company.

When their glasses were empty, Sebastian ordered them to be refilled. Yet after only a couple of sips, Morag raised a hand delicately to her brow and said primly, 'Oh my. I think this wine is going straight to my head.'

Having investigated the laundress before making initial contact, the spy knew Morag was fond of a tipple and wasn't as inebriated as she made out. Nevertheless, because he hadn't discovered where Princess Lilyanna was being kept, he played along anyway and thoughtfully replied, 'Perhaps something to eat might help.'

Pleased such a handsome man was willing to wine and also dine her, Morag replied demurely, 'Yes, I think it would.'

Sebastian ordered the food with the same pretentious air he'd used when ordering the wine. But the tavern keeper didn't mind, he'd been around arrogant peacocks like this one long enough to know the more he fed his customers' egos the fatter his own purse became.

Having forgone her snack, Erosmay could hardly bear it when the steaming plates of food arrived. She'd hidden herself high upon a shelf behind a rather large ugly jug in order to eavesdrop on the couple sitting below and was afraid the wafting aroma was going to cause her stomach to rumble. Then fortunately, when she scooted a little closer and saw how greasy the food was, she lost her appetite.

As the evening progressed, Sebastian and Morag spoke of many things. However, it wasn't until the laundress mentioned a woman of importance had recently arrived and Robin, the white-haired witch, had been reinstated as lady-in-waiting to attend her, Erosmay became interested.

Crouched down behind the jug, the little dragon stretched her neck along the top of the shelf just as far as she possibly could to better hear the conversation. And the more she listened to what was being said, the more apparent it became Sebastien was interested too. Because several times afterwards, he skillfully guided the conversation back to the same topic.

Flattered her companion hung on her every word, Morag confided Elrod's guest was staying in the same east wing apartment his deceased wife had occupied. And, as well as sleeping in his dead wife's bed, she'd also been seen wearing her jewelry.

Already suspecting Elrod's guest was Princess Lilyanna, this snippet of information was all the confirmation the spy needed.

Keeping in character, Jerhal didn't let his excitement show. Instead, he lifted an eyebrow and roguishly suggested a romance might be in the air.

Morag giggled conspiratorially. Then, she leaned a little closer and whispered he might be right, because the lady only left her rooms in the evenings to dine with him.

Sebastian flashed a knowing smile. Then, having learned all he needed to know, he picked up his glass and slowly drained the last of its contents.

Still smiling, the spy looked into Morag's eyes and said, 'I bet the meals they share aren't half as enjoyable as this one has been. But regrettably, I have an early start in the morning.' Then, he stood and held out his hand, leaving the laundress no other alternative than to put her hand in his, rise to her feet, and accompany him out of the tavern.

As they strolled towards her home, Morag wished the evening would never end. But alas, the inevitable happened and they arrived outside her door all too soon.

Hoping Sebastian might ask to come in, the laundress stood bosom heaving and weak kneed with expectation. Yet ever the gentleman, he kissed the back of her hand goodnight instead and, as she tried to think of an excuse to invite him inside, walked away.

Still feeling Morag's eyes upon him as he rounded the corner, Jerhal was relieved this part of his mission was over. Because even though he lived to serve his king and country, bedding the laundress was a BIG ask far beyond the call of duty.

Erosmay was already winging her way back to the fortress by the time Jerhal had successfully extricated himself from Morag with his dignity intact.

When the little dragon arrived outside the chamber she shared with Robin, she tucked in her leathery wings, darted through the open window, and then landed gently on the bed.

'Hello,' the white-haired woman greeted Erosmay fondly in mind-speech. 'What have you been up to?'

Erosmay replied unabashedly, 'I've been watching and learning.'

Trying to hide her amusement, Robin walked over and sat down on the bed beside the inquisitive dragon. 'You mean snooping,' she corrected fondly.

Knowing full well Erosmay could've been up to just about anything, the white-haired woman waited while the little dragon climbed onto her lap and made herself comfortable. Then, she asked, 'Just what did you learn this time?'

Erosmay replied seriously, 'Men are here looking for the princess.'

Robin was stunned. Although she knew King Dallin would be searching for his missing daughter, she hadn't expected his men to arrive so soon and exclaimed, 'Tell me everything!'

Needing no further encouragement, the little dragon eagerly launched into a detailed account of what she'd learned, even describing Morag's strange behavior, which wasn't pertinent but made the white-haired woman smile.

'I have just one more question,' Robin said when Erosmay had finished. 'What were you doing in the stables to begin with?' But before her linked companion could answer, the white-haired woman laughed and added, 'Don't bother. I think I already know. You went there for a between meals snack.'

The dragon looked up at her and answered seriously in mind-speech, 'I'm a growing dragon. I need to eat.'

'Yes, and that's our dilemma,' Robin replied as she lovingly stroked the top of the little dragon's scaled head. 'But, I have a feeling our luck and your diet are going to change real soon.'

'Good. I thought their horses looked tasty.'

Unable to tell if the dragon was joking, the white-haired woman decided to play it safe and admonished, 'Erosmay, you can't go around trying to eat horses, especially the horses belonging to these men.'

The dragon shook her head in disappointment. So to help cheer her linked companion up, Robin gave Erosmay some well-deserved stroking, and in no time the little dragon was fast asleep.

Later that evening, when almost everyone had returned to their homes, Robin pulled up the hood of her cape to hide her distinctive long white hair and slipped out of the fortress.

Although the grey clouds had cleared, the temperature had dropped with the setting sun, and Robin could smell the familiar scent of woodsmoke wafting from the chimneys of the buildings she passed as she made her way down the deserted cobblestone streets towards Far View Inn.

Flying high overhead, Erosmay served as escort, ready to swoop down out of the darkness and nip anyone who harassed Robin with her razor-sharp teeth.

When they finally neared the inn and the dragon had confidently confirmed it was safe to travel the rest of the way unaccompanied, the white-haired woman asked her linked companion if she would do a bit of snooping on her behalf, which of course the inquisitive dragon was more than happy to do.

While Erosmay took the more direct route and darted eagerly ahead, Robin wove her way down the last few cobbled streets alone. And by the time she arrived at the inn, rosy-cheeked from the cold and slightly out of breath, the dragon had already peered through the building's upstairs windows and told her which room the men from White Cliff were occupying.

After taking a moment to compose herself, Robin strode confidently through the doorway, straight up the stairs and down the hallway. When she reached the last door on the right, just as Erosmay had directed, she stopped and took a couple of deep calming breaths. Then, with chin up and shoulders back, she lifted her hand and quietly rapped upon it three times in rapid succession.

A moment later, Jerhal opened the door and saw the cloaked woman standing before him. From the wisp of white hair that had escaped from beneath her hood, he knew immediately who she was. 'Robin!' he exclaimed, not bothering to hide his astonishment. 'Come in.'

Robin wasn't surprised the tall bearded man knew who she was; Erosmay had already told her Morag had mentioned her to him by name. But she didn't know, even as she knocked upon their door, the three men were busy discussing the best way to approach her.

She nodded and quickly stepped inside.

As Jerhal closed the door behind her, Robin pushed back the hood of her cloak and bobbed her head in acknowledgement to the others in the room. Then, she turned back and looked Jerhal directly in the eyes. 'I believe you've been asking about me and an acquaintance of mine.'

Recovered from the shock of her unexpected arrival, Jerhal returned her gaze evenly. But rather than confirm her statement, he asked, 'How do you know this, or are you really a witch like everyone claims? I thought that was just fortress gossip.'

Ever since Erosmay had come into her life, Robin had encouraged the rumors to protect the little dragon. And even though she believed she could trust these men, she was still hesitant to divulge any information which might endanger her linked companion.

Electing to keep up the pretext a little longer, she answered, 'Let's just say a little bird told me.'

From out of nowhere, Erosmay's objection sounded loudly in her mind, 'I'm not a bird. Dragons are superior to birds.'

Realizing Erosmay hadn't waited outside like she'd asked and feeling the tall man's eyes upon her, Robin tried to keep her face expressionless. Then after what felt like an eternity, the man seemed to come to a decision and said, 'Since you haven't brought any of Elrod's soldiers to arrest us, I trust we're allies.'

Although Robin was worried for Lilyanna's safety and had been desperately seeking a way to help the princess escape, she was also concerned for her linked companion. And, it was because of this, she answered, 'I'll help you rescue the princess on one condition. You must take me and,' she paused as she sought the right word, 'my little bird with you.'

Aware of Robin's situation at the fortress, Jerhal understood why she'd asked to come along. However, he also knew adding members to their small group would create complications, so he glanced over questioningly to Zarak and Dare.

After both men had nodded their approval, Jerhal surprised Robin by stepping forward and shaking her hand to formally seal their pact. And by this one simple act, the last of her niggling doubts vanished and she knew she could trust them.

'Robin, we have you at a slight disadvantage. We all know who you are, but you don't know us,' the spy said with a smile. 'I'm Jerhal, but here in Greystone I'm also known as Sebastian. This is Zarak. He's a soldier and as strong as an ox. And, this is Dare. He's a locksmith by trade and a picklock by necessity.'

When Robin heard the word picklock, her eyes lit up. Because for lack of a key, the alternate escape route she'd discovered had been impassable. But, she also realized before she could share the plan with her new associates, there was one last introduction to be made. So instead of using mind-speech to communicate with the dragon like she normally did, she spoke aloud for them all to hear. 'Erosmay, you can show yourself. There are people here I'd like you to meet.'

17 TUNNEL

The following morning the three men from White Cliff made their way in the cold to the concealed entrance located outside the fortress ramparts Robin had told them about the night before. And true to the white-haired woman's word, Erosmay was there waiting for them, perched upon the branch of a spindly pine growing nearby.

It transpired the inquisitive creature had happened upon the ancient tunnel system during one of her excursions. And, had the tunnel's barred door not been locked and blocked with vegetation, Robin had said she and the little dragon would have used the forgotten passageway to make their escape from Greystone Fortress weeks before. However, now with the princess's abduction and their arrival, she thought this route was the best option available for them all.

Allied with the white-haired woman, the men had come to inspect the tunnel wearing the old weapons Sire had given them and carrying a small pack filled with various items they thought they might need, including the trusty hatchet Zarak had blazed their trail with through the Dread Wood.

It didn't take them long to hack their way through the troublesome vegetation, taking care not to disturb the area too much and only clearing enough space to allow them single file access to the disused entrance. Then, as Zarak and Jerhal began to fashion torches from some of the saplings they had chopped down, Dare dropped onto his knees in front of the iron door, slipped several picklocks from his leather cuff, and started working on the door's rusted lock.

He'd seen worse, having picked many an old lock at his father's smithy. So when the lever inside didn't release straightway, he wasn't daunted and had a rummage through the pack they had brought for the small jar of cooking grease they had obtained from the innkeeper earlier that morning.

With jar in hand, Dare hunkered back down in front of the barred door, scooped up some of the grease with his picklock, and dabbed the lubricant into the keyhole. Next, he reinserted the picklock into the keyhole and gradually worked the grease between the wards. Then after a lot of wiggling and jiggling, the smith firmly turned his wrist and the rusted lever inside the lock released with a click.

His task completed, Dare retrieved his tools and moved away from the narrow entrance so Zarak could take his place in front of the rusted door.

While the smith slipped the picklocks back into his leather cuff, the soldier took hold of the door's cold bars and pulled with all of his might. But, its hinges had rusted and the door wouldn't budge.

Zarak breathed onto the palms of his hands and rubbed them together to warm them. Then, he grabbed hold of the cold bars and pulled again. This time, the door begrudgingly started to swing open, but its rusted hinges let out such an ear-piercing screech he immediately stopped pulling for fear someone might hear.

'Here,' Dare said calmly from behind him. 'Use some of this.'

Zarak glanced over his shoulder and saw the smith was holding out the jar of cooking grease. 'Good idea,' he muttered softly as he accepted the jar. Then, he turned back to the door, scooped out a big dollop of grease with his cold fingers, and applied it liberally to the rusted hinges until the screech was eventually smothered and the door swung freely.

When he was satisfied they would be able to come and go without attracting unwarranted attention, Zarak then cleaned his hands by wiping the excess grease onto the clothbound ends of the torches to help fuel them.

Erosmay's mouth had started to water the moment she had smelled the cooking grease. And by the time the soldier had finally resealed the pottery jar, she could hardly bear it. So to take her mind off her empty stomach, the little dragon spread her leathery wings and glided into the disused passage to have a look around, scarcely noticing it was pitch-black inside because her eyesight was just as keen as her sense of smell.

She had only flown a short distance when she came across a number of small bones scattered across the tunnel floor and realized, although the door's iron bars kept large animals out of the tunnel, they were too far apart to block the way of smaller ones. And, at some point, after she and Robin had explored the tunnel, either a fox or stray dog had used it for a den.

Never one to miss an opportunity, the peckish dragon landed gently amongst the bones in hope of finding a tasty titbit. But before she had the chance to find anything, she saw the flicker of torchlight dancing upon the tunnel walls and knew her travelling companions were fast approaching.

Like the dragons of old, Erosmay could be a very dignified creature when she chose to be, and this just happened to be one of those occasions. Fully aware the men from White Cliff would think her no more than a common scavenger if they saw her searching through the bones for food, the dragon put her hunger aside for a second time and flew back to rejoin them.

When Zarak, who was leading their small column because the tunnel was too narrow for the men to walk abreast, reached the spot where the bones lay scattered across the tunnel floor, he lowered his torch for a better look and quickly came to the same conclusion the dragon had. Then, after warning the others to keep on their guard for creatures of both the two and four-legged kind, the soldier continued down the passageway, only now Erosmay had boldly caught a ride and sat perched upon his shoulder. And if Zarak minded, he was much too professional to let it show.

Although Jerhal and Dare both thought this funny and exchanged an amused glance behind the soldier's back, they followed Zarak's good example and didn't say anything either.

When the smith first stepped into the tunnel, he hadn't known what to expect and was a little surprised the passageway smelled of damp. That was until a cold droplet landed on his face and he realized surface water, or at least that's what he hoped it was, was slowly seeping into the tunnel through tiny fissures in the rock.

He wiped the droplet from his cheek and tried to concentrate on the way ahead, because in the flickering torchlight it was difficult to see and he did not want to lose his footing.

Between glancing down at the uneven floor and back up to the back of Jerhal's rhythmically bobbing head as the spy walked in front of him, the smith soon lost all track of time. But fortunately, just when it began to feel like the tunnel walls were starting to close in on him, they reached the chambered juncture Robin had told them about.

Here, the rock face abutted the fortification's foundation and the tunnel system split in two directions; the passageway on the right leading to the fortress garrison and the stone-cut steps on the left ascending into the fortress itself.

Dare thought it looked exactly as the white-haired woman had described. Directly in front of him, the texture of the chamber wall was smooth and he could clearly see the large staggered stone blocks of the fortress's foundation, whereas the surfaces of the rest of the chamber were rough, having been crudely hacked into the rock by pickaxe.

As the smith slipped the pack from his shoulders to give his muscles a rest, he realized his companions were just as pleased as he was to be out of the cramped confines of the tunnel, because Jerhal set down the spare torches he had been carrying with a relieved sigh and Erosmay suddenly leapt from Zarak's shoulder and glided down to the chamber floor.

Free of his passenger, the soldier unslung the waterskin from across his chest and passed it to his companions.

After Dare and Jerhal had each taken a couple of sips, the smith held the torch for Zarak so his friend could have his turn. And when the soldier had finished, just as Dare had seen him do many times for the horses on the journey there, Zarak poured some water into his cupped hand and held it out so the dragon could also drink.

Erosmay walked over and lapped up the water. Then, as if to thank Zarak for his thoughtfulness, the little dragon rubbed the back of the soldier's wet hand with her little scaled face.

On impulse, Zarak reached out and stroked the dragon in the same manner he would have one of his horses. And when the creature didn't bite him with her razor-sharp teeth, Dare realized she liked it.

When Zarak stood and slipped the strap of the waterskin back into position across his chest, the dragon flew to the passageway on the left, landed on one of its stone steps, and looked at the soldier as if to remind him which passage he should take.

Dare wasn't surprised when Zarak thanked Erosmay aloud, because he was used to the soldier talking to the horses. But when he saw the little creature nod her head in acknowledgement, he was momentarily taken aback, until he remembered Robin's claim the creature communicated with her and realized there really was some truth in the dragon lore he had heard.

Up until now, he had mistakenly thought of the dragon as some kind of strange pet. And, as the little creature flew back and landed upon Zarak's shoulder, the smith looked upon her with new eyes and a growing respect.

'I think the break is over fellas,' the soldier said, wearing an amused grin.

If Jerhal thought things odd, he didn't let it show. Instead, he simply agreed. 'Yes, onwards and upwards.' And with that, he reached down and picked up the spare torches he had set down upon entering the chamber.

◆◆◆

Robin had stayed in contact with Erosmay via mind-speech throughout the morning. And when her linked companion told her the men from White Cliff had reached the chambered juncture, the white-haired woman carefully concealed Lilyanna's cloak within her own before draping them over her forearm so it would appear she only carried one. Then, she picked up her trusty sewing basket, bade the princess farewell, and headed for the paneled room with the secret doorway she had told the rescue party about the evening before.

While Robin strode down the hallway to meet her new allies, King Dallin's men ascended the roughly hewn stone steps to the left of the chamber in the flickering torchlight, and then slowly proceeded along the dark passageway towards the secret doorway located on the ground level of the fortress.

When they eventually came upon the wall-mounted sconce marking the recessed entrance the white-haired woman had told them about, Jerhal and Dare silently set aside the items they were carrying and, despite the narrowness of the passage, eagerly crowded around Zarak as he lifted the torch towards the opening.

Behind the thin veil of cobwebs, they could clearly see the rectangular outline of the secret door and, about a quarter of the way down from the top, there was the plugged spyhole cleverly fashioned from a knot within the wood, exactly as Robin had described.

Zarak quickly burned the cobwebs away with the torch. Then, he placed it into the wall sconce to free his hands so he could work the plug free from the spyhole, like a stopper of a bottle, and peer through.

The meeting room was of average size and sparsely furnished. But more importantly, Robin was there to cover any noise the door might make when they opened it. And by the way she had overturned one of the chairs beside the large table her opened sewing basket was sitting upon, Zarak knew this was how she planned to do it.

As if reading his thoughts, the white-haired woman turned towards the secret entrance and smiled.

Realizing the dragon must have told Robin he was looking at her, the soldier watched as she signaled him to wait and then walked across the room to the door leading to the hallway and peered out to ensure no one was about.

After receiving the all-clear, rather than sliding the bolt to unlock the door himself, Zarak stepped aside so Jerhal could take his place. Then, he drew his battered sword alongside Dare, just in case they ran into any trouble Robin couldn't handle, and watched as the spy slowly began to free the bolt from its keep.

It made a grating sound, but the noise was not loud enough to attract anyone's attention.

After shooting his colleagues a relieved 'so far so good look', Jerhal then pushed on the door to open it, but it did not budge. So, he tried again, only this time he pushed harder using both hands. However, when the door still did not open, the spy realized the damp air from the tunnel must have warped the wood and a more forceful approach was necessary.

Jerhal shook his head resignedly and whispered, 'I'm going to try and force it.' Then after peering through the peephole once more to ensure it was still safe to continue, and despite his sore ribs, the spy put his bodyweight into it and rammed the door hard with his shoulder.

As the door swung open with a loud crash and Jerhal stumbled into the paneled room, Robin glanced back into the corridor just in time to see one of the more stringent fortress guards come tearing around the corner.

Fearing her new allies would be discovered, she spun on her heel and warned them in a hushed voice, 'Guard.'

As Robin ran to the overturned chair, Zarak grabbed Jerhal's shirt and yanked the spy back through the secret entrance.

In his rush to discover the cause of the noise, the guard failed to notice a section of paneling on the far wall stood slightly proud from the rest. He just saw the white-haired woman bending down to right the meeting room chair and assumed she had knocked it over.

Robin looked up at him and exclaimed nervously, 'It was the biggest rat I've ever seen!' And with a trembling finger, she pointed in the opposite direction of the secret entrance and added, 'I think it ran over there.'

Clearly annoyed she had wasted his time, the guard informed her, 'You'll need to tell the ratcatcher. I've more important things to do.' Then filled with disgust, he turned and strode from the room.

The white-haired woman busied herself with the contents of her swing basket until the guard's footsteps had faded away. Then once she was sure the coast was clear, Robin signaled the men to come out of hiding.

Eager to be reunited with her linked companion, Erosmay flew past the men and landed on Robin's shoulder, where she lovingly began to rub the white-haired woman's soft cheek with her scaled one.

Robin smiled and reciprocated in kind, her response so spontaneous she failed to realize how strange it must appear to others until she noticed the way her new allies were looking at her.

The white-haired woman did not lose her smile. But, she did speak aloud when she asked the dragon to watch the hallway and warn her if anyone was coming while she spoke with the men. Then as Erosmay glided from her shoulder to position herself as guard on the floor beside the door, Robin asked Jerhal in a hushed voice, 'So?'

'Our only hitch is the noise from this warped door and it's too risky to try and plane it,' the spy quietly answered.

The white-haired woman thought about it a moment, and then she suggested, 'We could use candlewax. I use it sometimes on drawer runners.'

'That just might work,' Jerhal replied as he glanced towards Zarak.

The soldier nodded his head and promptly removed a couple of candles from the small candelabrum on the table beside them.

While Zarak and Dare commenced to rub candlewax along the edges of the warped door, Robin handed Jerhal the cloaks she had brought along with a small bundle she had concealed in her sewing basket and told him, 'The rest of the things you asked for are tucked inside.'

'Excellent,' the spy replied as he accepted the offering. Then, he warned, 'When we close the door behind us, you might want to be ready with another one of those large rats of yours.'

'Fingers crossed, I won't have to,' she replied with a nervous smile.

Once the edges of the door had been waxed sufficiently, the men bade Robin farewell and the spy advised, 'Try to get some sleep. We've a long night ahead of us.'

'I'll try,' the white-haired woman replied softly as she went to relieve Erosmay as lookout. 'But, I don't think the butterflies inside me will settle.'

Although none of the men replied, they knew exactly what she meant, because each had been contending with a flutter of their own all morning.

Having missed her snack, Erosmay wasn't concerned about her companions' stomachs. She was famished and only interested in filling her own. So when she heard Robin planned to take a nap, the dragon decided to stay with the men and flew over to the tunnel to join them.

Knowing Erosmay as well as she did, Robin realized her linked companion must be ravenous by now, so she wished the dragon good hunting in mind-speech and then signaled the men it was alright to close the secret door.

Unsure if the candlewax had remedied the problem, the white-haired woman stood guard with her heart in her mouth watching the corridor for anyone who might come to investigate if it hadn't. But, luck was on their side. And although she could hear the sound of the warped door being closed behind her, it wasn't loud enough to attract anyone's attention.

Once Zarak had relocked the door and plugged the spyhole, Robin walked over to the nearest chair and sat down wearily, totally drained and wondering if it was possible for her hair to have turned even whiter than it already was.

The men from White Cliff had no time for such luxury. Instead, they swiftly stuffed the cloaks into their pack, swapped the burning torch in the sconce with a spare unlit one in preparation for the evening, and began to retrace their steps back down the dark passageway.

As they headed towards the chambered juncture in the flickering torchlight, Dare realized he felt more at ease. Whether this was because he was familiar with the route and knew what to expect or because the moment of danger had passed, the smith could not say. But in either case, he was pleased they had achieved what they had set out to do and were leaving the ancient tunnel system.

Because this leg of their journey was relatively short, in next to no time the men found themselves descending the cut-stone steps back into the small chamber they had decided to use as a staging area.

During the course of the morning, the three men had travelled in silence lest someone hear and discover their whereabouts. But now they had seen how far the chamber was from the paneled room, they knew they could talk without fear of detection. So, as Jerhal unrolled the small bundle Robin had given him, the spy casually told his companions, 'If I had any doubts about Robin before, I sure don't now.'

'Me either,' Zarak agreed. 'She's true to her word and calm under pressure.' Then, he added with a chuckle, 'You should have seen the look on the guard's face when she told him about the rat.'

'What rat?' Dare asked, because he had been standing too far away from the secret door to hear anything that had transpired within the paneled room.

Happy to oblige, Zarak explained how Robin had tricked the guard into thinking she had been so frightened by a rat she had knocked over a chair in her panic to get away from it. And then totally out of character, the soldier ended his tale by mimicking the guard, 'You'll need to tell the ratcatcher. I've more important things to do.'

'Cleaver woman,' Dare laughed appreciatively as he set down the cloaks he had just removed from his pack.

'Yes,' Jerhal agreed, as he reached over and handed the smith the packet of assorted needles from the center of the cloth bundle. 'And from what I've heard, she's had to live by her wits for quite some time now.'

Dare accepted the packet but did not ask Jerhal what he meant, because he had travelled with the spy long enough to know, despite his occupation, Jerhal still respected a person's right to privacy and, if Robin wanted anyone to know her story, he thought she should be the one to tell it.

As the smith stuffed the packet of needles into his pack and Jerhal started to tear one of the two pillowcases which had made up the rest of the small bundle into long strips, the torch Zarak was holding began to waver.

The soldier quickly grabbed one of the spare torches and held it to the dwindling flame. There was a couple of sputtering pops as the cooking grease ignited, then the cloth binding at the top of the torch caught fire.

With their lighting renewed, Jerhal wound the long strips of cloth into bandage-like rolls so they would be easier to use later. Then, he walked over and placed them with the other pillowcase on top of the cloaks Dare had set down.

Because it was difficult to fly within the confines of the tunnel, when the preparations for this stage of the mission were complete, Erosmay retook her place upon Zarak's broad shoulder and the rescuers resumed their trek back to the barred entrance.

By now, the little dragon was so hungry she felt sure her ribs were showing. And despite her resolution to stay with her new allies until they were safely out of the tunnel, when Erosmay finally saw the first pinhole of daylight streaming into the passageway, she leapt from Zarak's shoulder and flew directly towards it.

Her response was so impulsive, Erosmay did not realize what she had done until it was too late and she found herself outside the tunnel. So to rectify her mistake, the famished dragon flew around the surrounding area to ensure there were no nasty surprises awaiting the men.

It did not take her long to fly the circuit. And because she had not seen anyone suspicious lurking about, when Erosmay spotted a young squirrel scurrying amongst the undergrowth, she decided to take advantage of the opportunity.

Tucking in her leathery wings, the dragon darted downwards arrow fast. Then just before she reached the ground, she spread her wings, stopping her freefall, and seized the squirrel with her sharp claws, ending the hunt nearly as soon as it had started with her quarry oblivious to the danger.

Never eaten a squirrel before, the hungry dragon flew over and perched herself upon the same sturdy branch she had occupied earlier that morning near the tunnel entrance. And filled with mouthwatering expectation, Erosmay then took her first succulent bite.

To her dismay, however, she swiftly discovered squirrel tasted just like rodent, and she had grown tired of rodent ages ago. But, Erosmay was hungry. So, she gobbled it down anyway and, by the time the men began to emerge from the tunnel, the only evidence she had eaten a snack was a small tuft of red fur at the corner of her mouth.

'That was sure easier than I thought it was going to be,' Dare remarked in a hushed voice as he followed Zarak out of the narrow passageway.

'Yes, it was,' the soldier agreed as he removed the stopper from his waterskin and doused the flame of the torch. 'Now, all we need to do before nightfall is buy a horse for Robin and some rope.'

'I think we should buy a padlock and chain too,' Jerhal added mischievously as he placed the last spare torch within easy reach of the tunnel entrance and pulled the barred door closed.

Dare and Zarak laughed in appreciation, knowing how frustrating it would be for a pursuer to suddenly find his way barred and having to retrace his steps.

'But first, let's get something to eat,' the spy continued as he tossed some of the vegetation they had chopped down earlier in front of the entrance to screen it from view. 'My head's beginning to think my belly's got a hole in it.'

Of this, Erosmay fully agreed. Because even though she had just eaten a squirrel, the growing dragon could always find room for a little more.

18 RESCUE

Under the pretext of bringing Lilyanna her midday meal, Robin had informed the princess King Dallin's men planned to implement their rescue plan that evening. Then after delivering the message, the white-haired woman had returned to her own small chamber to take the nap Jerhal had suggested. But with thoughts of escape swirling in her mind, sleep never came, so she finally gave up the idea and got up.

Glancing around her sparsely furnished room, Robin's eyes came to rest on the sewing basket she had been given during her apprenticeship with the fortress dressmaker. Having used it nearly every day since then, Robin realized it was the only thing in the entire fortress she would actually regret leaving behind.

On impulse, the white-haired woman picked the basket up and carried it over to the bed where she sat down on the thin straw-filled mattress and lifted the basket's lid for a nostalgic look inside.

Seeing her wooden thimble, its grain now darkened with age and dotted with needle pricks, Robin placed it on her finger and smiled sadly, recalling how Allyce and the other women at Greystone Fortress used to jest lightheartedly that she wielded her needle like a wizard waved his wand, working magic on whatever she sewed. But then, those were happier times, before her friend had been murdered and women had shunned her.

Knowing there was nothing but heartache in store for her and Erosmay if they stayed, Robin returned the thimble to the sewing basket, closed the lid, and set the basket on the floor beside the faded dress she had stripped off before lying down to take her nap.

Feeling the cold, the white-haired woman shivered and then carefully lifted the only other dress she owned from the wooden chest she used to store her few possessions in. It was her best dress, the one she wore in the evenings when she attended the princess at dinner.

She slipped the dress on over her shift and smiled as she began to do up the lacing, pleased things had worked out differently than she had originally planned. Because now, instead of making her escape on foot disguised as a dark-haired orphan boy donned in castoffs, she was going to ride away on horseback, with her hair uncut, and wearing her best dress.

Once the lacing was done, the white-haired woman sat back down on the bed and looked inside her right shoe to ensure the map Lilyanna had smuggled off the Venture was still safely hidden inside. Then, she slipped her shoes onto her stocking-bare feet.

As she began to replait her pillow-ruffled hair, Robin realized Erosmay must think her still asleep, so she contacted her linked companion via mind-speech and asked the dragon what she was doing.

'Having a snack,' came Erosmay's prompt reply, which the white-haired woman had come to know really meant the dragon was gorging herself on some unfortunate creature. And, even though Robin thought she already knew the answer to her next question, she asked anyway, 'Will you be returning to the fortress soon?'

'No. I'm going to stay here for a while,' the dragon answered matter-of-factly.

The white-haired woman understood. Normally Erosmay had to sneak around the fortress during the day so as not to be seen. But outside the ramparts, the inquisitive little dragon could enjoy herself unconstrainedly. 'Alright then, I'm on my way to the east wing, so I'll talk to you later.'

'Yes. Later,' Erosmay agreed before bluntly breaking contact, which lead Robin to suspect another poor animal was about to meet its doom.

Their conversation ended, Robin took one last look around the small room which, up until meeting Erosmay a few months ago, she had thought she would spend the rest of her nights in. Then, with no idea of what the future held for herself or her linked companion, she stepped out into the corridor and closed the door.

Feeling emboldened, the white-haired woman bravely headed towards the east wing and her uncertain destiny. When she encountered a servant or passed one of Elrod's men, Robin self-consciously wondered if they could sense the change in her. But she quickly realized there was no need to worry, they were used to shunning her, and when they saw her this is exactly what they did.

By the time she finally reached Lilyanna's apartment, however, Robin's newfound confidence had begun to wane and her heart was pounding so hard she was certain the guard at the door would hear its loud thumping and question her. But accustomed to the white-haired woman's comings and goings, he allowed her admittance without challenge.

Robin managed to maintain her composure until the door had been closed behind her. Then, because her legs were trembling so badly, she leaned against it for support.

Seeing this, Lilyanna ran to her friend's aid and helped Robin to the nearest chair. 'Are you alright?'

'Yes,' the white-haired woman answered shakily. 'But, I'll be glad when this is all over.'

'Me too,' Lilyanna agreed reassuringly.

Although the princess had conducted herself with dignity, never once voicing her fears, Robin knew Lilyanna was just as scared as she was. So, she reached out and hugged the princess like a sister, the first human embrace she had shared since the passing of Allyce.

◆◆◆

While Erosmay spent the remainder of the afternoon enjoying her freedom outside the ramparts and the women whiled away time until they were summoned to the Great Hall for supper, the three White Cliff men finished their rescue preparations and returned to Far View Inn to rest and share a much earlier evening meal of their own.

Having frequently accommodated the man he knew as Sebastian over the past two years, the innkeeper was more than happy to serve Jerhal and his companions the early meal they had requested, because he knew he would be well compensated for his trouble. And, aware this was the last proper spread they would share until they were safely out of Elrod's domain, the men took their time eating it.

When they finally wiped their plates clean and pushed their chairs away from the table, Jerhal sang the cook's praises to the innkeeper just as he always did. Then, much to the man's delight, the spy settled their account handsomely in advance while explaining they had an early start the following morning and would not require his services further.

As the innkeeper began to clear their table, the men from White Cliff returned to their lodgings to collect their things. And with no intention of returning, even though Jerhal had told the innkeeper otherwise, the rescuers slipped quietly out of the inn.

Swim Tail heard their approach long before they reached the stables and nickered, as if in greeting, when they stepped through the entrance of the small building.

Dare fondly wished he had an apple to give the trusty shaggy-haired horse who, after surviving the shipwreck, had carried him safely through the Dread Wood. But, he didn't, so he walked over and stroked the Greystone Steed affectionately on the neck instead.

When Swim Tail nickered again, it was a slightly different sound. And as odd as it seemed, Dare got the impression the horse was trying to talk to him. Amused, the smith stroked the horse's neck a few more times, and then gently slipped the bridle on over the animal's head.

With the assistance of the groom, all five horses were saddled in no time. Then after the supplies had been loaded, Zarak took point and lead his companions, each with a spare mount in tow, out of the stables.

Riding in single file, the small rescue party wound their way downwards through the cobbled streets within the defensive towering walls of the fortress's middle bailey. Their progress was steady and, for the most part, unhindered by other travelers because of the late hour.

Bringing up the rear, Dare fastened the top button of his new jacket with his rein-free hand to keep out the cold draft which was beginning to settle in his bones.

Realizing he was trailing farther behind his colleagues, the smith urged Swim Tail forward to make up the distance. And in so doing, the horse he was leading received an unexpected tug on its guide rope, forcing it to increase its pace as well.

By now Dare was familiar with the way, having already travelled the route twice that day. So when they reached the heavy doors at the gateway to the outermost bailey, he knew to prepare himself for the muddy squalor inside.

Each time he travelled through this rundown area, he felt a pang of sorrow for the people living and working there. The further they rode from the actual fortress, the poorer and hungrier the inhabitants of Greystone appeared. And not for the first time, Dare realized how fortunate he was to have been raised in White Cliff.

When the twin towers of the barbican finally came into view, the smith knew they were nearing the outer wall. The guards positioned there had only stopped him and his companions twice. And on both occasions, it had been when they were entering the fortress, not leaving it. So, he suspected they would pass unchallenged this time too.

When the three riders eventually reached the fortified gateway, the guards were more interested in warming themselves beside the braziers, so the rescue party rode quietly past them. But instead of turning left and following the major road downward towards the coast, the White Cliff men guided their horses to the right and took the less used trail up the mountain slope.

Skirting the rampart wall, the rescue party slowly zigzagged their way ever higher along the winding trail until they were out of view from below. Then, they dismounted and cautiously led their horses off the trail across the rough terrain to the large fissure in the mountainside they had discovered while exploring the area.

Although the location was not ideal, because it was a fair distance from the tunnel entrance, the fissure was large enough to hide all five horses from anyone using the trail without the need to guard them. So after they had picketed the horses, the trio commenced to make their way in the fading light to the mouth of the tunnel by foot.

Even though she could hear the men approach from a long way off, having been a greedy gut that afternoon, Erosmay decided it was an unnecessary waste of energy to fly out to meet her new allies and elected instead to doze on her perch near the tunnel entrance to allow a little more time for her food to digest.

By the time the men finally arrived, the dragon's belly felt a bit better. So, she spread her leathery wings and glided down from the sapling she had been resting on and greeted them.

Once the formalities were over, Zarak and Dare walked over and began to remove the vegetation screening the tunnel entrance while Jerhal slipped off the heavy pack he had insisted on carrying, fished out the padlock and chain they had purchased earlier in the day, and placed them conveniently outside the entrance. Then when they were ready to proceed, the soldier swung open the barred door, stepped inside the narrow passageway and, striking steel to flint, lit the torch they had previously positioned there.

Seeing her allies were about to enter the tunnel, Erosmay flew over and unashamedly landed upon Zarak's broad shoulder, fully expecting the soldier to carry her just as he had before.

Noticing the marked increase in his passenger's weight since the morning, Zarak glanced towards Erosmay and, seeing her bulging belly, wondered how she had managed to get off the ground. But, he liked the little creature and did not want to offend her. So, he simply asked, 'Are you ready?'

As Erosmay nodded in reply, his companions answered 'Yes' in unison, mistakenly assuming Zarak had been talking to them. Then, the soldier commenced to confidently lead them down the narrow passageway.

Having already made their way through the tunnel system twice that day, their pace was much faster than before and they soon reached the place where the animal bones lay strewn across the tunnel floor.

Still suffering with indigestion, Erosmay was not the least bit tempted when she heard the sound of bones snapping beneath the men's booted feet. But to pass the time and take her mind off her discomfort, she contacted Robin via mind-speech and asked the white-haired woman what she was doing.

'We're on our way to the Great Hall.'

Sensing the stress within her linked companion's reply, the dragon immediately tried to reassure her, 'Be brave. After tonight we will be free of this place.'

'I sure hope so,' agreed Robin, feeling a little more at ease.

'Just remember to breath and act normal.'

'I'll try,' Robin replied, glad for her linked companion's support. 'We're nearly there, so hopefully I'll see you soon.'

'Yes, soon,' Erosmay repeated as their telepathic conversation came to an end.

While the rescue team continued to the chambered juncture, Robin and Lilyanna, along with the guard escorting them, entered the Great Hall. As usual, they were among the last to arrive but, having grown accustomed to their presence, the other diners no longer stared and whispered amongst themselves when they stepped into the room.

Armed with the knowledge this was the last meal they would share with Elrod, the two women obediently followed the guard to their accustomed table and seated themselves. Then, duty done, the guard left to enjoy a meal of his own.

Outside of Lilyanna's chambers, neither Robin nor the princess spoke unless they were addressed by someone else. Initially, this was because they did not want anyone to suspect they had formed a friendship. And now, with so much at stake, they did not want to draw needless attention to themselves. So, trying to appear calm, they sat and quietly listened to the buzz of soft voices around them.

When the room fell silent, the two women knew without looking Elrod had arrived, and they stood just like everyone else until he had taken his place at the center of the high table.

The evening then commenced with the serving of wine and the nobles vying for Elrod's favor by lifting their glasses to him in toasts and tossing compliments his way like he was the grand prize at a ring toss. And even though everyone, with the exception of Robin and Princess Lilyanna, tried to pretend otherwise, the atmosphere in the room never recovered after his arrival.

The two women watched the proceedings with detached interest, silently biding time and sipping their wine sparingly.

When the first course was served, Robin and Lilyanna forced themselves to eat even though they had little appetite, knowing they would need their strength later to escape.

For Robin, the meal seemed to pass much more slowly than usual. And by the time the last course was finally served, she could sense the uneasy tension in the air that habitually came at the end of the evening meal, when Elrod liked to amuse himself with a twisted little game of give and take where, seemingly at random, he would call someone forth for sport and either reward or, more often than not, cruelly debase them depending upon which way his mood took him.

She found herself remembering one particular evening, not long ago, when Elrod had summoned Lilyanna and complimented the princess on how she had worn her hair. Then in the very next breath and for no other reason than to see the look on her face, he had offhandedly informed Lilyanna her brother had not died from illness like everyone thought, but from an undetectable poison he had acquired especially for the occasion.

The white-haired woman suppressed a shudder and, not for the first time, wondered if Elrod had tortured small animals as a child simply to watch them suffer.

Assuming this evening would be no different, Lilyanna would eventually receive Elrod's attentions. And even though the thought was sickening, both women knew they would not be allowed to leave the room until after the princess had played her part in Elrod's sadistic game.

It was because of this, Lilyanna found herself strangely looking forward to the moment and Robin felt a guilty relief when the Black Hawk finally beckoned her friend forth with a wave of his bejeweled hand.

With all eyes upon her, Lilyanna delicately dabbed the corners of her mouth with her napkin. Then after setting the cloth aside, she rose with dignity from her chair while Robin contacted Erosmay via mind-speech to ready the men, and strode regally to the high table where she curtsied, albeit ever so slightly, before him.

Although Elrod had watched the princess approach with a predatory gaze, when he spoke to her it was with the honeyed tone of a lover. 'Good evening my pet,' something he had taken to calling her ever since she had defiantly told him only pets wore collars. 'I've decided to end your suspense and grant you the marriage of state you wanted, with one exception.' He paused, searching her face for a reaction. But seeing none, he continued, 'I'll be the groom.'

Even though Lilyanna had steeled herself, she could not hide the revulsion reflected in her eyes.

When the Black Hawk noticed this, the corner of his mouth lifted in pleasure and he purred just as honey toned as before, 'I see the thought of our coupling excites you too.'

Earlier in the day, Lilyanna had worried the knowledge she was about to escape might make her appear overconfident. But now, knowing he intended to force himself upon her, Lilyanna realized she need not to have worried. She was horrified and he knew new it. So, she fought back with the only weapon she had, her tongue, and vehemently replied, 'You disgust me.'

Elrod laughed, amused by her obvious revulsion. 'I was hoping you'd say something like that. I do so enjoy a challenge.' Then, he leaned towards her and added softly, 'And rest assured my pet, I won't disappoint. You'll soon find I have ways to make you moan you haven't even dreamed of.'

Lilyanna's throat suddenly felt very dry. And, as she tried to swallow, Elrod gave her another smile which held no warmth and said, 'Now, you had best get some rest. You've a busy day ahead of you tomorrow, trying to satisfy me while producing my heir.'

Unable to stomach his presence any longer, Lilyanna turned and headed straight for the door at the opposite end of the hall while Elrod and his cronies laughed dirtily and Robin, who had been providing Erosmay with a running commentary, hurried to catch up with her.

◆◆◆

Receiving the signal from Erosmay, Zarak nodded to his companions and whispered. 'It's time. And if we do this right, we won't even bloody our swords.' Then without waiting for a response, he slowly opened the secret door and stepped into the paneled room.

With the others following closely behind, the soldier carefully crept across the dark room towards the sliver of light shining through the narrow gap of the partially opened door and peered out into the corridor.

As the women strode into view, Zarak heard Robin ask Lilyanna if she was alright, but the princess did not answer until they had reached the doorway of the paneled room. Then, she stopped in such a way her escort was left standing with his back towards the door and said, 'Just give me a moment.'

Zarak opened the door lightning fast and grabbed the unsuspecting guard from behind, covering his victim's mouth with one hand and holding a knife to the man's throat with the other. Then, he warned menacingly, 'Do as I say or I'll slit your throat.'

Caught by surprise, the guard was unaware Zarak's bark was worse than his bite and that the soldier preferred to kill only if someone was trying to kill him first. All he knew was he had a knife pressed against his jugular and, if he wanted to keep on breathing, he had better do as his captor demanded. So when Zarak ordered him to back into the paneled room, he did as he was told.

Within a few heartbeats the corridor was deserted once more and the guard, never once seeing his captors, sat bound to one of the chairs in the meeting room trussed up like a goose on Feast Day, blindfolded, hooded, and gagged with the pillowcases Robin had supplied.

Whilst Jerhal commenced to lead the women through the secret entrance into the narrow tunnel and Dare followed as rearguard, Zarak incapacitated his captive with a well-aimed blow so the man would be unable to hear their movements and report them to Elrod. Then, he quickly re-bolted the paneled door and plugged the spyhole before hurrying to catch up with the others in the vanishing torchlight.

Still reeling from her encounter with Elrod, Lilyanna felt weak at the knees and forced herself onwards, blindly trusting her father's men.

In an effort to cover as much ground as possible before the princess's escape was discovered, Jerhal lead the party swiftly down the ancient tunnel while Erosmay, able to see in the dark, darted ahead, the tips of her outstretched wings narrowly missing the tunnel walls.

When the small group reached the chambered juncture, they only stopped long enough for the ladies to don their cloaks and catch their breath. Then, they set off again, but it was all the time Lilyanna needed to compose herself.

Jerhal continued to set a fast pace even though it was difficult to watch their footing in the flickering torchlight. From time to time he would hear someone behind him let out a painful gasp, and he knew without looking one of his companions had stumbled upon the uneven tunnel floor.

Without any obvious landmarks it was difficult for the spy to accurately judge the distance they had travelled within the tunnel. All he had to go by was his gut instinct, and it told him they had long since past the halfway point.

The dragon flew ahead of him. And every once in a while, on the fringe of the flickering torchlight, he would catch a glimpse of her iridescent scales as they shifted in color from sage green to copper. Then with a powerful beat of her wings, she would disappear into the darkness.

When Jerhal suddenly felt a bone crunch beneath his foot, he realized they were much closer to the tunnel entrance than he had thought. However, as he turned to tell the others the good news, the torch he was holding started to sputter as the last of its cloth binding burned away.

The spy quickly spun on his heel and thrust the nearly spent torch into Lilyanna's hands. Then, he stripped off his jacket so he could use the shirt underneath to refuel the torch. But before he could slip the garment over his head, there was a burst of light from further up the tunnel.

Surprised, he and his companions looked towards the source. And by the last dim flicker of their torch, they saw the dragon exhale a second small jet of fire.

Robin was more stunned than the others. Having known Erosmay since the day of her hatching, never once had she seen the dragon breathe fire. But, this was not the time for questions. And when Jerhal ordered them to place one hand on the shoulder of the person in front of them, she complied. Then, guided by short bursts of dragon fire, the small party walked as a human chain the rest of the way to the mouth of the tunnel.

While Jerhal padlocked the barred door, Robin seized the moment to speak with her linked companion. 'You never told me you could breathe fire.'

'Never needed to,' Erosmay replied matter-of-factly. 'Besides, it's not polite to smoke indoors.'

'What?' Robin asked in mind-speech, so shocked she nearly bumped into Lilyanna as the small group started to pick their way across the rough terrain in the darkness. Then, realizing this was something the dragon must have overheard, she asked Erosmay, 'Is this something you watched and learned?'

'Yes. Cook said so.'

Despite the circumstances, Robin suddenly found herself struggling not to laugh. 'Cook's husband smokes a pipe. I think she must've been talking about that.'

Although the white-haired woman had tried repeatedly to explain the varying shades of grey concept to Erosmay, the dragon would have none of it. To her everything was either black or white, and she answered flatty, 'Smoke is smoke.'

Knowing she was fighting a losing battle, Robin was wise enough not to reply. Instead, she simply pulled the hood of her cloak a little further over her head and concentrated on her footing.

Having previously viewed the area through the barred door of the tunnel entrance, she had known the landscape was treacherous. Yet even so, Robin never imagined just how difficult it would be to travel across the jagged rock and the straggly vegetation in the dark, with unseen branches snagging her clothing and slapping her stingingly across the face.

In her haste, she slipped and grazed her knee. But knowing a bloody knee would be the least of her worries if Elrod's men caught them, the white-haired woman picked herself up and hurried to keep up with the others.

From somewhere up ahead, Robin thought she heard the nicker of a horse. But, she was too busy scrambling down the rocky slope in the drizzle and the darkness to think about it further and failed to notice the large V-shaped formation their mounts were tethered in until she reached the base of the incline and had a chance to glance around.

In spite of the lack of light, Robin instantly recognized three of the horses were Greystone Steeds, the sure-footed breed native to the area. And although she did not know much about horses, she did think their stocky frames were better suited for the harsh environment than the other two horses picketed with them.

Having planned the escape to the last detail, the men from White Cliff quickly lead the horses out of the crevice. Then, with Jerhal taking point followed by Lilyanna and then Dare, Robin found herself next in line.

Fearing the men might not take her if they discovered she didn't know how to ride a horse, the white-haired woman had deliberately not told them. It never occurred to her the men had assumed this all along. So, when she reached to take the reins of her mount from Zarak and he said, 'She's gentle. Just follow the others and Dare will show you what to do once you reach the trail.' Robin was so surprised, she just mumbled thank you and quickly led the horse away.

The soldier watched her just long enough to ensure she had control of the animal; a sturdy mare with an even temperament named Misty. Then, he coiled the picket rope, stuffed it into his saddlebag, and lead his own mount from the fissure.

He could vaguely see Robin and her Greystone Steed, like ghostly apparitions up ahead in the drizzly darkness. There was no sign of the woman's linked companion, but the soldier knew the little dragon would be flying nearby.

By the time he reached the trail, Dare had already helped Robin onto her horse and was explaining the rudiments of horseback riding to her. So, all Zarak had to do was step into his stirrup, grateful to take the load off his stone-bruised feet and let his mount do the walking while they cautiously zigzagged their way down the steep trail towards the main road.

Robin had been a little tense at first. But, their slow pace gave her the opportunity to get the feel of her horse. And after a while, she began to relax and loosened her white-knuckled grip on the reins.

The downwards trek towards the barbican was uneventful. At times the riders would catch an occasional glimpse of light shining through the structure's arrowslits or the braziers positioned at its arched gateway. Then, the trail would bend and the light would disappear from view until the winding track switchbacked again.

When they finally reached the bottom of the steep slope, the small party quietly continued to follow the narrow track alongside the fortress's outermost wall, steadily heading towards the main road which converged with the trail just in front of the barbican's heavy gates.

Having worked his way through the ranks and pulled more stints of guard duty than he cared to remember, Zarak wasn't surprised to find the stronghold appeared to be deserted, because anyone with a lick of common sense would have sought refuge from the bad weather.

It was not until the riders actually drew near to the barbican's entrance, two of the unfortunate guards emerged from the shelter of its arched gateway. But then, when they saw the riders were only passing by the stronghold, they quickly disappeared back to the warmth of their abandoned brazier.

From his position at the back of the small column, Zarak didn't see the rain-soaked horseman with the unruly mop of red hair approaching from the main road. However, Lilyanna did and reached up to pull the hood of her wet cloak further over her face so Scary Hairy wouldn't recognize her.

The tactic might have worked had her former kidnapper not ridden close enough by then to spot her signet ring. Then when he did, he grabbed hold of her horse by one of its reins and pulled the animal to a halt.

Realizing the princess was in danger, Jerhal turned his mount sharply while Dare spurred his horse between Lilyanna's and her accoster's. And for one tense moment, the smith nearly drew his sword. But then, the red-haired man laughed and told Lilyanna, 'I thought I recognized the ring. But until I'm ordered to hunt you down, I won't. And hopefully by then, I'll be so drunk I will have forgotten I've ever seen you.'

Flooded with relief, the princess smiled and thanked him. 'You're a good man.'

'Don't say that,' Scary Hairy chided. 'Someone might hear, and then my reputation will be ruined.' Then, he gave his horse a nudge with the heels of his boots and rode on.

Pleased her charm offensive had worked, Lilyanna breathed a sigh of relief. Then, when she glanced over to Jerhal and saw his questioning look, she answered. 'We shared a drink on the way here.'

19 DREAM WOOD

The princess's escape went unnoticed until changeover early the following morning when her guard's replacement arrived at the east wing apartment and discovered it deserted. A thorough search of the fortress then ensued and the missing guard was eventually found trussed up in the meeting room near the Great Hall with a large egg-sized lump on his head.

Even though the men from White Cliff had gone out of their way not to kill the man, the soldier's life had been forfeited the moment Zarak held his knife to the man's throat. Because, when the unfortunate guard was brought before Elrod for questioning and found unable to provide any useful information, the royal usurper was infuriated.

As the panicked guard finished repeating his account of events for a second time, Elrod casually pulled his dagger from its sheath and commented, 'They did overlook one thing. When you hold a knife to someone's throat, you finish the job.' Then, like a hot knife through butter, he slit the man's throat from ear to ear.

The helpless guard raised his hands to staunch the pulsating flow, but his efforts were futile. And, as the blood gushed between his fingers, he dropped to the floor like a stone.

Stunned, the others stood unmoving and watched in horror as Elrod callously wiped his blade clean on the dying guard's uniform while the man bleed out at his feet.

As he returned his dagger to its sheath, Elrod ordered, 'See if the white-haired witch fled with the princess and release the birds accordingly.' Then, as his men turned to obey, the Black Hawk added, 'And get rid of this incompetent fool, he's staining the carpet.'

After witnessing Elrod's displeasure, the soldiers did not need to be told twice. Two of the men immediately lifted their fallen comrade and carried him away while the others began the search for Robin.

◆◆◆

Travelling steadily down the mountainside throughout the night with her allies, Erosmay was enjoying her newfound freedom, either darting about energetically or, when she grew tired, napping comfortably behind Robin on the back of the white-haired woman's Greystone Steed.

With the coming of the sun, her human counterparts were able to see the road more clearly and increase their pace, pushing on until late morning when they and their bone-weary horses were eventually forced to stop and rest.

Erosmay, on the other hand, was not tired in the least. Refreshed from her napping, the dragon wanted to continue the greatest adventure of her short life and enthusiastically informed Robin she was going to fly back to see if any soldiers were in pursuit.

Unable to tell if Erosmay was actually looking forward to the prospect, Robin wearily told her to go ahead in mind-speech, which was all the little dragon needed to hear and she immediately spread her leathery wings and took flight.

'Where's she off to in such a hurry?' Zarak asked Robin as he strode up beside her.

'Erosmay wants to see if any soldiers are pursuing us yet.'

'That's a good idea. I hadn't thought to use the dragon as a scout. Can you tell her to let us know if she sees anyone?'

'Sure,' Robin replied, pleased she and her linked companion were able to contribute.

While the rescue party commenced to water their horses and bed down behind the screening of nearby trees, Erosmay winged her way back towards the fortress, observing the road from high above yet flying a more direct route than she had earlier.

The further she flew, however, her enthusiasm began to wane as her hunger grew. So much so, she started to pay less attention to the road below and more to the rumblings of her empty stomach.

Fortunately, just when Erosmay thought she might be too weak to return to the makeshift camp, she saw four pigeons flying straight towards her. Using her successful and finely-honed hunting technique, she immediately darted higher into the air and hovered in wait until her unsuspecting quarry had flown past. Then, she tucked in her wings and dived directly towards the straggler of the bunch whose soft feathers and small beak were no match for the dragon's strong talons and razor-sharp teeth.

Unaware one of their number had just become dragon fodder, the small flock flew on whilst Erosmay landed with her prey.

The famished dragon was just about to take her first mouthwatering bite when she noticed a metal ring fastened around one of the pigeon's legs and realized it must be one of the fortress messenger birds. So, out of love for Robin, she forced her hunger aside and took to the air once more.

Approaching from behind, the dragon commenced to methodically dispatch the other three birds one by one. Then famished from her exertions, Erosmay landed and ate all but the banded leg of her last kill, which she intended to show Robin once her linked companion woke up. However, when she returned to the spot where her human companions were resting, Zarak, who was standing watch, saw her and quietly greeted, 'Hello little friend. What have you got there?'

Having established a rapport with the soldier, Erosmay landed gently on the ground in front of him and placed the severed leg at the soldier's booted feet. Then, she tilted her little head to one side and looked up at him to observe his reaction.

Seeing there was a message affixed to the band, Zarak picked up the small leg and slipped the narrow strip of paper from its tube. Then knowing how peckish Erosmay always was, he returned the leg to her, a gesture she deemed particularly thoughtful.

Normally, Erosmay would never have dreamed of communicating with anyone besides Robin. But these were special circumstances and, because the soldier treated her with respect, when he asked her how many birds there were, she lifted her clawed foot and scratched four lines in the soil with her talons.

'I see,' Zarak said with concern. 'Did any of them get away?'

Erosmay shook her head no and then, since there were limits to how much a respectable dragon should associate with anyone other than their linked companion, extricated herself by flying over to where Robin was sleeping.

The wind gradually changed direction while the rescue party rested. And by the time the horses were refreshed enough to continue, the clouds had broken and the seemingly endless drizzle had ceased.

While Zarak distributed rations they could eat as they rode, he enthusiastically told the others about the messenger birds Erosmay had intercepted, and Robin could not decide who was more proud: the dragon, the soldier, or herself. The thought her linked companion had communicated with Zarak never even crossed her mind.

To provide the soldier an opportunity to rest, even if it was only dozing in the saddle, Dare swapped places with him at the back of their group, serving as rearguard in the soldier's stead.

As the smith's clothes began to dry and the cold slowly melted from his body, Dare's mind drifted back to the time Zarak had told him a smart swordsman tried not to bloody his blade. He hadn't appreciated what the soldier had meant back then. But, he had grown up a lot since leaving White Cliff, and now understood it was better to avoid a fight rather than be in one. And with the dragon's aid, the rescue party could hide from patrols they might otherwise have encountered, thus preventing unnecessary injury while simultaneously improving their chances for success.

Electing not to take the same route back, the rescuers had deliberately passed the first left turning where the road skirted the outer edge of the Dread Wood. Then unfamiliar with the area, when they eventually came upon the second small turning, the riders halted their horses to discuss whether or not they should take it.

Common sense dictated it would be safer for them to leave the main road. But, not knowing where this less travelled road lead, both Jerhal and Zarak were hesitant to take it for fear they would lose valuable time and end up in the middle of nowhere.

Aware she still had the map Lilyanna had given her for safekeeping, Robin quickly slipped off her shoe and held forth the folded piece of paper. 'Here, this might help.'

When they unfolded the paper and saw what it was, they were astonished, because this wasn't just a map. It was a map so detailed even the small left-hand juncture they were stopped at was clearly depicted upon it. And on closer inspection, they discovered the road lead towards the area of coastline where they had originally planned to drop anchor at the beginning of their mission.

The fact the road bordered the Dream Wood, once part of a much larger ancient forest called the Drea Wood before it was split in half during the War of Magic, was something they took in their stride, since they had been prepared to travel alongside it at outset of their journey anyway. So decision made, they returned the map to Robin and took the rutted left-hand turning off the main road.

Having experienced the Dread Wood first-hand, Dare had no idea why the forest on this side of the Great Rift was called the Dream Wood. However, he was certain he would have preferred to stay on the main road and take his chances. But, being the youngest member of the rescue party, he bit his tongue and kept his opinion to himself.

It was dusk when they stopped for the night. Erosmay flew one final sweep of the area and then, once she had made certain there was no one about, Jerhal and Zarak began to erect a simple shelter from the low-hanging branches of nearby trees while Dare looked after the horses.

After the smith had finished his task, he walked over to Lilyanna to ask if he could examine the locking mechanism on the collar she wore. And when she glanced up at him, he was startled to see the look of fear reflected in her eyes. She had been so quiet, it had not occurred to him she was terrified, and he regretted he had been too tired to notice earlier.

Robin observed the exchange and wasn't surprised by the smith's stunned reaction. She knew the look all too well, having seen it two years before in the eyes of Allyce. And because of this, she had feared for Lilyanna ever since the evening she had seen the collar locked around the princess's neck.

'Can I do anything to help?' Robin asked, trying to keep her voice even. Since learning Dare was a picklock, she had clung to the hope he would be able to remove the golden collar. But now the moment had arrived, she was suddenly afraid the poisonous creatures within the open-backed gems might awaken and frenziedly attack her friend.

'Yes,' Dare answered. 'Could you face the princess and hold the collar so it won't shift while I work?'

'Of course,' Robin replied as she moved to take up position. After withdrawing the small packet of assorted needles from his pocket, Dare examined the clasp at the back of the collar carefully, and then gently slid its little cover aside to expose the tiny keyhole hidden beneath.

Realizing she was holding her breath, Robin forced herself to breath and gave Lilyanna a smile of encouragement. But when the princess smiled back, the white-haired woman could tell something was terribly wrong.

Oblivious to the exchange, Dare selected one of the needles from the pack and began to blunt its sharp tip on a nearby stone.

'I don't feel right,' Lilyanna confided to Robin in a hushed voice, not realizing the collar's serpentlike creatures had woken and numbed her skin with toxin while they slowly burrowed into her flesh.

Despite her growing concern, Robin encouraged cheerfully, 'Let Dare see if he can open the lock, then you can rest.'

Using the blunted needle as a picklock, the smith inserted its tip into the keyhole and quickly discovered that the wizard, who had gone to such great lengths to create the enchanted collar, had fitted it with a very simple locking mechanism. He turned the pick to the left, pressed it in a little deeper, and then turned it to the right. And with a barely audible click, the tiny lock snapped open.

Dare grinned triumphantly over Lilyanna's shoulder and announced, 'That was easier than I thought it was going to be.'

'It's done?' Robin asked, unable to believe her ears.

Still grinning, Dare nodded his head and replied, 'Yes. It's simple when you know how.'

Relieved her friend's terrible ordeal was finally over, Robin smiled back and gently started to lift the jeweled collar from Lilyanna's neck. But, the smile froze on her face when she met resistance and realized, without the shawl as a protective barrier, the serpentlike creatures had awoken and started to burrow into her friend.

When the princess felt the numbed tug, she understood exactly what had happened, because on the second day of her captivity at Greystone Fortress she had asked Robin to tell her everything she knew about the collar. 'I'm alright. But, I want rid of this thing. So no matter how much it hurts, pull hard.'

Knowing what had to be done, Robin nodded. Then, she tightened her grip on the collar and pulled with all of her might.

Despite the anaesthetizing effect of the toxin injected into Lilyanna's system, it failed to numb the pain as the tiny creatures were pulled from her body and she cried out in agony, whilst Robin, still clutching the collar, fell backwards upon the ground.

Dare reached out and caught the princess as she collapse in front of him, while Jerhal and Zarak, having heard her scream, rushed to them.

When the spy saw Lilyanna's wounds and deathly-pale face, he turned to Robin and accused, 'You could have killed her!'

Robin didn't cower. But instead of reminding him she and Lilyanna had been holding the creatures in the collar at bay for days and that the parasites hadn't had time to burrow deeply, she firmly countered, 'I just saved her life.'

Cradled within Dare's protective arms, Lilyanna weakly agreed. 'She did right.' And even though her voice was no more than a whisper, it was commanding.

Realizing he had been out of line, Jerhal turned back to Robin and apologized. 'I'm sorry. I thought you'd put the princess's life at risk.'

'I understand,' Robin replied, looking him directly in the eyes. 'But know this, you reacted out of loyalty for the princess, whereas I acted out of love for my friend.' Then, the white-haired woman turned to Dare and asked him to assist Lilyanna to her sleeping blankets, where she tenderly treated the princess's wounds with pine balm before tucking her in like a small child for the second time since they had met.

Robin's nerves felt frayed. The stress of the past few days had been overwhelming and it had taken the last of her determination to stand up to Jerhal. So after seeing to the princess's needs, the white-haired woman slipped quietly out of the encampment.

Tired from her exertions, she had only intended to walk a short distance, just far enough into the ancient woodland to find a tranquil place where she could collect her thoughts. But even in the dim light, the unexpected beauty of the Dream Wood filled her with awe and she soon found herself standing at the edge of a small glade.

Seeing what looked to be a restful spot at the base of a nearby tree, the white-haired woman walked over to it and sat down. A gentle tingling sensation skipped lightly across her skin as she leaned her back against the tree's thick trunk. And assuming it was goose bumps, she pulled her cloak more tightly about herself to keep out the cold evening air.

Willing the tranquility of the Dream Wood to wash through her, Robin took in a deep breath, held it for a couple of heartbeats, and then slowly released it. Feeling a little less stressed, she closed her eyes and repeated the process until eventually all of the tension within her had drained away.

Unaware the magic of the Dream Wood was settling upon her like a fine mist and reluctant to return to the encampment, Robin sat there simply breathing in the fresh air while listening to the soft sounds of the forest, something she had never envisioned doing before. And, as her eyelids slowly began to close and she drifted off into a peaceful sleep, she had no idea her skin was starting to sparkle with light-blue magic.

As she slept, dreaming of things as she wished them to be and not as they really were, the evening shadows gradually blended into the darkness of the night.

When at last the white-haired woman opened her sleepily eyes, she saw the flutter of small wings darting about the light of a flame flickering in the middle of the glade, and it took her a moment to realize she was no longer dreaming. Then, fearing the forest had caught fire, Robin scrambled to her feet.

It wasn't until then, she noticed the music. Confused, the white-haired woman blinked to clear her vision and discovered the winged creatures she had mistaken for moths were fairy folk, dancing naked around what appeared to be a little bonfire.

A faint voice warned Robin from deep within she should rejoin her companions and leave the fairies to their dancing, but it was already too late. Having fallen under the spell of the Dream Wood whilst she slept, her entire body now sparkled with its light-blue magic. And when the music intensified, she found she no longer cared what the voice of her subconscious was saying.

In a dreamlike state, she started to walk towards the bonfire at the center of the clearing. As she neared, Robin could see it was not a real fire, but some kind of glowing vortex. Yet unable, and strangely unwilling to stop herself, the white-haired woman continued forward.

With each step she took, the music quickened, the vortex grew, and her heart beat a little faster. Then, as the music began to pulsate through her veins, her limbs took on a life of their own and she started to dance.

Vaguely aware her body was shrinking, Robin was glad to be free of her cumbersome clothing as it fell away and the binding slipped from her long hair. Because, it seemed perfectly natural she too should be fairy sized dancing naked in the glade.

The fairies welcomed her, happy for the tiny human to share the joy of the dance. At times they danced in twos and threes, while at other times they danced by themselves or in large groups. They danced on the ground and they danced in the air. And because Robin had no wings, the fairies would lift and spin her breathlessly around.

The more they danced, the more enthralled they became, laughing with lightheaded merriment. None of them noticed the music's tempo continued to grow faster as the fiery vortex at the center of the clearing stretched higher into the night sky like the funnel of a tornado, stripping the magic from the fairies nearest it and discarding their lifeless bodies like husks onto the ground.

As the fairy magic was sucked upwards into the vortex, it was transformed into crackling-red bolts of contaminated power which were then flung across the clearing and exploded high in the air.

The dancing of Robin and the remaining fairies became more frenzied as small particles of corrupt magic settled upon them, instilling an irrepressible desire to enter the vortex and feel its sweet release.

Erosmay woke with a start. Alarmed by the strange emotions she sensed emanating from her linked companion, the little dragon glanced over at Robin's blankets and saw they were empty.

Realizing something was seriously wrong, Erosmay immediately took to the air in hope of spotting her linked companion somewhere amongst the nearby trees. However, when the only human she saw moving about was Dare, who was on guard duty, she frantically began to widen her search by flying in an outward spiral around the encampment just as fast as her little wings could carry her.

Then suddenly transported, Erosmay found herself hovering high above the glade just as one of the male fairies flew into the whirling vortex. There was a burst of blue light as the magic was ripped from his tiny body and a popping sound, and then the fairy was no more.

With no time to wonder how she had teleported there, the little dragon saw several more of the mesmerized fairies dancing frenziedly closer to the deadly vortex.

Knowing she must act, Erosmay called upon her dragon wisdom of old, tucked in her wings, and dived towards the center of the vortex. Then just as she started to feel its pull, she spread her wings to stop her descent and blasted the spinning shaft with the largest breath of fire she could.

The heat intensified as the dragon fire made its way down the whirling funnel. Then when the fire reached the core of the vortex rooted deep in the forest floor, there was a ground-shaking explosion and the vortex began to wobble like a misshapen vessel on a potter's wheel as it imploded until nothing remained but a smoldering hole in the ground.

With the enchantment broken everything happened at once. Frightened by the dragon hovering above them, the fairies scattered in all directions, leaving the tiny human to fend for herself. And in Robin's confused state, she failed to recognize Erosmay and ran from her linked companion just as fast as her little feet could carry her.

Realizing she was frightening Robin, Erosmay landed so she would appear less threatening. But as to what she should do next, not even her dragon wisdom held the answer.

The white-haired woman's thinking did not begin to clear until she neared the edge of the glade and her body started to revert to its original state. Then short of breath, she chanced a quick glance over her shoulder and recognized Erosmay, who had only appeared enormous due to her own small size. Yet even as Robin contacted her linked companion in mind-speech, she kept running, wanting to distance herself from the nightmare of the glade.

When Robin eventually stopped to catch her breath, her heart was beating so hard she could hear the blood pounding in her ears. Then, realizing she was covered in nothing but tangled hair and sweat, she started to laugh, a giddy kind of laugh that took a while for her to get under control.

Erosmay stayed long enough to ensure her linked companion was alright. Then after pointing Robin in the direction of their camp, the little dragon flew back to the deserted glade to retrieve the white-haired woman's clothes, which was difficult because Erosmay was so small and could only carry one article of clothing at a time. So little by little, Robin dressed as she walked. And by the time she neared the pine-bough shelter, she was fully clothed, albeit for one missing shoe.

Several hours had passed since the white-haired woman had slipped out of the encampment. And when she saw the relieved look on Dare's face upon her return, she realized he must have been worrying about her the entire time she had been away. Yet when the smith asked her where she had been, Robin was too embarrassed to tell him the truth and doubted he would believe her even if she did. So, she told him she had lost her way. Then before Dare could notice her shoe was missing, she excused herself and headed for her blankets for some badly needed sleep.

20 PATROL

While the enchantment of the Dream Wood restfully spun the desires of his sleeping companions into dreams fulfilled, Jerhal ended his stint on watch by rekindling the campfire and preparing a cooking pot of rolled oats so, at first light when he woke the others, they could eat and be quickly on their way.

An early riser by nature, Robin opened her eyes before the spy had gone to rouse her, feeling oddly well rested despite her midnight adventure with the fairies.

As the white-haired woman pushed her woolen blankets aside and sat up, she noticed her missing shoe, along with the map still tucked inside, had found its way back to her.

Pleased, Robin slipped her cold shoes onto her dirty feet and thanked the dozing dragon curled up beside her in mind-speech, fully expecting Erosmay to launch into an exaggerated account of her difficult search. However, the sleepy dragon surprised her by replying she hadn't.

It took Robin a moment to realize the fairies must have found the shoe, an act of true kindness on their part. So to show her appreciation, she looked up and whispered 'thank you' on the off chance one of them was watching. Then, she got up and went to join Jerhal beside the fire.

Everyone was famished when they awoke. Having eaten nothing but dried meat whilst on the move the previous day, the steaming porridge went down a treat. Even Princess Lilyanna liked it, and she had sworn off the stuff after her captivity aboard the Venture.

When the pot was empty and their hunger satisfied, the rescue party wasted no time in striking camp. Then with the creaking of saddles, they mounted their horses and resumed their journey towards the coast.

Still weary from the previous night's adventure, Erosmay promptly landed on the back of Robin's mount and stretched herself across its back with the intension of dozing a bit longer. But just as soon as she made herself comfortable, Robin asked her in mind-speech, 'How did you know what to do last night?'

'I used my dragon wisdom and remembered it from before.'

It had taken the white-haired woman a while to get her head around what Erosmay actually meant by 'dragon wisdom'. But over time, Robin had come to the realization, unlike animal instinct, dragons possessed deep-seated memories passed down from one generation to the next which they could recall when needed, and she found this latest revelation very interesting.

They rode in silence as the white-haired woman mulled this over. Then, just when Erosmay was beginning to nod off, Robin asked her, 'Why weren't you affected by the magic in the glade?'

Realizing Robin was full of questions from the night before and she wasn't going to get any sleep, little dragon shook herself awake and explained, 'As a creature of old magic, it has no effect on me.'

The answer stunned the white-haired woman. She had always thought of Erosmay as a friend who just happened to be a dragon. It had never occurred to her the dragon was a magical creature. But before she could enquire further, another thought struck her. 'And the vortex in the glade, was it also of the old magic?'

'Yes, very bad magic which should have been nullified in the war.'

If Robin was stunned before, she was absolutely shocked now. 'What are you talking about?'

'The War of Magic that ripped the Drea Wood apart when the fairies and dragons fought the warlocks,' Erosmay stated matter-of-factly, wishing humans could recall memories like dragons instead of allowing events to get lost in the mists of time. Then knowing this revelation would lead to more questions, Erosmay ended their conversation by informing Robin she was going to see if anyone was following them yet and flew off in the opposite direction, leaving her linked companion with much to contemplate.

The land bordering the Dream Wood was much less barren than the region they had travelled through the day before, populated with trees and bushes which no longer had to struggle to survive. And at times, had it not been for the narrow road separating the two areas, the riders would have been unable to distinguish the one from the other.

Without the poisonous collar locked around her neck, Lilyanna could breathe easily for the first time since her abduction. Totally trusting in the people with whom she travelled, she felt free. And even though they were still far from the safety of her father's kingdom, she knew with each step their horses took, it would be a little more difficult for Elrod to recapture her.

Erosmay had only travelled a couple of leagues before she caught a whiff of wood smoke in the air. Having flown reconnaissance over the area the evening before and found it uninhabited, the dragon immediately assumed Elrod's soldiers had ridden their mounts late into the night and bedded down near the road just as her travelling companions had.

With this in mind, Erosmay continued on her current course, flying high enough to observe the general area whilst keeping an eye on the road below.

The further she flew, the stronger the smell became. And shortly thereafter, the little dragon spotted a plume of smoke.

As Erosmay drew nearer, she glimpsed a splash of red through the trees and knew her assumption had been right, because the distinctive red uniforms of Elrod's soldiers were unmistakable.

Relieved her human companions had risen at the crack of dawn and were already on their way, Erosmay warned Robin in mind-speech, 'Elrod's red men are here.'

Having expected a message of this sort ever since fleeing the fortress, Robin was prepared and calmly asked, 'How far behind us are they? And, how many soldiers are there?'

'Their camp is at the top end of the Dream Wood and I'm not sure how many red men there are. But, I'll watch and learn.' And with that, the dragon broke contact, stretched out her leathery wings, and glided steadily downward towards one of the trees near the smoky campfire.

After gently landing upon a suitable branch where she could observe the soldiers without being seen herself, Erosmay tucked in her wings and began to watch and learn, something she had not been able to do for several days now. Only this time, concern for the humans she was travelling with overshadowed the excitement she usually felt, and the snooping wasn't nearly as fun.

The stealthy dragon quickly discovered the soldier she had spotted from the air was responsible for stoking the smoky campfire. Having pulled the last shift of guard duty, he was in the midst of preparing a pot of rolled oats for his colleagues just like Jerhal had for the rescue party. However, the similarity ended there. Because when it was time to wake the others, instead of doing it quietly like Jerhal had, the soldier hammered the side of the cooking pot with a large metal spoon and shouted, 'Time to get up you lazy toerags or Elrod will have your guts for garters!'

There was a lot of grumbling and cursing. But knowing he spoke the truth, the other soldiers sleepily staggered to their feet.

As the red men congregated around the cooking pot, Erosmay counted ten in total: a quarter of a platoon. But, she continued to watch and learn just in case she heard something of importance before she contacted Robin. Then, after the soldiers struck camp and had ridden far enough away not to notice her, the hungry little dragon decided to see to her own needs and took to the air.

Having glimpsed several juicy-looking fish swimming in the river whilst searching for the source of the smoke, Erosmay had developed a desire to try one for her breakfast.

The little dragon soon reached the river. And when she spotted a rather large fish swimming just below her, she extended her wings, glided gently downwards, and snatched the unsuspecting creature out of the river with her claws.

Although the fish thrashed to free itself, it didn't stand a chance. Erosmay was determined and famished, a lethal combination. Gripping her wriggling breakfast vice tight, the dragon refused to relinquish her hold and flew erratically towards the riverside. Then just as soon as she cleared the water's edge, Erosmay dropped her catch onto the rocky shore, landed, and dispatched the fish with her razor-sharp teeth.

Concentrating on her hard-won repast, the dragon ignored the insects darting about the riverbank and hungrily tucked into her catch, quickly discovering the fish had more bones than meat. So after wolfing down what there was of it, Erosmay caught another and consumed it with as much relish as she had the first.

She was about to take flight when she heard someone say, 'Dragon friend, we thought the last of your kind had perished during the War of Magic and are pleased this is not so.'

Turning towards the sound of the voice, Erosmay realized it belonged to a blue fairy she had mistaken for a dragonfly whilst she was busy eating.

Although the dragon stood more than twice his height, the small fairy boldly continued, 'It has been several centuries since the last pocket of corrupt magic worked its way up from deep beneath the bedrock. And for this reason, many of my people had become complacent and are no more. Thank you for your intervention and for reminding us, as guardians of the Dream Wood, we have a duty of care. We also owe you a great debt which will not go unpaid.'

Knowing fairies were not like humans, because they didn't lie and they remembered events from long ago, Erosmay bowed her head courteously in acknowledgement. Then, she spread her leathery wings and flew back from whence she had come so she could keep an eye on Elrod's soldiers.

Once the little dragon had caught up with the red men, she resumed her aerial surveillance, stealthily following the detachment and providing Robin with updates on their movements via mind-speech. So when the soldiers stopped to rest, Robin and her travelling companions could do likewise. And thus, as the rescue party left the Dream Wood behind, they managed to maintain the distance between themselves and the soldiers searching for them, or so they thought.

Unaware Elrod had sent messenger birds to even the most remote outposts, as the small band rushed away from the detachment of soldiers behind them, they were riding headlong towards a fast-approaching patrol from the cost.

At twilight, when the first of the stars could be seen and Robin's legs were so saddle-sore the white-haired woman doubted she would be able to dismount her horse, Erosmay informed her that the soldiers pursuing them were stopping for the night and, because she was too tired to fly back, she planned to spend the night near their encampment.

Grateful for the news, Robin and her travel-weary companions reined their horses to a halt.

As the white-haired woman began to climb woodenly from the back of her Greystone Steed, Lilyanna noticed her stiff movements and confided, 'And to think, a few weeks ago I rode for pleasure.'

In their exhausted state, the pursuit seemed so ridiculous they both started to laugh. And because every muscle in their bodies hurt when they did, they laughed all the more.

Observing the exchange, Jerhal could tell the women were nearing the end of their endurance. So, he swiftly located a level spot beneath the sheltering branches of two large pines and asked the ladies to spread the bedrolls under the trees while he and his colleagues saw to the horses.

Given the easier of the two tasks, the two women quickly completed theirs. And when the men returned, they found Lilyanna and Robin, nestled comfortably under their blankets, fast asleep.

While Dare, having volunteered to stand first watch, commenced to build a small campfire, Zarak and Jerhal lowered themselves, boots and all, onto the carpet of pine needles beneath the other tree. And within minutes, they were carried to the land of slumber by the night rider.

Bone-weary, the smith found himself hoping the only thing his tired eyes would set sight on outside their encampment was a dark night. But having noticed the ghostly presence of a winter-starved wolf appearing and disappearing alongside them throughout the day, he thought the chances extremely unlikely.

Aware the safety of the rescue party was dependent upon him, Dare tried to keep alert by walking around the camp and periodically checking on the horses.

Now and again, an owl would hoot to keep him company. But aside from that, all was quiet until he neared the end of his watch and heard the eerie howl of a wolf much too close for his liking.

Knowing the hungry animal was somewhere nearby, the smith diligently searched the darkness for movement, but saw none. Then, just as with the termightiest, the horses started to move about restlessly.

Dare pulled his battered sword from its homemade scabbard. But, he was already too late, because the wolf sprang snarling out of the darkness and tried to hamstring the horse nearest it.

As the frightened horse bucked to fend off its attacker, the smith ran to its aid and hurriedly swung his sword. But in the frenzy, the blade did not bite true. So, Dare planted his feet and swung again. And this time, the sharpened steel sliced deep into the wolf's neck.

Before the dead animal's body hit the ground, Zarak and Jerhal arrived by Dare's side with their swords in hand ready to dole out another slice of death to the next comer. But when no further attack came, they lowered their blades. And, when Zarak examined the smith's kill, the soldier swiftly concluded the animal was a lone wolf, because the only thing holding the old alpha male together was sinew and a scarred pelt.

Aware the smell of fresh blood would attract further predators, Zarak and Jerhal disposed of the flea-bitten carcass by dragging it deeper into the woods. Then, deciding it was pointless to return to his blanket, the soldier relieved Dare early and, except for the occasional snarling of scavengers fighting over Dare's kill, the remainder of the night passed without further incident.

When it was light enough to travel the following morning, Jerhal ended his shift at watch by waking his companions once more to the smell of hot porridge which took longer to prepare than it did to consume. Then, the rescue party struck camp and was on its way well before Erosmay informed Robin the soldiers she was watching were on the move.

Pleased they had been able to increase their lead, the five riders slowly made their way towards the foothills of the Greystone Mountains.

By midmorning, Dare could clearly see the highland conifers were gradually being replaced by the ash and alder Zarak had taught him to recognize on their journey to the fortress. And, he was secretly pleased to be leaving the high altitude of the mountains, where every task required greater effort in the thin air and the cold never seemed to leave his bones.

He pulled the collar of his jacket up and, not for the first time, wished he was with his father sitting beside the fire in their cozy home above the locksmith shop instead of riding on horseback during the day and sleeping on the hard ground at night.

Shortly after leaving White Cliff, he had swiftly come to realize life on the road was not all he had thought it would be. But, it had taken this journey for him to be able to distance himself from the smithy before he was able to appreciate it.

His musings were interrupted when Robin suddenly announced the patrol behind them was stopping. So, he and his fellow travelling companions reined their horses to a halt so they too could rest and tend their tired animals.

As Dare wearily slipped his foot from the stirrup to dismount, he noticed Robin was having trouble climbing down from Misty, her Greystone Steed. Unaccustomed to riding until a few weeks ago himself, the smith knew the white-haired woman's entire body must be aching, because his did even though he was physically fit from years of sword practice and working at the forge. So, just as soon as his feet touched the ground, he walked over to lend her a helping hand.

Several leagues away, Erosmay had landed and was stealthily creeping through the damp foliage towards the soldier in charge of the patrol.

The snippets of conversation she overheard on the way did not surprise her because, other than for the occasional complaint involving someone's saddle-sore buttocks, the subjects of conversation were the usual soldier-speak she had listened to many a time back at the fortress garrison: drinking, whoring, and wagering. But on the off chance she might glean some useful information she could pass on to Robin, the dragon kept her head down and crept silently on.

It was a good thing she did too. Because just as soon as she was within earshot of the lead soldier, she heard one of the red men ask him when they would be meeting up with the patrol coming from the south.

Alarmed by this new revelation, the dragon realized her human travelling companions were riding directly into the arms of the enemy. Yet despite her trepidation, she remained statue still and waited for his reply.

'We should come across them sometime this afternoon.'

Aware the rescue party's attempts to increase their lead on the patrol behind them had inadvertently shortened the distance between them and the soldiers approaching from the coast, Erosmay immediately contacted Robin via mind-speech and warned her of the danger.

After the white-haired woman had passed on the warning, Zarak replied in his usual droll manner, 'It looks like we're caught between a rock and a hard place.' Then, he turned serious and told Robin, 'You'd better tell Erosmay to join us. We're going to need her eyes and ears here.'

While Robin complied, the soldier instructed Jerhal, 'Find a safe place for us to holdup. And once I've covered our tracks, I'll catch up with you.'

'Sounds like a plan to me,' Jerhal agreed with a firm nod of his head because, even though he was in charge of the rescue team, he was not opposed to Zarak taking the lead when the situation warranted it. And in the next heartbeat, he turned to the others and announced, 'You heard the man, this way.'

As Jerhal guided his horse from the road and the two ladies followed with theirs, Zarak dismounted and handed the reins of his mount to Dare so the smith could lead the tired animal away while he swept away their tracks with a bough broken from the far side of a nearby pine. Then, once all trace of their passage into the woods had been removed, the soldier started to work his way back up the road from whence they had come.

Working hastily, Zarak managed to cover about the length of a tall ship before he heard the sound of horses approaching from the south. And knowing he had run out of time, the soldier hurriedly left the road, brushing away his own bootprints as he went.

Although Zarak did not stick around to see what happened next, Erosmay arrived just in time to glimpse him as he vanished into the trees. And having heard the patrol too, the little dragon darted into the foliage so she could watch and learn as the coastal patrol rounded the bend and headed her way.

Unaware the princess and her traveling companions were in the vicinity, Elrod's men failed to notice the rescue party's oncoming hoof prints until it was too late and the patrol's horses had trodden over them. Then in an attempt to rectify the situation, the soldier in charge ordered his men to search the immediate area.

After making a right pig's ear of it by contaminating the area further with even more prints, the patrol leader eventually decided they had found nothing to indicate the mysterious riders were anyone other than the usual peasants and woodsmen they had sporadically encountered during their journey northwards, or at least that is what his report would say, and ordered his men to remount.

Having watched the disorganized proceedings from her hiding place, Erosmay stayed hidden until the enemy patrol had ridden far enough away not to notice her. Then, she took to the air and disappeared in the same direction as Zarak.

Since leaving the road, Jerhal had steadily guided his small contingent down the wooded slope until they had come upon a small stream. Then with their freshwater needs met, he continued to lead them along the streambank until they eventually ran across a clearing with sufficient grass for their horses as well as enough space for them to stay comfortably hidden until the enemy patrols had left the area.

As the riders dismounted and fell into the familiar routine of stripping the horses of their packs, bedrolls, and saddles, Zarak was following and sweeping away the tracks their tired animals had made down the wooded slope just as quickly as he could. And by the time he had reached the stream, the horses were already hobbled near the water's edge so they could spend the remainder of the day leisurely drinking and grazing without roaming too far.

When the soldier finally stepped into the clearing, breathing heavily and looking a bit worse for wear from his exertions, Dare took one look at him and jokingly chided, 'Now all of the work's done, you show up.'

'It's the first thing every good soldier learns,' Zarak replied, slightly winded but taking the ribbing in good stride. 'The second is knowing when to keep your mouth shut.'

Dare didn't have to be a psychic to predict what was coming next. Having heard Zarak's tale about when, as a fresh recruit, his muddied platoon had returned to the garrison after a week's maneuvers and their sergeant had asked if they wanted clean uniforms. Then when four of his companions eagerly admitted they would, the sergeant had ordered the rest of them to strip and march naked to the bathhouse, so the four volunteers could do the laundry.

Although Zarak told a more carefully worded version of the account this time, because there were ladies present, the mental image of ranks of bare-bottomed soldiers marching off in formation still brought lighthearted laughter from his listeners, even if a couple of them were slightly red in the face.

The little dragon arrived just in time to hear Zarak's anecdote. And even though she understood the humor, Erosmay decided she was much too dignified a creature to join in. However to make amends, she did magnanimously offer to guard the camp so her human counterparts could rest.

21 EROSMAY

It felt strange, waking up leisurely beneath the shelter of the lean-to and seeing daylight. But then, Lilyanna remembered the dangerous game of hare and hound the rescue party had been playing with Elrod's men since fleeing Greystone, and she sat bolt upright.

Resting nearby, Robin saw the princess's startled reaction and reassured, 'Don't worry. We're safe. Jerhal thought it best to wait until the coastal patrol has travelled a bit further south before we set off behind them.'

Lilyanna smiled self-consciously and pulled her blanket more snuggly over her shoulders.

The two women sat together quietly for a while. Then, Lilyanna broke the silence by wishfully saying, 'You know, I could get used to this, sleeping in and relaxing like a princess ought to.'

'And on such a fine featherbed too,' Robin laughing added, referring to the pine boughs the men had spread to cushion the bottom of the shelter.

After days of stress, this was the first real opportunity the two women had to spend private time together. Feeling stiff from riding, they leisurely got up and strolled to the stream and refreshed themselves. Then still chatting softly and looking much more presentable, they joined the men for an unhurried breakfast.

The unplanned break in their journey seemed to have done them all a world of good, and everyone appeared to be in high spirits as they made ready to depart the small encampment.

The horses seemed eager to be off as well, or at least that's what Dare thought when he walked across the clearing and Swim Tail greeted him with a whicker and shake of his shaggy mane.

'It's good to see you too,' the smith murmured fondly as he reached out and affectionately stroked the sure-footed animal's neck. Then once their hellos were completed, Dare got down to business and gently slipped the bridle over the horse's muzzle and positioned the bit, an action now so routine he no longer feared one of his fingers would be bitten off, before buckling the throatlatch to keep the bridle in place and removing the hobble.

Working together, the small band soon saddled the remaining horses, broke camp, and resumed their journey southwards through the foothills of the Greystone Mountains towards the coast. Only this time, because of the dragon's invaluable aid, the shoe was on the other foot and they were following the soldiers who had been pursuing them.

While Erosmay slept or was flying reconnaissance elsewhere, the men from White Cliff had taken to sending a rider ahead to serve as lookout. Then, when the lookout saw someone approaching, he would signal so the women could hide amongst the trees until the road was clear again.

This tactic worked fairly well until the following day, when the land began to level and the vegetation started to change. With fewer large trees to contend with, small farmsteads had started to spring up. And knowing it was just a matter of time before one of the local inhabitants saw the women, Jerhal suddenly announced, 'This won't do. We need some way to travel openly without anyone seeing the ladies or Erosmay.'

'Yes,' agreed Zarak. 'I think some kind of covered wagon or large cart would do the trick. But, it might be difficult to get one of the farmers to part with theirs and, on this road, the ride is going to be rough.'

They could have easily stolen what they needed, but Jerhal and Zarak were honorable men who did not believe in stealing from hardworking people unless it was absolutely necessary, so theft was not an option. However, understanding human nature as well as he did, Jerhal knew every man had his price; it just depended on how empty the man's purse was at the time. Hence, he corrected the soldier, 'Not difficult, just costly.'

'Won't the farmer wonder why we need a wagon since we have horses to ride?' Dare interjected.

For a split second the smith thought he saw a knowing look pass between the two older men, but the conversation changed to which horses they should trade for the wagon. And when they decided to keep Robin's and his, Dare was so relieved he forgot about what had transpired until a short time later when he found himself stretched out in the middle of the road near a smallholding that had the wagon they needed.

With a bandage wrapped around his head and a crude splint made of branches strapped to his left leg from boot to hip, Dare tried to ignore the pointed stone digging into his back as he chided himself for being played like a fine fiddle. Then as instructed, when he heard the sound of the wagon approaching, he began to groan in agony.

Just as soon as the wagon rolled to a stop and the farmer started to secure the driving lines, Jerhal climbed down from the wagon and rushed over to Dare. 'How are you feeling?'

'Terrible,' Dare gasped.

As the weather-beaten farmer joined them, the smith pressed his back against the stone gouging him and let out a painful moan. And because it really did hurt, the man swallowed the ruse hook, line, and sinker. However, this still did not stop him from shrewdly trading up, even though he grumbled the horses were of no use since they couldn't pull a plough, by swapping his pair of worn-out draft horses for Jerhal's mount and the other horse tethered nearby, which he presumed was Dare's.

Although Jerhal knew the farmer would make more than enough money to purchase a much younger replacement team when he sold their mounts at market, the spy played along. And then, when the man went on to demand a goodly handful of coins to cover the cost of the old wagon and harnessing, which Jerhal knew he would, the spy haggled just long enough to keep up appearances before handing him some of the money he kept hidden in the heel of his boot.

It was not until after Jerhal and the farmer had shook hands to seal their bargaining they finally lifted the injured smith from the ground and placed him in the back of the covered wagon. Then, after their farewells were said, the two men from White Cliff and the hard-bartering farmer went their separate ways.

While the spy drove the wagon down the bumpy road towards the large cluster of trees screening the other members of their party from view, Dare pushed the bandage from his head and began to saw through the bindings of the splint with the pocketknife his father had given him. And by the time they reached their companions, the smith had managed to successfully free himself without cutting off his leg in the process.

The moment Jerhal pulled the team to a halt, the smith and the ladies, accompanied by Erosmay, quickly swapped places. Then, while Dare took charge of Swim Tail and the women adjusted the canvas cover so no one could see inside the wagon, Zarak secured Misty's reins to the tailboard. And in no time, the rescue party set off down the rutted road with no one the wiser.

To all outward appearances, it looked as if Jerhal was transporting cargo with Zarak and Dare, still wearing their battered swords, riding alongside serving as guards to deter any bandits he met along the way.

Inside the wagon was another story. Because the vehicle lacked springing to absorb the shock as its wheels rolled along the uneven road, the ride was even rougher than Zarak had predicted, and its occupants were tossed about like grain in a winnowing basket.

When they encountered someone travelling upon the road, the men would give the women advanced warning so the ladies would know to keep the noise down until they were safely out of earshot, no matter how bone-shaking the ride was.

The slower pace of the draft horses only served to contribute to the monotony of the journey and the afternoon seemed to pass even more slowly than the morning had. However, Dare did not mind since he knew once this stage of their mission was over, he would have to leave Swim Tail behind, and he had grown genuinely fond of the horse.

By late afternoon the rescue party came upon the small village one of the local farmhands had told them had a shop that sold provisions, including loaves of freshly baked bread prepared each morning by the shopkeeper's wife. So armed with this information and a hardy appetite, Zarak appointed himself the task of replenishing their supplies whilst his colleagues continued their journey.

Being the professional he was, the soldier soon purchased the foodstuffs they needed. And when he caught up with his travelling companions, his saddlebags were not only bulging, there were a couple of roasting chickens dangling beside them.

Except for the dragon, they had all lost a little weight since fleeing the fortress. So when Dare saw the hens Zarak had purchased, his melancholy over the impending loss of Swim Tail was instantly replaced by mouthwatering thoughts of roast chicken.

Seeing the hungry look on the smith's face, Zarak laughed and told him, 'You pluck em and I'll roast em.'

'It's a deal,' Dare replied enthusiastically, unaware Jerhal now wore an amused smile beneath his dark beard because they hadn't included him in the dirty work.

It was early evening when they finally reached the coastal road and took the right-hand turning towards the Port of Hesketh where Jerhal, under the guise of Sebastian, planned to book them passage aboard ship via some of his contacts.

They travelled until dusk. Then, Jerhal drove the wagon from the road and pulled the draft horses to a halt behind the screening of a large thicket so they could setup camp for the night.

Pleased to be stopping, the ladies and Erosmay emerged from the back of the bone-rattling wagon. And when Zarak asked Lilyanna and Robin to gather dried wood for the fire, they were happy for the opportunity to do something useful whilst stretching their legs.

Unable to assist with either the firewood or the horses, Erosmay silently watched the proceedings from the thicket until Dare carried the two hens towards the perimeter of the camp. Then, always a little peckish, she glided down from her perch and followed him in hope of a morsel or two.

The smith had other plans. When he noticed the opportunistic dragon tagging along, he was too hungry to be tender-hearted and informed her in no uncertain terms she had better find a bird of her own because there was not enough to go around.

Erosmay wasn't offended. She was just trying her luck, but nothing ventured, nothing gained. So, she followed Dare's advice and took to the air to see what she could find.

While the smith got on with his plucking, Zarak lit a cooking fire from the dried wood the women had gathered before pushing a couple of sturdy Y-shaped branches into the ground on either side of it. Then once he was satisfied the Y-shaped supports were relatively level and embedded deep enough not to give way while he spit-roasted the hens, he picked up his hatchet and went to chop a spit out of green wood long enough to comfortably span the two supports.

By the time Dare finished plucking the chickens, Zarak had fashioned a crude spit with three bluntly trimmed branches at one end and two sets of double pronged branches in the middle.

Interested in what Zarak would do next, Dare handed his friend one of the hens and watched as the soldier slipped the branchless end of the long skewer inside the bird past both sets of prongs. Then with a sharp tug, Zarak pulled the hen back onto the prongs nearest it and impaled the chicken in the middle of the spit so it would not slip whilst being turned above the hot coals.

After the second hen had been impaled next to the first, the two men lifted the spit onto the Y-shaped supports at either end of the cooking fire. However, because the weight was not distributed evenly, when they relinquished their hold the large skewer spun on its supports and came to rest heavy side down nearest the hot coals.

Realizing their dinner was going to be burnt on one side and undercooked on the other, Dare reached for the spit so they could reposition the birds.

'Not so fast,' Zarak forestalled in his usual easy going manner. 'We still need to hammer in a positioning stick.' Then, he picked up a sturdy branch the smith had mistaken for firewood and, with a few swings of his hatched, chopped one of its ends into a point which he slipped between two of the spit's three trimmed branches, before hammering it into the ground with the butt of his hatchet.

'Simple, but effective!' Dare exclaimed with a grin when he saw how the positioning stick stopped the spit from spinning freely yet, because it was made from flexible green wood, still enabled them to disengage and rotate the spit when needed.

'Don't forget the years of practice,' Zarak added, enjoying the camaraderie. 'But I must admit, the first rabbit I ever roasted moved about more on the spit than it did when I was trying to catch it.'

They both laughed. Then, when they noticed Jerhal, freshly groomed in preparation for the following day, sitting on the tailboard of the wagon trying to buff the shine back onto the ridiculous shoes he wore when disguised as the foppish Sebastian, they laughed all the more.

'I thought dressing chickens was bad, but being dressed-up like a peacock must be even worse,' Dare chuckled.

The spy didn't let the remark ruffle his feathers. Instead, he casually spat on the shoe he was trying to polish and replied in like manner, 'Wearing these wouldn't be so bad, if the wages weren't so paltry.'

'Did you say paltry or poultry?' Zarak asked just as the ladies returned with the last of the firewood.

'It doesn't matter,' Jerhal answered as calm as ever. "In either case, it's still chicken feed.'

'What's chicken feed?' Lilyanna asked as she set down her armload of firewood.

'To put it in an eggshell, we were just swapping some fowl jokes,' Dare replied with a lopsided grin.

As Robin rolled her eyes skywards, the princess said, 'If this is the quality of the humor around here, I'm glad I missed it.' And then, they all laughed.

By now, Jerhal had given up trying to polish his buckled shoes. So when he went to put them in the wagon, the rest of the small party made themselves comfortable around the fire to wait for the chickens to finish roasting. And to satiate their hunger in the meantime, Zarak surprised them with a wizened apple each he had purchased earlier in the day.

The apples weren't the only treat the soldier had in store that evening. Because just before it was time to carve the roast chickens, he reached into his saddlebag and produced a large loaf of crusty bread he then proceeded to cut into five big slices with his battered sword and distribute evenly amongst them.

When Erosmay arrived back at camp, her stomach swollen from gorging on seagull, she found her travelling companions happily munching away.

Being the coldblooded creature she was, the dragon settled next to Robin beside the campfire so she could enjoy the warmth while she listened to the humans talk softly amongst themselves.

Her belly full, Erosmay soon nodded off, but her little ears instinctively perked later when she heard the sound of unfamiliar voices coming from the direction of the road and she warned Robin immediately via mind-speech.

Robin hurriedly alerted the others of the approaching danger. And since this wasn't the first game of sneak attack Jerhal and Zarak had played, they swiftly jumped into action, the spy motioning for Lilyanna and Robin to follow him in the darkness from the camp while Zarak and Dare readied themselves for a fight.

Jerhal and the women were safely away by the time Elrod's men had crept near enough to observe the encampment. And when the leader of the patrol saw Zarak and Dare standing in the firelight with swords in hand ready to defend themselves, he knew they had lost the element of surprise, so he raised both of his hands to indicate they meant no harm and stepped out of the darkness.

'Don't move! We're here in the king's name,' he announced to the two men before him.

'We thought you might be thieves,' Zarak said by way of explanation, and then he and Dare lowered their swords like loyal subjects.

With the confrontational part of the encounter over, the patrol leader dropped his arms and got down to business, 'Where are you bound?'

Knowing any soldier worth his pay would have already examined their wagon tracks to determine which direction they were heading, Zarak answered truthfully. 'Hesketh.'

While his subordinates went about searching the camp, the patrol leader boldly continued, 'What business do you have there?'

To account for the extra horses they had with them, Zarak calmly replied, 'We're selling some horses to buy grain for spring planting.'

'I see,' the patrol leader said, his eyes searching Zarak's for a glimmer of a lie. But when the White Cliff man returned his gaze evenly, the patrol leader decided to believe him.

An uncomfortable silence then ensued while the three of them waited for the other soldiers to finish conducting their search. But, because Lilyanna and Robin had gathered firewood instead of spreading the sleeping blankets like they usually did, there was no obvious evidence Zarak and Dare were with anyone else, even if Jerhal's Sebastian costume in the back of the wagon raised an eyebrow or two. So when nothing suspicious was found, the leader of the patrol eventually ordered his men to withdraw, and they departed with little more than a curt apology for the intrusion.

It was only after the soldiers had disappeared back into the darkness Zarak and Dare sheathed their swords and Erosmay, having sat watching and learning from the thicket, disappointedly gave up her desire to see Elrod's men off with a nip to their backsides with her razor-sharp teeth. However, the dragon did follow them long enough to ensure they really were leaving the area before she notified her linked companion the soldiers had gone.

When Erosmay returned, she found the five humans casually sitting around the campfire quietly discussing their plans for the following day as if the incursion never happened. So as curious as ever, the little dragon landed and curled up comfortably on the ground beside Robin where she could hear all.

By the way Robin reached down and fondly stroked her back, the dragon knew her linked companion had missed her. And because she hadn't had a good backrub for some time, or at least not since the wagon had rolled to a stop, Erosmay scooted closer so the white-haired woman could do a better job.

The dragon was just beginning to feel relaxed when Zarak, with whom she had been getting along with perfectly well until then, cut her backrub short by suggesting they turn in for the night. Then much to her annoyance, she was left waiting near the campfire while her travelling companions collected their sleeping blankets from the back of the wagon.

For propriety's sake, the men always sleep apart from the women so the ladies could have some privacy. And shortly after climbing beneath their blankets, they were all fast asleep, with the exception of Dare who was standing guard.

The night passed without further incident. And early the following morning, Zarak had another surprise in store for his sleeping companions. Having requested the last watch, the soldier ended his stint on guard duty by filling the cooking pot with water. But instead of adding oats like usual, he sprinkled in a handful of tea leaves. Then, while the tea brewed, he took out his sword and sliced the large wedge of cheese and remaining loaf of bread he had purchased from the village shop the day before into large chunks.

Once the tea had infused sufficiently, Zarak woke the others. And when they discovered what he had been up to, they were well pleased, including Erosmay who, partial to a bit of cheese herself, decided to forgive the soldier for interrupting her backrub the evening before.

After they had eaten, the rescue party broke camp and set off towards Hesketh once more, fully aware the closer they got to their destination the greater the risk became, because Elrod's men would be on high alert around the harbor area.

When they eventually reached the turning shown on Robin's map, they split up. The spy, mounted on Zarak's horse and disguised as Sebastian, continued on the coastal road towards the port in the hope his contacts might be of help, whilst the rest of the rescue party headed downwards to the sea along the side road which was even worse than the potholed road they had travelled on the day before.

Sitting on blankets in the back of the wagon to cushion the ride, Erosmay and the two women soon found themselves sliding sledgelike towards the front of the vehicle. Whereas Lilyanna and Robin were able to grab hold of the sides of the wagon to stop themselves from slipping, the little dragon could only grip the shifting blankets helplessly with her clawed feet until she skidded to a stop by bumping her head into the front of the bed.

The land levelled slightly after that, although the road was so rough the three passengers continued to bounce about the back of the covered wagon like a box of frogs until Zarak pulled the team to a halt.

Even though Robin had known they were travelling on a coastal road, it was not until she clambered out of the covered wagon that she caught her first sight of the sea, and the impact hit her. 'I've heard stories, but I never thought I'd actually see it. It's so vast.'

Having grown up beside the sea, Dare had taken the view for granted. But now, seeing it through Robin's eyes, he could appreciate what she meant. Although, he mischievously replied, 'And very wet.'

Zarak knew where the conversation would eventually lead, because he too felt the urge to pull his boots off and run to the water's edge just to feel the cold waves lapping his feet. However, he also knew this was not the time to let their guard down. So putting their mission first, the soldier reminded them, 'There'll be plenty of time to enjoy the sea once we're safely out of here. But for now, we'd best get settled and not draw any unwanted attention to ourselves while we await Jerhal's return.' And, that is exactly what they did.

When the spy finally rejoined them, the news was not good. Other than for a couple of military crafts anchored in the harbor, the next merchant ship was not expected for several days and Venture, the only friendly vessel in the area they knew they could count on, had set sail that morning.

Realizing all was not lost, Robin asked Erosmay in mind-speech, 'Do you think you could catch up with the Venture and deliver a message to the captain?'

'If it's light, I can try,' the little dragon answered.

'Alright,' the white-haired woman replied. Then, she turned and announced to the others, 'Erosmay thinks she might be able to deliver a message to the captain of the Venture if it's light enough for her to carry.'

Relieved, the other members of the rescue party started to talk at once.

'We'll need something to write on,' Dare eagerly stated the obvious.

'How about the map?' Lilyanna chimed in. 'Captain Nagrom should recognize it because I tore it from one of his charts.'

As Robin slipped off her shoe to retrieve the map, Jerhal agreed. 'Yes, and we can mark our exact location!'

'Good,' Zarak replied enthusiastically. 'Now we just need some charcoal to write with.'

The words had scarcely left the soldier's lips when Erosmay contributed by blowing a jet of flame towards a small piece of driftwood near Dare's feet.

As the surprised smith jumped aside, the dry wood instantly caught fire. And a few seconds later, they had the charcoal they needed.

'Well done!' Jerhal exclaimed. Then he turned to Lilyanna and instructed, 'Nagrom knows your handwriting, so you'd better write it. But, keep it brief.'

The princess nodded. Then just as soon as the charcoal had cooled to the touch, she wrote the message, rolled it up, and slid her signet ring around the small scroll to make doubly sure the captain would know the message was genuine.

Although Erosmay did not read, she could recognize shapes. So after Jerhal had written the word 'VENTURE' on the ground with a stick and she knew which ship to look for, the little dragon set off on her important errand, fully aware the Venture had half a day's lead and was still moving.

Preoccupied with the urgency of her task, it took a while before Erosmay began to think of other things, like her stomach. But encumbered with the message she carried, the peckish dragon was unable to catch any of the tempting creatures swimming in the water beneath her.

From time to time Robin would contact her via mind-speech to see how she was getting on, and the distraction helped Erosmay take her mind off her growing hunger and thirst, which was quite a feat considering she was surrounded by water and food she could neither drink nor eat.

As the afternoon wore on and the dragon began to tire, she was forced to slow her speed and ride the air currents, but even this was not enough to rest her little wings.

With nowhere to land, Erosmay knew if she did not find the ship soon she would never see her linked companion again. But for Robin's sake, she bravely kept this information to herself and battled on.

It was not until the sun was beginning to set and the dragon was so worn out she thought she might drop from the sky like a stone, she spotted a small dot of white on the horizon. And realizing it must be the sails of a ship, she adjusted her course.

Try as she might, it seemed to take ages before the small dot grew and the exhausted dragon noticed she was shortening the distance between herself and the vessel. But it was not until Erosmay heard the faint voices of sailors carried on the wind, she believed she might actually make it.

Spurred on, the winded dragon dug deep within herself and, ignoring the pain in her burning lungs, somehow found the strength she needed.

Ever so gradually, the sailors' voices began to grow louder. Then, when she had finally flown close enough to see the lettering emblazoned boldly on the ship's stern, her heart nearly skipped a beat, because it read 'VENTURE'.

Shifting the message from her clawed feet to her mouth, Erosmay extended her leathery wings and glided downwards to one of the ship's yardarms where she silently landed so she could watch and learn which of the men on board was Captain Nagrom while she caught her breath.

The sailors working on the weather deck directly beneath her seemed a friendly lot and, under normal circumstances, the dragon would have enjoyed listening to their banter. But, time was of the essence, and she swiftly concluded none of these men were likely to be the captain, especially when she learned one of them was called Fish Bait.

Erosmay wearily spread her aching wings and flew over to the next yardarm. It was taller than the first and the view was better despite the fading light. From here she discovered the ship looked a bit like a building because it had a couple of doored rooms and what appeared to be a small stairway leading downwards into the belly of the vessel.

Outside one of the doors were two men and a boy. The older man was sitting on a small crate leisurely smoking a pipe. And by the food-stained aprons he and the boy wore, the dragon knew through experience they worked in the galley.

The other man, however, was dressed much smarter than everyone else she had seen on the ship thus far. And by his bearing, Erosmay sensed he must be a person of some importance. So, she listened carefully to what they were saying in the hope he might be the captain.

Luck was on her side, because a short time later the well-dressed man asked the cook, 'So, how's your apprentice working out?'

The cook removed the pipe from his lips and replied, 'He's a keeper Captain.' Then, he looked over to the boy and said, 'If you keep working as hard as you have, you'll be ready to take my place in a month or so.'

This was all the exhausted dragon needed to hear. As the boy beamed with pride and earnestly promised he would, Erosmay startled them by gliding down from the yardarm and dropping the message on the deck in front of the captain.

Unable to believe their eyes, the three humans just stood there staring down at her. So with the last of her strength, Erosmay nudged the small scroll closer to the captain with her nose.

Recovering first, Nagrom understood the dragon's intent and picked up the little scroll. As he started to slide the gold band from the rolled paper, he realized it was not a band, but a ring. Then, his eyebrows raised when he saw the ring's seal, because he recognized it. And, it belonged to none other than the princess of White Cliff.

Having unwittingly assisted in Princess Lilyanna's abduction, Nagrom slipped the signet ring onto his little finger to free his hands. Then, he unrolled the tattered paper and began to read.

Captain,
Have escaped.
Require transport.
Location on reverse.
Please hurry.
Princess L.
P.S. Look after dragon.

By now Erosmay was beginning to feel lightheaded, but determined to see her mission through, she stood and watched Nagrom turn the paper over.

When his eyes widened as he saw the map, she could tell he recognized it as the missing portion from his chart. Then exhausted from her exertions, the little dragon's vision started to blur and, as her legs gave way, she heard him say 'Change of plan. It looks like this business with the princess isn't over yet'.

22 SEEING-SIGHT

Archie, the lad with the dirty apron Erosmay had seen on the weather deck when she had delivered the princess's message, sat in the galley gently cradling the dragon's limp body in the crook of his arm while, ever so slowly, feeding her spoonfuls of warm broth.

The warmth and nutrients of the broth, combined with Archie's body heat, gradually began to revive the exhausted dragon. And after several hours of tender ministrations, the boy was rewarded when the helpless creature began to stir.

Flooded with relief, he talked softly to Erosmay as if she was the puppy he had always wanted. 'Everything's alright. Rest now and regain your strength.'

Although Archie had heard dragons were of the old magic, the young apprentice did not actually believe she could understand him like the tales claimed. Yet, he continued to talk soothingly to Erosmay as he stroked her, because he thought she seemed to respond to the sound of his voice.

Back onshore, things were very different. When Robin had asked the dragon if she could find the Venture, it had never occurred to the white-haired woman her request was dangerous. But as the day wore on, a deep foreboding began to grow within the pit of her stomach, despite Erosmay's assurance everything was alright.

Then just around sunset, all communication between them abruptly stopped. And for the first time since the dragon's hatching, Robin could not feel her linked companion's presence.

Overwhelmed by a great sense of loss, the white-haired woman stood numbly staring out to sea, trying to understand what had happened and slowly coming to the conclusion her naivety may have cost Erosmay her life.

When Lilyanna noticed Robin standing alone on the shore, the princess assumed her friend was waiting to greet Erosmay on the dragon's return. So, she grabbed a couple of blankets from the back of the wagon to ward off the evening chill and went to join the white-haired woman, totally unaware of Robin's inner turmoil.

'I thought you might like some company,' Lilyanna said warmly as she drew near. But when Robin turned and her face was as white as her hair, the princess knew something was terribly wrong. 'What's happened?' Lilyanna asked, her voice full of concern.

'I can't feel Erosmay,' Robin chokingly sobbed as the tears rolled down her pale face. 'And, it's all my fault. I asked her to go.'

Reacting on impulse, Lilyanna dropped the blankets and rushed to comfort her friend.

Pained to see Robin so distraught, she hugged the white-haired woman reassuringly while frantically trying to think of something, anything, which might help. Then out of nowhere, the princess recalled Urba, the court wizard, had mentioned distance and strong emotion blocked his searching. And although she knew little about the science of magic, or having a linked companion for that matter, it stood to reason Erosmay would be exhausted from her long flight and Robin's own agitation over the dragon's safety could affect her ability to sense her linked companion.

Breaking the embrace, Lilyanna held Robin firmly by the shoulders and looked straight into her friend's tear-filled eyes. 'Is it possible your fear is blocking your connection with Erosmay?'

Even though Robin heard what the princess was saying, it took her a moment to comprehend what Lilyanna meant. Then, she sniffed back a sob and replied, 'I don't know. I guess so. I've never been this worried about her before.'

'Alright then,' the princess said decisively. 'Let's wipe those eyes and get you calmed down.' And for the first time since they had met, it was Lilyanna's turn to take care of Robin.

While the princess quietly began to tell the white-haired woman everything she could remember Urba say about his seeing-sight, she collected the blankets and led Robin from the encampment to a spot where they could sit undisturbed.

Then once they were both wrapped warmly in the blankets, Lilyanna sat beside Robin and held her friend's hand for support while the white-haired woman tried to still the turmoil within herself by breathing in the sea air, holding it a short time, and then slowly exhaling, something Robin had not done since the evening they had camped on the edge of the Dream Wood.

When the white-haired woman finally felt ready, she nodded to Lilyanna. Then, she closed her eyes and tried to re-establish her link with Erosmay, but nothing happened. So, she took another deep breath, slowly released it, and tried again. Yet still, nothing happened. And after several failed attempts, she began to panic.

Even though the white-haired woman knew the princess never intended for her to try such a thing, in her desperation, Robin decided to visualize herself leaving her body and flying out over the sea to search for her linked companion just like Lilyanna had described. And to her surprise, it was amazingly simple.

As Robin's seeing-self rose into the air, she glanced down detachedly and saw her body was still sitting beside Lilyanna's. Each of them was surrounded by the glimmering glow Urba had described to the princess as an aura. And oddly, there was a fine trail, like stardust, marking the way her seeing-self had travelled from her body to the point she now hovered. But, concern for her linked companion overrode her curiosity. So, Robin headed out to sea, leaving behind a shimmering trail as she went.

It took the white-haired woman's seeing-self much longer than she had expected to spot the ship in the distance. And miraculously, as she drew nearer to the vessel, she felt the connection between her and her exhausted linked companion slowly begin to re-establish itself.

Relieved, Robin's seeing-self continued towards the Venture. And as she did so, their bond grew stronger as the distance decreased.

When she finally thought the connection was strong enough, Robin shouted to Erosmay in mind-speech. 'Are you alright?'

Awoken from her slumber, the spent dragon replied, 'Tired.'

Flooded with relief, Robin continued, 'Thanks for turning the ship around. Sleep well. I'll see you tomorrow.'

'Yes, tomorrow,' Erosmay agreed as she closed her eyes and fell back to sleep.

Content in the knowledge her dearest friend was safe and the Venture was returning to collect them, Robin began to withdraw her seeing-self along the glimmering trail of her aura back to the shore, unaware she had travelled further than any unsupervised novice studying the science of seeing magic would have been allowed.

High above the wave-capped sea, the white-haired woman realized, too late, she had overextended herself and her only option was to continue. So, trying to ignore her growing weariness, she continued doggedly on.

This tactic worked fairly well at first, but as Robin's life force waned so did the glimmering trail she was following, and the white-haired woman began to fear she might not be able to reunite her seeing-self with her physical body.

Back on shore, Lilyanna had sat quietly holding Robin's hand. And when she felt her friend's fingers growing colder, the princess had assumed the white-haired woman was simply chilled from the night air.

It was not until Robin's body slumped limply against her own, the princess knew something was seriously wrong.

Afraid to move lest she disturb Robin and break her concentration, Lilyanna pushed down her rising panic and tried to remember if Urba had mentioned anything that might help.

Then it occurred to her, this situation was similar to when the creatures of the collar had fed upon her life force energies, draining her aura, and weakening her. Therefore, it might be possible for her to reverse the loss of Robin's by sharing her own life force energy with her friend.

With no thought of her own safety, the princess squeezed Robin's hand firmly and selflessly willed her life force energy into the white-haired woman.

Floundering above the sea, it would have been easy for Robin to simply let her seeing-self sink beneath the waves and disappear like the dwindling trail of her aura, now barely discernible in the night sky. Yet out of love for Erosmay and Lilyanna, she struggled on.

At first, the princess could not tell if her ridiculous notion was working. But then, as the waves slowly rolled in and out, she thought she could feel Robin's hand grow warmer.

Unsure if this was wishful thinking on her part, the princess doubled her efforts. And even though she was unable to see the trail marking the passing of Robin's seeing-self, it began to glimmer more brightly.

As Lilyanna's life force energy continued to flow out of her body and into her friend's, Robin gradually became less lethargic and, better able to distinguish the trail from the darkness, the white-haired woman urged her seeing-self onwards.

So near death, Robin did not notice the trail was a slightly different hue until after her seeing-self had reached the shore and reunited with her body. Then, realizing Lilyanna's life force energy was sustaining her, the white-haired woman used the last of her strength to let go of the princess's hand and broke the connection between them.

Having seen the two women settle themselves further down the shore, the men had assumed Lilyanna and Robin wanted some privacy. So, to honor their wishes, the men had tried not to disturb them. However, several hours later when Dare woke Zarak for second-watch and informed him the ladies had not returned, the soldier decided it was time to stop being courteous, and told the smith so in no uncertain terms as he pulled on his boots.

Although Zarak and Dare choose their footing carefully in the darkness, their approach was far from quiet because of the loose stones. Yet, the women appeared to be fast asleep when the men reached them. So to wake the ladies, Dare chided, 'Alright sleepy heads, time to come back to camp.'

When neither of the women stirred, Zarak and Dare exchanged quizzical glances. Then, the battle-hardened soldier took a more direct approach and reached out to shake the princess gently by the shoulder. But as soon as he touched Lilyanna, her limp body slumped forward like a rag doll and, without the princess for support, Robin's fell sideways behind her.

Stunned, it took a moment for the men to react. But then, Zarak's training kicked in and he immediately began checking to ensure the ladies were still breathing.

Watching his friend in action, Dare was relieved Zarak was there, because he hadn't a clue what to do. And before he could shake his paralysis, the soldier turned to him and said, 'Their body temperatures are low. We need to get them warmed up.'

Without waiting for a reply, Zarak lifted Lilyanna's limp body in his arms and began to carry her up the slope, leaving Dare to pickup Robin's and follow him back to their camp.

Aboard the Venture, Erosmay had revived enough to groggily overhear the ship's cook saying, 'By the look of those teeth, it's a meat eater.'

Now the cook would not have got a faster result even if he had waved smelling salts under the dragon's nose. Always peckish at the best of times, Erosmay was absolutely famished after her exertions. And at the mere mention of the word 'meat', she opened her eyes, squirmed upright, and leapt onto the table. Then, she walked over to Stewpot, looked him straight in the eye, and told him she was with a firm nod of her little scaled head.

Archie laughed and replied, 'I think you got your answer.'

Stewpot agreed. So, he got up and walked over to the stove where he fished out a small chunk of mutton from the previous evening's leftovers with his trusty ladle. Then, he placed the meat on the table and Erosmay wolfed down the entire piece before he had even returned the ladle to the pot.

Realizing the dragon must be ravenous, the cook walked back over to the stove and gave the pot a good stir in order to find another piece of mutton. And when he did, the hungry dragon gobbled it down just as quickly as she had the first.

Once all of the meat was gone, Archie and Stewpot quickly discovered the dragon liked the cooked potatoes and carrots in the soup too. And, it wasn't long before the empty pot was the only reminder of the previous evening's meal.

Totally stuffed, Erosmay let out a burp and walked back over to Archie, fully expecting to resume her place within his warm comfortable arms. But, Stewpot and the lad had other plans, like preparing the morning meal for the crew. So, she curled up on a shelf near the stove where she could absorb the heat from its fire and, lulled by the gently swaying of the ship, quickly fell back to sleep despite all of the banging of pots and pans which ensued.

Captain Nagrom hadn't passed the night so easily. Just as soon as he had finished reading Princess Lilyanna's message, he had charted a new course to the location marked on the map fragment and ordered the ship turned about. Then, he returned to his cabin to get some sleep so he would be mentally alert for the morrow. But when sleep did not come, he decided to gather up his things so the princess could use his quarters during the voyage back to White Cliff.

By the time the sun had risen and the first of the crew went to line up outside the galley for their morning meal, they found the captain, dressed in his best suit of clothes, awaiting their arrival.

Knowing something was up, the sailors stood a little straighter and, when Nagrom wasn't looking, whispered speculations amongst themselves. However, not in their wildest imaginings had they thought anything as strange as what the captain finally told them. Then, when he had finished, he commanded, 'After you've broken your fast, you'd best get the ship and yourselves cleaned up. We're officially in the service of the crown now and need to make a good impression.'

The crew respected their captain and would have willingly followed his orders regardless of the fact they had inadvertently assisted in Princess Lilyanna's abduction. However, because fear of the king's reprisal was still fresh in their minds, they hurriedly broke their night's fast and began to swab the decks and polish the brass with surprising vigor.

Erosmay woke up amidst the racket, her little wings feeling leaden and achy from her long flight, blissfully unaware of the lengths Robin had gone to in order to restore the link between them.

She took a long drink of water from the wooden bowl Archie had thoughtfully placed on the shelf beside her. Then, once she was more alert, she contacted her linked companion via mind-speech.

Hearing the dragon's voice, Robin awoke, too drained to tell Erosmay about her reckless actions during the night. Yet knowing the little dragon would sense the fatigue within her, the white-haired woman explained her tiredness away by saying she had not slept well before quickly ending the conversation and falling back to sleep.

Lying alongside her, Lilyanna had fared much better. When the princess awoke a short time later, other than feeling slightly disorientated, she had already slept long enough to replenish most of the life force energy she had expended while assisting Robin.

'Are you alright?' she heard the concerned voice of Jerhal ask.

Lilyanna turned her head and saw the spy sitting nearby, protectively watching over her like a governess.

'Yes. I think so,' Lilyanna replied as Zarak and Dare joined them. Then, she tried to explain what had happened, but it was obvious only Jerhal understood.

Having spent several hours with the court wizard before he had left White Cliff, the spy asked, 'Could you sense if the dragon reached the ship?'

Lilyanna thought about it for a moment, and then answered. 'Yes. I don't know why, because Robin and I haven't spoken. But somehow, I'm certain the Venture is on its way back to collect us.'

'Very well then, that's good enough for me,' Jerhal replied approvingly. 'Now, I bet you're hungry.'

'No,' Lilyanna corrected him with a slight smile. 'I'm absolutely starving.'

As the princess began to munch away on cold rations and the Venture sailed steadily towards their location, Erosmay was busy finding fun ways to entertain herself, like exploring the nooks and crannies of the ship whilst eavesdropping on the crew. Yet, she kept to herself, believing she had already interacted with the humans on board the ship far more than any self-respecting dragon should.

Other than for being separated from her linked companion, Erosmay soon discovered she had everything she ever wanted; she could fly about without having to sneak around, unless she chose to of course, there were delicious sea creatures vying for her to taste them, and Archie and Stewpot genuinely seemed to like her, which in the little dragon's opinion was the perfect relationship because they were in charge of the food and she loved to eat it.

Back on shore, life wasn't as exciting for the rescue party, since there was little to do other than keep watch for Elrod's men and the ship. Then eventually, when the Venture's white sails were spotted in the distance, Dare's heart sank because he knew it was time to say goodbye to Swim Tail.

Keeping his feelings to himself, the smith turned and started to make his way towards the trusty Greystone Steed. But as usual, he had only covered half the distance before the shaggy-haired horse heard his approach.

Once he reached him, Dare smiled sadly and, fondly stroking the horse on its muzzle, said, 'You're a good fellow.' And, when Swim Tail nickered as if in agreement, the smith chuckled despite his heavy heart.

Having followed quietly behind his friend, Zarak laughed too and added over Dare's shoulder, 'I've got something for you.' Then, the soldier handed Dare the last of the wizened apples he had bought two days earlier.

Knowing how partial the Greystone Steed was to apples, Dare accepted the shriveled offering with husky thanks, and then fed it to Swim Tail.

The smith stayed with the horses until the Venture dropped anchor and the sailors began lowering the gigs so they could row to shore and collect their passengers. Then, one by one, Dare untied their other mounts and released them, saving Swim Tail for last.

As the freed horses began to roam down the shore, the smith gave the Greystone Steed one final pat and untethered him, fully expecting the stallion to follow the others. But instead, Swim Tail merely stood there and looked at him.

'I'll miss you too, fella,' Dare told the Greystone Steed fondly. Then, just when it looked like he might have to apply a firm hand of encouragement to the animal's hindquarters to get him moving, Robin's mare whinnied and, being the healthy stallion he was, Swim Tail turned and trotted off to join her.

23 FIRE BREATHER

When Erosmay flew back to shore, the little dragon was surprised to find her linked companion in a weakened state. And when she had asked Robin about it, the white-haired woman forestalled her, saying she would explain once they were aboard the Venture. So even though it went against Erosmay's nature, she waited patiently until they had been ushered into the privacy of the captain's quarters before demanding the truth.

Being so near death the night before herself, Erosmay had only a foggy recollection of speaking with her linked companion. Yet, as the dragon listened to Robin describe her seeing-search, dormant memories deep within Erosmay's subconscious surfaced and the dragon recalled her ancestors had assisted the wizards in the use of this very same magic. However, she also remembered her kind had suffered terrible loss as a consequence. And because of this, she chose not to share this newfound wisdom with Robin.

Meanwhile on the upper deck, Captain Nagrom was working under the assumption Elrod's patrols would have spotted his ship and were on their way to Hesketh to sound the alert. So, as soon as everyone had climbed aboard the Venture, he ordered his crew to weigh anchor and they set sail.

Aware the captain was an experienced seaman, the members of the rescue party had no way of knowing Nagrom was also an experienced naval officer, having worked his way through the ranks in the king's navy before resigning his commission to tend his ailing wife. Then after her passing, he had purchased the Venture and returned to sea; the only reminder of his lost love was a lock of her hair he kept in a small silver box inside his desk.

Running a profitable shipping business ever since, Nagrom was in the process of sailing the Venture back to White Cliff when Erosmay had arrived with the princess's message. And having seen the sleek-lined military vessels of Elrod's anchored in the Port of Hesketh the previous morning, the captain knew, with the Venture's full hold, it would be nearly impossible for his heavy-laden ship to outrun them. Nevertheless, he also knew he had to try.

Drawing upon his naval training, Nagrom had briefed his men in advance and divided the crew between himself and Rowan, his first mate. Then working in shifts, whenever they noticed the slightest change in the wind, they trimmed the sails so they could put as much distance between themselves and the enemy ships which they knew would soon follow. And admittedly, they made good time. But despite their best efforts, early the following morning the dark shapes of Elrod's two ships could be seen in the distance.

Dare stood at the stern with his companions, struggling to fight down the growing nausea within him as he watched their adversaries slowly draw nearer. Yet despite his queasiness, he chuckled when Zarak said he wished he had a bow powerful enough to rain fire arrows on the ships.

Jerhal was still thinking about fire arrows when the order rang out for the crew to start jettisoning the ship's cargo. Then, as the sailors started to rush towards the hold to lighten the load, it suddenly occurred to him they had something on board even more effective. 'That's it!' the spy exclaimed to no one in particular. But instead of explaining what he meant, he turned and headed towards the cabin the ladies were occupying.

Zarak and Dare exchanged a questioning look, and then hurried after him. And by the time they caught up with Jerhal, the spy was already hammering on the women's cabin door with his fist.

Just as soon as Lilyanna swung open the door and the men had stepped inside, Jerhal told the women about Elrod's ships. Then, he turned to Robin and asked, 'Do you think Erosmay has recovered enough to fly out and breathe fire on the enemy's sails?'

The white-haired woman turned towards the dragon and said in mind-speech, 'You heard him. Do you feel up to it?'

'Sounds like fun,' Erosmay replied enthusiastically, eager to practice her fire breathing and thrilled she could infuriate Elrod at the same time.

Still pale from her exertions, Robin smiled fondly at the dragon. 'I thought you'd think so.' Then, she turned back to Jerhal and told him what Erosmay had said.

Although the excited dragon wanted to set off straightway, she was forced to delay her new adventure while Robin warned her to be careful and not to take any unnecessary risks, which Erosmay thought was a bit rich considering her linked companion was still recovering from the effects of her own reckless actions. Then after what seemed an eternity, Robin finally wished her good luck and opened the cabin door. And before anyone else could hinder her, the eager dragon spread her leathery wings and took to the air.

'This should be interesting,' Jerhal remarked candidly. Then, he added, 'I'd better go tell the captain he can stop throwing his cargo overboard now.'

As the spy went to deliver his message and the rest of the rescue party made their way to the stern of the ship so they could watch the upcoming spectacle, the little dragon flew steadily towards the enemy ships while mulling over her attack options. And recalling how successfully she had picked off the messenger birds by striking from behind, she decided to use this tactic once more.

To conserve her strength, Erosmay glided on the thermals until she drew nearer to the vessels. Then, heedful of Robin's warning to be careful, she dropped altitude and began to stealthily fly just above the crest of the waves to avoid being noticed in the morning light.

Giving the ships a wide berth, the dragon circled silently behind them. Then, once she was aligned with the stern of the last vessel, she began to rise higher with each beat of her little wings, cleared the craft's railing and, after taking a deep breath, exhaled her first jet of flame onto the tinder-dry canvas of the mizzen sail at the back of the ship.

Erosmay did not glance back to admire her work. Instead, she took another deep breath and darted determinedly towards the main topsail, slightly higher and further along the ship. And when she breathed out again, she blasted the sun-bleached material with dragon fire just liked she had the mizzen sail.

As deckhands and soldiers alike rushed aft to put out the sudden flames, they failed to notice the little dragon high above them. But even if they had, the time for intervention had already passed, because Erosmay was swooping down towards her next two targets at the bow of the vessel. And in rapid succession, she swiftly ignited the fore topsail and the spirit sail.

As the fire began to spread throughout the ship and the people on board struggled to douse the flames, Erosmay left the disabled ship behind and headed to her next target.

Fully aware the fire would have attracted the attention of the men aboard the lead ship and they would have raised the alert, the little dragon kept low just as before. But this time, she reversed her plan of attack and flew around to the bow of the ship where she started with the spirit sail and worked her fiery way to the stern of the vessel.

Meanwhile on board the Venture, word of the dragon's mission had spread faster than the fire she breathed, and Erosmay's travelling companions found themselves crowded together at the stern of the ship with the merchant seamen cheering as she methodically disabled Elrod's ships.

Still weak from performing her seeing-search, Robin had insisted on being there too. Then when the spectacle was over and the small crowd began to disperse, the white-haired woman told the princess she wanted to wait until she was certain Erosmay was safe. So, the two women stayed at the stern and watched as the smoke plumes from the burning sailcloth rose ever higher into the sky.

To not distract the dragon during her mission, Robin had refrained from contacting her. But just as soon as she caught sight of Erosmay, still only a speck in the distance winging her way back to the Venture, Robin asked her linked companion via mind-speech if she was alright. And when the dragon promptly replied burning sails was thirsty work and she was hungry, the white-haired woman knew Erosmay had suffered no ill.

"I bet you are,' Robin replied fondly in mind-speech. Then after promising the dragon there would be food and water waiting for her back in the cabin, the white-haired woman allowed Lilyanna to assist her from the railing.

Too drained to collect the items herself, Robin asked the princess if she would do it for her, and Lilyanna agreed straightway, out of appreciation for what Erosmay had done.

Having taken a liking to the little dragon, the cook and Archie would have willingly fed her anyway. But now Erosmay had disabled the enemy ships, they couldn't do enough for her and they piled Lilyanna's arms so full with food the princess had to set the bowl of water down in order to open the door when she returned to the cabin.

Because the little dragon had caught most of her own food during their journey from Greystone Fortress, Lilyanna had no idea how much Erosmay actually consumed and thought she had been given way too much food, that was until the dragon returned and ravenously devoured nearly everything.

When Erosmay's hunger was finally satiated and her belly felt like it would burst, the tired dragon then curled up beside Robin on the berth and fell fast asleep, leaving Elrod's disabled ships to slowly vanish on the horizon.

The two linked companions slept soundly until late the following morning when, as per Lilyanna's instructions, Captain Nagrom rapped lightly upon the cabin door to inform her they had reached the deepest part of the sea.

While the princess retrieved the collar she had been forced to wear, Robin asked Lilyanna if she would like her to accompany her. But, the princess smiled her thanks and replied, 'No. I've got this.' And by the confident sound in her friend's voice, Robin could tell she did.

As unofficial guardian of the collar, Lilyanna had Dare lock it closed and disable the mechanism so no one else would ever be harmed by it again. Then to avoid touching the accursed thing, she had wrapped it in a piece of lining torn from the inside of her cloak and painstakingly tried to keep the small bundle cool so the vile creatures residing within the gems would not reawaken.

After slipping on her cloak, Lilyanna picked up the innocuous looking bundle and headed for the back of the ship where she could dispose of it properly. Then once she reached the stern, she walked over to the railing and unceremoniously dropped it over the side of the ship with a little splash, leaving the dormant creatures within the collar's gems to sleep for eternity in the deep's dark cold water.

Recognizing the bundle Lilyanna had dropped overboard, Jerhal joined her at the railing and commented, 'Best place for it.'

'I thought so,' Lilyanna agreed, pleased to be free of the unpleasant burden.

Then, like two old friends, the couple strolled back towards the bow where Lilyanna casually observed, 'Dare looks better today.'

'Yes. It was a close-run thing, but in the end the fish went hungry.'

'Not the sailor type then,' Lilyanna replied lightheartedly.

'No. He's a landlubber through and through.'

As the spy finished speaking, they both felt the tingling sensation of Urba's seeing-sight dance lightly across their skin and they knew he was checking up on them.

Jerhal cringed as if shaking off a chill and said, 'I'll never get used to it.'

Lilyanna simply laughed, having known the wizard her entire life, she was familiar with the sensation and found it as comforting as the touch of his hand.

◆◆◆

A short while later, the wizard sent his apprentice to inform King Dallin the ship carrying the rescue party would arrive the following afternoon. And, because the king could not greet his daughter personally at the dock lest he add an element of truth to the rumors circulating around the citadel, he did arrange for a couple of nondescript carriages to transport Lilyanna and her travelling companions to the castle.

◆◆◆

Dare stood on the upper deck next to Zarak and Robin, the sea breeze ruffling his dark blonde hair, watching as the familiar green-capped chalk cliffs slowly grew larger.

'Beautiful. Isn't it,' the soldier commented beside him.

'I've never seen anything like it,' the white-haired woman added, having grown up in Greystone where the place name aptly described its gloomy landscape.

'Will you be staying?' Zarak asked her.

'Yes,' the white-haired woman answered with a smile. 'Erosmay has already informed me she likes it here because it's warm and there's more to eat. And, Lilyanna said she would arrange accommodation for us. So, that just leaves employment and, since I'm a seamstress by trade, that shouldn't be a problem either.'

'Sounds like you've got everything all stitched up then,' Dare replied with a grin.

Even though the wordplay was bad, both Robin and Zarak laughed, simply because they were happy and it felt good.

Later that day, after the Venture had docked and the rescue party had said farewell to Captain Nagrom and his crew, the small band disembarked the vessel and everyone, except for Lilyanna and Jerhal, was surprised to find two carriages awaiting them at the pier.

As the coachman assisted Lilyanna into the first carriage, she gasped in surprise. Then, the princess turned to Robin with an enigmatic smile and abruptly told her she would meetup with her later. And with that, the coachman briskly closed the carriage door and the vehicle pulled away, leaving the white-haired woman standing there stunned.

'What was that about?' Erosmay asked Robin in mind-speech.

'I have no idea,' the white-haired woman replied as she was bustled into the second carriage with her male travelling companions.

Up ahead, Lilyanna was locked in a tight embrace. She still could not believe Arlo was actually there, holding her as if he would never let her go and kissing her lips, her cheeks, her hair.

When they finally pulled apart, they both started to talk at once.

'How did you?' Lilyanna asked breathlessly.

'Your father,' Arlo interrupted excitedly. And then, they both started to laugh, the happy sound of two people in love.

Inside the other carriage, the atmosphere was much different. Although all of the passengers were pleased to be in White Cliff, Zarak and Jerhal knew their mission was not officially over until they had been debriefed and written their reports. However, being the junior member of the team, Dare was not required to do either, which was a good thing considering the young smith was chomping at the bit to get home. And as for Robin and Erosmay, the white-haired woman sat quietly taking in the sights while the dragon, always a little peckish, flew excitedly overhead on what she called 'a food-finding expedition'.

With the state wedding fast approaching, the streets of the citadel had grown even more congested than they were when the rescue party had left. And because of this, it was not long before both carriages were slowed to a crawl.

Growing more frustrated by the minute, Dare soon had enough and commented disgustedly, 'I can walk faster than this.'

Zarak understood. 'Suit yourself. You're the only one who doesn't have to be here.'

'You're right,' the smith agreed, happy for his friend's go-ahead. 'I'll see you all at the wedding.' Then without wasting a second more, he stuck his head out of the window and shouted for the driver to stop the carriage. And just as soon as he had, Dare got out, waved goodbye to his travelling companions, and strode off in the direction of his father's locksmith shop.

Other than for the side streets now being as congested as the main streets were, Dare did not notice any major changes since he had left the citadel weeks before. But it still didn't feel like home until, he opened the door to the smithy and heard the familiar doorbell tinkle in greeting as he stepped across the threshold.

His father heard the bell too and emerged from the workroom at the back of the shop expecting to attend his next customer. But when he glanced towards the door and saw Dare, his face split into a wide grin and he rushed over to greet him.

'When did you get back?' the master locksmith asked as he embraced his son tightly.

Dare hugged his father back equally as hard, man enough to no longer feel boyishly self-conscious like he had when they parted. 'Not long. But the streets were so crowded, it was difficult to get here.'

'Good for business though', the master locksmith replied as he took a step back to get a better look at his son. 'You've lost weight.'

'Nothing a few days on firm ground won't cure,' Dare assured him.

'I was afraid of that.'

'You were?'

'Yes,' his father replied with a knowing smile. 'Let's just say, you come from a family of smiths, not sailors, and leave it at that.'

'Why didn't you warn me?'

'The subject never came up,' the master locksmith replied as he turned the sign on the door from 'open' to 'closed'. 'Then when it did, I didn't want to put you off.'

As they carried their conversation upstairs, the other members of the rescue party were being ushered into the secluded room in the west wing of the castle the king had used as a base during the search for his missing daughter.

Jerhal, who had been there before, entered first and swiftly realized the debriefing was going to be formal because the tables had been abutted to form a single much longer one, behind which sat the wizard, King Dallin, Lord Talmen, and Karl, Talmen's scribe. So, he bowed his head in homage to the king and quietly took a seat facing the panel beside Princess Lilyanna and Prince Arlo. Then, once Zarak and Robin had taken their places, the debriefing commenced.

Taking it in turns, the members of the rescue party recounted their version of events, only stopping when one of the men sitting before them asked a question.

For the most part, the briefing was fairly straightforward, until it was Lilyanna's turn. And even though she had stoically not blinked an eye as she described Elrod's plans for her, they did have to take a short break so she could compose herself after she told them how the Black Hawk had boasted about poisoning her brother.

When at last it was Robin's turn to explain her role in the escape, the panel dismissed Zarak and Jerhal, saying the princess would be able to assist them if they had any queries. So, the two men took their leave, pleased their part in the debriefing was over and, because Karl had already recorded their statements, there was no need for them to file any further reports.

Robin started her account by telling them about the evening she had met Lilyanna. But when she got to the part where she said she had recognized the collar locked around the princess's neck, Urba interrupted and asked when she had first encountered it. So, Robin was forced to tell them about the horrific death of her friend, Allyce. And when she mentioned her hair had turned white from the shock of it, the wizard sat a little straighter in his chair.

Robin then went on to describe their escape from Greystone Fortress just as the others had. But too embarrassed and tired to explain her encounter with the fairies in the Dream Wood, she omitted to tell them, even though Erosmay, having snuck into the room during the break to earwig, reminded her of it. And in the end, the white-haired woman was glad she had, because the wizard asked her, and Lilyanna, dozens of questions about the seeing-search she had performed, which was exhausting.

By the time Robin thought she had answered every conceivable question the members of the panel could possibly have, the wizard surprised her by asking if she had left any loved ones behind. So, she told him she was orphaned and the closest thing to family she had was Erosmay.

Urba nodded. Then, he asked, 'Before we draw this meeting to a close, would it be possible for us to meet Erosmay?'

'It's up to you,' Robin told her linked companion in mind-speech.

'I'm hungry,' the dragon replied. 'If it means we can get out of here, I'll do it.'

Robin smiled and told the wizard, 'She said yes.' And as if by magic, the little dragon landed on the table in front of them.

24 WEDDING

The following day, Zarak and Jerhal were given temporary assignments at the citadel so they could attend the royal wedding; the soldier placed in charge of training a platoon of new recruits, and the spy detailed to track down the source of the map Princess Lilyanna had acquired from Captain Nagrom.

As for Dare, having gone off the idea of adventuring, he had hung his sword over the mantelpiece in his home above the smithy, to serve as a memento of the mission and a reminder not to volunteer for another one, and contentedly gone back to work with his father.

Things had not worked out like either of the women had planned. Having returned within days of her wedding, Princess Lilyanna discovered she had lost weight and was busy with last minute fittings because all of her dresses, including her bridal gown, required alterations. And surprisingly, instead of resuming her previous occupation as seamstress and moving into the lodgings Lilyanna promised to organise, Robin found herself apprenticed to the wizard and was so busy improving her reading skills and memorizing the laws governing the science of magic, she had little time for anything else.

Erosmay, on the other hand, had quickly discovered life at White Cliff was even better than on the Venture. She and Robin now shared a private chamber at the very top of the tower in the castle's west wing with a window so large she could come and go without even banking her wings to fly through it. And as for food, the dragon had only to fly as far as the castle kitchen if she was hungry. But if she felt like catching something on her own, she also had the options of surf and turf, by fishing in the sea or hunting in the nearby woodland. However, being the greedy gut she was, most days she ate all three.

❖❖❖

The morning of the royal wedding, Robin and Erosmay got up early and went downstairs to the cluttered workroom one flight below to break their fast with Urba and Garan.

Although the room looked similar to Elrod's converted library at Greystone Fortress, because there were lots of books and strange things stacked all over the place, the similarity ended there and Robin usually did not feel the least bit uncomfortable. However, on this occasion when she entered the room, the white-haired woman could tell something was definitely afoot.

Seeing the questioning look on her face, Urba merely pointed towards a large bundle sitting on the far end of the worktable and said, 'This just arrived for you.'

'For me?' Robin asked in surprise.

'Yes, and we've been sitting here trying to figure out what it is, Garan interjected. 'So, why don't you put us out of our misery and open it already.'

Still unable to believe anyone would be sending her anything, Robin and Erosmay went to examine the parcel, and clearly written in a delicate hand was a note addressed to her slipped beneath the sky-blue ribbon which bound the mysterious bundle.

The white-haired woman tentatively slipped the small piece of paper from its restraints and unfolded it.

The note read:

Dearest Robin,
As my Maiden of Honour, this is for you.
See you at the wedding.
Your friend,
Lilyanna

Robin could not believe it. Since she had not seen the princess since the afternoon of the debriefing, she had sadly assumed, as so often happens, the two of them had gone their separate ways and, after attending the wedding, they would never see each other again. But now, the white-haired woman realised no matter how busy they both were or where life led them, their friendship would endure.

Robin looked over to the men with tears in her eyes and said, 'Lilyanna wants me to be her Maiden of Honour.'

'As well she should,' Erosmay remarked in mind-speech, even as Urba and Garan uttered similar comments out loud.

After setting aside the note, Robin carefully untied the ribbon securing the bundle. And to her delight, she found the princess had sent her a beautiful dress and a pair of dainty shoes, the same shade of sky-blue as the ribbon, for her to wear to the wedding.

◆◆◆

Dressed in ceremonial uniform, buttons shining and boots highly polished, Zarak stood alongside Dare and his father, quietly waiting as one of the castle guards inspected their invitations before directing them across the courtyard towards an arched entranceway, adorned with garlands made of yellow primroses and pine boughs, the couple ahead of them were disappearing through.

When they finally reached the Great Hall, the three men were stopped once more so the attendant at the door could examine their invitations and instruct a page to lead them to their assigned seats at one of the tables skirting the inner walls of the large room.

Looking around the hall, it was obvious the majority of the people there were of lesser rank, because they were seated at the back of the room furthest from the head table. And being of low-born status themselves, Zarak, Dare, and his father fully expected to be joining them. So, when they were escorted to the table directly adjacent the head one and shown their places, side by side facing the hall, they were pleasantly surprised.

Once the page was out of earshot, Zarak leaned over to his companions and confided in a hushed voice, 'I sure didn't expect this.'

'Me either,' Dare agreed, not bothering to hide his delight.

The three continued to chat quietly amongst themselves while the room slowly filled with expectant wedding guests and the musicians played softly in the background.

When the herald's trumpet sounded a short while later, they stood along with everyone else as King Dallin and Queen Leah entered and took their places at the high table. And, they remained standing until King Gestmar, the groom's father, joined Lilyanna's parents and the music resumed.

Fully expecting the Maiden of Honour to enter next, everyone looked towards the entrance. However, the princess had asked Erosmay to join the wedding party which surprised them all, including the musicians, and they watched wide-eyed as the little dragon flew through the doorway straight up the center of the room. Then, she banked sharply and soared high above their heads once around the Great Hall before extending her leathery wings and gliding to a gentle landing directly in front of the head table.

Privy to his daughter's surprise, King Dallin waited for the room to fall quiet. Then, he rose to his feet and announced in a strong voice, 'This is Erosmay. From this day forward, treat her with respect. She is not only a creature of the old magic and last of her kind, she is also a friend to the crown and our honored guest.'

To show her mutual respect, the dragon dipped her head to the king. Then, she lifted her wings and flew to her place at the left side of the high table where Robin, as Maiden of Honor, would join her.

When the music started again, the white-haired woman entered the hall on the arm of the gentleman serving as Prince Arlo's Chosen Man. They were both dressed in sky-blue and Robin's white hair, freed from its usual plait, cascaded down her slender back like a waterfall.

Upon reaching the head table, the couple bowed in homage to the royalty before them. Then, they separated, Robin taking her place on the bride's side to the left beside Erosmay and the Chosen Man taking his place on the right.

Prince Arlo came next. Tall and muscular in his wedding finery, he looked every bit the prince. And by the pleased expression on his handsome face, it was obvious to all he had been looking forward to the day.

Just like the couple entering before him, when the prince reached the high table, he nodded his head formally out of respect for the nobility seated before him. Then, he turned to await his bride.

As the music grew louder, Princess Lilyanna stepped through the entranceway, so radiant in her silk gown no one would have suspected the hardship she had undergone to be there.

When she reached her intended, Lilyanna paused and smiled at Arlo before curtsying in deference to her parents and future father-in-law sitting behind the table before her. Then, she turned, handed her primrose bouquet to Robin, and the music stopped.

Although this was no ordinary wedding, because it was also the union of two kingdoms, the ceremony itself was a simple affair. The two lovers joined hands and made their pledges freely one to the other under the eyes of God, the crown, and before witnesses.

After the vows had been made, Robin set aside the bridal bouquet and, as Maiden of Honor, poured wine from the pitcher of plenty into the nuptial cup which the Chosen Man then presented to the couple so they could each take a symbolic sip.

Once the cup had been returned to its place on the high table, the newlyweds kissed and Robin handed the bouquet back to the princess. Then, the music resumed and everyone stood and cheered as Lilyanna and Arlo walked arm in arm as man and wife back through the entrance from which they came, followed by Robin, the Chosen Man, and Erosmay.

While the servants commenced to carry the marriage feast into the Great Hall, the wedding party began to make its customary way across the courtyard so the royal newlyweds could climb the stone steps beside the castle gate and wave to the people on the other side of the defensive wall who had gathered to celebrate their happiness.

When the gamekeeper and guards awaiting the couple's arrival saw them approaching, they too were caught up in the spirit of the occasion and, disregarding formality, began to cheer.

Lilyanna and Arlo laughed and waved back happily. Then, as they neared and the princess noticed the gamekeeper was trying to conceal several large boxes covered with tarpaulin, she asked him, 'What have you got there?'

'It's something your father requested,' he replied, smiling broadly and tapping the side of his nose.

None the wiser, the princess and her new husband began to climb the stone steps. And just as they reached the top and the crowd began to cheer, the gamekeeper threw off the tarpaulin and released dozens of white doves into the air.

As the crowd gasped in awe, Erosmay decided to start her feasting early and began to spread her leathery wings. But before the peckish dragon could take flight and mar Lilyanna's special day, Robin fondly warned in mind-speech, 'Don't even think about it.'

ABOUT THE AUTHOR

V. G. Bratt's life changed on the day she was introduced to a Hobbit, Bilbo Baggins to be precise. Up until then, her life on the cattle ranch had been pretty mundane. But after that fateful day, even the childhood adventures she shared with her siblings could not compare to what she believed awaited her on Middle-earth.

For many years, she strove to ignore the calling by trying diverse things, like graduating from university, writing questions for a quiz show, and even military service. Yet, as if drawn by magic, she ended up moving across continents to live in a shire, where she is enjoying the greatest adventure of all with her loving husband and family.

Printed in Great Britain
by Amazon